HELLIONS OF HALSTEAD HALL

"Another sparkling series with winning potential"
(*Library Journal*) from the *New York Times* and *USA
Today* bestselling author of the "warm, wickedly
witty" (*RT Book Reviews*) School for Heiresses series

SABRINA JEFFRIES

Praise for

HOW TO WOO A RELUCTANT LADY

"Jeffries delivers a delightful addition to the scandalous Sharpe
family saga. . . . Quick pacing, witty dialogue, and charmingly
original characters set Jeffries's books apart, and this one is sure
to please old fans and make plenty of new ones as well."
—*Publishers Weekly* (starred review)

"The latest addition to Jeffries's exceptionally entertaining
Hellions of Halstead Hall series is richly imbued with steamy
passion, deftly spiced with dangerous intrigue, and neatly
tempered with just the right amount of tart wit."
—*Booklist*

**All of the Hellions of Halstead Hall titles
are also available as eBooks**

A HELLION IN HER BED

"A perfectly matched pair of protagonists who engage in a spirited battle of wits and wiles and a lively plot blending equal measures of steamy passion and sharp wit come together brilliantly in the second addition to Jeffries's tempting new Hellions of Halstead Hall series."

—*Booklist* (starred review)

"Wonderfully original. . . . It's more than the original plotline that captures readers; it's Jeffries's sense of humor, her engaging characters, and delightfully delicious sensuality that spice things up!"

—*RT Book Reviews* (4 ½ stars)

"Rich with family interaction and overflowing with scintillating wit and heart-stopping sensuality, this addition to Jeffries's addictive series satisfies while cleverly doling out tidbits that will keep readers eager for the next installment."

—*Library Journal*

"Engaging . . . fun and moving."

—*Romance Reviews Today*

"A winning hand of hearts and spades!"

—Fresh Fiction

"Another enjoyable romance that will entertain readers from cover to cover."

—Reader to Reader

"*A Hellion in Her Bed* enchants with its likable characters. . . . Amusing and poignant."

—Single Titles

"Yet another delicious love story from Sabrina Jeffries."

—Romance Junkies

"A lively, energetic romance with two smart, strong-willed protagonists that are sure to capture your heart."

—Joyfully Reviewed

THE TRUTH ABOUT LORD STONEVILLE

"Jeffries pulls out all the stops with a story combining her hallmark humor, poignancy, and sensuality to perfection."

—*RT Book Reviews*

"The first in a captivating new Regency-set series by the always entertaining Jeffries, this tale has all of the author's signature elements: delectably witty dialogue, subtly named characters, and scorching sexual chemistry between two perfectly matched protagonists."

—*Booklist*

"Lively repartee, fast action, luscious sensuality, and an abundance of humor."

—*Library Journal*

"*The Truth About Lord Stoneville* has the special brand of wit and passion for which Sabrina Jeffries is recognized, where each enthralling scene will thoroughly capture your imagination."

—Single Titles

"Sabrina Jeffries . . . starts another excellent series which will alternately have you laughing, crying, and running the gamut of emotions."

—Romance Reviews Today

Sabrina Jeffries

To Wed a Wild Lord

POCKET STAR BOOKS

New York   London   Toronto   Sydney   New Delhi

Pocket Star Books
A Division of Simon & Schuster, Inc.
1230 Avenue of the Americas
New York, NY 10020

This book is a work of fiction. Names, characters, places, and incidents either are products of the author's imagination or are used fictitiously. Any resemblance to actual events or locales or persons, living or dead, is entirely coincidental.

First Pocket Star Books paperback edition December 2011

POCKET STAR BOOKS and colophon are registered trademarks of Simon & Schuster, Inc.

For information about special discounts for bulk purchases, please contact Simon & Schuster Special Sales at 1-866-506-1949 or business@simonandschuster.com.

The Simon & Schuster Speakers Bureau can bring authors to your live event. For more information or to book an event contact the Simon & Schuster Speakers Bureau at 1-866-248-3049 or visit our website at www.simonspeakers.com.

Cover illustration by Jon Paul Ferrara
Handlettering by Iskra Design

Manufactured in the United States of America

10 9 8 7 6 5 4 3 2 1

ISBN 978-1-4516-4240-7
ISBN 978-1-4516-4248-3 (ebook)

To Susan Williams, who's always been there for me.
Thank you for all the wonderful years!

And to my beloved brother, Craig Martin, the adrenaline
junkie of the family, who inspired Gabe's character.
Stay safe!

Acknowledgments

Much thanks goes to Nicole Jordan, for her invaluable input concerning horses and racing. You're a doll, Nicole, for reading it so quickly!

And to Deb Marlowe for loaning me her books on horse racing in England and for giving me her usual helpful information. What would I do without you?

Dear Readers,

I am at my wits' end with my grandson, Gabriel. It is because of him I demanded that all my grandchildren marry within a year or be disinherited. His best friend died racing Gabe, yet nearly seven years later, the reckless lad broke his arm racing another fool on the same treacherous course! That is what set me off. And no wonder—people call Gabe the Angel of Death precisely because he courts it at every turn.

Now, his best friend's sister, Virginia Waverly, has some notion about seeking vengeance by beating him in a race on that same course, and instead of ignoring the girl's mad challenge, Gabe wishes to court her! I believe he may have lost his mind. Granted, she is a spirited, pretty little thing, but her grandfather, General Waverly, will never approve the marriage. The man is too stubborn and willful for words. Why, the cavalry general had the audacity to call me a "she-devil"! No man gets away with that, no matter how handsome and spry he may be for his age.

But I digress (General Waverly distracts me unduly). I cannot decide what I think about Gabe's interest in the pert Miss Waverly. I do want him to marry, but he is still grappling with his guilt over what happened to her brother—how can I be sure that she won't make that situation worse? My only consolation is that she seems as fascinated by my grandson as he is by her. Only today General Waverly and I stumbled upon them after what may very well have been an intimate encounter! Her lips were decidedly red, and Gabe looked as if someone had just jerked his horse out from under him. The man is clearly unused to dealing with respectable women.

Meanwhile, I am getting too old for this. If this courtship does not turn out well, I may just have to tie Gabe up in the barn until he sees sense. Wish me luck, dear friends!

Sincerely,

Hetty Plumtree

Prologue

People were yelling again.

Seven-year-old Gabriel Sharpe, third son of the Marquess of Stoneville, tried covering his ears to blot out the sound. He hated the yelling—it made his stomach knot up, especially when Mother yelled at Father.

Only this time Mother was yelling at his oldest brother. Gabe could hear it plain as day, because Oliver's bedroom was right below the schoolroom. Gabe couldn't make out the words; they just sounded angry. It was strange for Oliver to be yelled at—he was Mother's pet. Well, most of the time. She did call Gabe "her darling boy," and she never called his brothers that.

Was that because they were almost grown? Gabe scowled. He should tell Mother he didn't like being called "her darling boy" . . . except that he did. She always said it right before she gave him lemon tarts, his favorite.

A door slammed. The yelling stopped. He let out a breath, and something loosened up inside him. Perhaps everything would be all right now.

He gazed down at his primer. He was supposed to be reading a story, but it was stupid, about a robin who got killed:

Here lies Cock Robin,
Dead and cold.
His end this book
Will soon unfold.

It told about all these creatures who did things for the dead Cock Robin—the owl who buried him, and the bull who tolled the bell. But though it said how Cock Robin died—the sparrow shot him with an arrow—it never said why. Why would a sparrow shoot a robin? It made no sense.

And there were no horses, either. He'd flipped ahead through the pictures, so he knew that for sure. Lots of birds and a fish and a fly and a beetle. No horses. He'd much rather read a story about a horse running a race, but there were never any children's stories about that.

Bored, he glanced out the window and saw his mother head for the stables with long, strong strides. Was she going to the picnic to tell Father on Oliver?

Gabe would love to see that. Oliver never got into trouble. Meanwhile, Gabe *always* did. That's why he was sitting in this stupid schoolroom with this stupid book, instead of having fun at the picnic—because he'd done something bad and Father had ordered him to stay home.

But Father might forgive him if he had Oliver to be

mad at. If Mother was going to the picnic, Gabe might even convince her to take him, too.

He glanced across the room; his tutor, Mr. Virgil, was dozing in the chair. Gabe could easily sneak out and ask Mother. But only if he hurried.

Keeping an eye on his tutor, he slipped off his chair and edged toward the door. As soon as he reached the hall, he broke into a run. He ran down the stairs, then half-slid and half-ran along the tiled hall at the bottom before vaulting out into the Crimson Courtyard.

A quick dart across and he was in his favorite place in the whole world—the stable. He loved the sweaty smell of the horses, the crunch of hay underfoot in the loft, the way the grooms talked. The stable was a magical place, where people spoke in quiet, even voices. No yelling, because it bothered the horses.

He looked around, then sighed. The stall holding Mother's favorite mare was empty. She was gone. But he didn't want to go back to the schoolroom and that stupid book about Cock Robin.

"Good day, young master," said the head groom, Benny May, who was shoeing a horse. He used to be a jockey for Gabe's grandfather, back when the Sharpes put lots of horses in races. "Lookin' for someone?"

Gabe wasn't about to admit he'd wanted Mother. Instead, he puffed out his chest and tucked his thumbs in the waistband of his breeches like the grooms did. "Just wondering if you need help. Looks like the grooms are gone off."

"Aye, to the picnic. I imagine a lot of folks will be

tramping in and out this afternoon. The fine ladies and gentlemen will tire of the outdoors before long." Benny kept his gaze on the horse's foot. "Why aren't you at the picnic?"

"Father wouldn't let me go on account of my putting a spider in Minerva's hair and refusing to apologize."

Benny made a choking sound that turned into a cough. "So he said you could come to the stables instead?"

Gabe stared down at his shoes.

"Ah. Gave Mr. Virgil the slip again, did you?"

"Sort of," he mumbled.

"You ought to be nicer to your sister, y'know. She's a sweet girl."

Gabe snorted. "She tattles. Anyway, I came to check on Jacky Boy." That was Gabe's pony. Father had given it to him on his birthday last summer. "He gets cranky sometimes."

Benny's hard stare softened into a smile. "Aye, that he does, lad. And he always settles right down for you, don't he?"

Trying not to show his pride at the compliment, Gabe shrugged. "I know how to curry him the way he likes. Does he . . . um . . . need grooming?"

"Well, now, it's funny you should ask, because I do believe he could use a little care." He jerked his head toward the tack room. "You know where we keep the combs."

Gabe sauntered off to the tack room. He quickly found what he needed, then let himself into the stall. Jacky Boy sniffed him, hoping for a lump of sugar.

"Sorry, old chum," Gabe murmured. "Came out here in a hurry. I didn't bring you anything." He began to curry the pony, and Jacky Boy relaxed.

There was nothing better in the whole world than grooming Jacky Boy—the soothing motion of the comb, the pony's breathing quieting to a soft rhythm, the feel of Jacky Boy's silky coat beneath his fingers . . . Gabe never tired of it.

Out in the stable, people came and went, but in the stall it was just Gabe and Jacky Boy. Occasionally, something would disturb his reverie—a haughty gentleman demanding a change of mounts, a groom apologizing to some rude lady for not getting her mount as quick as she liked—but for the most part, it was silent except for the sound of Benny's hammer tapping another shoe into place.

Even that sound ended when Benny was called away to help with an approaching carriage. For a few minutes Gabe was in a state of pure bliss, alone with his pony. Then he heard boots tromp down the aisle.

"Anyone here?" a man's voice called out. "I need a mount."

Gabe shrank onto the floor in the front corner of the stall, hoping not to be noticed.

The man must have heard him, for he cried, "You there, boy. I need a mount."

He'd been discovered. When the man came closer, he called out, "Sorry, sir, I'm not a groom. I'm just looking after my horse."

The man stopped outside the stall. Since Gabe sat on

the floor with his back to the stall door, he couldn't see the man. He hoped the man couldn't see him, either.

"Ah," the man said. "One of the Sharpe children, are you?"

His stomach got queasy. "H-How did you know?"

"The only children who would own horses stabled here are the Sharpe children."

"Oh." He hadn't thought of that.

"You're Gabriel, aren't you?"

Gabe froze, frightened of the clever man. He was in for it, if his father heard of this. "I-I . . ."

"Lord Jarret is out at the picnic, and Lord Oliver chose not to go. That leaves only Lord Gabriel. You."

The man's voice was soft, even kind. He didn't say things in that lofty tone grown-ups usually used with children. And he didn't *sound* as if he wanted to get Gabe into trouble.

"Do you know where the grooms are?" the man asked, his voice moving away.

Gabe relaxed now that the subject was off him. "They went to meet a carriage."

"Then they probably won't mind if I saddle my own mount."

"I guess not."

Oliver saddled his own mount all the time. So did Jarret. Gabe couldn't wait until he was big enough to saddle a mount. Then he wouldn't have to ask Father's permission to ride Jacky Boy.

As the man chose the horse from the next stall, all Gabe could see was his beaver hat showing above it.

After he rode off, Gabe started to wonder if he should have found out the man's name, or at least tried to get a better look at him. Sudden panic gripped him. What if the man was a horse thief, and Gabe had just let him ride right off?

No, the man had known Gabe's name and all about the rest of them. He *had* to be a guest. Right?

Benny came back in the stable and, before Gabe could say anything, called out, "The guests are returning from the picnic, lad. You'd best run up to the house if you don't want your father catching you here."

Gabe's panic returned. If Father learned he'd snuck out of the schoolroom again, he'd get his hide tanned. Father was strict about their studies.

He ran for the house. When he reached the school-room, his tutor was still snoring. With a sigh of relief, Gabe settled into the chair and took up the boring book again.

But he couldn't think about the dead Cock Robin. He kept wondering about the unknown man. Should he have said something to Benny? What if there was a hue and cry about a stolen horse? What if he got into trouble?

He was still fretting over it after dinner in the nursery with Minerva. Celia, who'd been sick with a cough, was already asleep when a footman, Nurse, and Mr. Virgil came to fetch them. Grandmother Plumtree wanted to talk to him and Minerva downstairs, the footman said solemnly.

Gabe's pulse leaped into a gallop. The man in the

stable *must* have stolen a horse, and somehow Gran had found out that Gabe had let him do it. But then, why bring Minerva into it?

The footman brought them into the library, leaving Celia with Nurse and Mr. Virgil. When Gabe saw Oliver standing there with his hair wet and his eyes red, wearing different clothes than he'd worn earlier, he didn't know what to think.

Then Jarret appeared, summoned by another servant. "Where's Mother and Father?"

Oliver's face hardened to granite, and his eyes turned scary looking.

"I have something to tell you, children." Gran spoke more softly than usual. "There's been an accident." Something caught in her voice, and she cleared her throat.

Was she crying? Gran never cried. Father said she had a heart of steel.

"Your parents . . ."

She broke off and Oliver flinched, as if struck. "Mother and Father are dead," he finished for her in a voice that didn't even sound like his.

The words didn't register at first. Dead? Like Cock Robin? Gabe stared at them, waiting for someone to take it back.

No one took it back.

Gran wiped her eyes, then straightened her shoulders. "Your mother mistook your father for an intruder at the hunting lodge, and she shot him. When she realized her error, she . . . she shot herself, too."

Beside him, Minerva began to cry. Jarret kept shaking his head and saying, "No, no, it can't be. How can that be?" Oliver went to stand by the window, his shoulders quivering.

Gabe couldn't stop thinking about that stupid poem:

> Then all the Birds fell
> To sighing and sobbing,
> When they heard the bell toll
> For poor Cock Robin.

It was just like the poem, except without the bell. Gabe didn't know what to do. Gran was saying that they weren't to speak of it to anyone, because there would be scandal enough without that, but her words made no sense. Why would he want to speak of it? He couldn't even believe it happened.

Perhaps this was a nightmare. He would wake up, and Father would be here.

"Are you sure it was them?" he asked in a wavering voice. "Perhaps it was somebody else who got shot."

Gran looked stricken. "I'm sure. Oliver and I saw the—" With a grimace, Gran stepped over to put her arms around him and Minerva. "I'm sorry, my darlings. Try to be strong. I know it's hard."

Minerva just kept weeping. Gran held her close.

Gabe thought of the last time he saw Father, riding out to the picnic, and Mother, hurrying to the stable. How could that have been the last time? Now he could never tell Father he was sorry for putting the spider in

Minerva's hair. Father had died thinking he was a bad boy who wouldn't apologize.

That's when tears welled in his eyes. He couldn't let Jarret and Oliver see—they would think him a stupid girl. So he darted from the room, ignoring Gran's startled cry, and dashed toward the stable.

It was quiet; the grooms were at their supper. As soon as he reached Jacky Boy's stall, he collapsed on the floor and began to cry. It wasn't right! How could they be dead?

He wasn't sure how long he lay there sobbing, but next thing he knew, Jarret had entered the stall and bent down to lay his hand on Gabe's shoulder. "Come now, lad. Buck up."

Gabe shoved Jarret's hand away. "I can't! Th-They're gone, and they're n-never coming back!"

"I know," Jarret said, his voice unsteady.

"It's n-not fair." Gabe gazed up at Jarret. "Other children's p-parents don't die. Wh-why should ours?"

Jarret bit his lip. "Sometimes things happen."

"It's j-just like that s-stupid book about Cock Robin. M-Makes no sense."

"*Life* doesn't make sense," Jarret said softly. "You mustn't expect it to. Fate has a hand in everything, and nobody can explain why Fate acts as it does."

Jarret still didn't cry, though his eyes were hollow and his face was screwed up in an odd way, as if somebody had stepped hard on his foot.

Gabe had always liked Jarret the best of everyone, but right now he hated how calm Jarret was. Why wasn't his brother angry?

"We have to be strong," Jarret went on.

"Why?" Gabe shot back. "What does it matter? They're still d-dead. And we're still all a-alone."

"Yes, but if you let Fate have the upper hand, it will drag you down. You must refuse to be cowed. Laugh at it, tell it to go to hell. It's the only way to beat it."

It wasn't Life that made no sense. It was Death. It took people away for no reason. Mother oughtn't have shot Father, and sparrows oughtn't shoot cock robins. Yet they were all still dead.

Death could take him away, too, any time it wanted. Fear gripped him by the throat. He could die *any minute*. For no reason.

How was he to stop it? Death seemed to be a sneaky bastard, coming up from behind to deal low blows. If it came after *him* . . .

Perhaps Jarret was right. There was nothing to do but stand up to Death. Or even try to ignore it. Gabe had played with plenty of sneaky bastards, and the only way to deal with them was not to cower, not to show that they hurt you. Then they went off to torment other chaps and left you alone.

He thought of Mother and Father lying somewhere dead, and tears stung his eyes again. Wiping them ruthlessly away, he stuck out his lower lip. Perhaps Death could get him the way it had grabbed Mother and Father, but not without a fight.

If it wanted him, it would have to drag him kicking and screaming. Because he would not go easy.

Chapter One

Eastcote, August 1825

Virginia Waverly could hardly contain her excitement as the carriage hurtled toward Marsbury House. A ball! She was going to a ball at last. She would finally get to use those waltz steps her second cousin, Pierce Waverly, the Earl of Devonmont, had taught her.

For a moment, she let her mind wander through a lovely fantasy of being danced about the room by a handsome cavalry officer. Or perhaps by their host himself, the Duke of Lyons! Wouldn't that be grand? She knew what people said about his father, whom they called "the Mad Duke," but she never paid attention to such gossip.

She did wish she had a more fashionable gown—like the one of pink *gros de Naples* she'd seen in *The Ladies Magazine*. But fashionable gowns were expensive, which is why she had to make do with her old tartan silk one, bought when Scottish garb was all the rage. How she wished she'd picked something less . . . distinctive to make over. Everybody would take one look at her and know how poor she was.

"I can see that you're worried," Pierce said.

Virginia stared at him, surprised by his insight. "Only a little. I tried to make this gown more fashionable by adding a net overlay, but the sleeves are still short, so now it just looks like an outdated gown with strange sleeves."

"No, I meant—"

"Surely people won't fault me too much for that." She thrust out her chin. "Though I don't care if they do. I'm the only woman of twenty I know who's never been to a ball. Even the farmer's daughter next door went to one in Bath, and she's only eighteen!"

"What I was talking about—"

"So I'm not going to let my gown or my inexperience on the dance floor keep me from enjoying myself," she said stoutly. "I shall eat caviar and drink champagne, and for one night pretend that I'm rich. And I shall finally dance with a *man*."

Pierce looked affronted. "Now see here, *I'm* a man."

"Well, of course, but you're my cousin. It's not the same."

"Besides," he said, "I wasn't talking about your gown. I meant, aren't you worried about running into Lord Gabriel Sharpe?"

She blinked. "Why would *he* be there? He wasn't at the race today."

A few years ago, the Duke of Lyons had started an annual race—the Marsbury Stakes—run on a course on his property. This year her grandfather, Pierce's great-uncle, General Isaac Waverly, had entered a Thoroughbred stallion from their stud farm. Lamentably, Ghost Rider had lost the race and the Marsbury Cup.

That's why Pierce was accompanying her to the race ball tonight, instead of her grandfather—Ghost Rider's poor performance had keenly disappointed Poppy. It had disappointed her, too, but not enough to keep her from attending the ball.

"Sharpe is Lyons's close friend," Pierce said. "In fact, he was at the race in Turnham Green with Roger."

Her stomach sank. "That can't be! The only people there were Lord Gabriel and some fellow named Kinloch—"

"The Marquess of Kinloch, yes. That was Lyons's title before his father died and he ascended to the dukedom."

She scowled. "No wonder Poppy refused to attend tonight. Why didn't he tell me? I wouldn't have come."

"That's why. Uncle Isaac wanted you to enjoy yourself for once. And he assumed that Sharpe wouldn't be there since he wasn't at the race."

"Still, I'll have to face the duke, who let Roger run that awful course in Turnham Green despite knowing the risks. Why did he invite us? Doesn't he realize who we are?"

"Perhaps he's holding out the olive branch to you and Uncle Isaac for his own part in Roger's death, small as it was."

She snorted. "Rather late, if you ask me."

"Come now, you can't blame Lyons for what happened. Or Sharpe either, for that matter."

She glared at Pierce. They'd had this argument many a time in the seven years since her brother had died in a dangerous carriage race against Lord Gabriel. "His lordship and Kinloch—Lyons—took advantage of Roger's being drunk—"

"You don't know that."

"Well, no one knows for sure, since Lord Gabriel refuses to speak of it. But Poppy says that's what happened, and I believe him. Roger would never have agreed to threading the needle with Lord Gabriel when sober."

The course was called "threading the needle" because it ran between two boulders with room enough for only one carriage to pass. The racer coming behind had to rein in to allow the other to drive through. Roger hadn't pulled back in time and had been thrown into a boulder. He'd been killed instantly.

She'd hated Lord Gabriel ever since.

"Men do stupid things when they're drunk," Pierce said. "Especially when they're with other men."

"Why do you always make excuses for Lord Gabriel?"

Pierce cast her a shuttered look from eyes the exact shade of brown as Ghost Rider's. "Because although he may be a reckless madman who risks his neck every chance he gets, he's not the devil Uncle Isaac makes him out to be."

"We'll never agree on this," she said, tugging at her drooping gloves.

"Only because you're stubborn and intractable."

"A family trait, I believe."

He laughed. "Indeed it is."

Virginia gazed out the window and tried to regain her buoyant mood, but it was no use. The ball was doomed to be ruined if Lord Gabriel showed up.

"Still," Pierce went on, "if Sharpe does come, I hope you'll refrain from mentioning the challenge you gave him a month and a half ago."

"And why should I?"

"Because it's madness!" His eyes narrowed on her. "It's not like you to do something so irresponsible. I know you didn't mean to issue that challenge—you were just angry—but to continue would be foolish, and you aren't that."

She glanced away. Sometimes Pierce had no clue what went on inside her. He and Poppy insisted upon seeing her as some pillar of domestic virtue who kept the farm running and wanted the same things all women her age wanted—a stable home and a family, even if it was just with Poppy.

It wasn't that she didn't want those things. She just . . . didn't want them at the sacrifice to her soul. To the part of her that felt boxed in sometimes by constant work and responsibility. The part of her that wanted to dance at a ball.

And race Lord Gabriel Sharpe.

Pierce went on lecturing. "Besides, if Uncle Isaac ever hears that you challenged Sharpe to a race on the same course that killed Roger, he'll put a stop to it at once."

True. Poppy was a mite overprotective. She'd been only three years old when he'd left the cavalry to take care of her and Roger after their parents, his son and daughter-in-law, had died in a boating accident.

"How will he hear of it?" Virginia batted her eyelashes at Pierce. "Surely you wouldn't be so cruel as to tell him."

"Oho, don't try your tricks on *me*, dear girl. They may work on Uncle Isaac, but I'm immune to such things."

She stiffened. "I'm not a girl anymore, in case you haven't noticed."

"Actually, I have. Which is why you must stop tormenting Lord Gabriel. This ball is your chance to find a husband. And chaps don't like it when women go about challenging men to foolish races."

"I'm in no hurry to marry," she said, giving him the same lie she always gave her grandfather. "I prefer to stay with Poppy as long as possible."

"Virginia," Pierce said softly, "don't be naïve. He's sixty-nine. The likelihood of him living much longer—"

"Don't say it." The very thought of Poppy dying made her stomach roil. "He's in good health. He could live to be a hundred. Surely one of our horses will win a good prize in the coming years, enough to increase my pathetic dowry."

"You could always marry *me*." Pierce waggled his dark brown brows. "You wouldn't even have to leave home."

She gaped at him. Because of Roger's death, Pierce would inherit Waverly Farm, but he'd never before suggested marriage. "And who would be sleeping in the room adjoining yours—me or your mistress?"

He scowled at her. "Now see here, I'd give up my mistress."

"For me? The devil you would." She smirked at him. "I know you better than that."

"Well," he said sullenly, "I wouldn't keep her in the same house, at least."

She laughed. "Now *that* is the Pierce Waverly I know. Which is precisely why I could never marry you."

Unmistakable relief crossed his face. "Thank God. I'm too young to be leg-shackled."

"Thirty isn't young. If you were a horse, Poppy would put you out to pasture."

"Good thing I'm not a horse," he quipped, flashing her the lopsided grin that had every silly girl on the marriage mart swooning over him.

She straightened. "Look, we're almost there! I think I see the house!" She smoothed her skirts as she faced him. "Do I look *too* much a country mouse?"

"Not at all. A *city* mouse perhaps—"

"Pierce!"

He laughed. "I'm joking, you little widgeon. You look perfect—eyes sparkling and cheeks blushing. That's why I offered to marry you," he teased.

"You didn't offer marriage. You offered a convenient arrangement wherein you got to have your cake and eat it, too."

He grinned. "Isn't that always my plan?"

She shook her head at him. He was hopeless. "I should hope I'm not yet so desperate that I need to marry for convenience."

"The trouble with you is you have your head in the clouds. You want some damned union of souls, with cooing doves flying overhead to bless the conjugal bed."

Surprised that he'd even noticed that about her, she said, "I just think two people should be in love when they marry, that's all."

"What a disgusting thought," he muttered.

That was why they could never wed. Pierce had a distinct aversion to marriage. Besides, he preferred women with big bosoms and blond hair, neither of which she had. And he liked them wild, too. Pierce's reputation was less than stellar—though she suspected that half of it was whipped up into a froth of scandal, outrage, and intrigue by the gossip of worried mamas whose daughters were enamored of his dark good looks and devil-may-care manner.

Then there was the fact that he was practically her brother. He spent as much time at Waverly Farm as he did at his estate in Hertfordshire. She could no more picture him as her husband than his coachman.

The carriage stopped and Pierce climbed out, then helped her down. She stared open-mouthed at the famous Marsbury House—three long expanses of flint dressed with stone and anchored by four copper-domed stone towers.

The inside was even grander—marble columns and statues everywhere. As servants escorted them to the ballroom, she glimpsed rich tapestries, huge paintings in gilded frames, and silk draperies.

Oh, Lord. She didn't belong here.

Could Pierce be right? Could the duke have invited

her because he felt bad about Roger's death? No, that made no sense. He hadn't even attended the funeral.

Still, what other reason could there be for the invitation? The race ball at Marsbury was an exclusive affair, and although Poppy *was* the third son of an earl, he'd spent more of his life riding over battlefields than at fine parties like this. Having never had a formal debut, she wasn't exactly high society, either.

When they entered the ballroom, Pierce guided her to a secluded corner so they could catch their bearings. Done all in gold and cream with gaslit chandeliers, the ballroom held a warm glow that made her heart race with anticipation. What if she *did* meet someone here tonight? Wouldn't that be lovely?

After all, she wouldn't *mind* finding a husband, though she feared that her requirements were unreasonable. The man would have to be willing to live at Waverly Farm until Poppy died, he'd need his own fortune, and he'd have to overlook the fact that she meant to race Lord Gabriel. All of which was a tall order.

Suddenly Pierce's face tightened, and he bent to murmur, "Don't look now, but Sharpe himself is leaning against that pillar over there."

She looked at once, of course, then wished she hadn't. Because Lord Gabriel Sharpe's appearance had materially altered since the last time she'd seen him.

When she'd challenged him at Turnham Green, she'd been blinded by rage, and he'd been covered in dust from the race he'd just won against Lieutenant Chetwin. Tonight, however, he looked every inch the Angel of Death.

Oh, how she hated that nickname! People had given it to him after Roger's death, and he did everything to reinforce it. He dressed entirely in black, down to his shirt and cravat, which were said to be specially dyed for him. He'd even painted his phaeton black and fitted it out with a matched pair of coal-black horses.

Angel of Death, indeed. He was using the tragic race against Roger to enhance his reputation as a fearless driver. He ought to cower in shame in a remote corner of his family's estate—not take on every fool who demanded that he race him. How dared he strut about society without a care in the world? How dared he *look* so much like an Angel of Death?

Not just the death part, either. Grudgingly, she admitted that aside from his clothes, he was the very image of an angel. His gold-streaked brown hair looked as if the sun had run its fingers through its waves. And his face was like something sculpted by Michelangelo—a classic nose, a full Italian mouth, and a stubborn chin. Though she couldn't see his eyes just now, she'd observed their color before—a mossy green with brown flecks that reminded her of secret forest glades.

She snorted. She must be mad. His eyes were those of the man who'd killed her brother. She'd only noticed him because she hated him so thoroughly that it seemed an outrage for him to be that sinfully attractive. That was the only reason.

"You're staring," Pierce muttered under his breath.

Oh, Lord, she was. How *dared* Lord Gabriel get her to stare at him?

"Come, let's dance." Pierce offered her his arm.

She took it, grateful to be saved from herself. Then, as they joined a long line of dancers, she saw Lord Gabriel catch sight of her. His gaze widened, then slid down her figure with rude interest.

And the last thing she saw, as Pierce whirled her into the dance, was the curst Angel of Death look straight into her eyes and smile.

LORD GABRIEL SHARPE watched as Miss Virginia Waverly danced down the length of the hall with the Earl of Devonmont. Thank God she had come. If he'd had to endure an entire blasted ball without accomplishing his purpose, he'd have blown his brains out.

Fortunately, he was well prepared for her appearance here. Jackson Pinter, the Bow Street runner helping his siblings look into the deaths of their parents, had discovered a great deal of sobering information about Miss Waverly. And Gabe meant to use it to his advantage.

"There goes your nemesis," said Maximilian Cale, the Duke of Lyons.

Lyons was a fellow Jockey Club member and Gabe's closest friend. He had a stable of Thoroughbreds that Gabe envied, one of which had won the Derby twice and another that had won the Royal Ascot. Gabe had bought the progeny of the latter horse last month, after he'd scraped together enough money from his wager winnings to afford it.

"Miss Waverly hardly qualifies as a nemesis," Gabe said dryly.

Lyons snorted. "Has she renewed her challenge to you yet?"

"She hasn't had the chance," Gabe said, feigning nonchalance. That damned challenge had been bandied about society ever since Turnham Green, and tonight he meant to put an end to it.

"Surely she won't." Lyons sipped his wine. "She can't possibly be as hotheaded as her brother."

Gabe stiffened. Seven years, and he still couldn't forget the sight of Roger lying twisted in the grass, his neck broken. If only . . .

But "if only" was for priests and philosophers. Gabe was seeking neither absolution nor understanding; he couldn't change what had happened.

But perhaps he could assuage the dire results, now that he knew about them. "I suspect that Miss Waverly is not only hotheaded, but stubborn." Gabe followed her with his eyes as Devonmont led her down the narrow row. "She came here tonight, didn't she? She had to guess I might be here."

"If she mentions the challenge again, will you accept it?"

"No." He was done with running that course in Turnham Green.

Lyons smirked at him. "Afraid that the chit will beat you?"

Gabe knew better than to rise to the bait. "More afraid that she'll run her rig over my best team of horses."

"They say she beat Letty Lade. That's no small feat."

He snorted. "Letty Lade was nearly seventy by then; it's a miracle the woman didn't fall off her perch. Leave Miss Waverly to me. After tonight, there will be no more talk of a race."

"What do you mean to do?"

"I intend to marry her," Gabe said.

What else could he do? Clearly her grandfather over-indulged her, and that scoundrel Devonmont probably encouraged her for his own amusement. Miss Waverly needed a man to take her in hand. And since he was partly to blame for her present situation, he'd be the one to do it. In the process, he could solve his own problem.

Lyons gaped at him. "Marry her? Why the hell would you do that?"

Gabe shrugged. "Gran is demanding that my siblings and I marry, and Miss Waverly needs a husband. Why shouldn't it be me?"

"Because she blames you for Roger's death?"

Gabe forced a smile. "Once she realizes that what happened with Roger was truly just an accident . . ."

He trailed off, bits of memory plaguing him. Roger rousting him out of bed for the race. Lyons looking green about the gills as they arrived at the course. Gabe's blood running high as he approached the boulders . . .

An uncharacteristic anger boiled up in him, and he tamped it down with effort. He didn't generally get angry. Long ago, he'd buried his emotions in a grave so deep that they could never be unearthed.

Or so he'd thought. Ever since Miss Waverly's chal-

lenge, he'd been volatile, prone to irrational bouts of
fury. It made no sense. How could one stupid challenge
churn up the cold ground inside him? And yet it had.
Everything seemed to tax his temper.

But tonight he must hold his anger in check, or he'd
never succeed in his plans. So he fought his emotions
back into the grave that felt shallower by the day.

"Why not find someone more compliant to marry?"
Lyons asked.

Because her lack of compliance oddly attracted Gabe.
Since he had to marry, he didn't want some placid,
toadying society chit. He wanted a wife with spirit.
Who had more spirit than a woman brave enough to
publicly challenge a man to a race?

Besides, after everything he'd heard about Miss Waverly and the sad life she'd been leading, he couldn't let
that situation continue. Not that he could tell Lyons
that; the duke wouldn't understand that he was only
doing what was right.

He put on his usual grin. "You know me. I always like
a challenge."

Looking unconvinced, Lyons sipped his wine. "So it
wasn't your grandmother's idea for you to marry Roger's
sister?"

"Gran didn't specify whom we marry, just that we all
do so—or none of us will inherit. And by the way, that's
not common knowledge, so I'd appreciate it if you kept
it to yourself."

"I suppose Miss Waverly wouldn't *like* hearing that
she's the key to your gaining your inheritance. But do

you need the money that badly? Oliver seems to have the estate well in hand, Jarret convinced your grandmother to give him the brewery anyway, and Minerva now has a husband who can afford to give her whatever she wants. Surely you can rely on them to lend you money if you run short."

"It's not that." Given more time, he hoped to support himself on his own anyway. "I'm worried about Celia."

"Ah, yes. I forgot about her."

Gabe glanced over to where his sister was dancing with some foreigner twice her age and looking decidedly annoyed. She'd told Gabe only last week that she had no intention of marrying as long as Gabe stayed unmarried. *We two should hold firm*, she'd said, *and Gran will have to give in. She's got three of us paired off— that should satisfy her.*

Gabe gritted his teeth. Gran wouldn't be satisfied until she had the entire family marching in step to her tune. And as long as he refused to marry, Celia could blame *him* for the fact that they were all disinherited.

But then she would be the one to suffer. While he was putting his plans for financial independence into place, she would be shuffled from relation to relation. She said she didn't need or want a man, but with no dowry to compensate for the weight of the family scandal on her marital prospects, she'd have no choice but to become a spinster.

He refused to be responsible for that. If Celia still wouldn't marry after Gabe got himself leg-shackled, at least she couldn't blame *him*.

"I don't suppose you're looking for a wife," Gabe said hopefully.

Lyons eyed him askance. "Your lovely sister? I'm not sure I *want* a wife who can shoot me dead at twenty paces."

Gabe smiled ruefully. "That seems to be the objection most men have to Celia."

And given Lyons's family background, he would have more of an objection than most.

Lyons returned his attention to Miss Waverly, who was sashaying into a turn. "I suppose she's pretty enough. A bit underendowed, though."

Underendowed? Hardly. But then, Gabe had never been attracted to women with bosoms like overstuffed chair cushions. Made them look unbalanced. He liked breasts he could take in his mouth without feeling smothered.

He'd wager Miss Waverly had fine little breasts beneath that martial gown . . . and a shapely little derrière to match. In fact, she was damned near close to perfect. Taller than the average female, with a trim figure that bespoke hours of walking and riding.

Then there was her beautiful hair, glossy black and swept up into some arrangement of feathers and plaid ribbons and dangling ringlets that made a man itch to take it down. And her face, too—all pert and pretty, from her saucy chin to her high, aristocratic brow. Not to mention her eyes. A man could wander for days in the depths of those cool lake eyes.

Lyons drained his wine glass and placed it on the tray

of a passing footman. "Her hatred of you will be a serious obstacle to winning her. Especially since you're not good with women."

"What? Of course I'm good with women."

"I don't mean the doxies and merry widows who pursue you because you're the Angel of Death. You don't have to do anything to get *them* to like you—they just want to see if you're as dangerous in bed as you are on the race course." Lyons glanced back at Miss Waverly. "But she is a respectable woman, and they require finesse. You have to be able to do more than bed them. You have to be able to talk to them."

Gabe snorted. "I can talk to women perfectly well."

"About anything other than horses? Or how lovely they look naked?"

"I know how to turn a woman up sweet." The dance ended, and Gabe saw Devonmont leading Miss Waverly from the floor. When the orchestra struck up a waltz, Gabe arched an eyebrow at Lyons. "Ten pounds says I can get her to dance the waltz with me."

"Make it twenty, and you're on."

With a grin, Gabe sauntered off toward Miss Waverly. Devonmont was headed for the punch table. Good. That should make things easier.

As he approached her another man also did so, but Gabe took care of that with one warning glance. The man paled, then headed in the other direction.

There were definite advantages to being the Angel of Death.

She seemed oblivious to what had just happened.

Tapping her foot to the music, she stared bright-eyed at the couples taking the floor. Clearly she was eager to dance again. This shouldn't be too hard.

Gabe made a wide circuit so he could come up behind her. "Good evening, Miss Waverly."

She stiffened, refusing to look at him. "I'm surprised to see you at such a dull diversion, Lord Gabriel. *My late brother* always said you disliked balls. Not enough danger, I suppose, and few opportunities to create mayhem."

He ignored her emphasis. "Every man needs the occasional break from mayhem. And although I dislike the insipid punch, insincere smiles, and inevitable gossip, I enjoy the dancing. I'd be pleased if you gave me the honor of the next one."

A sharp breath escaped her, and she finally turned to fix him with a cold gaze. "I would rather immerse myself in a vat of leeches."

The vivid image made him bite back a smile.

"Thank God." When she blinked at him, he added, "I was worried you might accept, and then we'd have to discuss that racing nonsense."

He turned as if to walk away, and she said, "Wait!"

Ah, he had the fish on the line. He faced her again. "Yes?"

"Why can't we discuss it right here?"

He cast a meaningful glance at the people straining to overhear the conversation between the notorious Angel of Death and the notorious female rumored to have challenged him to a race. "I'd have thought you'd prefer the privacy of a waltz for that, to prevent any chance of your grandfather finding out what you're contemplating, but if you don't care—"

"Oh." She glanced nervously about. "You do have a point."

"It's your decision," he said casually. "You would probably just as soon forget the whole thing, in which case—"

"No, indeed." She lifted her chin and said in a carrying voice, "I'd be happy to dance with you, Lord Gabriel."

"Very well." With a cordial smile, he took her to the floor, casting a triumphant glance back at Lyons. When the duke lifted his eyes heavenward, Gabe grinned.

Not good with women, hah! What did Lyons know about it?

True, he rarely had dealings with respectable females, but he could get a woman to marry him. He was eligible enough, despite the scandal that surrounded his family, and he was generally accounted to be handsome. And he should soon inherit a tidy fortune.

Granted, Miss Waverly had a certain bias against him, but her current situation was very precarious. All he need do was show her his good side, soften her up a bit, and then point out the practical advantages to a marriage between them.

How hard could it be?

Chapter Two

As Lord Gabriel took her to the floor, Virginia's mind wandered to a fantasy of race day. Unlike her brother, *she* wouldn't be too drunk to win. She would reach the finish line ahead of Lord Gabriel, having cut him off before he reached the boulders. Crowds of people would cheer, saying, "Those Waverlys certainly have pluck." His friends would jeer at him for losing to a woman.

She'd show him *she* wasn't intimidated by his black phaeton and clothes and reputation. She would end his posturing as the Angel of Death, so Roger could finally rest in peace. And she could stop feeling as if Lord Gabriel tromped all over her brother's grave every time he ran another reckless race.

"You're looking very lovely tonight," Lord Gabriel said.

His remark took her off guard. "What has that got to do with anything?" They were supposed to be talking about the race.

He blinked. "I was just saying that you look nice in that gown."

She stared at him. "Do you think I don't realize my gown is three years out of date? I know the sleeves look ridiculous, but I did my best with remaking it, and—"

"Miss Waverly! I'm *trying* to pay you a compliment."

Color rose in her cheeks. "Oh." Her eyes narrowed. "Why?"

"Because that's what a gentleman does when dancing with a lady," he said irritably.

"Not when he's only got the space of one waltz to discuss a matter of great importance," she countered. "We're supposed to be talking about when to have our race. And we don't have much time."

"Oh, for God's sake," he muttered under his breath.

"Did you think that if you flattered me, I'd forget the whole thing?"

His eyes looked a brighter green under the candles—less like a forest and more like an ocean. "No. I was hoping to remind you of your place in the world."

"Which is?"

"As a respectable member of society. One who attends balls and is sought for dances." His voice deepened. "*Not* one who is ostracized for engaging in a scandalous race."

Perish the man, he was as bad as Pierce. "Racing you isn't scandalous," she said tartly. "People do it all the time."

"The rules are different for men than for women, especially unmarried ones, as you well know. Racing me will instantly reduce your prospects for marriage."

Why did he care? "You assume that if I *don't* race you,

lords and rich merchants will drop at my feet like beggars at a feast."

His eyes became carefully blank. "Is that what you want? For a lord to beg to marry you?"

"No, indeed," she said as he led her expertly in the turns. No great surprise that he was a good dancer. He was probably good at anything that involved manhandling women. "I want to stay at home and take care of my grandfather until he dies. No lord would allow that. Even if I could find one who begged."

"I see. And what does your grandfather think of that plan?"

Heat rose in her cheeks. "That is none of your concern."

"Ah, but it is." He drew a deep breath. "Because of Roger's death, you'll lose your home when the general dies. Waverly Farm is entailed upon your cousin."

A chill ran down her spine. "How did you know that?"

"I hired a Bow Street runner to look into your situation after you challenged me to that race."

She gaped at him. "You . . . you . . . *what*?"

"He tells me that things have been difficult. Your grandfather had planned on Roger's inheriting the stud farm and helping him run it. Then Roger died. And when you turned sixteen, the general was thrown from a horse and incurred serious injuries, so it has taken him some time to—"

"How *dare* you!" she hissed. He'd dug into her family's private affairs? How mortifying! "Poppy is fine. *We* are fine, you . . . you presumptuous wretch."

She tried to break free of him right there, but he gripped her hand and waist so tightly that she'd have to make a scene to get him to release her. And she wasn't about to humiliate herself before him and his lofty friends, who were probably laughing about it this very minute.

He bent close, his expression oddly resolute. "The stud farm is struggling, and he can't afford to give you a season or a sufficient dowry. So don't pretend that your refusal to marry is a choice. The truth is, your situation makes it difficult for you to find a husband. You're just making the best of the bad hand dealt to you."

She wanted to sink into the floor. No, she wanted to *slap* him for his unemotional recitation of their problems.

"This ball tonight is the first you've ever attended," he went on. "And you're only here because I persuaded the duke to invite you and your family."

She fantasized driving a stake through his heart. "I should have known. You want to humiliate me before your friends, as revenge for my making you a laughing-stock with my challenge."

"Oh, for the love of God—" He blew out a frustrated breath. "Even if you *had* made me a laughingstock, which you haven't, I have no desire to humiliate you." He stared her down. "I got you invited so I could make you a proposition. Since I doubted that your grandfather would allow me to call on you, I had to arrange matters myself."

His gaze on her was intent, serious . . . disturbing. It filled her with a strange feeling of wariness. "A proposition having to do with our race?" she asked, her heart beating violently in her ears.

"Damn it to blazes, no! I'm not interested in racing you."

"Aha! Now the truth comes out. I hadn't thought you a coward."

Something glittered in his eyes. "And I hadn't thought you stupid."

The edge in his voice made her shiver, and not entirely with fear.

She hadn't known Lord Gabriel when he was Roger's friend. Roger had considered her too young, at thirteen, to hang around with him when he was with his lordly friends. Besides, the men had generally been at school, and when not there, they'd met in London, either at some tavern or at the town house owned by Lord Gabriel's grandmother, Mrs. Plumtree.

So she'd seen him only once—at Roger's funeral. Even that had been a mere glimpse, since Poppy had ordered him off the grounds the moment he'd arrived.

Still, that glimpse had been enough to make her hate him for surviving the race that her brother had not. Though perhaps he wasn't quite what she'd thought.

"All right then, not a coward," she conceded. "So I don't understand your reluctance to race me. You seem to race whoever challenges you."

"Not women." His gaze burned into her. "Not Roger's sister."

"As if that matters," she scoffed. "You've never shown any interest in my family before."

"That's because I was unaware that you— No matter

what you think of me, Roger was my closest friend. I cared enough about him that I don't want to see his sister embroiled in a scandal. I'd like to propose something else instead."

She couldn't imagine what that might be.

"I want to court you," he finished.

For a moment she thought she'd misunderstood him. Then she noticed the expectant look on his face and realized he was perfectly serious.

"*You*? Court *me*?" She imbued the words with as much contempt as she could muster. "That's the most ludicrous thing I've ever heard."

He didn't look the least bit insulted. "Hear me out," he said as he whirled her about on the highly polished wood floor. "Thanks to me, you have no one to provide for you. If Roger had lived, he would have inherited Waverly Farm and you would have always had a home, but since he didn't, you'll lose it when your grandfather dies."

"And your solution to that is that I marry you," she said, still hardly able to believe what he offered.

"It's the least I can do. I don't expect you to leap into it willy-nilly, but surely you could consider a courtship." His eyes gleamed at her beneath the warm glow of the gas lamps. "You might find I'm not so awful once you get to know me."

"I know enough already to tell me that you're arrogant, nosy, prone to make assumptions—"

"I spoke the truth about your situation. Admit it."

"You overstepped your bounds," she said stoutly. "You had no right."

He muttered a low curse. "I'm *trying* to help you."

Humiliation washed over her. The only thing worse than being proposed to by your worst enemy was being pitied by him. "I don't need your help, sir. And I certainly don't need—or want—you as a husband."

The scoundrel didn't even flinch. "Only because you've heard some foolish gossip about me. Give me a chance. I might surprise you." He flashed her a cocky smile. "Your brother liked me well enough."

"Yes, and he ended up dead for his pains," she shot back.

A stricken look crossed his face, and she almost wished she could take back the words. Until that vestige of grief vanished, replaced by a steely determination that frightened her.

"That's exactly why I'm offering to make amends by marrying you," he said with a cold lack of emotion. "Because you have a grim future ahead of you if you don't find a husband."

What a monstrous thing to say, even if it *was* true. She tipped up her chin. "I'm perfectly content living with my grandfather."

"He won't live forever. And when he dies—"

"I'll find a position as a lady's companion."

Lord Gabriel scowled. "And be subject to your patron's every whim?"

"As your wife, I'd be subject to *your* whims. Why is that better?"

"Because I would have your best interests at heart. Your patron would not."

"Then I'll become a governess."

"You'd throw yourself upon the mercy of some dragon-faced matron and her seven children? How could that be satisfying to a woman of education and good breeding?" His gaze played over her face. "And what if your beauty puts you at the mercy of a philandering husband or lecherous son?"

Ignoring his second surprising compliment to her looks, she glared at him. "You assume that everyone has *your* morals, sir."

"Those aren't my morals," he snapped. "But many men have them, and I'd hate to see Roger's sister fall prey to such."

There it was again, his reference to her as Roger's sister. Did he really feel guilt over what had happened? The day she'd confronted him at Turnham Green, he'd shown a great deal of remorse, but she'd assumed that was only in front of his family, whom he didn't want to think ill of him. Yet here it was again.

She snorted. It wasn't remorse he was showing, but arrogance. How typical. The way he strutted around town laughing at death, as if Roger's accident hadn't touched him one whit, made her steaming mad.

Besides, his offer of marriage didn't fit his character. Though she didn't move much in society, she had heard about the Sharpe brothers' exploits with women. Why did he want to marry all of a sudden? And why *her*?

She didn't for one minute believe that he genuinely wished to make amends. He hadn't tried to do so since the letters he'd written to Poppy right after Roger's death. And this would be an extreme way to make amends—

to leg-shackle himself for life. No, he must have some ulterior motive. She just didn't know what it was.

Not that it mattered. She wouldn't marry him for any reason.

"As flattered as I am by your eagerness to improve my circumstances, sir," she said in a cutting tone, "I'm afraid I must decline your offer. The only thing I want from you is a chance to race you. If you're not interested in that, I see no reason to continue this conversation."

Lord Gabriel looked frustrated, which gave her a wicked satisfaction.

The dance was ending, thank goodness. She would find Pierce and leave, now that she knew her invitation had merely been a ruse.

"What if I agree to a different race?" he said, as the last notes of the waltz sounded. "Not on the course that killed your brother, but on another course."

She stared at him in surprise. "A carriage race," she said, to confirm what he meant.

He led her from the floor, covering her hand with his. "Between you and me. If you win, I'll race you at Turnham Green as you've been plaguing me to do." He shot her a challenging glance. "But if *I* win, you let me court you."

She sucked in a breath. She might get her race at Turnham Green after all. If she won this new race he was proposing.

"You can even pick the course," he said.

Her blood began to pound. If she picked the course, she'd have an even better chance of winning. And wouldn't that be delicious—to beat him twice, especially after all his presumptuous talk about marrying her? He'd never be able to hold his head up around his friends again!

"Any course I like?" she asked.

He nodded. "You could even use the same one you ran against Letty Lade."

Not a chance. She'd raced Lady Lade at Waverly Farm, when the Lades had come to have a mare covered by one of Poppy's studs. She and Lady Lade had raced down a dirt track only a mile long. Expecting the notorious Angel of Death to race her along *that* tame course would be embarrassing.

But another sprang instantly to mind. "What about the one near Ealing that you and Roger raced all the time?" And that she'd driven her curricle along a hundred times. Roger used to bring her over there when he wanted to practice, and she was the one he'd practiced against.

He raised an eyebrow at her. "You know about that?"

She feigned nonchalance. "Roger always talked about his races against you. It annoyed him that he couldn't beat you more often."

"He beat me often enough," Lord Gabriel said tersely. *Just not when it counted.*

They were halfway around the room from the corner where Pierce was standing, holding two goblets of punch and watching her with narrowed eyes.

She ignored her cousin. "So is it a bargain? We race the course near Ealing?"

Lord Gabriel's gaze bore into her with unsettling intensity. "Do you agree to my terms?"

She hesitated. But really, how could she not? It didn't matter that his terms involved courtship—she was going to win. Her horses knew that course well. He might have a fast rig, but so did she, and she had the advantage of being smaller and lighter than he.

"I agree to your terms."

A smile broke over his face that nearly took her breath away. It was truly vexing how handsome he could look when he wanted.

"Very well then," he said, "the course near Ealing. Is this Friday too soon for you?"

That gave her little more than three days to prepare, but it would suffice. "Certainly, as long as it's after one p.m., so my grandfather thinks I'm off on my afternoon ride." Slowing her steps as they neared Pierce, she lowered her voice. "And don't tell my cousin. He'll go right to Poppy with it."

A knowing look crossed Lord Gabriel's face. "Does that mean we're to have a secret race? Just the two of us?"

Something in Lord Gabriel's lazy smile put her on her guard. And made her heart pound the teeniest bit faster.

She scowled. "Don't be ridiculous. Pierce has to be there. Someone must make sure you don't cheat."

"For God's sake—"

"But I won't tell him until the last minute. That worked well when he brought me to Turnham Green." She lifted her chin. "I can get Pierce to do whatever I please."

"Except not tattle on you to your grandfather," Lord Gabriel said dryly. "I suspect there are limits to even Devonmont's indulgence of your whims."

"None that I've reached."

"Yet."

Lord Gabriel didn't understand her friendship with her cousin. She was practically a sister to him.

But as Pierce came up to them, too impatient to wait for their approach, she wondered if there *were* limits to his indulgence.

"Good evening, Sharpe," Pierce said in a cool voice. He thrust a goblet at her. "You said you were thirsty."

"Indeed I am. Thank you."

Pierce glanced at Lord Gabriel. "I was surprised to see you two dancing, Sharpe, given Virginia's dislike of you."

"That's water under the bridge," Lord Gabriel said with a dismissive smile.

Virginia eyed him askance. The man had an annoying tendency to believe whatever suited him.

A gentleman sauntered up to join them who looked familiar, and both Pierce and Lord Gabriel stiffened at his approach.

"Well, well," the man said, taking in the little group with a gaze of keen interest, "what a surprise to see you here, Sharpe. You missed the race today."

Lord Gabriel shrugged. "No reason to come. I knew Jessup's filly would win."

"What do you say to that, Miss Waverly?" the stranger said with oily condescension. "Too bad you didn't consult with Sharpe. Your grandfather could have saved himself the trouble and just kept Ghost Rider home."

Virginia took an instant dislike to the man. "I'm sorry, sir, but I don't believe I know you."

Pierce stepped in to introduce the man as Lieutenant Chetwin. "Chetwin was the one who raced his rig against Sharpe's at Turnham Green," he added.

"Ah, yes, I remember." Another reckless scoundrel willing to do anything for the thrill of it, no matter whom it might hurt. She was surprised that Pierce knew him, though. He'd never mentioned the man.

"Tell me, Miss Waverly," the lieutenant said with a smirk, "is Sharpe still balking at racing you?"

"I hardly see how that is any concern of yours," she said coldly.

That banished his smirk. "I merely wondered if he's as skittish about racing you as he is about racing me. I keep trying to convince him to race again at Turnham Green, but he won't. Last time, I had to insult his mother to prod him into threading the needle."

"And yet I beat you," Lord Gabriel drawled, though his eyes glittered. "If not for clipping that boulder and destroying my phaeton the first time we raced there, I would have beaten you twice."

"Yes, but not hitting the boulders is rather the point, old boy," Lieutenant Chetwin sneered. "Don't you agree, Miss Waverly?"

Was the dreadful man referring to her brother's death? "It seems to me that *winning* is the point, sir. And you lost."

Lieutenant Chetwin's gaze turned frigid. "Only because one of my horses' hooves picked up a stone, as Sharpe well knows. And because I had the good sense to pull back before I could be dashed upon the rocks."

She was stunned into silence at the reference. What sort of boor trampled on someone's grief?

"That was beyond the pale, Chetwin. But then, you never did learn how to speak properly to a lady," Lord Gabriel growled.

Chetwin flicked a dismissive glance over her. "A lady doesn't challenge gentlemen to races she never intends to run."

"I *do* intend to run it!" she said hotly. "As soon as I beat Lord Gabriel in Ealing on Friday!"

The moment the words left her mouth, she could have kicked herself.

"If you'll excuse us, Miss Waverley agreed to stand up for this next dance with me," Lord Gabriel said, and whisked her back onto the floor.

This time the dance was a reel. Appropriate, since her mind was reeling.

Lord Gabriel had defended her to that nasty Chetwin. And until she'd blurted it out herself, he'd kept her secret about the race, too, when he could just as easily have countered the lieutenant's insinuations by bragging to the man about it. Given his apparent flair for the dramatic, that was rather strange.

He caught her about the waist to dance her up the line and said, "Sorry about that, Miss Waverly. Chetwin is an arse."

"I agree. Why does he hate you so?"

A muscle ticked in Lord Gabriel's jaw. "I won a race against him in front of his entire cavalry regiment and humiliated him before the men under his command.

He's resented me ever since. That's why he keeps badgering me about racing him at Turnham Green again."

"That's no excuse for his behavior to *me*," she said before they were separated again.

When they were together in the dance again, he drawled, "You reminded him that I beat him. That's reason enough for him to dislike you. Why did you do that, when you purport to hate me, too?" His eyes gleamed at her as if he had drawn some spurious conclusion from that.

She sniffed. "If anyone is to criticize you, Lord Gabriel, it's going to be *me,* not some vile fool whose mission in life seems to be making trouble."

He laughed, and the dance separated them again.

After that they spoke no more, but she was very aware that something had shifted between them.

The lieutenant's words drifted into her mind: *Last time, I had to insult his mother to prod him into threading the needle.* Was that really why Lord Gabriel had raced that vile fellow—because of an insult to his mother?

It didn't change anything, of course. But it did . . . well . . . mitigate it somewhat, since his parents had died scandalously.

She'd heard all the rumors ages ago about the late Lord and Lady Stoneville. The official story was that Lady Stoneville had killed her husband by accident, then killed herself out of grief, but all sorts of other tales abounded. That their eldest son, the present Lord Stoneville, had murdered them for his fortune. That

Lady Stoneville had killed her husband out of jealousy over one of his many indiscretions.

No wonder Lord Gabriel had felt compelled to accept the man's challenge.

She frowned. How could she make excuses for him? He was a reckless fool with no sense of decency, an arrogant rogue who thought she ought to be grateful that he wanted to marry her . . . And a man who'd lost his parents in a horrific way at seven, and somehow still managed to find some joy in life.

She glanced at him as they turned with their alternate partners in the dance. The woman he was twirling beamed up at him, and he grinned back.

All right, so she could see how some women *might* find him charming. He had a way of making a woman feel she had his entire attention when she was with him.

Every time the dance brought them back together, he smiled, and every time he did, her pulse gave a little flutter.

Clearly she didn't get out into society nearly enough. Her pulse had no taste in men whatsoever.

They finished the dance, and he led her from the floor. "Since the cat is out of the bag," he said, "what will you do about your cousin?"

"Leave Pierce to me. I'll meet you Friday at one-thirty. Just make sure you're there."

Pierce could squawk all he wanted. She would race Lord Gabriel, and she would win—first at Ealing, then at Turnham Green. Then she would put him and his fine looks and wild reputation out of her mind for good.

Chapter Three

etty Plumtree had been sitting in the library of Halstead Hall for at least an hour. Her youngest grandson should have been home by now. The rest of the family had returned from the ball at Marsbury House some time ago. And given what they had told her, she did not know what to think of Gabe's continued absence.

But then, he never behaved as expected. The rapscallion had a rebellious streak that ran all the way to his toes. She remembered one time when he—

"You didn't need to wait up," said a voice practically at her elbow.

She jumped, then swatted at him with her cane. "Are you trying to give me heart failure, sneaking up on me like that? Where did you come from anyway, you little devil?"

Her six-foot-two grandson laughed and pointed to the open window behind her. He bent to kiss her cheek, and she smelled the musky scent of horses on him. He must have lingered in the stables to groom his own mount, which alarmed her. He only did that when something had disturbed him.

"Where have you been?" she snapped. "Everyone else has been home for hours."

"Last I checked," he drawled as he dropped into the chair opposite her, "I wasn't required to report on my comings and goings."

"Do not be impertinent," she grumbled.

He just laughed again. It was Gabe's way of thumbing his nose at the world. He pretended that his heart hadn't been sliced open twice already in his young life; first on his parents' deaths and again on the day Roger Waverly died.

Gabe plastered over the wounds with a few jokes and a reckless smile, but over the past six weeks, the plaster seemed to be cracking. He couldn't see it, but she could. And when those wounds began to bleed again, all the jokes in the world were not going to stanch the blood.

"So how was the ball?" she asked, wondering how to broach the subject she really wanted to discuss.

His smile faded. "You know perfectly well how it was. I'm sure the others told you all about it."

If he could lay *his* cards on the table . . . "They said you danced with Miss Waverly. Twice."

"I did."

"You are not thinking of taking her up on her challenge, are you?"

"Actually, I'm thinking of marrying her."

Hetty gaped at him. "Even though she hates you?" Was he serious?

He scowled. "Why does everybody keep saying that?"

"Because it is true."

"She can't possibly hate me—she doesn't know me. She hates that her brother died racing me, but that doesn't mean she hates *me*." He crossed his arms over his chest. "I got her to dance with me, didn't I?"

"What did you do—hint that you would agree to race her if she would dance with you?" When he shrugged, she snorted. "What you lads do not know about women could fill up an ocean. Manipulating a woman gets you nowhere with her in the long run."

"Yet you continue to try manipulating us," he said dryly.

"That's different. What are grandparents for if not to plague their grandchildren?"

Staring at his set jaw and haunted eyes, she felt a sudden clutch in her chest. She had always had a soft spot for Gabe, with his easygoing nature, lack of fear, and death-defying grin. But she had always felt helpless to reach him.

"This is not what I wanted for you," she said softly. "I wanted love and life and happiness. Not some woman who will make your life hell."

The blunt words seemed to upset him, for he went perfectly rigid. "Then you shouldn't have laid down your ultimatum."

"You do not have to choose the one woman who has every reason to hate you."

"Thanks to me, she'll be destitute when her grandfather dies. I figured marrying her was the least I could do."

She cast him a skeptical glance. "And she agrees?"

"She will. Eventually."

"Gabriel—"

"Enough," he said, rising to his feet. "As long as I gain a wife, you have no reason to complain."

"You have to live until the wedding for it to count, you know," she snapped as he walked away.

He turned to stare at her. "What do you mean?"

"If you're planning to race her—"

"Ah. You think I'll kill myself threading the needle at Turnham Green."

"You have been lucky three times. No one's luck lasts forever."

His brow furrowed. "What if I swore never to thread the needle again, against Miss Waverly or anyone else? What would you give me?"

She hesitated. Such a vow would eliminate her greatest worry—that he would run that blasted course and kill himself or someone else. Either scenario could put him beyond the reach of his family forever.

Still, bargaining with her grandchildren was dicey. It had worked to her benefit with Jarret, but Gabe was another matter entirely. "What do you want?"

"I want you to rescind your ultimatum for—"

"That will never happen," she broke in. "Besides, you said you wished to marry Miss Waverly to help her."

"I do. But it's not me I want you to rescind it for. It's Celia."

She gaped at him. "Why?"

"You'll already have four of us paired off. I realize the rest of us let it go too long, but she's only twenty-four. Let her find a husband in her own time. Or not find one at all, if that's what she prefers. I don't want to see her marry some fortune hunter, and neither do you. You got lucky with Minerva, but Celia is . . . different."

"You mean, because she shoots guns for entertainment."

"Because she'll hold firm in resisting your ultimatum. She'll force you between a rock and a hard place. You don't really want to disinherit us all. And you certainly don't want to do it if everyone complies but her."

He was right, though she wasn't about to say that to him. "I will do what I have to."

His lips thinned into a line. "Then I'll race whomever I want, on whatever course I want."

She scowled at him. "Remember what I said. If you die before you marry, then no one gets anything."

"Really? You'd punish my grieving siblings just because I had the audacity to die and cheat you out of seeing your plans come to fruition? I hardly think so." Then that impudent light came into his eyes, the one she knew so well from when he was a boy and would sneak out to the stable, no matter what punishment she invented for making him stay put. "Besides, haven't you heard? I'm the Angel of Death—I can't die."

A chill coursed down her spine. Damned fool. Saying such a thing was tempting Fate.

He stepped nearer, his voice low. "And I'm going to live just to watch Celia make you squirm, Gran. I suspect that after she takes her turn at finding a spouse, you'll regret you ever came up with this plan of yours. Never say I didn't warn you."

When he turned again to leave, she said, "I'll think about it."

He paused to look at her.

"I am not saying I will take you up on your offer. But I shall consider it."

"You'd better consider it soon," he drawled. "I'm racing Miss Waverly in three days." He strode off.

Damn that boy! It seemed he had inherited every bit of her skill at manipulation. If she was not careful, he might gain the upper hand in this battle.

She used her cane to push herself to a stand.

But she had come this far without caving in to her grandchildren's complaints. She was not about to give in because of Gabe's threats.

Still, as she hobbled to her bedchamber, his words rang in her head: *I'm the Angel of Death—I can't die.* She knew better than anyone that Death could seize you when you least expected it. And she could not bear to think of losing someone else she loved to its greedy hands.

GENERAL ISAAC WAVERLY was hunched over his breakfast of shirred eggs and bacon when his great-nephew entered the room. Still smarting over the loss of the Marsbury Cup yesterday, Isaac didn't even look up.

Ghost Rider should have won—the colt had lost by a mere nose. How was Waverly Farm supposed to get out of debt if its horses couldn't win purses?

Stud farms lived and died on the careers of their race-horses, and he hadn't had a spectacular winner in some time. He was pulling in less and less money from stud fees, and his few tenants were struggling because of the recent drought. It had been a hard year for many a squire, but he needed to set funds aside for Virginia.

He vastly feared that she wouldn't find a husband with her small dowry. Between her lack of a season and her inability to hold her tongue when she should, she needed all the help she could get. And he owed it to her. The girl had given up her future to take care of him after his injury—she deserved something more than a life of looking after a cranky grump like him.

He glanced over at Pierce. "How was the ball? Did our girl dance with anyone?"

Pierce poured himself a cup of tea. "You could say that."

"Anyone I know?"

His nephew hesitated, then glanced toward the door leading into the kitchen, from which came the sounds of Virginia's happy chatter with the servants.

It was no surprise to Isaac that she was as comfortable in the kitchen as she was in a drawing room. In those long months after he was thrown from a horse and unable to leave his bed, Virginia's only company, aside from the occasional visit from Pierce, had been the servants.

They adored her. His cook snuck her ginger cake when she was low, his housekeeper consulted her on the accounts and the menus, and his grooms let her have whatever mount she chose, even the ones that he'd instructed were strictly forbidden to her.

The girl had her mother's energy and her father's

temper. They argued about everything as she bustled about creating order in his widower's household. Sometimes he found it easier just to let her have her head.

"So whom did she dance with?" he prodded Pierce.

"Gabriel Sharpe."

A sense of foreboding caught him by the ballocks. "Why the devil would she dance with that cocky bastard?"

His nephew grimaced. "There's something I should have told you a month ago, when it happened. But I figured you had enough on your mind, and I really didn't think she'd go through with it. Now I'm not so sure."

"Go through with what?" he asked, his blood running cold.

In a few terse words, Pierce laid out exactly what his spitfire of a granddaughter had been up to.

Isaac leapt up from the breakfast table like a charger hit in the rump with birdshot. "Virginia Anne Waverly!" he shouted. "You come in here right this minute!"

The little sauce-box entered the room with a plate of toast in one hand and a salver of butter in the other, wearing an expression of pure innocence that didn't fool him for one minute. "Yes, Poppy?"

He scowled. "Pierce tells me that you mean to run some fool race against Lord Gabriel Sharpe."

She shot her cousin a foul glance as she set the plate and salver on the table. "See if I ever embroider a pair of slippers for *you* again."

Pierce eyed her coolly over his cup of tea. "If you embroider me any more slippers, I shall have to grow extra feet."

"You know perfectly well that you need an inordinate number of slippers," Virginia said. "You wear them out faster than—"

"I don't care about Pierce's damned slippers!" Isaac shouted. "I want to know what possessed you to challenge Sharpe to a race! It's not like you to do something so foolish."

Anger flared in her face. "It's nothing to worry about, just a quick carriage race along that course in Ealing. You remember the one—it's not the least dangerous."

"Any kind of racing is dangerous, young lady!"

"Poppy, sit down," she said firmly as she came to his side and took his arm. "You know the doctor says you must avoid upset."

"Then stop upsetting me!" He batted her hand away. "Pierce tells me you actually challenged the man to thread the needle—what were you thinking?"

A hot flush rose in her cheeks. "I thought that I would beat him and he would finally stop strutting around town, showing off his prowess at getting people killed."

That reined in Isaac's temper right quick. Roger's death had hit them both hard, but it had been harder on her. She'd idolized her brother, and his death had put a fine patina on the giant monument she'd been building in his honor ever since she was a girl. She couldn't see straight when it came to Roger.

"Oh, lambkin," he said. "You have to stop fretting over Sharpe. I hate the fellow as much as you do, but—"

"If you had only seen him last month at the race,

bragging about how he'd beaten Lieutenant Chetwin."
She balled her hands into fists. "He didn't give a fig for
the fact that Roger died running that course! Someone
needs to put Lord Gabriel in his place, to teach him
some humility, some . . . some sense of decency!"

"And you think it should be you?"

"Why not?" Her voice turned pleading. "You know I
can do it. You said yourself that I can tool a curricle better than any man you've ever seen."

"I'm not going to watch you risk your life—and your
future, I might add—trying to race that man, of all men.
Get your bonnet. We're paying a visit to Lord Gabriel
Sharpe. You, my dear, are going to tell him that you've
seen the error of your ways and you refuse to race him."

"I'm not doing any such thing!" she sputtered. "I refuse to let him think I'm a coward."

"And *I* refuse to lose another grandchild to that arse!"

She paled. "You won't lose me, I swear."

"You're damned right, I won't," he said, feeling a
clutch of fear in his heart. "I couldn't bear it."

After his wife had died of pleurisy while accompanying him and the cavalry on the Peninsula, he'd had
a rough time. Then his son and daughter-in-law had
died, and he'd come home to run the stud farm, bitter
over his losses, wanting nothing more than to crawl into
a hole and grieve alone.

He'd planned on finding a relative to take in Virginia
and Roger, until he'd seen the girl—three years old and
inconsolable. She'd gazed up at him with trembling lips
and said, "Papa gone?"

A lump had stuck in his throat as he'd answered, "Papa is gone, lambkin. But *Poppy* is here."

Staring at him with huge, tear-filled eyes, she'd thrown her chubby little arms around his leg and said, "Poppy stay."

In that moment, she'd clutched his heart in her tiny fists. He'd become her "Poppy," and she'd become his "lambkin."

And he was *never* going to lose her. "We're getting you out of this race with Sharpe, or I swear to God, I'll lock you up in your room and never let you out again."

The girl argued with him every step of the way. She protested while they waited for the carriage to be brought. She pleaded as they set off for Ealing. But as her efforts yielded nothing during the hour's drive to Halstead Hall, she lapsed into a brooding silence. He didn't know which was worse.

By the time they neared Halstead Hall he'd worked himself into a fine temper, further fueled by the sight of the large, impressive manor house. He'd always known that Sharpe was brother to a marquess, from a family as old as England itself. Indeed, that was one reason he hated the fellow.

If Sharpe hadn't lured Roger into a life of wild and reckless living, the lad would surely be alive today. Roger had worshipped the young lord, willing to do damned near anything to impress his friend.

While they'd been at school, Isaac hadn't worried about their friendship. Exposing Roger to a higher class could help the lad in the long run. He himself hadn't reached the rank of general without making advantageous friendships, so he knew the value of it.

Even the racing hadn't bothered him. Young men would be young men, after all. But then Roger had begun spending all his time in the stews in London, drinking and gambling beyond his means, and Isaac had started to worry.

Seeing Halstead Hall brought it all back. No wonder Roger had fallen in with Sharpe and that duke's son—how could the boy not have been seduced by such advantages when his own were so modest?

Isaac should have put his foot down while he had the chance. He shouldn't have waited until Roger's funeral to toss Sharpe off his property.

Well, he wasn't allowing another tragedy to happen.

All too soon, they pulled up to the massive front doors. Halstead Hall was one of those sprawling Tudor manors suitable to house a king—which was apparently who'd owned it before it was given to the Sharpe family over two hundred years ago.

"Now see here," he said to Virginia as footmen and grooms came running toward their carriage. "You'll let me do the talking until we meet with Sharpe. Then you'll inform him that you've changed your mind about racing him, and that will be the end of it. Understood?"

"But Poppy—"

"I mean it, Virginia." When she crossed her arms over her chest in a gesture of defiance, he sighed. "If you do as I say, I promise to buy you some new gowns. We could even go to London for a ball or two. I'm sure Pierce could wrangle us an invitation somewhere."

Though how he would afford lodgings for such a thing just now, he didn't know. They couldn't exactly stay in Pierce's bachelor quarters.

A hurt look crossed her face. "Even if there *was* money for gowns and balls, I'm not some ninny-headed society girl to be swayed by them. There's a principle involved."

With a deep sigh, she stared out the carriage window.

Damn, damn, damn. His lambkin certainly knew how to strike for the heart. Offering her gowns had wounded her dignity, and if the lass had one thing, it was oceans of dignity.

The door opened, and they got out. When he gave the servant their names and announced that they'd come to call on Lord Gabriel, they were led through a long archway and across a courtyard into a great hall that would cow the average fellow.

But this was the world Isaac had grown up in. One where "good breeding" was defined as the ability to put an upstart in his place, where men were judged by the cut of their coats, not the cut of their character.

He hated this world of vanity and empty promises. He'd been happy to leave it as a young man to become a commissioned officer and do something important with his life. He'd lived through the battles at Vimeiro and Roliça, and stared into the face of evil too many times to count. Some titled family with a passel of hell-raising children wasn't going to cow *him*, by God.

Virginia, he wasn't too sure about. She stared at the ancient carved oak screen that took up one end of the hall and the massive marble fireplaces that punctuated the flanking wall, her mouth hanging open.

"Is this really where Lord Gabriel lives?" she whispered as the servant went off, presumably to fetch the man.

"So I hear." Isaac frowned at her. "Surely you knew his background."

"Well, yes, but I never realized . . . I mostly paid attention to his exploits."

"Halstead Hall is famous in these parts for its size— three hundred sixty-five rooms. Its gardens are huge, and it has one of the largest mazes in England. Last I heard, the estate had seventy tenants."

"Sweet Lord," she said. "His family must be enormously wealthy."

"Wealthy enough to buy whatever and whomever they choose. Keep that in mind when you're thinking to do a fool thing like race one of them." He didn't bother to modulate his voice; he wasn't going to let these Sharpes intimidate *him* with all their wealth. "Though I hear that their money comes from the mother's side of the family, not from the marquess's."

"You hear correctly, sir. My grandchildren get their money from me."

Startled, he looked over to see a woman about his age descending a painted staircase. Her steps were slow, which lent her a regal quality that momentarily put him in awe. It was only when he saw the cane in her hand that he realized her slow gait was due to some weakness in her legs.

He idly rubbed the arm that hadn't worked right since

his tumble from that horse. He knew what it was to be betrayed by one's own body, to be incapable of doing everything one desired. It gave him instant sympathy for the lady.

He squelched that ruthlessly.

"You must be General Waverly," she said as she came toward them. "I'm Hester Plumtree, grandmother to—"

"I know who you are," he said sharply.

Who didn't know of Hetty Plumtree, famous for running a brewery empire with an iron fist and forcing all the male brewers to give ground?

But he'd expected some dragon-faced matron with the voice of a harpy, and a mannish demeanor. Not this fragile-looking creature with a roses-and-cream complexion and a smile that made a man's aged blood run hot again.

Damn it all, he was letting the woman get to him. "We've come to see Lord Gabriel," he barked. "This matter doesn't concern you, madam."

She didn't flinch or frown at his boorish words. "I'm afraid I'm not sure exactly where he is at the moment. But while the servants are looking for him, perhaps you'd like some tea? You must be parched after your long drive."

"I don't want any tea," he spat, knowing he was behaving like a grouchy old arse but unable to stop himself.

"I would love some tea," Virginia said with a bright smile. "Thank you."

Now the girl chose to behave like a well-bred young lady? She was going to drive him into an early grave.

Mrs. Plumtree ordered the servant to bring them tea

and told him they'd have it in the library. "This way," she said as she gestured toward a hallway. "We might as well be comfortable while we chat. And this room is so cavernous, don't you think? It makes me feel as if I'm conducting a lecture."

Isaac didn't know how to answer. Was she trying to throw him off by being cordial, lulling them into letting down their guard? It wouldn't work. No slip of a woman was going to get the best of him, no matter how fine a figure she cut.

Once they were ensconced in the library, she said, "I gather that this is about the race that my grandson and your granddaughter agreed to run?"

"I told you, it's none of your concern."

"Of course it is. I don't want to see either of them hurt any more than you do. And that course at Turnham Green—"

"Turnham Green!" He scowled at Virginia. "You told me you planned to run the course at Ealing!"

"We do, Poppy, I promise!"

"Then what is the woman talking about?"

"Forgive me, sir," Mrs. Plumtree put in. "I must have misunderstood my grandson. Now that I think of it, he never actually said what course they were running. I just assumed . . ." Her eyes narrowed. "I can see he and I need to have another conversation."

"It doesn't matter what course it is. They shouldn't be racing."

Virginia leaned forward. "I keep explaining to my grandfather that it's perfectly safe."

"Safe!" Isaac roared. "To race a rig down some rutted track against a man who's known for recklessness, a man who will do anything to win?"

"My grandson would not let her be hurt, if that is what you are implying, sir," Mrs. Plumtree said stonily.

Ah. The dragon lady emerged at last. "Forgive me, madam, but I've seen what havoc your grandson wreaks when he races."

"Surely such an innocuous course could not cause any harm," she countered.

"That's exactly what I keep telling him, Mrs. Plumtree," Virginia piped up. "Honestly, Poppy, it would hardly—"

"Enough, girl." He scowled at her. "Go wait in the hall while I talk to Mrs. Plumtree alone."

"But—"

"Now, Virginia!"

With a sniff, she rose and stalked out.

As soon as she was gone, he glared at Mrs. Plumtree. "How dare you encourage her in this mad idea!"

She gazed at him, steely eyed. "So you have had success squelching her mad ideas in the past?"

The words took him aback. "She hasn't *had* any mad ideas in the past. Until your grandson came along, she was responsible and levelheaded and—"

"My grandson did not change her character, sir. Perhaps he just exposed what was already there."

"You don't know my granddaughter."

"I know young women. I have two granddaughters of my own, and a daughter before them. I am well aware of how stubborn young females can be, especially those of a passionate nature, like your granddaughter. If you hold firm, she is likely to go behind your back. When did you first learn that she had challenged my grandson to a race?"

He eyed her balefully, then rose, annoyed to have his incompetence as a guardian thrown back in his teeth. "Today."

"She challenged him over a month ago. That should tell you something."

"Well, if you could keep your damned grandson from doing foolish things like racing that blasted course at Turnham Green—"

"I do my best," she said stiffly. "But consider that you have only one grandchild to corral. I have five."

He couldn't dispute that. Hell and damnation, what would he have done if he'd found himself at an advanced age the guardian of five children? It didn't bear thinking on.

"Besides," she went on, "at twenty-seven years old, he is quite grown. He is not going to listen to what his grandmother tells him."

He strode up to stand over her. "You could cut him off, reduce his allowance—"

"I have already threatened something of that sort. So far, it has not curbed his behavior to any great degree."

"Clearly, or he wouldn't be agreeing to race Virginia."

Ignoring the position he'd taken deliberately to intimidate her, she pushed herself to a stand and faced him down. "And what of your granddaughter? Your tactics do not seem to carry much weight with *her*."

They were so close that he could see into her fathomless blue eyes and smell the rosewater on her. The woman was maddening. The woman was exciting. It had been years since he'd found a woman exciting, not since his Lily died. But this woman . . .

He stiffened. "So what are you proposing that we do? Let them kill each other?"

"Oh, please," she said tartly. "You men always exaggerate. They will not kill each other. If you allow the race, then you have control of when and where and how it happens. We can both be there to monitor the situation. Your granddaughter will be so pleased that she will stop fighting you, and racing my grandson will purge her desire for vengeance. Then you need not worry about more encounters between them."

"And if I don't allow it?"

"They will just find a way to arrange it in secret. You cannot keep her locked up all the time, you know."

Much as he hated to admit it, her words made sense. He could recognize a master strategist when he met one. "It sounds to me, madam, as if you've had quite a bit of experience at manipulating matters regarding your grandchildren. I'm surprised they aren't more cooperative."

"So am I," she said blithely.

A laugh escaped him despite himself.

At the sound of it, her eyes softened. "Actually, I have managed to get three of them married and well settled in the last few months. So in truth, they are vastly more cooperative than they used to be."

"You'll have to give me lessons on how to achieve such a feat," he said with a smile.

"I would be honored." A coy smile curved her own lips. She had pretty lips, he couldn't help noticing.

Then he caught himself. What was he doing? This was Sharpe's grandmother, for God's sake! The scoundrel had clearly come by his recklessness honestly; Isaac could well imagine Hester Plumtree driving a carriage neck for leather down some track. And woe be unto the fool who stood in her way.

"I must see to my granddaughter," he muttered, turning away. He needed to escape the woman and her machinations before he foundered on the rocks.

It had been a mistake coming here. He would just lock the girl up on Friday; let Sharpe come after her if he wanted his race.

He strode out to the hall. "Virginia, we're going home."

There was no one there.

"Virginia!" he shouted.

No one came, and there was no sign of where she might have gone.

"Damnation! Where the devil is my granddaughter?"

Chapter Four

$\mathcal{V}$irginia followed the detailed directions that the kind footman had given her to the stables. This mansion was unbelievable. Who lived in such a place?

No wonder Lord Gabriel was so sure of himself. He'd been handed everything on a silver platter from the time he was born, so he assumed he had a right to it all.

Well, she would take him down a peg.

It was a pity that Poppy was being so stubborn about the carriage race. Didn't he *want* to see Lord Gabriel publicly humiliated?

Well, she had a plan. If she could get a look at the horses Lord Gabriel used to pull his phaeton, she'd have some ammunition for her arguments with Poppy. She would detail their strengths and weaknesses, then point out exactly how she could beat them with her own horses. She had a whole stud farm to draw from, after all. She doubted that Lord Gabriel had *that*.

It wouldn't hurt to survey his rig, either. There might be some way she could improve her curricle. If she could just convince Poppy that she couldn't lose this race, he might relent.

She neared a large building that obviously housed several horses, a short distance from a smaller building that also seemed to be a stable. Oh, dear, which one held his horses and phaeton? And how was she to gain the grooms' help in looking at them without showing her hand?

Suddenly a groom emerged from the larger building carrying a bucket. She ducked into a doorway to watch as he called for a younger groom. As soon as the younger one came flying, the older handed him the bucket and said, "This is the special mash Lord Gabriel wanted for his new horse. Make sure that the beast eats all of it. It'll ease her digestion."

The young groom hurried across to the smaller building and ducked inside with the bucket, then came out shortly afterward without it.

Virginia let out a breath. Lord Gabriel's new horse must be for his phaeton. Since the small stable wasn't nearly as busy as the large one, perhaps she could get in to see it without being spotted.

She edged toward the entrance, looking about for any grooms who might emerge from the larger one. When she heard voices coming her way, she darted into the small stable.

Then she stopped short. Because standing in the narrow aisle was Lord Gabriel himself.

He held the bucket of mash in his hands and was feeding it to the horse whose nose she could just see sticking out of a stall. His lordship wore no coat or cravat, just a waistcoat and a shirt with the sleeves rolled up exposing his fine, muscular forearms.

She caught her breath. In shirt sleeves, riding breeches, and top boots, he was a rather astonishing figure of a man, lean and fit and handsome. Too handsome for any woman's sanity.

"There now, my little filly," he crooned to the horse. "This should make you feel better."

His soothing voice did something fluttery to her insides. It was hard not to be charmed by a man who could treat an animal so tenderly. It made her wonder how he would be with a woman.

She cursed inwardly. She didn't wonder any such thing. She did *not*!

"And stop fighting the grooms, will you?" Lord Gabriel told the filly. "You must save that fine energy for the St. Leger Stakes. You're going to knock them back on their heels, my pretty girl. You're going to run like the wind and leave all those silly colts far behind."

He planned to enter a Thoroughbred in the St. Leger Stakes? Sweet Lord, so did Poppy. And if Lord Gabriel caught her here . . .

With her heart in her throat, she began to back away. Then a horse near her whinnied, and Lord Gabriel's head swung round. He took her in with a narrowing gaze, set the bucket down, and came toward her.

She turned tail to run, but he was beside her in two steps and grabbing her by the arms. "Whoa, there," he growled as he turned her to face him. "What the blazes are you doing here?"

"I . . . um . . . well . . . my grandfather wanted to pay a visit to you, but he is talking to your grandmother, and . . ." She thought quickly. "And I heard that you had a spectacular maze, so I went looking for it. Then I got lost and ended up here."

"Because you were looking for our maze," he said skeptically.

"I love mazes."

"So it has nothing to do with trying to observe your competition." His eyes bored into her.

"No, indeed! I had no idea you have a Thoroughbred that you intend to— I mean . . ."

"You heard me talking to Flying Jane," he accused. "Why, you sneaky little vixen."

Oh, dear, now she was really in trouble. The racing world was rife with subterfuge. Since odds were laid based on knowledge of a horse, touts often sneaked into stables or spied on secret trials to gain their information. So any Thoroughbred owner grew suspicious if a competitor came near his horses—especially before a big race like the St. Leger Stakes.

"It was purely accidental, I swear!"

"And now you'll run off to tell your grandfather about his competitor."

"No!" At his arched eyebrow, she added, "I won't tell a soul. I would never do that."

"Really." His grip slid from her shoulders down to her arms. "You got lost and decided to enter a stables alone, knowing that several male grooms would be about."

"I live on a stud farm. I go into stables alone all the time."

"But your own grooms know better than to lay a

hand on the owner's granddaughter. These grooms don't know you."

His hold on her unsettled her. He was keeping her far too close, and it made her nervous. Especially with him dressed so casually. His black shirt was open at the throat, exposing a little dusting of chest hair.

"They would have treated me better than you, I dare say," she retorted with a tilt of her chin. "Please let go of me."

"So you can spy on me some more?" he drawled.

"I was *not* spying."

"Then you had some other reason for coming in here," he said, his voice deepening. "Perhaps some reason more . . . personal."

"Personal?" she squeaked.

His gaze played over her, growing more heated. "Perhaps you were looking for *me*."

Oh, but he was a cocky one. "Certainly not. Why would I look for you here, of all places?"

"Because the footmen undoubtedly told you that I often spend my mornings here." His voice was husky now, and his hands moved up and down her arms, warming them, making her heart race unaccountably.

"I didn't ask the footmen . . . I mean, I asked them about the sta—The maze, but I . . ." She was babbling like some smitten schoolgirl, for pity's sake. "I didn't know you were here," she finished lamely. "You're being ridiculous."

"Judging from your blush, I'm not being ridiculous at all," he murmured.

Her hand went to her cheek. Was she blushing? Good

gracious, she was. "I am not one of those tarts who swoons at your every word, you know."

"It's not the words they swoon at." He encircled her waist and pulled her even closer. "And though you're not the least bit a tart, that doesn't mean you're not curious about me."

Her breath refused to obey her commands, quickening feverishly. She should be slapping him, shoving him away. "That's absurd. How could I possibly be curious about a . . . a scoundrel with your reputation?"

"Because you want to know how I got that reputation. If it's deserved. If I really do make women 'swoon' in my bed."

Her jaw dropped. He should not be saying things like that to her. And she should definitely not be letting them make her pulse race and her hands grow clammy. What was wrong with her?

"I tell you what," he rasped, bending his head toward her. "Why don't I satisfy a bit of your curiosity?" He covered her mouth with his.

She froze at the intimate assault. How appalling. How unacceptable.

How intoxicating. His lips moved over hers with the surety of a man who'd kissed many women. An instant thrill swept down her spine that did the most delicious things to her insides.

She could feel her mouth soften beneath his, feel her breath stutter against his lips, feel her blood race rampantly through her veins. This was wrong, so wrong. And it felt completely and utterly right.

"Ah, vixen," he whispered against her lips. "What a kissable mouth you have."

Did she? No man had ever kissed her before.

"Lord Gabriel, I really don't think—"

"Gabe," he murmured. "My friends call me Gabe."

"I'm not your friend."

"You're right. You're something more . . . intimate. So call me Gabriel. Hardly anyone does. Or better yet, call me 'darling.' No one ever calls me that, sweetheart." Before she could balk at that effrontery, he took her lips again.

But this time his lips were firmer, hotter. He pulled her flush against him and opened his mouth over hers, coaxing it open so he could plunge his tongue inside.

Lord have mercy on her soul. What was *that*? She'd never imagined . . .

It was glorious. He coaxed her tongue to twine with his, then he played with it. Oh, how he played. His mouth consumed hers, and his tongue drove inside her with slow, silky strokes that made her want things, *need* things she didn't understand.

Before she knew it, he'd pressed her against the wall between two stalls, his lips seducing hers. She couldn't breathe, couldn't think.

She laid her hands on his chest, meaning to push him back, but her fingers curled themselves into his waistcoat like little traitors.

Within moments, the whole world narrowed to this man with his mouth on hers and his hands roaming up and down her ribs and her waist, his thumbs brushing the undersides of her breasts as they swept—

A sudden sharp pain in her arm made her cry out against his mouth and shove him away. "What the dickens?"

"Jacky Boy!" he growled at the pony that had just nipped her. "None of that!"

She turned her head to look at the pony whose lips were drawn back to show his teeth. If ever a beast could be said to glare, this one was doing so.

Gabriel examined her arm with great concern. Seeing that the bite hadn't even cut through the cloth, he turned to the pony. "You know better, lad," he scolded. "You can't go around biting ladies."

The pony nudged Gabriel with his head, shoving in between them as if to separate them.

Stifling a laugh, Virginia moved out of range. Gabriel might call it "lad," but the aging pony was clearly well beyond its prime. The poor thing probably had only a few more years left in him. And a decided attachment to his owner.

Thank heaven. She'd been on the verge of doing goodness knows what.

"I'm sorry," Gabriel said. "Jacky Boy was the first mount I ever owned, so he tends to be possessive. He's jealous of anyone I show attention to. He's already annoyed by Flying Jane's arrival in the stable, so he took it out on you."

"He has no reason to be jealous of me," she said.

Gabriel's eyes darkened as he came toward her. "He most certainly does." His gaze swept down her body with such heat that her breathing quickened again. "But he'll have to get used to it."

The intimation that they had some sort of future together alarmed her as nothing else had. She backed away, horrified that she'd gone so far with him.

"No, no," she said, shaking her head. "I am *not* taking up with my brother's murderer."

His face turned to stone, but his eyes blazed with a heat that singed her. "Don't you ever grow tired of that argument, Virginia?" he bit out, as if it took every ounce of his will not to throttle her. "I didn't murder your brother. Murder implies intent. What happened was a tragic accident—"

"That you brought on by taking advantage of him while he was drunk," she countered. "Roger was too drunk to know what he did."

"When we raced, he was perfectly sober."

"That's not what Poppy says."

"Your grandfather wasn't there. He needs someone to blame, so he blames me. But that doesn't mean he has a reason for it."

"He . . . he has no reason to lie about it, either."

"People deceive themselves sometimes." He headed toward her again. "It's better than facing the truth, that your brother—"

"What the devil is going on here?" came her grandfather's voice from the entrance.

Gabriel halted. "Good morning, General," he said, though he kept his eyes locked with hers. "Your granddaughter and I were just discussing a race."

As her grandfather drew himself up, she added hastily, "I came to the stables to see if I could get a glimpse of Gabriel's . . . I-I mean, Lord Gabriel's rig and horses, Poppy, and I found his lordship instead."

Might as well admit the truth. At least then, Gabriel wouldn't persist in thinking she had come looking for him. Or worse, spying on his Thoroughbred to help Poppy gain an advantage for the St. Leger Stakes.

"You have no business wandering the stables alone," Poppy snapped.

"His lordship was just telling me the same thing. He was about to escort me back inside."

With a skeptical expression, her grandfather glanced from her to Gabriel. She prayed that he couldn't tell she was lying. That he couldn't tell she'd just been kissed senseless.

At that moment, Mrs. Plumtree hobbled into the stable, then halted. Her gaze seemed to take in more than Poppy's, for she fixed it on Virginia's probably reddened mouth for so long that Virginia had to drop her eyes.

"Well, isn't this cozy," she said. "The secret meetings have already begun."

Poppy stiffened and shot Mrs. Plumtree a baleful glance. Then he glowered at Gabriel. "All right. This is how it's going to be. You two will have your race on Friday. Mrs. Plumtree and I will be there to make sure it's done fairly and safely. Afterward—"

"We will all come back to Halstead Hall for dinner," Mrs. Plumtree put in. "What do you say, General? Wouldn't that be a pleasant way to end the day?"

"Aye," he growled. "And a pleasant way to end our families' association, too."

Virginia sucked in a breath. She didn't dare reveal that after this race, she would either be racing Gabriel at Turnham Green or he would be courting her. If Poppy heard that, he would lock her up in her room and throw away the key.

"Sounds like an excellent plan to me," Gabriel drawled.

"Yes," she agreed. Once the race was over, she and Gabriel could manage the rest of their bargain more discreetly.

"Very well." Poppy held out his arm. "Come, my girl, we're going home."

She took his arm, not daring to look at Gabriel for fear of what she might see in his eyes. And what it might make her feel.

"Miss Waverly!" Gabriel called after her.

She stopped to look back. "Yes?"

His gaze locked with hers. "I meant what I said about Jacky Boy. He has every reason to be upset. Because he knows I won't give up."

She swallowed hard. She wasn't quite as horrified as she should be by his reminder. Plague take him.

"Persistence isn't always enough, sir," she said, then walked out with her grandfather.

As they headed for the other stable, where their carriage now sat waiting, Poppy said, "What was that all about?"

"We discussed his lordship's training methods for his horses," she lied. "I was giving him some pointers."

Poppy snorted. "I hardly think Sharpe needs any pointers."

No, he knew exactly what he was doing—with horses *and* women. More was the pity.

"Is there something going on between you and Sharpe that you're not telling me?" Poppy asked.

She caught her breath. "Why would you say that?"

"It's been pointed out to me that young women can sometimes be different than they appear."

Lord, much as she wanted Poppy to see her for what she was, she didn't want him to see the part of her that had recklessly enjoyed kissing Gabriel. "I'm always your lambkin, Poppy. You needn't worry about that." It was an evasive answer, but she couldn't bear lying to him.

Fortunately, it seemed to satisfy him. "That's what I thought."

Guilt kept her silent.

While they were headed home, something occurred to her. "Poppy, was Roger drunk when he raced Lord Gabriel?"

Her grandfather stiffened. "Why do you ask?"

"Because of something Lord Gabriel said."

"Roger was definitely drunk when he agreed to the challenge."

Her breath stuck in her throat. "So Lord Gabriel was definitely the one to lay down the challenge?"

He stared grimly ahead. "He must have been. Otherwise, he would have blamed it on Roger a long time ago."

She thought back through what Gabriel had said. He hadn't mentioned who'd made the challenge. But obviously he'd lied to her about Roger's drunkenness. "So Roger *was* drunk when he ran the race."

A long pause ensued. Then Poppy let out a low oath. "I don't know."

"What do you mean?"

"It was hours later. They raced at noon."

A ball of lead settled into her belly. "But I thought Lord Gabriel challenged him after they'd been drinking all night and half the morning. Then they went right out and ran the race."

"Not quite."

Her world shifted. All this time, she'd believed . . . "Then what *did* happen?"

"Why does it matter?" he snapped. "Isn't it enough that he convinced Roger to race him when the lad was drunk, then dragged him out on that damned course later to die?"

"I suppose," she said quietly.

Though that wasn't entirely true. She'd always assumed that Gabriel had purposely coaxed Roger into getting drunk so he could beat him. But if hours had lain between the time Roger had agreed to the challenge and the two men had run the race . . .

She stiffened. No, Poppy was right. Gabriel had still taken advantage of Roger. Her brother never would have run that race if he'd been sober.

She kept telling herself that all the way back to Waverly Farm.

Chapter Five

Gabe didn't know which bothered him more—that Gran was about to discover the new Thorough-bred he'd been keeping under wraps . . . or that she'd nearly caught him kissing Virginia.

Probably the latter. Having a reputation for being good in the bedchamber was one thing; having one's grandmother nearly witness that talent was quite another.

Especially when it had thrown him so off-balance. Virginia Waverly had one damned sweet mouth. He wished he could have plundered it longer. He wished he could have laid her down in the straw and discovered what secrets lay beneath today's outdated gown—a yellow and white muslin thing that made her look like a lemon drop. Which was only appropriate, since he wanted to unwrap her and suck her and savor her, to satisfy his sweet tooth by devouring her whole.

"You lied to me," Gran said without preamble.

That shattered his pleasant fantasy. Trying to think what Gran meant, Gabe went to fetch the mash bucket he'd left outside Flying Jane's stall. He had to get Gran out of here before she noticed the horse; she had a decided bias against his racing. "What about?"

"You said that you and Miss Waverly were going to thread the needle at Turnham Green, when you're really planning some simple race at Ealing."

Ah, *that*. A pity she'd found out so soon. He'd hoped that worry for him might make her agree to let Celia out of the marriage ultimatum.

Although perhaps he could still manage that.

"I didn't lie." He snagged his coat and headed toward her at the stable door. "Miss Waverly and I are racing to determine whether we will thread the needle. If I win, then she lets me court her. If she wins, then we thread the needle."

Gran snorted. "You know damned well you are going to win."

With a shrug, he left the stable, handing the mash bucket to the first groom who came running. "Races are unpredictable." He shot her a sly glance. "And there's nothing to say that I won't be hurt while racing her in Ealing."

She rolled her eyes at him. "If you hurt yourself on that tame course, you deserve to lose. So I shall wait to see who wins before I decide whether I want to release Celia from my demand."

"Suit yourself." He turned toward the house, matching his stride to her halting gait.

"Miss Waverly has turned into a very pretty girl. I'm not surprised; her mother was stunning."

"You knew her mother?"

"She came out at the same time as yours. The chit had her eye on your father, but Prudence was having none of that. Lewis utterly dazzled your mother, poor girl. Once she met him there was no one else, and she wasn't going to let any other woman have him, either."

"A pity that he didn't feel the same," Gabe snapped. Unlike Oliver, Gabe didn't blame their father for everything that had gone wrong in his parents' marriage. But Father's infidelities had made it awfully difficult for Mother to overlook their other problems.

Gran shot him a long look. "That's a harsh statement coming from you, who are never without a female in your bed."

He gritted his teeth. He entertained a widow or barmaid from time to time, but most of his days were spent with his horses. He wasn't the whoremonger she seemed to think. He certainly had never rivaled his father for debauchery. Or even his older brothers.

"At least I believe in fidelity, which is more than I can say for Father," he told her. "I fully intend to do better in my own marriage."

"Assuming that Miss Waverly agrees to marry you."

He flashed her a cocky smile. "Have you ever seen me *not* gain a woman I wanted?"

"Women of the sort you've been gaining don't count—they can be bought. I doubt that Miss Waverly can."

"Thank God," he said coldly, "since I only get money from you if Celia also marries, and that's by no means certain."

They entered the house and headed toward the drawing room.

"What will you do if you marry Miss Waverly and then I end up cutting you off?" she asked, her tone carefully distant.

"I have prospects," he said evasively.

"What sort of prospects? Do they have anything to do with that new Thoroughbred filly you're hiding?"

He stiffened. Damn Gran and her observant eye. "What makes you think I'm hiding her?"

Her eyes narrowed on him. "She was in the old stables, which have only held Jacky Boy for years. I hope you don't have some fool notion about entering her in a horse race. Your father had to marry precisely because *his* father—"

"I know, Gran. I've already heard the lecture."

Numerous times. Their paternal grandfather had been horse-mad. Unfortunately, he'd also been cursed with bad trainers and even worse horses. He'd sunk hundreds of thousands of pounds into his stables so he could race Thoroughbreds, none of which had ever won him any money.

Which was why Gabe hadn't wanted Gran to know he hoped to build his own stable of Thoroughbreds. She'd never believe that he could succeed. He had a keener eye for horses than his grandfather ever had, and he could train them himself as long as he could find the right jockey to ride them.

But Gran thought Thoroughbred racing was a gambler's sport, and gambling was a waste of good blunt to her.

Not that he cared. She'd ruined his life enough with this marriage business. She wasn't going to ruin his future in racing, too. This was his insurance policy in case Celia chose not to marry.

"So what do you plan to do with the Thoroughbred?" she prodded.

"That's none of your concern," he said as they neared the drawing room. "It's my horse. I bought it out of the funds I've accumulated from wagers I win in carriage racing. Whatever I do with it is my own business."

She walked into the drawing room. "Not if you use Oliver's stables to—"

"What's Gabe using my stables for this time?" Oliver asked from his seat on the settee.

Gabe started as he saw Oliver, along with the rest of his family, ranged around the room. The only ones missing were Jarret's stepson George, who was visiting his family in Burton, and Minerva's husband Giles, who was probably too busy with a trial to come. But Jackson Pinter, the Bow Street runner, was here.

Damn, he'd forgotten that he'd asked Pinter and his siblings to assemble in Halstead Hall's drawing room at noon today. Now there was an audience for this discussion.

"I bought a horse that I'm keeping in the old stables," Gabe said, preparing for a fight. "I mostly see to Flying Jane myself. But if that's a problem—"

"I didn't say it was a problem," Oliver countered.

"It's not just a horse," Gran snapped. "Gabriel has bought a Thoroughbred. For racing, no doubt."

"Good for him," Jarret said. When Gabe's jaw dropped, Jarret winked at him. "It's about time the Halstead Hall stables were used for something other than our few riding and carriage horses. There's plenty of room for Thoroughbreds."

Gran looked as if she might explode. "That's easy for you to say. The stables aren't yours to maintain."

"No," Oliver said sharply, "they're mine. You keep forgetting that, Gran. The estate is well on its way to supporting itself. So you don't have a say in what I allow in my stables."

Oliver was agreeing with him, too? Gabe couldn't believe it.

Gran looked utterly flummoxed. She glared at Oliver, then at him. How gratifying to see her at a loss for words.

Gabe grabbed the opportunity to explain himself. "I'm paying for the filly's upkeep myself and giving the grooms extra to take care of her when necessary. I'm not relying on Oliver for anything but space in the stables, which, as Jarret pointed out, there's plenty of."

"Are you really planning to race the horse?" Jarret's wife Annabel asked.

He hesitated. But since they were all being so reasonable . . . "I'm training her for the St. Leger Stakes," he admitted.

"You've lost your mind," Gran grumbled.

"And he loses it so brilliantly, too," Minerva said, her green eyes twinkling. "I can't wait to see how Gabe's new venture turns out."

"Stop encouraging him," Gran snapped. "It's a fruitless endeavor."

"At least we don't have to worry about him killing himself, since he won't be riding in these races," Celia pointed out.

"Of course not," Gabe said, pleased that his siblings were taking this so well. "Though I'll need to find a jockey."

"I know of a decent jockey looking for a position," Jarret offered.

"So do I," Pinter said, to Gabe's surprise.

"You're all mad," Gran said with a sniff. "Every last one of you."

Taking pity on her, Gabe looped his arm about her shoulders. "Relax, Gran. I'm doing my best to marry, too. Isn't that enough?"

Minerva's eyes lit up. "You've chosen someone?"

"I have."

Celia gave a start that shot him through with guilt.

Although there were three years between him and his younger sister, and only two between him and his older one, he and Celia had always been closer in spirit. Minerva had mothered them both while Jarret and Oliver were off at school, so he and Celia had become partners in crime. He'd been the one to teach her to shoot; she'd lied for him whenever he snuck out to races.

Now the look of betrayal in Celia's eyes cut him to the heart. But her plan to have them both hold firm against Gran would never have worked, so he had to try things his own way. If he played his cards right, he might still win her freedom.

"Whom are you planning to marry?" Annabel asked, all smiles and eager anticipation.

"Is it someone we know?" Minerva prodded.

"Come on, man," Jarret said. "Tell us who it is."

"It's Miss Waverly," Gran said.

An incredulous silence fell over the room.

It was punctuated by Minerva's cry, "But she hates you!"

"She does not hate me." She had given him ample proof of that in the stable.

His family began to talk all at once.

"Speaking of fruitless endeavors . . ." Oliver muttered.

"Does she know you mean to marry her?" Jarret asked.

"What about her grandfather?" Minerva asked. "He'll never allow it."

Celia sat there smirking, obviously less worried now that she knew who his prospective wife was.

Gran surprised him by answering for him. "Miss Waverly is well aware of Gabe's intentions, and I believe she is not as opposed to the idea as she pretends. She was just here to arrange a race with your brother. And I am hoping you will all attend. Might as well show her we are not the monsters she has created in her mind since Roger's death."

That sparked a new round of questions which Gabe answered, though he refrained from mentioning the wager attached to the race. When he started explaining about the Waverly family's dire financial situation, Celia rounded on the Bow Street runner.

"I should have seen your meddling hand in this," she snapped.

Pinter blinked, clearly taken off guard by her attack. "I beg your pardon?" he asked in his thick, raspy voice.

"As well you should." Celia rose and strode over to glare down at him with her hands propped on her hips. "You probably suggested the woman to Gabe. You won't be satisfied until you see us all married and miserable."

Pinter's eyes narrowed, and he looked on the verge of a hot retort when Oliver said, "Here now, Celia, I'm not miserable. And as far as I can tell, neither is Jarret."

"Nor am I," Minerva put in.

"This doesn't concern you lot!" Celia cried. "It concerns *my* future! And if Gabe marries, it means that I . . ." She trailed off with a huff of frustration. "Oh, you wouldn't understand. I thought Gabe did, but clearly he's in Gran's pocket, too."

She turned on Pinter again, her eyes alight. "And you, sir, ought to be ashamed of yourself to let Gran buy you, body and soul."

Pinter stood, his brow lowering into a black frown. "While *you*, my lady, ought to be ashamed to fight her so. Be careful that in biting the hand that feeds you, you don't break your teeth on it."

Her cheeks rosy, Celia thrust her face up to his. "It's not your purview to lecture me, sir."

He towered over her. "I'm merely pointing out that your grandmother has your best interests at heart, something you seem incapable of recognizing."

"Because unlike you, who are paid to support whatever she says and does, I can see that she's wrong. So if you think I'll stand here and listen to my grandmother's *lackey* lecture me—"

"Celia!" Gabe snapped, noting the sharpening of Pinter's gaze. The man had a dark side that he hid very well, but one of these days he was going to let it fly if Celia kept provoking him. "Pinter came all the way out here today at my request, so I'd appreciate it if you'd treat him civilly."

She scowled at Gabe, then at Pinter. "If I must," she said stiffly, then turned to go back to her chair.

Pinter's eyes followed her retreat with an interest that gave Gabe pause. Could Pinter *want* Celia?

No, the idea was absurd. They fought constantly. And Gabe knew for a fact that she despised the man.

The way Virginia despises you?

He shoved that unsettling idea from his mind as he took a seat. "Pinter, I asked you here so I could tell you what I know about the events of the day my parents were killed."

That got everyone's attention.

"What do you mean?" Oliver demanded.

Gabe took an unsteady breath. This wasn't as easy as he'd expected. But after their despicable cousin, Desmond Plumtree, had revealed that he'd seen a man riding *toward* the hunting lodge after he'd heard their parents being shot, it had set Gabe to wondering again about the man he'd met that day.

"I was in the stables shortly after Mother rode out to the hunting lodge." He told them everything about his encounter with the man that he could remember, then added, "You remember how Desmond said that the horse he saw was black with a face blaze and one white stocking on the left hind leg? Well, I'm fairly certain that the stranger in the stable that day chose such a horse."

Oliver leaned forward, his black eyes stormy. "That business with Desmond was almost two months ago. Why didn't you say anything then? For that matter, why didn't you tell us about the man years ago?"

"Until earlier this year, when you finally deigned to discuss your argument with Mother that day," Gabe said, "none of us knew that Gran's story of what happened wasn't entirely accurate. I had no reason to believe that the man I saw had anything to do with our parents' deaths."

With a muttered curse, Oliver settled back in his chair. His wife, Maria, took his hand. Her pregnancy was beginning to show, and she had a sweet glow that seemed to soothe Oliver's dark mood.

For some reason, Gabe felt a stab of resentment. No one had ever leaped to soothe *his* dark moods. "Then you and Jarret decided that Desmond might have killed them, so I still had no reason to think the stranger was involved. Even after Desmond admitted to having seen a man ride toward the scene, I couldn't see how it was relevant. The man was kind to me. He didn't seem upset, or interested in finding anyone. I figured it was pure coincidence that he'd ridden near the scene."

"Except that he never told anyone what he saw," Jarret pointed out, his eyes flashing in the candlelight.

"Yes, I considered that. But would *you* tell anyone if you'd stumbled across two dead bodies? Wouldn't you worry that you might be implicated in their deaths, even if you'd done nothing? And that's assuming he went inside and found them."

Silence fell upon the room, only broken when Minerva asked, "If you considered his presence there irrelevant, why are you telling us now?"

Gabe threaded his fingers through his hair. "Because we haven't gotten anywhere in our efforts to find out the truth. It's been two months, and Pinter seems to have lost track entirely of Benny May, our old head groom."

"I haven't lost track of him," Pinter countered. "I just can't find him."

"You found him easily enough a few months ago, when Jarret sent you looking for him," Gabe said. "Don't you find it odd that he disappeared only a couple of months after revealing how Mother cautioned him not to mention to Father where she was going that day?"

"He didn't disappear," Pinter said coolly. "He went up to visit a friend near Manchester. That's what his family said."

"Yet they haven't heard from him."

"Benny couldn't exactly write a letter to them," Gran said. "He isn't literate."

"True," Gabe said. "But Pinter's trip to Manchester last week didn't turn him up."

"Only because he took a different road there," Pinter said. "Once I picked up his trail in Manchester, I was only a few days behind him. But he must have stopped off somewhere near Woburn, since that's where I lost him. Nor has he returned to his family."

"Which I find troubling," Gabe said. "I suppose it's possible he may just not want to be found. Perhaps he knows something. Perhaps he too saw the man, but recognized him."

"Did you not recognize the man yourself?" Annabel asked.

"I didn't see his face. I was hiding down in the stall, afraid of getting into trouble. All I heard was his voice. And that was no help in figuring out who he was. I was nursery age so I didn't meet any of the guests."

"We're not even sure he *was* a guest," Jarret pointed out.

"He had to have been," Oliver said. "No one else would be so bold as to walk right in and steal a horse. Besides, Gabe said he knew our names and guessed Gabe's identity. That was no horse thief."

"If we could find Benny, we could learn whether the horse was ever returned to the stable, and by whom," Minerva said.

"That's why I haven't broached this subject until now," Gabe told them. "I knew we couldn't move forward without speaking to him. I was hoping he would turn up and identify the man."

He rose to pace. "But it's been too long. I've begun to worry about Benny. If he did see or know something, and he did approach the man . . ." He shook his head. "I have an uneasy feeling about his disappearance."

This time the silence that fell upon the room mirrored his unease. It seemed the more they delved into their parents' deaths, the more nasty business they uncovered. Sometimes Gabe wondered if they were making a mistake even trying to get to the bottom of it. It had been nineteen years, after all. Nothing could bring Mother and Father back. And yet . . .

If it *had* been murder, then his parents deserved justice. And their killer deserved to suffer the full wrath of those he'd orphaned. Because what good was thumbing one's nose at Death when Death still got away with the worst crime of all?

"Has it occurred to anyone else that the man might have been Major Rawdon?" Jarret said. "He and his wife left in a hurry the evening of Mother's and Father's deaths. We assumed it was because of the incident with Oliver, but it might have been something darker. If his wife was cheating on him with Father—"

"She wasn't," Pinter put in.

They all gaped at him.

Oliver in particular scowled. "She had to be. Mother said, 'You already have *him*.' What else could she mean?"

"I don't doubt that your mother *thought* your father was cheating on her with Mrs. Rawdon, given his past actions," Pinter remarked. "But that doesn't mean he was. I tracked down your father's valet a few days ago. He said he knew all your father's secrets, and that wasn't one."

That shocked them all. "He could be lying," Jarret pointed out.

"He could, but I don't think he is. He's no longer in service and came into some money from his mother, so he has nothing to lose by telling the truth."

"Oh God," Oliver said hoarsely. "If that's true, then why did the woman seduce me?"

Pinter shrugged. "Because she could. Or perhaps she'd tried to seduce your father and failed, so she tried for you next. Or perhaps she just didn't like your mother."

Oliver shuddered. "I can't believe this." He gazed at Pinter. "So if Mother did kill Father out of anger over Mrs. Rawdon, it might have been for nothing? Because she was jealous?"

"I'm afraid so. I still wish to speak to the Rawdons, but the captain has been posted in India for some years. As soon as you mentioned their friendship with your parents, I sent a letter to him and his superiors with numerous questions, but it will be months before I receive a reply. And they may be reluctant to speak of your mother's penchant for violence in a letter."

"Mother did *not* kill Father," Minerva said stoutly. "Giles is almost sure of that. Or at least not in the way we originally assumed."

"We haven't ruled it out entirely, though," Pinter said with a pained look. "Besides, even if it was Captain Rawdon whom your cousin saw, he couldn't have been the one to kill them. Desmond made it clear that the mysterious man arrived at the hunting lodge after the murders."

"So we're back to needing to know what that man saw, and why he went there in the first place," Gabe said tightly.

"All right then," Oliver said. "Here's what we shall do. Pinter, go back and find the other grooms, the ones from your initial interviews who said they saw nothing, and find out if they remember that horse and who might have returned it. Ask about their association with Benny, too. Some of them may still see him from time to time."

"Very well," Pinter said. "And if you wish, I'll speak to Benny's family again, see if they know anyone else with information on his exact whereabouts. If all else fails, I'll make another trip to Manchester."

"Anything you can do will help," Oliver said.

"If you do head for Manchester," Gabe said, "let me know. I want to go with you."

The nagging sense that Benny might hold the key to what had happened that day just wouldn't leave him. Until he talked to the man and satisfied himself that Benny knew nothing, he couldn't rest easy.

Chapter Six

"It's a nasty day for a race," Virginia's grandfather said as they headed for Ealing.

She scowled out the carriage window at the dark sky that threatened rain. Her horses, which had been sent on ahead to the race site hours ago, ran like demons in good weather. Bad weather could scuttle everything, especially if the wind picked up. Horses did not like wind.

"Is the weather what's got you in such a foul mood?" Pierce asked. He would have returned home yesterday if not for the race. Apparently he was needed back at his estate.

"Of course," she lied.

Her foul mood had started the day she'd left the Halstead Hall stables. That devil Gabriel wouldn't get out of her head. She kept feeling the press of his firm body against hers. He had the kind of muscles that made a woman just want to dig in and hold on. Such a fine physique had to be criminal.

And the way he kissed? Pure heaven. She couldn't stop thinking about his hot mouth and wicked tongue exploring hers.

A blush rose in her cheeks. Sweet Lord, she was as wicked as he. She did *not* want that man to kiss her again. He was awful. Detestable. Despicable.

Unfortunately, that argument grew weaker by the day. Ever since Poppy had put doubts in her head about what had happened at Turnham Green, she'd been thrown off-balance.

But even if Gabriel wasn't entirely at fault for Roger's death, he was still an arrogant rogue who thought she should leap at the chance to marry him. She *hated* it when men thought they knew what was best for her, and how it should be accomplished.

By the time they arrived at the course, she'd worked herself up into a fine temper. Just let Gabriel attempt to kiss her today! She would give him a piece of her mind. She would tell him in no uncertain terms that she was *not* the sort of fool to fall for his fine muscles and gorgeous green eyes and cocky smile. No, indeed.

Then she spotted him on the course, dressed in his characteristic black and his shining boots, and her stomach did a little flip. Perish the man. Why must he affect her like this?

"Remember what I told you about feeling the horses' mouths lightly," Poppy said as they drew up beside her curricle. "You don't want to chafe their mouths."

"Yes, Poppy, I know. I've done this before."

"And keep the outside wheeler well in check while making the turns, or she'll scuttle the curricle."

"Or perhaps I should just give the horses their heads and see if they can run the race on their own," she said lightly.

He started, then scowled. "This is serious business, girl."

She patted his hand. "I realize that. But it's time for you to give *me* my head, and see what I can do."

"I don't like this," he grumbled. "Not one bit."

"You think I can't win?"

He shot her a long look. "If anyone can beat Sharpe, it's you."

"But . . ."

"But you don't have his reckless spirit. That might keep you from winning. You're sane. He's not."

She stifled a hot retort. How was it that Poppy never saw the real her? She wasn't always sane, and sometimes she was reckless. Or at least she yearned to be, though she got few chances of it.

But she had one now, and she was going to make good use of it. "He's not unbeatable, and I mean to prove it."

Poppy glanced out. "There's a crowd. Do you think you can handle that?"

She followed his gaze out the window. Good gracious, he was right. People lined either side of the course, leaning in to watch her descend from the carriage. "I understand why Lord Gabriel's family is here, but who are the others?"

"Are you joking?" Pierce said. "All it took was Chetwin spreading the word to have half of society trotting out here. There's nothing the *ton* loves more than a juicy, scandalous race."

For a moment, her heart failed her. She'd wanted Gabriel humiliated before his friends, but she'd also wanted a straightforward race. With so many people crowding in and no rails to restrain them, the race would not be straightforward.

Suddenly she felt Poppy's hand squeeze her shoulder. "Go give him hell, lambkin."

That bolstered her courage. "I will. Don't you worry."

Pierce leapt out to hand her down, then bent to kiss her forehead. "Time to beat the trousers off Sharpe, cuz. I've got twenty pounds riding on you."

She laughed shakily but noticed that Gabriel was glaring at Pierce. Had he overheard their conversation? Surely he didn't expect her cousin to bet on *him*.

As her grandfather and Pierce drove off toward the finish line where they would wait for her, she strolled up to her curricle, positioned to the right of Gabriel's phaeton.

When she climbed up and took the reins from the groom, Gabriel looked over and tipped his hat. "It's not too late to forfeit," he said with a smug smile that set her teeth on edge.

"Oh, did you want to forfeit?" she said sweetly. "I'm more than happy to accept."

That wiped the grin from his face. He picked up his reins, his eyes glinting at her in challenge. "May the best driver win."

"She will," she countered.

"Bravo!" cried a female voice, and Virginia turned to see a woman standing nearby with his family. It was the recently married Lady Minerva, who'd been at the race with Gabriel the day Virginia had challenged him. What was her name now? Oh yes, Mrs. Giles Masters.

"Good luck to you, Miss Waverly," Mrs. Masters called out. "If you beat my brother, I'll give you a whole set of my novels."

"Thank you for offering her an incentive to lose, Minerva," Gabriel said good-naturedly, apparently not the least concerned that his sister was encouraging his competition.

"Careful, little brother," his sister countered, "or I'll put *you* in one of my books. Just ask Oliver how he likes that."

"Ah, but then you'll finally have a hero worth his salt," Gabriel said gamely.

"What makes you think you'd be a hero?" Mrs. Masters said with a smug grin.

Virginia watched them, envious of their ribbing. She'd forgotten how comfortable it was to have a brother. Pierce was a good friend, of course, but it wasn't the same. There was something special about having a sibling around who shared a bond of blood with you and understood you when no one else could.

Gabriel had taken that away from her, she reminded herself, and she would make him pay.

The Duke of Lyons came to stand before their rigs. Gabriel explained that Lyons was not only a member of the Jockey Club, but also of the old Four-in-Hand Club. So he was perfectly suited to lay out the rules for the race. His fellow members of the Jockey Club were going to act as judges, if she was amenable.

Of course she was amenable. These men might be Gabriel's friends, but they were also gentlemen with a well-known, ironclad code of honor. They wouldn't judge a race unfairly.

"First rule," the duke said. "There will be no attempts to force the other carriage from the road, at risk of forfeiting the race."

As if she would ever do something like that. She wasn't one of these fool lords who would risk another person's life and limb to win.

"Second rule. Drivers must be bareheaded. We don't want to chance spooking the horses with a flying hat or bonnet."

As Gabriel tossed his hat to one of his brothers, she removed her bonnet. She loved feeling the wind in her hair, anyway.

"Third rule. No whipping of each other's horses, at risk of forfeiting the race."

Did people really do such things? Good gracious, that was beyond unfair.

"Fourth rule. If you fall from the carriage, you forfeit the race. If your carriage loses a wheel, you forfeit the race. If your horses collide—"

"You forfeit the race," Gabriel finished irritably. "Get on with it, Lyons."

The duke flashed him a smooth smile. "Very well. The starter from the Jockey Club will signal the beginning of the race with a flag." He glanced to Virginia. "Are you ready, madam?"

"Of course."

She noticed he didn't ask the same of Gabriel—whose manner had shifted most disturbingly. He looked remote, intent, and cold. The embodiment of the Angel of Death.

With a shiver, she returned her attention to the course.

The duke motioned to the starter, who stepped to the edge of the course and lifted his flag. "Prepare!" the starter shouted.

Virginia tensed and tightened her grip on the reins.

The starter dropped the flag, and they were off.

The course was two miles long, a good test of a pair, but after a few furlongs of flat terrain, it ran around half of a hill before finishing in another furlong that led to the finish line. So the part that skirted the hill would be tricky. As the challenger, she'd been given the less advantageous position at the start. If they remained neck and neck, Gabriel would have the inside track. She had to pass him before they reached the hill so *she* could take the inside track.

But the wind was so high, it whipped her hair from its pins and unsettled her horses. They pulled against the reins, tugging at her hands until her shoulders ached from the effort of controlling them. A glance at Gabriel showed him perfectly at ease. His attention seemed narrowed to the course and his pair.

He didn't seem to notice the people edging in from either side so tightly that the two rigs were soon barreling along a narrow lane scarcely big enough for both teams. Though she urged hers on, she knew she was holding back a little.

What if they struck someone in the crowd? She

couldn't put that fear from her head. This was utterly different from the many times she'd raced the grooms or Roger.

And the horses seemed to sense her reluctance, for they weren't running full out. Apparently, his horses were more used to crowds—she could see them straining at their bits, their coats well lathered, their eyes fierce.

He was almost a full horse's length ahead, and she gritted her teeth. She couldn't let him win! Urging her team on with a flick of the whip and a "Hi yah!" she made herself ignore the crowd. And her pair began to gain on his.

Yes! She could do this. She *could* beat him.

Exultant, she leaned halfway out of her seat, the thrill of the race firing her blood. She had to win. She must!

The two pairs thundered down the track, hooves flying, heads bobbing. She was edging ahead now; even the dust stinging her eyes couldn't keep her from her purpose.

Unfortunately, they were nearing the hill, and she couldn't pass him to take the inside track. She was only ahead by half a horse's length. She urged her pair on, but the increase in speed wasn't enough. So as they headed into the curve around the hill, she was still in the outside lane.

To the right of her, people crowded as near as they dared. To the left of Gabriel was the hill. She was halfway around it, managing to maintain her slight lead, when an onlooker fell into her path. She had only a second to choose between swerving into the crowd and swerving toward Gabriel. Hoping that he'd seen what happened and would rein in to let her pull into his path, she chose the latter.

But instead, he drove his team up onto the steep hill. As she passed the fallen man who was being pulled out of her path by other onlookers, Gabriel's rig teetered on its side next to her.

If his phaeton rolled, he could kill them both! With a curse, she slowed, praying she could control her pair when his rig tumbled over, taking him and his horses with it.

But it didn't roll. Miraculously, he maintained his speed and still managed to wrench his rig back down onto the track . . . and well ahead of hers.

Admiration at his deft driving rapidly twisted into anger. What was he thinking, to risk such a stunt? The man was mad! And dangerous and careless and a thousand things, none of them good!

She urged her team into a sprint that would have left anyone else in the dust, but Gabriel seemed to have heaven on his side, for his horses ran fleeter than the wind. By the time they reached the finish line, he was still a full yard or more ahead of her.

He'd won, the scoundrel! And nearly killed himself as well!

Seething with righteous fury, she reined in, jumped down, and handed the reins off to the grooms who came running. Then she marched over to where Gabriel was leaping down from his phaeton.

Ignoring her grandfather and Pierce, who were headed toward her, she walked up to Gabriel. "Are you insane? Only you could turn a tame course into a death trap!"

He blinked, then shrugged. "I'm the Angel of Death. What do you expect?"

Oh, that was too much! She slapped him across the face, hard. "I expect you to have some respect for human life!" Her blood still thundered in her ears. "You could have injured us both, and our horses, too!"

Eyes gleaming, he rubbed his jaw where she'd struck him. "Ah, but I didn't."

"Only because you have the devil's own luck!"

His gaze narrowed on her. "And because I know how to handle a team. You're merely angry that I won."

Ooh, that really took the cake. "I'm angry that you took such an enormous risk! If your phaeton had rolled over at that speed, you would have broken your neck!"

He arched one insidious brow. "So you were worried about me?"

The rotten devil *would* look at it that way. "I was worried about myself and my horses. I don't give a fig if you want to murder yourself racing, but I'd thank you not to kill me in the bargain!"

That finally cracked his uncanny reserve, for anger flared in his features. "I wouldn't have risked it if I'd thought you'd be hurt. In truth, I didn't think at all—I barely had time to react. You veered, and I veered. Realizing I was going up the hill, I figured the best thing to do was play it out."

That mollified her temper only a little. "You should have reined in. But you never do, do you?" she snapped, thinking of Roger. "You couldn't bear not to win."

"No, I couldn't." He was nose to nose with her now, his eyes alight. "Since winning was the only way to gain a chance of courting you, I had no choice."

As the crowd strained to hear every delicious word, she could only gape at him. He wanted to court her that badly? Really?

"Court you?" Poppy asked.

"Court you!" Pierce echoed.

Sweet Lord, she'd forgotten them entirely. So much for keeping the true stakes hidden from her family. And half the gossips in London.

By that point, the entire Sharpe clan had shown up and were encircling them like spectators at a boxing match.

"They made a wager," Mrs. Plumtree explained to Poppy. "If she won, he was to race her at Turnham Green. If he won, she was to let him court her."

"And you kept that information from me?" Poppy snapped at Mrs. Plumtree.

"I did not learn of it myself until after you left," the woman countered.

"I don't care what arrangement they made," Poppy shot back, "your grandson is *not* courting my grand-daughter!"

Gabriel glowered at Virginia. "Do you mean to renege on our wager?"

She straightened her shoulders. "Certainly not," she

said, ignoring Poppy's roar of outrage. "But courting me will do you little good if you mean to keep up such displays. I will never marry a man so reckless."

A grim smile touched Gabriel's lips. "Never say never, sweetheart."

Frowning to hear his granddaughter called "sweetheart," Poppy shoved between them. "I don't care what wager my granddaughter made with you, sir. I'm not letting you court her."

"Leave them be, General Waverly," Mrs. Plumtree said stoutly. "You should let *them* sort it out."

He rounded on her with a foul look. "That's what you said before. You convinced me to let them do this by telling me it would put an end to their association. But you knew it wouldn't. You're a devious, manipulative she-devil with a—"

"Watch it, sir," Gabriel cut in. "That's my grandmother you're maligning."

"And that's my granddaughter you're trying to seduce!"

"Poppy!" Virginia cried, as a blush rose in her cheeks.

"Enough!" The Marquess of Stoneville stepped into the fray and everyone fell silent.

Lord Stoneville strode up to stand between Poppy and Gabriel. "Tempers are understandably high at the moment. So before everyone starts slinging public accusations, it would be best if all the parties have the facts of the situation." He glanced about at the eager crowd beyond. "And such discussions are better accomplished in private."

He cast her grandfather a thin smile. "General, if you'll please accompany Miss Waverly to Halstead Hall, my grandmother has had a fine repast prepared for you and your family. On the way there, you can ask the young woman herself about what agreement she has made with my brother."

The marquess then turned to Gabriel, and his gaze turned colder. "In the meantime, brother, you will ride with me and explain why you arranged a wager with a respectable lady without telling her family of it." He shot Mrs. Plumtree a glance. "And Gran can explain why she kept it secret from both families."

Mrs. Plumtree merely sniffed.

Poppy stared down the marquess. "I'll do as you say, sir—but only because I don't enjoy supplying entertainment for your friends. Come, Virginia." He grabbed her by the arm and urged her toward the carriage.

As soon as they were out of earshot, he said, "You're in a great deal of trouble, young lady."

Why? Because I did something to satisfy my own needs for once? But that would only hurt his feelings, and he still wouldn't understand.

The minute that she, her cousin, and her grandfather were headed for Halstead Hall, Poppy began his lecture. "What do you think you're doing, making wagers with scandalous gentlemen and challenging them to races? You've lost your mind." He scowled at her. "Did you really agree to let that ass court you if he won?"

"I did," she answered as she repaired her coiffure. "But—"

"And *you*," her grandfather went on, turning his anger on Pierce. "Did you know about this?"

"Poppy, it isn't—" she began.

"Of course not," Pierce snapped. "She must have made the wager while she was dancing with Sharpe at that ball."

"I sent her off with you, thinking you'd look out for her. The next thing I know, she's embroiled in a wager that is sure to end in scandal and ruin her chances for marriage once and for—"

"Poppy!" she cried.

That finally got his attention. "What? What can you possibly say to make this any better?"

"I seriously doubt that Lord Gabriel genuinely wants to marry me." When she had both men's full attention, she added, "He probably just intends to court the woman whose family he wronged so everyone will like him better."

"Everyone already likes him just fine," Poppy gritted out. "You and I are the only people who blame him."

He had a point. "Well then, perhaps he has some other ulterior motive that doesn't come readily to mind. Or perhaps he really does want to make amends for what he did to Roger. That's what he says is the reason. And I begin to believe that he means it."

Pierce was frowning, his gaze flitting from her to her grandfather with disturbing intensity. Odd how he wasn't chiming in to voice his opinion as always.

"I'll tell you what he wants," Poppy said. "He wants to ruin you. I can see it in how he looks at you, as if he can see right through your clothes."

She snorted. "Oh, for pity's sake, he does not." At least, not when anyone else was around. That day in the stables, he'd certainly looked at her with a great deal of heat. And his kisses . . .

No, she was *not* thinking of those again, not with Poppy sitting right here, watching her every blush.

She must have given something away, for her grandfather flashed her a sudden dark glance. "Don't tell me you fancy him."

"Certainly not." That was the truth. Mostly. "Some women might find his devil-may-care manner attractive, but not me."

What she found attractive was his apparent concern for her and her family. Not to mention that infernal cocky grin of his, and the way his kisses seemed to heat the very air that entered her lungs and—

Sweet Lord, she must stop this madness!

"I'm not that shallow," she said, partly as a caution to herself. "I'm not swayed by dazzling good looks and fine muscles and an astonishing ability to drive a team with—" She broke off at the apoplectic look on Poppy's face. "I'm really not."

"And you weren't impressed that he took such risks on the course for the mere chance of courting you?" Poppy prodded.

"No! Well . . . not exactly. I suppose some women would . . . *might* find it terribly romantic to have a man nearly kill himself for a chance at courting them, but—"

"He does have an ulterior motive," Pierce broke in.

Virginia gave a start. He'd been so quiet up until now. "What do you mean?"

"Just what I said." Pierce wore a grim expression. "I only have the information secondhand, so I wasn't going to mention anything. But since you're clearly losing your head over the bastard . . ."

"What ulterior motive?" she demanded.

"He needs money," Pierce said tersely.

She stared at him, confused. "He's not getting any from me. You know that."

"Not from you." Pierce steadied a dark look on her. "From his grandmother. He can't gain his inheritance without marrying."

"What are you talking about?" Poppy put in.

Her cousin met Poppy's gaze coldly. "His grandmother gave him and his siblings an ultimatum—either they all marry before the end of next January, or she cuts them all off."

She stared at Pierce, trying to take in what he was saying. The whole thing, the race and the courtship, was merely so Gabriel could get his inheritance?

Her heart sank. So it *wasn't* a legitimate attempt to make amends for what he'd cost her family. Or even some grand attraction . . .

No, she'd never thought that. Had she?

But of course a tiny, foolish part of her had. The kisses and the dances and his determination to win the wager . . .

Tears stung her eyes and she struggled to keep them in check. "Are you sure?" She should have seen it sooner.

She'd known he was up to something, and his initial proposal had been coldly unemotional, more calculated than passionate. Why should she even be surprised by this news? It fit with everything she knew of him.

And still, it hurt. "Who told you about the inheritance?"

"Chetwin."

An odd relief coursed through her. "*Lieutenant* Chetwin? He despises Gab— Lord Gabriel. He's merely trying to make trouble for him, as always."

"Perhaps," Pierce said, "but I don't think so. Chetwin said he got it from a good source—someone who overheard two of the Sharpe brothers talking about it during a card game some time ago. And haven't you noticed that three of his siblings have married within just a few months? After going years without showing any interest in marriage?"

"Perhaps they all happened to meet the right person at the same time." That sounded inane, even to her.

"You said yourself that you thought he had an ulterior motive," her grandfather said.

She nodded, a lump clogging her throat. This shouldn't upset her. Everyone knew that Lord Gabriel was an utter scoundrel, and scoundrels didn't decide to marry for no reason.

But she'd really begun to think perhaps she'd been unfair to him. Was her judgment so very bad? And his kisses—

Stop thinking about his kisses! He's kissed a hundred women; it probably means nothing to him.

Which made it even more pathetic that it had meant something to her.

Fool. Idiot. She fisted her hands in her lap. How could she have been taken in so easily? This was what came of giving rein to her wilder urges. It brought nothing good.

Poppy glanced out the window. "We're nearly there. What do you want to do? We can head for Waverly Farm right now if you wish."

Oh, how she wanted to leap at that suggestion, to run away and just forget she'd ever met Gabriel Sharpe. But she couldn't. "No, that would be rude. Besides, I'd like to determine for myself what the truth is. No offense, Pierce."

"None taken," Pierce said. "I know you're not going to believe it until you have solid proof."

"Oh, I believe it," she said, fighting to keep her tone even. "But I want *him* to know that I know. So he'll understand why I can never accept his suit."

"Forget about his suit," Poppy growled. "You needn't even speak to that scoundrel again. We can just go home."

"I made a wager," she said firmly. "If I were a man and reneged, you would call me out. Why should it be any different with my being a woman?"

She could see the struggle on Poppy's face.

"So you mean to let him court you?" he snapped.

"Don't worry, it won't last long. I will put an end to it without reneging on our wager."

She would make him squirm. Make him regret his

pretense of caring about her and her family. She would expose the wretch, then cut him off at the knees.

"By the end of our dinner today, Lord Gabriel will have a decided change of heart about courting me. I'll make sure of that." She hardened her voice. "Because it'll be a cold day in hell before I let him marry me to gain his inheritance."

Chapter Seven

Gabe didn't know why he felt so irritated as Oliver's carriage lumbered toward Halstead Hall.

Winning a race usually made him feel like a king.

But Virginia's reaction to his winning had unsettled him.

"She was right, you know," Oliver said from where he sat next to Gabe, opposite Maria and Gran.

"About what?" Gabe snarled. He didn't have to ask who *she* was.

"The enormous risk you took on that course. You could have killed her and you both."

Blast it all, it was one thing to have *her* complain of it. It was quite another to have his brother chide him for it. "It wasn't as if I planned to go up the hill, for God's sake. *I* wasn't the one to veer."

"But you can't blame her for veering. It was either that or run into the crowd. She handled a difficult situation quite well and without panicking, which is more than many men would do."

Gabe didn't need to be told that. From the beginning of the race, she'd proved herself an excellent driver—

expert at controlling her team, adept at bringing out the best in them, and courageous beyond anything he would have expected of a sheltered young woman. "Once she made her decision, I did what was necessary to win." As he always had.

"You should have reined in," Oliver said.

He glared at his brother. "Why? I was in complete control at every moment."

"Really? Your phaeton came very close to tipping over onto her rig."

He said nothing. Oliver was right.

When he'd felt the balance of his rig shift, he'd had a moment of sheer terror. The very idea of his causing any accident that would hurt her . . .

He shuddered, then cursed himself for it. He'd always made it through these things by staring Death in the face, by not letting the idea of dying make him afraid. The fact that this race had done so—that *she* had done so—alarmed him.

Not wanting to live in fear was precisely why he'd avoided getting close to anyone outside his family. Having a mistress or a wife or children made a man afraid—of losing them, of having them yanked away from him, of dying and leaving them to suffer. The minute a man showed weakness, Death swooped in to conquer.

Look at how Death had come for his family. Mother had panicked at the thought that her son was being corrupted by her husband's mistress, so she'd struck out—murdering her husband. And then, she'd panicked at the thought of being without him, so she'd killed herself.

That's what he'd always thought, anyway. Now he wasn't so sure. He hadn't been sure of anything in the past few months. And that scared the blazes out of him.

He scowled. No, damn it! He was not going to let that scare him. And he was certainly not going to let Virginia plant fear in his mind with her ravings about his foolhardy actions.

"Life isn't worth living without risk," he said, though for the first time, the words rang a little hollow. "Even Miss Waverly recognizes that, or she wouldn't have challenged me in the first place."

"That may be, but if you're not careful, you'll forfeit any chance at winning her," Oliver said. "She lost her brother in a race. She won't want to risk marrying a man she could lose in one, wager or no wager."

Gabe crossed his arms over his chest. "Is this the part where you lecture me about setting up a scandalous wager with her? And lecture Gran about keeping it secret from her family?"

Oliver gave a rueful chuckle. "Lecturing Gran is pointless. She's never listened to me before, and I don't imagine that will ever change."

"I listen to you when you speak sense," Gran said with a sniff.

"You listen to me when I agree with you," Oliver countered good-naturedly. "Gabe doesn't even do that." He met Gabe's gaze. "But in this case, considering the outrageous subterfuges I used to gain my own wife, lecturing you on setting up a wager would be rather like the pot calling the kettle black."

"I should think so," Maria put in.

With one eyebrow raised at his wife, Oliver said, "Besides, Gabe, it looks as if you need all the help you can get with Miss Waverly. She stated she'd never marry a man as reckless as you."

"She can say it all she wants, but she doesn't mean it," Gabe retorted. "I saw the look on her face when I pointed out that I had to win to be able to court her. She was pleased as punch, whether or not she admitted it. Women love having a man risk his life for them."

Maria snorted. "Women like men who make intelligent choices. Not men who race madly into any reckless situation. A woman might be momentarily swayed by the romance of it, but in the end she wants a rational man."

"Women don't know what they want," he countered, irritated that she was probably right. "Not until they get it."

Oliver nudged his wife. "He's doomed."

"He is indeed." Maria stared at Gabe. "Does she know that you're marrying to gain your inheritance?"

Gabe tensed. "No. And I prefer to keep it that way until I can convince her to look past the accident with her brother and get to know me."

"If she learns of it before you can tell her," Maria pointed out, "you will lose your chance with her."

"Nonsense," Gran put in. "The woman needs a husband. Surely she will think sensibly when faced with the possibility of having a rich one."

"I'd rather she didn't know about the money just yet,"

Gabe said. "I need more opportunities to prove what I already know—that she likes me well enough to marry me. If I can just get her to stop thinking with her head and start thinking with her . . . her . . ."

"Yes?" Maria asked, her blue eyes bright with humor. "With her what?"

Gabe glared at Maria. "The point is, I know I can bring her round, given half the chance."

If he *got* the chance. General Waverly was the dark horse in this situation. If the general didn't allow Virginia to honor the wager, Gabe would have a fight on his hands. He could only hope Virginia was good at getting around her grandfather.

As soon as he and his family reached home, they were told that the Waverlys and Devonmont awaited them in the great hall. Gabe pulled his siblings aside and reiterated what he'd told Gran, Oliver, and Maria—that he wanted no mention made of Gran's ultimatum.

They agreed to it, though Celia did so grudgingly.

Now all he had to worry about was the general. Fortunately, when the two families met, the general looked quite a bit calmer than before. He didn't stay that way, of course—one glance at Gabe had him scowling—but he didn't look as if he'd just been ordering his granddaughter to renege.

And Virginia looked . . .

Gabe caught his breath. Virginia looked like some goddess out of a man's most erotic dreams. Her hair was still in disarray from the race, her cheeks were bright, and her eyes held a glint of cunning that would have given him pause if it hadn't also mesmerized him. In her royal blue carriage dress, she was everything a man could possibly want in his bed.

One thing was certain—he would have no trouble consummating the marriage. The thought of putting his hands on her and showing her how to satisfy her desires and his made his throat raw. They would make an excellent pair. She'd see that soon enough.

They entered the drawing room to have a glass of wine and wait for dinner to be served. For once, he was glad of the trappings of wealth Gran insisted that Oliver use for guests. Their crystal goblets might have a scratch or two and the upholstery on the settees might be old and worn, but it was good crystal and expensive fabric, and the wine was of an excellent quality. If ever he'd wanted to impress someone, it was now.

As soon as they were seated with their glasses, Gran formally introduced the family. Everyone but Minerva's husband was there, since he had to be in court.

Then his siblings began to behave with their usual nosiness, peppering Virginia with questions.

"So, Miss Waverly," Jarret asked, "you and my brother made a wager. I assume you mean to go through with it?"

"Of course." She sipped her wine, her expression enigmatic. "Women are no less honorable than men." She glanced over at Annabel. "Don't you agree, Lady Jarret? I understand that you and your husband met over a wager."

Annabel smiled. "We did indeed. Although I actually won, so reneging wasn't an issue."

"You lost *one* wager with me." Jarret's smile insinuated that it had been more scandalous than the one Gabe had witnessed.

Gabe's suspicion was confirmed when Annabel glared at her husband. "And I paid it—so I do agree with you, Miss Waverly."

"I'm actually looking forward to honoring my wager," Virginia said. "After attending my first ball the other night, I've been dying to attend more."

That put Gabe on guard. "What do you mean?"

"That's part of courting, isn't it? I wouldn't be invited to such affairs ordinarily, but as soon as word gets round that you're my suitor, I'm sure to receive many invitations. And you'll want to introduce me to all your friends. What better place than at a ball? The amiable people, the excellent conversation . . . Why, even the punch is delightful."

The vixen was deliberately echoing his litany of everything he hated about balls. As his brothers and sisters laughed heartily, he stifled a groan. Leave it to them to find this amusing.

Her grandfather seemed to do so as well, as did her cousin. Both looked rather smug.

"The season is over in London," Gabe pointed out. "I doubt there will be any balls in the coming months."

"Not in London, perhaps." Minerva's eyes gleamed with mischief. "But country balls abound now that the hunting season has started. We're invited to one in Ealing and two in Acton this month alone."

"And Miss Langston invited us to her birthday ball in Richmond," Celia added helpfully.

"Don't forget Lady Kirkwood's affair at the school to inaugurate the fall term for her girls," Oliver offered. "I promised Kirkwood we would all be there."

Gabe downed his glass of wine in one long swallow. Damn it to blazes. It looked like he had weeks of his worst nightmare ahead of him. "Well then, I'll be happy to accompany you, Miss Waverly," he lied through his teeth. "Assuming that your grandfather is willing to chaperone." If Gabe had to suffer, he would make the general do so as well.

"Nonsense," Gran said. "Any one of us is perfectly happy to provide you with a chaperone."

Of course they were. "You don't mind the hour drive to Waverly Farm and back?" Gabe pointed out. "In the wee hours of the morning?"

"Certainly not," Celia said with a sparkling smile. "I love a good drive. We all do."

Great. Now he had to go to balls with Virginia *and* his family. That was not what he'd had in mind. He'd envisioned picnics in the woods, chaperoned by a maid he could sweet talk into letting him have time alone with his prospective bride. Or long, rousing rides along deserted country lanes near Waverly Farm.

"I wouldn't want to inconvenience your sisters," Virginia said smoothly. "I'm sure Poppy would be happy to come along to any affairs we might attend. Not so much during the winter, when the weather plagues his injuries, but in the spring—"

"The spring?" Gabe cut in. "I hope we won't still be courting in the spring." Realizing how that sounded, he added hastily, "I mean, once we reach an understanding—"

"Oh, surely you don't think it will happen so quick as all that." Her innocent smile didn't fool him for one minute. "You said I needed to get to know you, and I quite agree. That's why long courtships are best."

"Long courtships," he echoed, his heart sinking into his stomach.

"My late son courted his wife for two years before they married," General Waverly said, with a suspicious glint in his eye. "I'd hate to see my granddaughter be hasty. What do you think, Pierce?"

As alarm built in Gabe's chest, Devonmont cast him a satisfied grin. "Oh, yes," he said, lifting his glass to drink. "Two years is plenty of time."

"Now, Pierce," Virginia chided him, "you and Poppy are being ridiculous. Two years is far too long."

Gabe let out a breath. "I should say so."

"A year is long enough." She cast Gabe a sly glance over the rim of her wineglass. "Though I suppose it could be shortened to six months."

At Gabe's groan, Celia burst into laughter. "How about that, Gabe? Miss Waverly wants a courtship that will last at least until February."

He bit back an oath. His brat of a sister was certainly going to have fun with this.

"There's no hurry, is there?" Virginia cast him another of those sweet smiles that gave him pause. "How can I make a judicious decision about my entire life in such a short time?"

Oh, God, could she have found out about Gran's demand? No, how could she? "No hurry at all," he muttered and got up to pour himself more wine.

"Besides," she went on in a suddenly steely voice, "you'll need that time to prepare for the move."

Gabe almost dropped his glass. "The move?"

"I assume that if we marry, you'll come to live at Waverly Farm with me and Poppy. You can't possibly mean for me to live here."

"Actually, I intend for us to have a house of our own," he ground out as he paced in front of the fireplace.

"Then who will look after Poppy? He needs me to run his household."

"Can't do without her," her grandfather said cheerily.

She cast Gabe a falsely pained look. "And forgive me for being indelicate, but given that you have no profession and I have a tiny dowry, well . . . I don't see how we could afford a house."

All eyes turned to him. Blast, blast, *blast*. He could tell they were enjoying this incredibly vulgar conversation. And what gently bred woman brought up her fiancé's future income as polite dinner conversation, anyway?

Gran didn't appear the least bit bothered by it. "I assure you, Miss Waverly, that my grandson will be able to support you."

"Oh, I never thought otherwise." Virginia's eyes glittered suspiciously. "But a lady has to be practical. I know that men like Lord Gabriel require wives who can bring something to a marriage. Since I cannot, I must do my best to help our situation."

Her manner deepened his alarm. She didn't seem apologetic or regretful. Plus, she was talking about their prospective marriage as if she really did mean to go through with it—quite a turnabout from earlier in the day.

He would lay odds that this vulgar discussion wasn't typical of her. What if she really *had* heard about Gran's ultimatum? But when? Surely not before the ball, or she would have thrown that in his face. Besides, it wasn't widely known beyond his family, except for some friends.

"I hate that marrying me will materially alter his lordship's life," she went on, rousing his suspicions even more. "He'll have to give up his rooms in town, not to mention his membership in any clubs. And I daresay there will be little racing after we marry. But I do hope our union will make up for those inconveniences."

"You must trust me in this, Miss Waverly," Gran persisted. "The lad has prospects."

"Oh? And what might those be?" Virginia's gaze met his, ripe with challenge. "One should never count one's chickens before they hatch, you know. I have to think practically."

He stiffened. She knew. He didn't know how, but she must have found out about Gran's ultimatum. And she was clearly eager to lay into him. She'd just been toying with him until now.

He walked up to her. "Miss Waverly, it looks as if dinner may be a while longer. Perhaps you would like to go view our maze? You seemed very interested in it the last time you were here, and I'd love to show it to you."

"I'd be delighted," she said, looking as if she were

spoiling for a fight. "We can discuss your 'prospects' some more."

Oh, yes. She definitely knew.

"Perhaps I should come along—" her grandfather began.

"No need," Gran interrupted. "The maze is close by—it won't hurt to let the young people have a short walk before dinner. It helps the digestion." She shot Gabe a long, stern glance. "And my grandson knows that if he doesn't behave, he'll have to answer to me."

"I'll be fine, Poppy," Virginia added as she slid her hand in the crook of Gabe's elbow. "This won't take long."

No, it wouldn't. Gabe intended to remind her of all the reasons she needed to marry, and all the reasons he was the perfect candidate. Her pride might be pricked at the moment, but she kept saying she was a practical woman—and she couldn't deny that his offer was as advantagous to her as to him.

But he wouldn't let her bow out of this, by God. He'd won that wager fair and square, and she owed him a courtship. He had Celia to think of, after all. He *had* to marry.

They both kept quiet as they walked through the halls toward the side door. There were servants everywhere, and Gabe didn't want anyone hearing this particular discussion.

The minute they emerged into the gardens and headed for the maze, he said in a low voice, "I take it that you've heard about my grandmother's ultimatum."

"Ultimatum?" she said with that false look of innocence.

It stirred his temper even more. "Don't play dumb, Virginia. It doesn't flatter you."

Leading her into the maze, he hurried her down the small lane between the close-cropped box hedges to find some privacy from any curious listeners.

"How would you know what flatters me?" she snapped. "You barely know me. Which is probably why you chose me for your mercenary plan."

Blast, blast, *blast*. "How did you find out about Gran's demands? How long have you known?"

She tipped up her chin. "Pierce told me just now in the carriage. Apparently he got it from an acquaintance who'd heard something of it at a card game you played in a tavern."

He'd forgotten all about that discussion, which had taken place in a public arena. "You're laboring under a false assumption. I chose you as my wife because I wronged your family," he bit out, annoyed at being painted in so poor a light. "Trust me, there are plenty of women eager to marry a marquess's son. I could have found one at any of your precious balls without having to go through the risk of racing you."

As soon as he spoke the words he regretted them, for the mention of other women seemed to inflame her further. Snatching her hand from his arm, she spat, "Then go do so. I want none of your scheme."

She turned to go back, but he blocked her path. He would make her listen, by God, if it was the last thing he did! "It isn't a scheme—it's a desperate situation. And yes, I was hoping you'd help me with it. Not for my sake, but for my sister's."

He could see curiosity warring with anger in her face. "Your sister's?"

"I don't know how much you've heard about Gran's demand, but she says we all have to marry by the end of the year, or none of us inherit. So if one doesn't marry, the others lose their fortunes as well. The three eldest of us are in good situations, so I'm not concerned about them. And I have enough income to support myself from racing. But Celia . . ."

He ran his fingers through his hair. "She deserves better than to be cut off without a penny just because she's too stubborn to give in. If I don't marry, she'll use my refusal as an excuse to refuse as well. But if I marry, she won't want to be the only one holding everyone else up. She'll do what she has to do."

She glared at him. "Sweet Lord, you're even worse than I thought. You want to force me into marrying so you can force your sister into marrying, as well."

"No, damn it!" He took a breath, expelled it, then took another, fighting for calm. "I don't want to force anyone into anything. If I had my choice, I'd go on as I'd always planned—racing whomever I want, living on my winnings, and trying to establish a decent Thoroughbred stable."

He stared her down. "But I *don't* have my choice. And neither does Celia. For that matter, neither do you. You want to live forever with your grandfather at your cozy farm, but we both know that can't happen. This courtship is the only way I could find to make all of us happy."

She eyed him skeptically. "So you don't care about the money."

"Of course I care about the money; I'm not an idiot. I know that my inheritance could allow me to reach my dream much more quickly than if I struggle on my own. But if Celia were already married and settled, I would tell Gran to go to blazes." God knows he wished he could.

"Instead," she snapped, "you've decided that I should give up my freedom so you and your sister can enjoy the fruits of your grandmother's labors."

He'd had enough, damn it! "You seem to forget that you, too, would enjoy those fruits. If I gain my inheritance, you'll have the money you need to help your grandfather in his old age, to restore Waverly Farm to its former glory, and to live like a queen if that's what you want."

She gaped at him. Clearly it hadn't occurred to her that if she married him, his gain would be her gain.

Then her expression hardened. "That's only if your sister also marries. What if she doesn't behave as you expect? What if she digs in her heels and refuses? Then I'll be saddled with a husband who's lost his 'prospects.'"

With a narrowing gaze, he bore down on her, forcing her to back up into a blind alley. "For a woman who's outraged that I would marry her in order to gain my inheritance, you seem awfully interested in my 'prospects.' You made quite a fuss about them a few moments ago."

"That was only because I was trying to provoke you! You know it was."

He did know it. Because when it came to him, Virginia was not practical. Practical women didn't challenge men to races in a fit of temper. Practical women didn't cut off their noses to spite their faces when a perfectly good marriage proposal presented itself, and practical women didn't turn down pots of money.

Romantics did that. She was a romantic.

God, he should have realized it before. He would never get anywhere by arguing the practicality of the thing. Her emotions ran too high. He needed to take a different tack.

"And do you know *why* you were trying to provoke me?"

"Because I was angry at you for being an arrogant, deceitful—"

"Because you didn't like the idea of my marrying you for money. Because you wanted me to marry you for other reasons."

When her cheeks pinkened, he knew he'd guessed right.

She squared her shoulders. "Don't be ridiculous. I don't want you to marry me for *any*—"

He lifted his hand to catch her chin. "You desire me. And you want me to desire *you*."

A panicky look came over her face. "That's the most absurd thing I've ever heard."

"Is it?" The time was past for talking. Instead, he kissed her.

For a second she was stiff and still, like a filly about to bolt. Then her lips softened and her body angled into him, and he knew he'd chosen right.

Because Virginia was more like him than she cared to admit. She was physical, susceptible to touch and taste, not words and arguments. And that was fine by him. With his blood still running high from the race and their argument, he burned to touch and taste her again.

He thrust his tongue between her tender lips to tease and explore. God, her soft mouth made him want to lose himself in it forever. She gave as good as she got, too, tangling her tongue with his, curling her fingers into his coat to hold him still so she could set his blood afire.

This was the woman he wanted, with her slender body and her smooth skin and her throaty laugh that was surely the envy of females everywhere. She was a wild forest enchantress succeeding in her merciless mission to drive him mad.

Suddenly she tore her mouth from his. "You can't just win the argument by kissing me senseless."

"I can try," he murmured against her impudent little chin. "You know damned well this isn't just about money. Every time I see you my blood runs hot, and I can think only of how badly I want to take you to bed."

The minute she stiffened he knew he'd spoken too bluntly, but he couldn't help it—words weren't his purview. Actions were.

"You're suffering under a grand delusion if you think that I—" she began.

He kissed her again. Only this time, he dragged her into his arms and ravished her mouth. It took a few moments for her to relax, but once he had her soft and eager, he laid a path of kisses down her jaw so he could bury one in the curve of her neck . . . her silky-skinned neck, with its scent of orange blossoms and almonds that made him want to devour her whole.

When he tongued her throat, she gasped. "I wish . . . you would . . . stop being so . . . naughty."

"No, you don't," he murmured and kissed her again.

By God, she was sweet, her body pressing up against his, clinging to him, driving him to an insane arousal. He ran his hands over her trim form, down her slender waist to her surprisingly shapely hips, then up to her ribs and the breasts he ached to touch.

Lyons's warning about how to treat a respectable woman came into his mind, but his hands seemed to have a will of their own as they slid up to cup her perfect little breasts, with their perfectly aroused nipples poking through her gown. He yearned to tear off her clothes and suck those tips until she moaned and melted in his arms.

But this was insanity. Anyone might come upon them. _Good,_ his mind whispered. Then she'd be compromised, and he could marry her without having to navigate the obstacle course of courtship.

If whoever found them didn't kill him first.

But he didn't care. As long as she would let him touch her, by God, he would. Because some things were worth dying for.

Chapter Eight

Virginia couldn't believe Gabriel had his hands on her breasts. It was shocking! Outrageous! Delicious.

How could something so scandalous feel so *good*? Bad enough that he'd kissed her, now he was wreaking havoc on her senses with his naughty caresses. It simply wasn't fair. He was cheating. And she was letting him.

She was a fool. She should make him stop. And she would, in a few minutes. After she figured out why she didn't want to.

He pushed her against the hedge, his body plastered to hers as he ravaged her mouth over and over. The clipped edges of boxwood pricked her through her gown, and its pungent smell wafted through her senses, but she was only conscious of how he made her feel, hot and eager and agitated. Pleasurably so. Especially with him kneading her breasts and thumbing her nipples through her gown. It was hard to tell where his rapid breathing ended and hers began. Sweet Lord, he was driving her wild!

And she must be doing the same to him; she could

feel the hardness rising in his trousers where he was pressed up against her. Raised on a stud farm, she knew precisely what that signaled. It ought to be a warning to stop this madness, but it merely made her exult. He'd told the truth about desiring her. When he was kissing her there was no sign of the cold and remote lord, and her feminine vanity thrilled to that.

But when he flicked open the top button on the front of her bodice, she balked and caught his hand. "You mustn't," she whispered, staring down at his other tanned hand, still caressing her breast. "It's unseemly."

His eyes gleamed at her. "Exactly the word I was thinking. Unseemly."

Awful man, for laughing at her. "And reckless," she chided, to keep her mind off the fact that he had undone two more buttons. "You're being very reckless." And she was dying to feel his fingers on her bare flesh. He might as well tip up her skirts and call her a soiled dove.

"What do you expect of a man like me?" He brushed a kiss to her temple. "Recklessness is my calling. Besides, you like that I'm reckless."

"I do not!" she said, but that was a lie. The feel of his bare hand sliding into her bodice was exquisite. It made her feel like a real woman. *His* woman.

Oh, she was mad.

He kissed her ear. "You like it because you've secretly got some recklessness in you, too."

Her heart raced. Why did he have to be the only one to notice her urges to be insanely irresponsible?

"Don't tell me you weren't swept up in the excitement

of the race this afternoon," he went on like a little devil sitting on her shoulder, whispering terrible truths. "I could see it in your face."

"Before or after you almost got yourself killed?" she choked out. Oh, Lord, he'd reached inside her corset cup to fondle her nipple through her shift. She longed to tear her clothes off so he could do it better.

His hand paused on her breast. "You really were worried about me."

What had she said? Oh, yes. She shouldn't have said that. "I meant, before you almost got *us* killed."

"Don't deny it—you were worried about me." He rolled her nipple between his fingers, making her weak in the knees. Why didn't she just make him stop?

Because she hoped he never stopped.

His breath thickened, falling heavily on her cheek. "No one but my family ever worries about me. Everyone thinks I'm invincible."

Something in his voice made her want to draw him in her arms and soothe him. Instead she pulled back to stare up at him. "That's because *you* think you're invincible, you daft fool."

His eyes held a bleakness that made her ache for him. "Actually, I just don't care if I am or not."

The words chilled her. Thank goodness, he'd stopped caressing her, because she really needed to think straight right now. "Then why marry, if you're just going to make some woman a widow?"

A raw, vulnerable expression came over his face before he masked it. "I told you why. Because Celia—"

"Ah, yes. Your sister needs you to." She didn't know whether to admire his loyalty to his family, or despise his arrogant assumption that his plan was best for everyone. "And you don't care what woman you hurt in the process."

With a sigh, he bent his head to nuzzle her cheek. "I'm not trying to hurt you. I need a wife, and you need a husband. Why not make it easy and marry each other?"

The words tore into her. "I don't want a husband who marries me out of pity for my situation. Or because he wants his sister to gain her inheritance."

His hand moved over her breast again, softly, delicately. "Does this feel like pity to you? Does this feel like mercenary intent?" When she sucked in a harsh breath, he added, "I've had seven months to find a wife, sweetheart, and you're the first woman I've even considered. Do you want to know why?"

Lord, yes.

"You rouse my blood. I have no other way to describe it. I'm not a poet, I'm not good with pretty compliments, and God knows I have little to offer except a possible inheritance. But I promise that at least in the bedchamber, I can make you happy. Perhaps that doesn't count for much, but people have married for less."

"I prefer to marry for more."

"So you have another, better prospect?" he asked, still fondling her, driving her to distraction.

He knew the answer to that.

"Give me a chance to show you how good we can be together," he whispered. "Just . . . one . . . chance . . ."

He was kissing her again, so sweetly it made her throat ache with the beauty of it. What if he was right? What if this was enough? Lord knows he roused her blood, too. If not for his mad need to be in danger at every moment—and her feeling that she was somehow betraying Roger by being with him—she could almost envision a life with him.

For a moment, she gave herself up to the pleasure he wound about her. He smelled of horses and leather and tasted of wine, intoxicating her with his kisses. His hot mouth moved down her chin to her neck to suck at the pulse that beat there, then skimmed lower toward her breast, making her moan and arch into him to grab at his shoulders.

His thickly muscled, magnificent shoulders. No wonder women threw themselves at him. He was a Thoroughbred among the cart horses, sleek and imposing. His masterful caresses made her feel like a mare in heat who'd trample over anything to mate with the stallion in the next paddock.

No man had ever provoked such wild feelings in her. She was sinking into them, drowning in the sensations—

"Virginia!" came a sharp voice, reaching through the fog in her addled brain.

Panic seized her. "Stop," she hissed. "You have to stop."

Gabriel pushed open her gown. "Keep quiet and he'll go away."

"Virginia!" the voice repeated, closer now.

"It's Pierce," she said, shoving Gabriel back. As he stood there blinking, she rebuttoned her gown. Sweet Lord, it was hanging half open! "He won't go away until he finds us."

When a half-dazed Gabriel reached for her, she slapped his hand. "Are you *trying* to ruin me?"

He raked his fingers through his hair, then glanced to the entrance of the blind alley. "It's not ruining you if I'm willing to marry you."

She gaped at him. So *that* was his plan—to compromise her and ensure their marriage that way. And she'd nearly let him do it!

Turning on her heel, she marched toward the entrance. "You aren't going to gain me like that, sir."

He followed her. "There's leaves and twigs on the back of your gown." He started brushing them off.

"Don't do that!" she growled, batting at his hands.

"Damn it, Sharpe, where have you and my cousin gone off to?" bellowed Pierce from very near. Then came an awful silence, followed by, "What the hell are you two doing?"

Gabriel took his sweet time about dropping his hands from her gown, the devil. "We're *trying* to tour the maze, Devonmont."

She glanced over to see Pierce standing at the head of the blind alley, regarding her and Gabriel with rank suspicion. As heat rose in her cheeks, it occurred to her that her hair was probably mussed from having Gabriel's hands buried in it. Oh, dear. How could she have been so foolish?

"Pierce, isn't this just the loveliest maze? I've been admiring the box hedges," she lied gamely.

"With Sharpe's hands on your behind?" Pierce said.

Her cheeks grew hot. Fie on Gabriel for that. "Don't be rude, Pierce. Lord Gabriel was merely helping me get leaves off my gown."

"I'll just bet he was," Pierce said dryly, his gaze going to Gabriel.

Who met Pierce's gaze with one that was far too smug. "You caught us, Devonmont—I admit it. I guess there's no stopping the wedding now."

Her cousin said, "No need for such dramatics. A man ought to be able to steal a kiss without finding himself leg-shackled, don't you agree?"

"I *quite* agree. Not that we were doing anything so scandalous," she said hastily, then scowled at Gabriel. "Because we weren't."

Gabriel glanced from Pierce to her. "It's all right, sweetheart. I'm more than happy to make this right."

"Of course you are," Pierce drawled. "You've got that tidy little inheritance waiting for you."

Fire blazed in Gabriel's face. "Not that it's any of your concern, but I was just explaining to your cousin why I'm not marrying her for my inheritance."

"Of course it's my concern," Pierce said. "She's family. And she deserves better than you—which is precisely why *I* intend to marry her."

For a moment, she and Gabriel just gaped at him.

Then Virginia found her voice. "What on earth are you talking about?"

Pierce shrugged. "You can have more than one suitor. I'm throwing my hat in the ring."

"The blazes you are," Gabriel growled and lunged forward.

"Stop it!" She grabbed him by the arm. "Can't you see he's just trying to provoke you?"

"Not in the least," Pierce said. "I'm perfectly serious. I'm a far more suitable husband for you than *this* scoundrel." He flicked a dismissive glance at Gabriel. "Since I'm the one who'll inherit your home, if you want to marry for an inheritance, you ought to marry for mine."

"I'm not marrying for anyone's inheritance," she said irritably.

"Then marry for love." Pierce's cool tone belied his sentimental words. "I love you madly, cousin. So I should have as good a chance with you as he does. Or better, unless Sharpe is claiming to love you madly, too."

She nearly burst into laughter. Pierce so clearly did *not* love her. If she had her head in the clouds, as Pierce claimed, then he had his firmly rooted on earth.

His declaration was having the oddest effect on Gabriel, who looked fit to be tied. How curious. Was he upset because he hated losing his future inheritance? Or because he hated losing *her*? She really needed to know.

Perhaps she should let Pierce continue this little farce. "Do you truly love me, cousin?"

When Pierce's gaze shot to her with a silent warning in it, she was glad she'd gone with her instincts. "Of course. I appreciate your intelligence and spirit and good heart. Sharpe just wants to get into your bed."

"And you don't?" Gabriel shot back.

"So what if I do?" Pierce drawled. "Isn't that normal for a man in love?"

He practically winced, and she had to stifle a snort. Surely even Gabriel could tell Pierce was lying; he practically choked on the word *love*.

But apparently Gabriel took her cousin's claim at face value. "You don't know the meaning of love, Devonmont. I'm well aware of your reputation, even if your cousin is not. You've left a string of mistresses behind you longer than my arm. If she marries you she'll always play second fiddle to your current mistress."

"Yet you plan to be faithful to her?" Pierce cast Gabriel a withering glance. "Once you get your hands on your grandmother's money, you'll be spending every night in the stews."

"You know nothing about what I mean to do with my grandmother's money," Gabriel bit out. "And you know nothing about me."

Pierce stepped closer. "I know I'm the best man for her."

"You're her cousin, for God's sake!"

"Second cousin. And there's no legal impediment to cousins marrying, anyway." He gave Gabriel a searching look. "I notice you haven't made any claims to loving her yourself."

A muscle worked in Gabriel's jaw, which was all the answer either she or Pierce needed. Not that she'd expected Gabriel to say he loved her—he barely knew her. And she didn't want him to claim a lie. That would prove him to be every bit as mercenary as Pierce seemed to think.

But some tiny part of her was disappointed. Which was utterly ridiculous. She didn't love him. Why should she want him to love *her*?

Pierce held out his arm. "Come, my dear. Uncle Isaac sent me to fetch you in to dinner."

As she walked forward, Gabriel growled, "Don't you dare go off with him!"

She stopped to face him with a frown. "I beg your pardon?" she said in her frostiest voice. "I was unaware you had any right to command me."

Pierce shook his head. "Not an ounce of gentlemanly civility in him."

Gabriel glared at Pierce. "Stay out of this!" Then he leveled an angry glance on Virginia. "You and I had an agreement. I won our race, and with it, the right to court you."

"Yes, but there was nothing in our wager to preclude anyone else courting me. Thank you very much for taking me around the maze, but now that my cousin has declared his intentions, I believe I shall let him take me in to dinner. It seems only fair that I give you both equal time."

At his look of outrage, she bit back a smile and took Pierce's arm.

Before they walked off, Pierce said, "You might want to take a few minutes, old boy, to . . . make yourself presentable." Pierce's gaze dipped down to Gabriel's groin, eliciting a curse from Gabriel.

Virginia blushed violently as Pierce added, "If you go in to dinner looking like that, and the general notices, not only will there be no wedding, but it'll be pistols at dawn. That won't do you any good."

They headed off together, leaving Gabriel to stew.

"You are very wicked sometimes," she said as soon as they were out of earshot.

Pierce's voice was hard. "Did he do anything more than kiss you?"

She swallowed. There were some things a lady definitely kept to herself. "Nothing." She slanted a glance at him. "You must tell me what you're up to. Because we both know that you don't want to marry me, and you certainly don't 'love me madly.'"

"Not madly perhaps, but I do love you."

She arched an eyebrow at him.

"I love all my family," he clarified, a devilish smile curving up his lips.

"So you love me as you do your mother, in other words."

He shrugged. "It's better than loving you as I do my dog."

"Play with words if you must, but at least tell me what your game is."

He lowered his voice. "Glance behind us."

She did so, and saw Gabriel coming out of the maze, his hands clenched and his eyes sending daggers into the back of Pierce's head.

"Is he watching us?" Pierce asked.

"Like a dog watches a bone being stolen from him."

Pierce shot her a long look. "Or like a man who doesn't want to lose a chance at a woman he desires?"

"It's the same thing."

"No, it's not." Pierce stared ahead at Halstead Hall. "Any woman will suffice to help Sharpe win his inheritance. He's irritated right now to have what he sees as an easy conquest taken from him. And if all he cares about is the money, he'll go on to another woman since there's competition. He has no time to fight a courtship war."

"And if he doesn't go on to another woman?"

"Then he desires you."

"How is that any better? In neither case does he love me."

"Come now, cuz, love is a farce for a man like Sharpe. The best you'll get from him is desire."

I promise that at least in the bedchamber, I can make you happy . . . People have married for less.

"That's not good enough for me."

Pierce cast her a pitying look. "Then you'll have to look elsewhere for a husband, dear girl. Or settle for the sort of love *I* offer and accept my suit."

"Your pretend suit, you mean."

He met her gaze solemnly. "It's not pretend. If the only way to help you is to marry you, I'm willing to sacrifice myself on the altar of matrimony."

"Thank you, but I believe I can do without a sacrificial lamb."

They entered the house in silence, Gabriel stalking after them. As they turned a corner, Pierce glanced back at the still glowering Gabriel. "There's a remote possibility that Sharpe might make you a good husband, my dear girl. But until I know his true intentions, we should give him some competition. Then, if he persists in his suit toward you, we can reexamine his sincerity."

She cast him a bemused glance. "Why would you want to help him?"

"I don't. I want to help *you*. Marriage is the only way to ensure your future." He searched her face. "And you fancy him, admit it."

Color rising in her cheeks, she stared down the hall. "I find him arrogant and too sure of himself."

"Yet you fancy him."

She gritted her teeth. Pierce might not always know her mind, but sometimes he was right on the mark.

"At the moment," she muttered, "I fancy the idea of being a governess. If I must deal with possessiveness and obnoxious demands, I'd rather it be from creatures small enough for me to send to their rooms."

Pierce chuckled. "I should like to see you try sending *Sharpe* to his room."

I'd only do that if I were going there with him.

Good gracious, where had that thought come from?

This was what came of letting a devil like Gabriel kiss her and put his hands on her. It fed the restlessness in her soul and provoked the most unwise thoughts and fantasies.

But perhaps Pierce was right. If she did want to consider Gabriel for a husband—which she wasn't at all sure of—it wouldn't hurt to give him some competition. And even if she *didn't* want to marry him, giving him competition would be a delightful way to torment him. At the moment, she found that vastly appealing.

"What shall we tell Poppy?" she asked.

"The truth. That I'm courting you, too."

"He won't believe it."

"I wouldn't bet on that." His expression turned solemn. "He'll swallow anything rather than face the possibility of Sharpe taking you away from him after doing the same with Roger."

He had a point. Poppy would never forgive Gabriel for getting Roger killed. She still wasn't entirely certain that *she* could. "Pierce, do you know what really happened?"

"What do you mean?"

"Was Roger drunk the day of the race? And was he the one to make the challenge, or was Sharpe?"

A shuttered look crossed Pierce's face. "You'll have to ask Sharpe."

"Do you think he'd tell me?"

"There's only one way to find out."

True. But part of her was afraid to learn the truth. Because if Poppy was right about Gabriel even as she'd been letting the scoundrel kiss and caress her . . .

Sweet Lord, she could never bear that.

Chapter Nine

They entered the dining room to find everyone else seated. Pierce led her to her chair, which was next to his.

"Where's my brother?" Lord Jarret asked as they sat down.

"They got separated, and Virginia was wandering the maze alone," Pierce lied. "So I used the opportunity to profess my desire to court her as well."

Audible gasps filled the room.

Virginia darted a glance at her grandfather, who looked stunned. Then he broke into a broad smile. Oh dear. She didn't want him getting his hopes up.

"This is rather sudden, isn't it?" Gabriel's sister Mrs. Masters asked.

"Very sudden," Gabriel said from the doorway. He sauntered in, his gaze narrowing when he caught sight of her sitting next to Pierce. "Apparently Devonmont isn't satisfied with gaining Waverly Farm. He wants the lady of Waverly Farm, as well."

"At least he wants the lady," Virginia shot back. "You just want to gain your inheritance."

As he scowled, his siblings let out a collective groan.

"You know about that?" Mrs. Plumtree asked.

"Yes, no thanks to any of you." She placed her hand on Pierce's, enjoying how it made Gabriel tense. "Fortunately, my cousin had heard the gossip and was kind enough to inform me on the way here."

"Kind enough?" Gabriel took his seat across from her, eyes ablaze. "Seems to me that he seized his chance to snatch you away from me."

Lady Stoneville motioned to the footman to serve the soup, and he began moving about the table.

"We're so sorry about the misunderstanding concerning Gran's ultimatum," Mrs. Masters said, with a hard glance at her brother. "We wanted to tell you, but Gabriel was against it. I think he's embarrassed. He's very enamored of you, and he knew you would misunderstand the situation if you heard of it."

Enamored of her, hah! Gabriel just wanted her in his bed. "So you lied for him."

"Not quite," Lord Jarret said. "More like . . . left out some of the truth."

"Important parts of the truth, wouldn't you say?" Virginia cast them a withering glance as she picked up her spoon. When they had the good grace to look sheepish, she added, "I find truthfulness in a husband essential."

"Gabe is generally quite truthful," Mrs. Masters insisted. "Almost to a fault."

"Mostly because he doesn't care what anyone thinks of him," Lady Celia added.

That brought Virginia up short. What had he said

when she'd accused him of thinking he was invincible? *Actually, I just don't care if I am or not.*

The vulnerable words brought an ache to her chest before she squelched it. How could she let herself be gulled by him still? He'd pursued her for ends entirely different than what he claimed, and she could not—should not—forgive him for that.

"He can be very stubborn about it, too. Do you remember that incident at Christmas with the tutor?" Mrs. Masters ate a spoonful of soup as she glanced at Lord Jarret. "The stolen plum pudding?"

"Oh, for God's sake," Gabriel muttered as he snapped his napkin out of its fanciful fold and dropped it into his lap.

Lady Celia paled suddenly, which roused Virginia's interest.

"Gabe was, what? Eight?" Mrs. Masters went on.

"Had to be," Lord Jarret said. "It was our first Christmas after Mother and Father—" He broke off. "Anyway, Gran's cook had left our Christmas pudding on the windowsill to cool, and it disappeared."

"Gabe had a particular fondness for plum pudding," Mrs. Masters continued, "and everyone knew it. So when it went missing, his tutor, Mr. Virgil, went up to the attic, where Gabe had made himself a sort of secret lair. He found Gabe surrounded by crumbs."

"But the lad flat out refused to admit that he'd stolen and eaten the pudding," Lord Jarret said. "He wouldn't deny it—that would be lying—but he wouldn't admit it, either. Mr. Virgil demanded that he confess what he'd done, but Gabe continued to refuse to answer him."

"I hope that tutor had the good sense to take a cane to the boy," her grandfather said as he dipped into his soup. "Got to be firm with a lad like that."

Virginia hid a smile. For all his blustering, Poppy had never caned either her or Roger, despite his threats to do so.

"Papa would probably have caned the truth out of Gabe," Mrs. Masters replied. "But Mr. Virgil was a mild-mannered scholar who merely lectured Gabe on the sin of stealing. He quoted Bible verses. He even brought up the specter of our dead parents, saying that they were looking down from heaven, disappointed in his actions."

"That only made Gabe dig in his heels," Lord Jarret said. "He refused to say a word."

Virginia could well understand that. Her nanny had tried that on her as a girl, and it had always infuriated her. She'd felt that if her parents had wanted her to behave, they shouldn't have gone away. Death hadn't been something she really understood. She'd just felt abandoned. No doubt he had, too.

An unwanted sympathy swelled in her. Thoughtfully, she ate her soup. Sometimes she forgot that they had the deaths of their parents in common. He was a little older when his died, but that only made it more awful for him. At least she didn't really remember hers.

"So his tutor said he couldn't go down to dinner until he admitted what he'd done," Mrs. Masters went on.

Gabriel's grandmother took up the tale. "He held out all Christmas Eve, and into the next day. The stubborn fool refused to admit anything—or to lie about it, either. It took his not appearing at Christmas dinner for me to learn the truth. Mr. Virgil had kept everything from me, afraid of being dismissed for not being able to handle Gabriel."

"Once Gran knew," Lord Jarret added, "she told Gabriel that what he'd done was wrong, that she would use his Christmas money to pay for another plum pudding at the bakery in Ealing, and then she caned him for stealing. There was no more talk of admitting anything. She realized by that point that she'd never get him to own up to it."

"That's because he didn't do it," said a small voice from down the table.

Every eye turned to Lady Celia.

"Celia," Gabriel said in a low voice, "it doesn't matter."

"Yes, it does," she said hotly, her eyes fixed on her brother. "They've had it wrong all these years, and I can't stand it anymore." She met her grandmother's gaze. "Gabe never took the pudding. That's why he wouldn't say that he did. *I* took it."

Everyone at the table seemed as surprised as Virginia.

"But the crumbs . . ." Mrs. Plumtree began.

"He put them there to cover it up," Lady Celia said. "By the time he found me in the kitchen with it, I'd eaten most of it. I was hungry, and there was a plum pudding. I didn't even realize it was for Christmas dinner."

"You were barely five," Mrs. Masters pointed out kindly.

"When he found me devouring it, he chided me for it, and I burst into tears." Lady Celia cast Virginia a rueful glance. "Gabe never could stand to see a girl cry."

Her heart full, Virginia glanced at Gabriel. He was staring into his soup, a flush reddening his ears. And it dawned on her that though he might like being the center of attention at a race, he didn't seem to like it at home.

His clear embarrassment tugged at her heart.

"Anyway," Lady Celia went on, "he heard Cook coming, so he grabbed my hand and what was left of the pudding and we ran."

Mrs. Plumtree stared at her grandson. "Why didn't you just leave her there? Cook would have been angry, but she always had a soft spot for Celia—"

"Celia didn't know that," he said quietly. "When I fussed at her, she asked, 'Will Gran go away because I've been a bad girl?' I told her no, Gran would never find out. Then I . . . just reacted. I carried her off, and I crumbled up the rest of the pudding in the attic."

But he'd refused to lie and say he'd eaten it. Or to say anything that might raise the question of who really *had* stolen the pudding.

Tears clogged Virginia's throat.

"Oh, Lord," Mrs. Plumtree said, her heart in her face. "Celia, girl, I never even knew you feared that I would go away."

"I thought that Mama and Papa had died because we were bad children," Lady Celia admitted.

The poor thing! "I understand that," Virginia said. "When we were children, Roger used to say that Mama and Papa had left us because we'd been naughty."

"I told the lad that wasn't true," Poppy said gruffly.

"But children feel things in their hearts, even when you tell them they're not logical," Mrs. Plumtree said. "It's hard for a child to lose a parent so young."

Poppy cast Mrs. Plumtree a long, thoughtful look. "Indeed it is," he said, his voice softer than before.

To Virginia's surprise, Mrs. Plumtree dropped her gaze, busying herself with her soup. A discomforting quiet fell on everyone.

Then Mrs. Masters took a look around the table and said, "Well, that story didn't turn out as planned. It has made you lot very dull indeed and put quite the damper on our dinner. So now I shall have to tell a happier story about Gabe. Oliver, do you remember the time . . ."

She related some tale of Gabriel accidentally shooting a hole in a boat when he and his brothers went hunting, sinking them in the river, guns and all, but Virginia couldn't stop thinking of Gabriel rushing to help his little sister. Every time she thought she had him figured out, she learned she had no idea of who he was. Could a man who cared so much for his family be all bad?

And did Lady Celia realize the sacrifice he was making just so she would have a future? It was terribly arrogant of him to assume that his sister would be better off married, but he was trying to do what he thought was right. Some brothers wouldn't if it meant they had to marry where they didn't wish to.

She studied him as he embellished his sister's tale with great glee, clearly eager to leave the sad story behind. She didn't know what to think of him. One moment he was neglecting to tell the truth about his true motives behind wishing to marry her, and the next he was refusing to lie about not loving her.

Because he *could* have lied. He *could* have denied the gossip about his inheritance entirely. His family would clearly have upheld his story. He could even have spouted some nonsense about having fallen in love with her during their two short encounters. Not that she would have believed him, but he could have tried.

He could have lied to Pierce when he'd had the chance, if only to save face. But when Pierce had asked him if he loved her, Gabriel had refused to answer.

His sister seemed to be right. Gabriel was truthful to a fault.

But that appeared to be his only virtue. He was still reckless and wild, willing to do any outrageous thing to win a race. And he still had caused Roger's death, though her understanding of what had happened became muddier with each new bit of information.

Yet, she fancied him.

She frowned at her soup. Could that ever be enough for a good marriage? Did she fancy him enough to risk watching him kill himself down the road?

Did she fancy him enough to forgive him for his part in Roger's death?

She simply didn't know.

HETTY DECLINED DESSERT when it was brought round. Sweets made her bilious these days, and the last thing she wanted to be right now was bilious. Especially with guests around.

The others seemed pleased by the orange trifle she and Maria had chosen, and the dinner had gone well. Miss Waverly certainly seemed less angry at Gabe.

Meanwhile, Gabriel had turned into jovial Gabe, joking Gabe, reckless Gabe who cared about nothing. It was his way of hiding, and hiding was as destructive for him as it had been for his brothers.

From the time their parents had died, Oliver had ruthlessly bottled up how he felt, suffocating his emotions so vigorously that when they'd finally erupted, after meeting Maria, he'd been an emotional wreck.

Jarret had dismissed his feelings as not useful to his aims, and had turned into a coldly analytical creature who genuinely hadn't cared about anything or anybody. Thank God, he'd finally met a woman who made him feel safe enough to rediscover the part of him that *could* care.

Gabe's approach was to battle his feelings. There was no ignoring them or dismissing them. His parents were dead? Fine, he would taunt Death to take him, too. He would scoff at torment and laugh at danger and never count the cost of any action. He would thrash Death into submission.

It was just another way of not facing the pain. Another way of not lancing the wound so he could heal. And Roger's death had made it worse, adding to the knot of agony that festered just beneath the surface.

The foolish lad thought he could patch it over by marrying Miss Waverly. In his usual reckless manner, he had thrown himself into action, going after her with the zeal he had for every challenge or conquest. He had managed to get far with her, too, until that blasted cousin of hers had come along.

But Hetty was not worried about Lord Devonmont. Miss Waverly clearly preferred Gabe, thank God. What worried Hetty was not being able to tell how Gabe felt about Miss Waverly.

And if she could not tell how he felt, then how could Miss Waverly? Young ladies liked to know where they stood with a man. Especially if they had another suitor waiting in the wings.

Maria rose from the table. "Ladies, shall we adjourn to the drawing room and leave the gentlemen to their port and cigars?"

"Of course," Hetty said, pleased that Maria was adapting so well to the habits of good English society. The girl might be American, but she had been willing to learn, and Hetty had been happy to teach her.

The ladies rose, eager to be away from the gentlemen so they could talk about babies and nurseries and fashion and all those things that bored men. With two of her granddaughters-in-law expecting, Hetty was just as eager to discuss such matters. She had been waiting for great-grandchildren a long time.

She was the last one out of the door as always, given her slow gait, and the general followed her.

"May I have a private word with you, Mrs. Plumtree?"

The others paused to look back and she motioned them to go on.

Once the hall cleared, she stared at him expectantly. With a glance at the open dining room door, he took her arm and led her down the hall to the library.

"What is this about?" she asked after they entered.

"I congratulate you, madam," the general said heatedly. "That was very cleverly managed."

She was not sure exactly what he meant. "Thank you, I think it went off rather well. The soup could have been a trifle warmer, but—"

"I'm not talking about the dinner, damn it! I'm talking about that tale of Lord Gabriel in his youth. I know you engineered that to soften Virginia's heart toward him. You have a knack for such things."

Her eyes narrowed on him. "While I do indeed have a 'knack' for managing people, I did not have anything to do with what occurred at dinner."

"Really?" he said skeptically. "Just as my girl is being reminded of what sort of creature your grandson truly is, lo and behold, your granddaughter relates a heart-rending tale that has her completely besotted again. And you expect me to believe you had nothing to do with that?"

She shrugged. "Even if I had urged my granddaughter to tell such a story about Gabe, she would not have listened. She always does exactly as she pleases. In this case, she wanted to paint her brother in a more attractive light. And since none of us, including myself, had any idea of Celia's involvement in the incident, I couldn't possibly have engineered *her* confession."

Honestly, he was such a suspicious old fool. If he were not also a very handsome old fool, she might have Oliver throw him out.

But she did enjoy looking at a fine man, even one who was nearly her age. Her grandchildren acted as if she were at death's door, but nothing was further from the truth. Especially when she was around the general. He made her feel like a girl again. And that was worth putting up with his silly suspicions.

He eyed her uncertainly. "You swear you didn't plan any of it?"

"I only wish that I had," she said, "since it has impressed you so."

She was not sure how he would take that remark; his expression was quite enigmatic. But then his face cleared and he gave a reluctant smile.

The man had a lovely smile. It made the corners of his eyes crinkle in a very attractive manner, even if it did hold a trace of smug self-assurance.

"Are you that eager to impress me, then?" he asked in the low, husky voice of a man who has drunk plenty of whiskey, smoked ample cigars, and seduced many a fine female in his youth.

Her late husband, Josiah, had been such a man, and she still missed him sorely. But Josiah had been dead for twenty-one years now. He would not mind if she had a small flirtation.

Not that she wanted the general to know what she had in mind; it never hurt to keep a man off-balance. "I am always eager to impress my guests," she said blithely. "One never knows when they can be of use."

The smugness left his smile, but the self-assurance did not. "And how can I be of use to you, Hetty?"

She arched an eyebrow. "I have not given you permission to address me by my given name, sir."

"Yet you will allow it, won't you?" He stepped nearer, towering over her. It had been a long time since any man worth his salt had tried to intimidate her, and she found his brazen lack of propriety rather . . . invigorating.

"I suppose I might . . . Isaac," she said in a silky voice. She decided to test the waters. "Especially since we are soon to be associated through the marriage of our grandchildren."

That brought a scowl to his brow. "I wouldn't be too sure of that, madam."

"You said that your granddaughter was besotted with my grandson."

"Perhaps a little. But she's no fool. She'll recognize his true colors in time."

It was her turn to scowl. "My grandson is not the devil you make of him. He has suffered over young Roger's death more than you can possibly know."

"As well he should," he snapped.

"I agree that it was reckless of Gabe to race Roger on that course, but we both know that young men will act however they please. And your grandson had some culpability in the accident, as well."

His blue eyes blazed at her. "It appears you and I will have to agree to disagree on this matter."

She wanted to argue the point further, but the man had his mind set and nothing so trivial as the truth was going to alter it. "I only ask that you not let your foolish opinions keep your granddaughter from a good marriage."

"Is that what it would be?"

"You think marrying her off to her cousin would be better?"

He gazed steadily at her. "As a matter of fact, I do."

"Then you are blind, sir. Anyone can see that they do not love each other. Not romantically, in any case."

"You don't know anything about them."

"I know that no matter how convenient it is for them to marry, it is not wise if they are not in love."

"I married my own wife in an arrangement," he said hotly, "yet I came to love her deeply. I don't see why it can't work for them. They're already quite fond of each other, and it's a practical solution to the problem of the entailment."

"Then why hasn't either of them suggested it before?"

He colored. "Lord Gabriel forced Pierce's hand, that's all."

"And you are not concerned about your great-nephew's reputation as a dissolute rogue."

"Not as much as I am over your grandson's reputation. Pierce wouldn't hurt her—I'm sure of that. I can't say the same for Lord Gabriel."

She sighed. He was so stubborn. And so narrow-minded. "You think I do not understand how you feel, but I do. You are worried about her. You both get older by the year, and you fear that if she waits much longer to marry, she will find no one and be left entirely alone."

"It's not good for a woman to be alone in this world," he agreed.

"It's not good for a man, either."

His gaze locked with hers. They were not speaking of their grandchildren any longer, and they both knew it.

She swallowed hard. It had been a long time since a man could read her thoughts. She had forgotten how unsettling it could be.

Clearing her throat, she glanced toward the drawing room. "Why do you think I laid down my ultimatum? My grandchildren would never have married if not for that."

"I'm sure you're right. I would have done the same thing. But I don't understand why you're so bent upon having *all* of them wed, and within a year, besides. With three married and two breeding, why force the other two to your schedule?"

She had asked herself the same thing. Was she being as stubborn and willful as her grandchildren?

She thought of Gabe, throwing himself into danger to avoid feeling the pain of what he had lost. And Celia, who barely remembered her parents but still fought to be as unlike them as possible.

It was no mystery to Gran why the girl loved to shoot. Celia had spent her life believing that her mother had been fool enough to shoot her father accidentally, so she had decided to learn how to use a weapon properly, to prove to the world that one Sharpe at least had good sense with guns.

What Celia would not admit was that she liked how her shooting made men wary of her. She need not risk falling in love with a scoundrel, the way her mother had. She need never again risk being abandoned by someone she loved.

Hetty dragged in a heavy breath. "Everything else I have tried has failed. They need love, all of them, but they fear it desperately. Giving them more time will not change that. I am hoping that if their feet are held to the fire, they will make an attempt to find love instead of hiding from it."

He snorted. "You women with your romantic notions. It has nothing to do with love. If it did, you would sit back and let Mother Nature take its course."

"Mother Nature is a fickle and forgetful bitch," she snapped. "She needs a helping hand, and I am trying to hurry her along for their sakes."

He did not even blink at her coarse language. "Balderdash. You're doing it for your own sake, so you can make sure it's done before you're no longer able to control matters. And you criticize *me* for encouraging Pierce's courtship of my granddaughter. You're no better."

She glared at him. "You cannot possibly understand. Unlike my grandchildren, your granddaughter wants to marry. Only circumstances have prevented it from happening until now. Nor do you have a vast fortune to pass on, that must be nurtured and managed by responsible heirs."

When he drew himself up stiffly, she regretted her sharp words. The one thing a woman should never do is attack a man's pride. Male pride was as sensitive as a woman's vanity.

"That's true," he said coldly. "If I did, Virginia would already be married and well out of the grasp of your grandson. But since I don't and she isn't, I make you this promise."

He leaned close, his eyes glittering. "I will gladly hand her over to Pierce before I let her be forced to marry just to suit your needs. I may not have your vast fortune, but I do have influence with her. And I mean to use it to encourage her to marry her cousin. One way or the other, I'll make sure that she *never* marries your scoundrel of a grandson."

He turned and stalked off.

She scowled after him, then headed for the drawing room. "We shall just see about that, sir," she muttered as she saw him go back into the dining room. "Because I mean to make sure that she does. And if you think that you and your unreasonable bias will prevent it, you have another think coming."

Chapter Ten

Hot—so hot. Perspiration poured down his back. Noon in the middle of summer was no time for a damned race, but Gabe could handle it. Despite the night's worth of drinking that now soured in his belly, he urged his horses into a run.

Must. Beat. Roger. The refrain clamored in his ears. Must. Win. Or Roger and Lyons would never let him live it down.

Even in his cropsick state, the blood rush of the race crept in, maddening him to increase his speed. He didn't look back to see how close Roger was, but could feel him right behind him. The boulders were closing in, heat shimmering off them, making them appear illusory.

But they were real, and Gabe was going to reach them first. Hah! He was ahead, well ahead as he drove through—

A cry sounded behind him, followed by the horrible crunch of wood against stone and the screams of horses. Looking back, he saw Roger hit the ground.

The blood rush changed to a sickening lurch. Frantically he dragged on the reins, pulling for all he was worth. He had to get to Roger! But the horses kept on. He couldn't turn *back. And now a strange new boulder loomed ahead, and he was headed straight for it, and he couldn't stop, couldn't stop, couldn't—*

Gabe woke in a cold sweat, as he always did. He lay staring at the ceiling with his heart pounding and his hands yanking on the sheets.

He struggled against his frantic breathing, and forced his hands to unclench the sheets. Then pushing himself up, he threw his legs over the side of the bed and stared out the window at the impending dawn.

His heart still stampeding in his chest, he fought for calm. He hadn't had the dream in almost two years. Why the hell was it back?

As his mind cleared, he knew why. Because of yesterday's race. Because of *her.* Virginia Bloody Waverly had brought it all back, blast her. He must have been daft to consider her for a prospective wife. Helping her was only stirring up the past.

He rose and went to the window, opening it to let in the cool night air, gulping it in so the chill would drive out his dream.

Gran was right. Just because he had to marry didn't mean he had to choose Roger's sister. He could go to any damned ball and find plenty of women who'd consider themselves *lucky* to be courted by a marquess's son. Besides, Virginia didn't even *want* his help. No, she wanted that fool Devonmont.

He scowled. The earl thought he could step in and make everything fine just by marrying her. And apparently she thought the same.

Do you truly love me, cousin?

Devonmont wouldn't know love if it walked up and licked his face. How could she fall for the tripe that fool spouted? How could she possibly consider marrying that whoremongering, conscienceless *arse*?

That *titled* arse with an estate, who was going to inherit her childhood home.

He groaned. All right, so it made sense if you looked at it from that perspective. On the surface, Devonmont certainly had more to offer Virginia than Gabe did. They had a family connection, Devonmont's fortune wasn't dependent on the success of Gran's ultimatum, and Devonmont didn't have a family scandal hanging over him. Nor had he been part of the accident that had killed Virginia's brother.

But a woman with Virginia's passion could never be happy with Devonmont, damn it! The bastard was incapable of fidelity—he'd probably be out trawling the stews on their wedding night.

Besides, it was *him* she desired—not Devonmont.

Gabe gripped the windowsill, remembering how softly she'd looked at him after Celia had confessed to stealing the plum pudding. How sweetly she'd melted yesterday in the maze when he'd kissed her and fondled her and . . .

Blast, blast, and *blast*.

He couldn't let her marry Devonmont. He had an obligation to save her and her family—that's what this courtship was about, and that hadn't changed. It could just as easily have been him broken and battered on that

field, and if it had been, Roger would have done his best
to make amends, too. So he owed it to the man to ensure that Virginia was taken care of.

Unbidden, Devonmont's words leaped into his head:
*I at least appreciate your intelligence and spirit and good
heart. Sharpe just wants to get into your bed.*

That was *not* why he was doing this! It had nothing to
do with how she heated his blood or made him laugh,
nothing to do with how her tart remarks and concern
for his safety tilted him sideways and inside out, and
made him want . . .

With a curse, he turned from the window. He didn't
want anything from her. He was fulfilling an obligation,
that's all. Never mind that she didn't appreciate it—it
had to be done. Somehow he had to convince her that
he was a better choice than Devonmont.

What had Lyons said? *She is a respectable woman, and
they require finesse. You have to be able to do something
more than bed them. You have to be able to talk to them.*

He'd tried talking to her, blast it. Then he'd tried kissing her. Neither of those had worked. She'd still gone
happily home last night without casting him a back-
ward glance. So he needed another plan.

He gazed out the window again at the rising sun. It
was too early to pay a call on her.

Then again, the woman *did* live on a stud farm.
Horses had to be fed and exercised, and stalls cleaned
out. No doubt she had duties as well. By the time he
dressed and rode over to Waverly Farm, it wouldn't be
that early. He might catch them at breakfast.

He wasn't sure what he would do after that, but he'd think of something spectacular on the way. He couldn't just wait around here hoping for something to happen. Devonmont already had the advantage by staying there.

Gabe hurried to the washbasin. The one thing he *mustn't* do is bungle things as he had in the maze. There must be no kissing and no fondling. *Definitely* no fondling. Lyons might be right about that—respectable ladies did seem to like other methods of courtship than kissing.

He'd just have to pray she wasn't wearing another of those frilly gowns with the bodices that fastened up the front, the ones that made him imagine unfastening each little button and unwrapping her like a Christmas gift . . .

He groaned as his drawers grew uncomfortably tight. What in the blazes was wrong with him? She was a respectable female. She was *not* supposed to incite him to lust.

But he could handle this slip of a female. Perhaps he'd take some flowers from the garden. Women liked flowers. He'd take those pretty purple ones—there were plenty of them. And more was always better than less.

Gabe donned his clothes and left before his family was up. Then he rode off for Waverly Farm with the flowers in hand. So now what? He doubted that a fistful of flowers was going to make up for his perceived sins.

He must show her he wasn't just the man she saw as her brother's killer. That he wasn't a reckless fool bent on killing himself, or a mercenary fellow bent on gaining his inheritance. He must show her that he could be a gentleman. That he could be a responsible husband.

But how to do that?

As he approached Waverly Farm, memories assailed him—of coming here for the funeral, sick to his stomach over the thought of seeing Roger laid into a grave in the estate cemetery. Of riding up to the house and having the general stalk out with murder in his eyes. Gabe had barely uttered a word before he was escorted from the property by two grim-faced grooms.

He shuddered. That very thing could happen again today. Waverly clearly hadn't forgiven him. Gabe wasn't even sure that Virginia had.

Yet he *had* to try to mend things between the families. It just seemed right. And Virginia was the key to that.

As he rode up to the manor house, he realized that he needn't worry about the early hour. There was already a ruckus coming from the paddock beyond the stables.

He rounded the stables to find a motley group assembled beside the paddock fence. They were intently watching the general, who was approaching a horse that was viciously fighting a groom. Was the man mad? He would be trampled! Why were the others just watching, for God's sake? Waverly was nearly seventy!

Riding up to the fence, Gabe leaped down from his mount and vaulted forward, meaning to drag the general from the paddock. But someone caught his arm.

When he shot the person a dark look, he found, to his astonishment that it was Virginia, dressed in a brown chintz morning gown with a plain white apron.

"What are you doing here?" she asked.

"Trying to save your grandfather!" he retorted as he shrugged off her hand.

She laughed and grabbed him again. "He doesn't need help. Just watch."

He followed her gaze to where the general had taken hold of the horse's halter. Ordering the groom away, he approached the stallion, speaking to him in a low voice. The stallion stopped rearing at once, though it still danced about, agitated. The old man stepped closer to stroke the horse's neck, murmuring to him all the while.

"What the blazes is he doing?" Gabe asked.

"Have you ever heard of a man named Daniel Sullivan?" she asked.

"Our head groom mentioned him a few times. Wasn't he that 'horse whisperer' fellow?"

She scowled. "That's a nonsensical name people gave him when they saw him whispering to the horses. It wasn't the whispering that did it—it was his methods of training."

Sullivan had been a legend in horse circles twenty years ago for being able to calm and train horses everyone thought to be intractable. Some said he'd learned his techniques from the gypsies, but no one knew for certain. "I thought he didn't share his methods with anyone."

"He and Poppy were friends. Before he died, he taught my grandfather some of what he knew. The rest, Poppy has developed on his own."

Gabe watched in amazement as a horse he would

have given up for impossible grew calm enough to allow a saddle to be put on his back.

"Sometimes when people have horses they despair of," she went on, "they bring them to Poppy. He does what he can to make them useful. He's been working with the gelding for weeks. That fool groom didn't listen when my grandfather told him how to handle the horse, so Poppy had to step in." She sighed. "Unfortunately, that probably means that Poppy will dismiss the groom. And we can ill afford to lose another."

In that moment, Gabe realized how to get close to Virginia so she could see his good side.

Waverly handed the stallion's halter to a laborer so the horse could be led off, then turned to lecture the erring groom. The young man argued with the general before stalking off to the stables. When he came out a few minutes later with his gear, Gabe stifled a smile. Now was his chance.

General Waverly watched the man until he'd left the property, then came toward his granddaughter. He halted when he spotted Gabe, and his already black scowl deepened as he strode toward them. "Rather early to pay a morning call, isn't it, Sharpe?"

"The two of you seem to be up and about."

"This is a working stud farm." With an obvious stiffness in his arm, Waverly opened the gate to the paddock. "We don't have time to loll about in bed half the morning like you London sorts. We've got more work than we can handle."

"I see that. And if you'll let me, I'm happy to help."

The general eyed him warily. "What do you mean?"

"Since it appears that you've just lost a groom, I'm offering to lend you a hand around here."

Waverly stared at him, then glanced to his granddaughter. "Was this *your* idea?"

"No." She looked at Gabe, her expression hard to read. "But it's a good one."

The general snorted, then surveyed Gabe. "You'll ruin those fancy clothes."

"I don't care."

"I suppose you don't. You've got enough money coming to you to buy you a fancy black shirt every day of the week."

Gabe ignored the bait. "I realize you don't like me, but my offer is sincere. Why not take it? You can work me to death, then kick me off the property when you're done with me. It's one way of punishing me for what I did to Roger."

Waverly flinched, then glanced away. "I don't want to punish you. I don't want anything to do with you."

"Then I'll just court your granddaughter. I'll come every day and sit in your parlor like any other suitor, and take her for rides in the country and—"

"The devil you will! She's not going riding with you."

"Poppy," Virginia began, "I *did* agree to—"

"That bloody wager," he grumbled. "Young women shouldn't make wagers with gentlemen."

"But if they do, they should honor them, don't you think?" Gabe pressed. "I'll consider this a part of the courtship if you let me help you."

"We could use the help," Virginia pointed out. "We've

lost two grooms in a month, and if Lord Danville does bring his mare to be covered—"

"All right, damn it." The general fixed Gabe with a cold gaze. "But don't think you're going to spend your time riding and showing off for her. There are horses to be fed and groomed—"

"I know how to feed and groom a horse. I've done it many a time."

"And have you mucked out a stables? I need a good deal of that." The general arched an eyebrow in clear challenge.

"I can do that, too."

The general cast him a skeptical glance. "I'd like to see a fancy lord like you muck out a stable. You won't last a day."

"Try me." He'd never mucked out a stable; the grooms had never allowed it. But he knew how it was done, and he was no stranger to other sorts of stable work.

Waverly crossed his arms over his chest. "I tell you what, Sharpe. You come here every day at this same hour, stay until dusk, and do whatever I ask, and at the end of a week I'll let you take my granddaughter for a drive. With me. After that, we'll see."

Gabe nodded. It was more than he'd hoped for.

As the general stalked off, Virginia asked, "Are you sure you want to do this?"

"I wouldn't have offered if I weren't." He suddenly remembered the flowers, and turned to get them from where he'd tucked them into his open saddlebag. He scowled. They looked wilted and beaten up after the hour's ride.

"Are those for me?" she asked.

He jerked around. "Well . . . um . . . they were supposed to be, but . . ."

"I love lavender," she said with a hesitant smile as she reached around him to take them out of the saddlebag. "How did you know?"

She buried her face in the tiny blossoms, and his throat went dry. She looked so fetching, even in her workaday gown and apron.

"Where's your cousin this morning?" he asked, to keep from imagining stripping that gown from her and laying her down upon the fragrant lavender.

Her laugh made something tighten in his chest. "Are you mad? Pierce never rises until well after noon." She cast him a sly glance above the flowers. "I'm surprised *you're* here so early."

"I always rise early. Can't sleep late."

"Really? Why?"

A bellow sounded from the fence. "Are you coming, Sharpe, or not?"

He gave her a bow and headed toward her grandfather. This wasn't going to be easy, but he would bear it for as long as it took. He was a Sharpe—and no curmudgeon of a cavalry officer was going to keep him from getting what he wanted.

Chapter Eleven

*F*ive days later, Virginia stood at the breakfast room window watching the drive. She'd hurried to eat her breakfast so she'd be ready. It was nearly eight.

Every day she'd expected not to see Gabriel again, and every day he'd appeared with the regularity of a paid laborer. And whenever he appeared, he chipped away at her defenses.

Why? They spent little time alone together—her grandfather and cousin made sure of that. She mostly saw him when she brought out sandwiches midday, as she'd always done. And if they did have a moment to themselves, he didn't attempt to kiss her. Not that she wanted him to. Just because she happened to think about his kisses occasionally, and wonder if they'd really been as amazing as she remembered, didn't mean a thing.

She found it interesting to listen while he and Poppy ate and talked of horse training, but that wasn't because she was falling under his spell. No, indeed. She merely got tired of working in the house sometimes.

That's why she went out to watch as they dealt with

a mare in heat or exercised a Thoroughbred. It wasn't out of annoyance that Gabriel seemed more interested in the horses than in her. Although he *was* supposed to be courting her. Not that she wanted him to. But when people said they were at a place to do a certain thing, they ought to do it, that's all.

She caught sight of Gabriel at the end of the drive, and her breath stuck in her throat. Sweet Lord, he looked fine. He sat a horse better than any man she knew: riding seemed as natural as breathing to him. He and the horse moved as one fluid beast, sinew and muscle flexing together, making her mouth go dry.

"He's here again, is he?" said a smooth voice behind her.

She jumped, then pressed a hand to her heart. "Pierce! Don't sneak up on me like that. What are you doing up so early, anyway? Poppy hasn't even come down yet."

Pierce strode up to her at the sideboard. "I told you yesterday that I was heading home this morning and planned to get an early start."

"I didn't believe you. You don't rise early for anything."

"I do generally make a point of enjoying my nights in some other way than sleeping," he said with a wink. "But sadly, my estate manager doesn't do the same, so if I don't get there before he retires for the evening, I'm not going to find out what was so all-fired important that he couldn't wait another week for me to return."

Pierce's steward had been sending increasingly urgent messages. She knew he'd been ignoring them for her sake, because of Gabriel's presence, but couldn't do so any longer.

He filled a plate with toast and cheese and sat down. "So, I take it that Sharpe showed up again this morning."

She couldn't hide her blush. "I have no idea," she said blithely.

He eyed her askance. "No, you were standing there precisely at eight to watch the hay men come in."

With a sniff, she left the window. "I merely enjoy looking at the sunflowers in bloom."

"I suppose that's also why you resemble a flower in bloom yourself these days," he said with a smug smile.

"She's wearing her best gowns for you, that's what it is," Poppy said cheerily as he entered the room.

"Yes," Pierce drawled, a devilish look in his eyes. "All for *me*. Isn't that sweet?"

Glowering at him, she tugged self-consciously at the lace fichu-pelerine she usually left off, then went to the sideboard to wrap a slice of bread about two sausages for Poppy. Otherwise he wouldn't eat breakfast at all. "I happen to like this gown, that's all."

She *did* like her pelisse-robe, mostly because the cut flattered her figure, and it had fancy little Spanish bows that made her feel pretty. Wearing it—or yesterday's striped gown with the handsome sleeves—had nothing to do with anyone. It certainly wasn't because of the heated glances of admiration Gabriel gave her whenever Poppy's back was turned. No, indeed.

"Well, you can tell she's happy to have you here,"

Poppy said, utterly unaware of Pierce's sly hints. "She's been spreading lavender all through the house to make it smell nice for you."

Pierce's laugh turned into a cough when she scowled at him. Virginia walked over to pour Pierce some tea. "I *like* lavender. It's got nothing to do with Pierce or anyone else."

Poppy winked at his great-nephew. "So you say. Meanwhile, we're about to choke to death on the smell."

Her cousin shot her a look of pure mischief. "Actually, Uncle Isaac, I believe she's getting the lavender from—"

"The garden," she said quickly. She held his teacup directly over his lap and began to pour hot tea into it. "Isn't that right, cousin?"

His eyes went wide. One slip of her hand and his nights were going to be decidedly less enjoyable. "Absolutely."

"Well, see that you don't clear out the garden entirely." Poppy wolfed down the remainder of his breakfast. "I know you use it for possets and such. You'll run out of it before winter at this rate."

"Yes, cuz, do be careful," Pierce said, eyes twinkling.

She glared at him as she set down the tea and poured a glass of milk.

"Got to go," Poppy said. Pausing only long enough to grab the glass she handed him and gulp down its contents, Poppy headed for the door. "Today I'm putting Ghost Rider through his paces, to see if I can get him up to snuff for the St. Leger Stakes. I've got to do it while Sharpe is out of the way."

"Out of the way?" Pierce asked.

Her grandfather grinned. "I'm having him muck out the stables again."

"Poppy!" she protested. "Wasn't it enough that you made him do it his first day? I'm sure he ruined his clothes."

That reminded her . . . She hurried to fetch Poppy's surtout, since their footman was nowhere to be seen.

"It's not my fault he wasn't dressed properly. And if he takes his bloody clothes off to work in the stables now, it's not my fault if he catches a cold."

She helped Poppy into his surtout. "A cold? It's summer, for heaven's sake. So you can't blame him for taking his coat off."

"That's no reason for him to go bare-chested. He'll catch his death if he goes about like that. It's not healthy, I tell you." Poppy headed for the door.

Gabriel went *bare-chested* in the stables? Surely Poppy didn't mean that he went without even a shirt.

"Might want to close your mouth, cousin," Pierce said dryly, "before you catch flies."

She whirled on him. "I wish you'd stop letting Poppy think you really mean to marry me."

"I *do* mean to marry you." Pierce grinned. "Assuming you don't run off with a bare-chested Sharpe first, adorned by all the lavender he keeps bringing you."

"How did you know about the lavender?"

"Don't insult my intelligence. I saw him give it to Molly for you one morning. He's been doing it every day, hasn't he?"

She couldn't prevent a small smile. "Yes." Her smile faded. "But Poppy doesn't know, and don't you tell him."

"I'm shocked he hasn't figured it out himself. Flowers are exactly the sort of boring gift a man like Sharpe would consider romantic."

"They're not boring at all!" She cursed herself for her quick tongue. But she couldn't help it; no one had ever brought her flowers before. She found it terribly sweet.

Pierce eyed her closely as he poured himself more tea. "Of course, volunteering to help around here was rather original. To be honest, I didn't expect him to last this long."

"Neither did I," she admitted. "Not that I care."

"If you don't care, then what are these doing here?" He flicked his hand toward a plate of lemon tarts on the sideboard. "I heard Sharpe tell Cook that first day that he loved lemon tarts. And ever since, they've been appearing on the sideboard for when he and Uncle Isaac come in for tea."

She lifted her chin. "I'm sure Cook is just trying to make him feel at home."

"Cook doesn't even make lemon tarts for *me,* my dear, and I'm her favorite. Besides, you're the one who tells her what to cook." He drained his teacup, then set it down. "Be careful, cuz," he said softly. "Sharpe isn't some stray dog you can lure into loving you with lemon tarts. Be sure that he's what you want, just as he is, before you tip your hand."

"I'm not trying to lure him into anything. I didn't

ask him to work on the stud farm—he chose to do that himself."

For me. To court me. Oh, how she wished that didn't thrill her every time she thought of it.

A knock came at the breakfast room door. "My lord, your carriage is ready."

"Thank you, James." Pierce finished his toast, then came around the table. "Will you see me out?"

"Of course."

She took his arm as they headed for the entrance hall. "I'm going to miss you, you know."

"I should hope so. I'm practically your fiancé."

"Oh, fie. Would you stop that nonsense?"

He laughed. "I will when it stops annoying you."

They went out onto the drive to find Gabriel coming back from the pasture where he'd apparently led a couple of horses, probably emptying the stalls in preparation for mucking them out.

Gabriel halted. "So you're leaving, eh, Devonmont?" He sounded rather pleased.

"Duty calls." Pierce turned to her. "That reminds me, I forgot to mention to Uncle Isaac that I went over all the books and they appear to be in order. But he does have a few bills of lading that are incorrectly entered, and he should press that farmer next door for payment. Neighbor or no, the man needs to pay the stud fee."

"I'll tell him, but he won't do anything about it. You know Poppy—he feels sorry for the fellow."

Pierce shook his head. "There's no point in helping him with his accounts if he ignores my advice."

"I know, but he does appreciate it. Truly." She leaned up to kiss his cheek. "As do I."

Pierce cast a sidelong glance to where Gabriel stood listening, and drawled, "Surely you can give your future fiancé a better thank-you than that."

And without warning, he grasped her head in his hands and kissed her hard on the lips. It wasn't restrained *or* brief. He *lingered*, for pity's sake.

"Now see here," Gabriel growled, "you can't do that to her."

Drawing back, Pierce winked at her. "I don't see why not. Cousins are allowed to kiss."

Gabriel came nearer. "That wasn't a cousinly kiss," he bit out.

"Virginia didn't mind." Pierce's eyes gleamed mischief at her. "Did you, dearest?"

She hardly knew how to respond. Pierce had never kissed her on the lips before. She'd have expected more of an impact. After all, Pierce was famous for his talent with women. But it had just been strange and uncomfortable, like kissing a brother on the lips.

"Well?" Gabriel snapped. "Did you mind?"

"I-I . . . no. Of course not." She didn't want Gabriel thrashing her cousin for some perceived insult to her honor.

"I see." Gabriel stalked off toward the stables.

As soon as he was out of earshot, she gave Pierce a shove. "What was *that* for?"

Pierce grinned. "Just having a little fun."

She let out a frustrated huff. "Now he's going to think

you and I have been . . . doing things that we haven't. And then there's the servants—"

"Who know perfectly well there's nothing going on between us, you little widgeon. It never hurts to make a man stew a bit. Can't have him thinking you're easy pickings, when you're throwing lemon tarts at him and dressing in your best gowns and watching for him out the window."

"Lower your voice," she hissed. "He doesn't know I'm doing those things."

"Then he's blind." He chucked her under the chin. "He already wants to marry you. You don't have to work so hard at convincing him it's a good idea."

"I'm not! And he only wants to marry me so he can gain his inheritance."

"Perhaps." He glanced toward the barn. "Perhaps not." Pierce suddenly turned very serious. "See here, cuz, if anything happens while I'm gone, send a note to Hertfordshire and I'll come back at once."

"I know. You're a dear." She crossed her arms over her chest. "A very wicked dear, but I suppose that's to be expected with the way you live when you're in London."

He fixed a disturbingly intent gaze on her. "That kiss didn't affect you at all, did it?"

She blinked. "It was . . . perfectly pleasant."

A rueful laugh escaped him. "Pleasant, eh? You really know how to cut a man off at the knees. Take care, will you?"

"I'll be fine."

But as he drove away, her smile faltered. She couldn't

stop thinking of the look on Gabriel's face when he'd said, "I see," as if somehow she'd betrayed him. She hadn't; there was no understanding between them. Nonetheless . . .

Glancing about, she realized that all the servants had disappeared. Poppy was off with Ghost Rider in the back pasture, and their two grooms were probably with him. Which left Gabriel alone in the stable.

Perhaps she should talk to Gabriel about Pierce. She could only imagine what Gabriel must think after Pierce's mischief, and she wanted to set him straight.

You just want to see if Gabriel really works in there bare-chested, her conscience said.

Stupid conscience. And it was wrong, too.

Still, she swallowed as she headed for the kitchen garden, which just happened to be next to the back entrance to the stable. And she was careful to make no sound as she slipped inside.

She halted next to the ladder that led up to the hay loft. Perhaps before she spoke to him, she should watch him at work. After all, Poppy didn't know for sure that he was doing a decent job—for all they knew, he was paying off one of the laborers to do the work.

You don't really believe that, her conscience said. *You just want to spy on him.*

With a scowl for her conscience, she hurried up the ladder, then crept through the hay until she could see him below.

She sucked in a breath. Sweet Lord in heaven, he *was* bare-chested. He had nothing on from the waist up.

And he was attacking the straw with a pitchfork as if it were an enemy soldier he'd met in battle.

A half-naked Gabriel in black buckskin breeches and boots was a sight to behold. The well-defined muscles in his arms flexed with each scoop of the pitchfork, and his back showed every ferocious stab, the sinews tightening in a marvelous dance. She'd never seen a man's naked back before, but she doubted that they all looked as spectacular as Gabriel's.

Then he bent over to pick up some tack that had fallen in the straw. His loose breeches tightened over his bottom, and she gasped. As he froze, she clapped her hand over her mouth. If he caught her watching him . . .

But then he straightened, and she let out an inward sigh of relief. He hadn't heard her after all. He bent again, and this time she took the chance to stare at his amazing bottom. Was it *supposed* to look that . . . well . . . firm?

When he finally returned to shoveling, she couldn't decide which she liked better—watching him bend over or watching him shovel. She wasn't surprised to discover that he had a most attractive form, but she hadn't known that seeing so much of it revealed would have this astonishing effect on her. With the sheen of perspiration making his back glisten, she could think of nothing but how she would like to touch his muscles. Which was absolutely ludicrous.

After a few moments lying enraptured in the straw, she began to crave more. *Turn around, turn around, turn around*, she chanted in her head, almost desperate to see the front of him.

And when he did, picking up the wheelbarrow handles and angling it toward the back door, she bit her fist to keep from sighing aloud. Lord have mercy on her soul. How had he come to be so exquisitely fashioned?

He had a little brushing of hair in the middle of his chest and circling his navel, but otherwise his entire upper body looked carved from oak. His flesh looked taut and unyielding, with ripples of muscles running down his belly. She could scarcely breathe at the sight of so much male . . . endowment.

She was almost glad when he disappeared out the back of the stable. At last she could catch her breath. She ought to climb down the ladder and wait for him at the bottom so he wouldn't know she'd been watching him, but what if he caught her?

No, she'd just wait until he was busy shoveling again. Then she would creep down and approach as if she'd come in from outside. That would work. And if he happened to—

"Enjoying yourself, are you?"

With a squeal, she scrambled to her feet and swung around. To her utter mortification, there stood Gabriel, a few feet away.

And judging from the black scowl on his brow and the fierce glitter in his eyes, he was furious.

Chapter Twelve

Gabe couldn't believe it. After all he'd endured this week, she had the audacity to spy on him! Wasn't it enough that she'd happily kissed her cousin while he stood there watching and seething?

And now she was probably in here making sure that he did exactly what her blasted grandfather wanted.

At least she had the good grace to be embarrassed; hot color crawled up her neck to her face. "I . . . I . . ."

"You were spying on me. Again." He crossed his arms over his chest. "Are you worried that your grandfather won't get enough work out of me? Or did he ask you to report on my progress? I guess it's not enough for him that he's got me working like some damned groom—"

"I wanted to talk to you, that's all," she blurted out.

His eyes narrowed. "About what?"

She bit her lower lip. "About Pierce."

That put the finishing touch on his anger. Now she was going to explain how she and her bloody cousin were perfect for each other, and Gabe could just go to hell. "What about him?"

She smoothed her skirts, refusing to look him in the

eye, which confirmed his suspicions. "My cousin and I are not . . . that is . . . we . . . the two of us . . . have never . . ." Taking a deep breath, she started again. "That was the first and only time he has ever kissed me . . . like that. I didn't want you to get the impression that we had been—"

"Intimate?" he said caustically.

Though her blush deepened, her gaze shot to his. "Yes. Intimate. I thought you should know that no matter what he implied, we don't have that sort of . . . friendship."

He stared at her a long moment, trying to take in what she was saying. So she wasn't dismissing his courtship? She was embarrassed to be accused of being "intimate" with her cousin?

"Are you sure *he* knows that?" he asked, all at sea.

"Of course!" She released a frustrated breath. "He did it just to annoy you. And it took me so by surprise that I didn't know what to say when you asked if I truly didn't mind it."

As it dawned on him what that meant, his anger ebbed.

"That is Pierce's biggest fault, you see," she went on. "He doesn't know when to leave well enough alone. He seems to delight in—"

"He'd make you a lousy husband," Gabe broke in.

She didn't leap to deny it. "What makes you say that?"

He pressed his advantage. "Devonmont takes you for granted."

She blinked. "That's absurd."

"Come now, sweetheart. I see how you take care of things around here. You hold this house together. You're the one who makes sure they're all well fed. Without you, that lazy cook of your grandfather's would give them stale bread and mutton, and they'd take it because he can't afford a decent cook."

Her eyes went wide. "I can't believe you noticed."

"I'm not blind," he snapped. "I see how things are. When you go off to town to shop, the two maids spend their time flirting with your absentminded footman and your grooms, and your housekeeper tipples whiskey until your return." As she gazed at him in apparent shock, he added, "But when you're here, they do their jobs, and damned near happily, too."

"Because they're afraid I'll dismiss them."

He snorted. "They know you can't afford that. That's not why." He groped for words to explain it to her. It suddenly seemed very important for her to understand her own worth. "It's because you're so blasted cheerful."

That had come as a complete surprise to him. He'd seen her only as the woman who found his very existence an outrage. But that was before he'd watched her in her element. Here at Waverly Farm she was a blur of happy female, bustling in and out, up and down, smoothing frayed nerves and stoking enthusiasm wherever she went.

"Who *wouldn't* want to make you happy?" he choked out. "You . . . well, you make them all somehow . . . find the strength to be better than they are." She did that to him as well, but he'd swallow gunpowder before he'd admit it. "You make do with the staff you have, and you do it brilliantly. Devonmont doesn't see that or care. He's used to having everything work as it should, so he doesn't notice that what goes on in this house is *your* doing."

Now she watched him with an openly vulnerable expression that made him angry. How could she not know these things about herself? How could none of them *make* her know it?

"Devonmont doesn't notice that when you're not around, your grandfather lapses into a darker mood. The earl's a selfish, condescending arse, and he doesn't deserve you." At her obvious shock, he muttered, "Forgive my language, but it's true."

Her intent stare made him uncomfortable. He uncrossed his arms, then tucked his thumbs beneath the waistband of his breeches in a gesture of defiance meant to show her that he was not quite the blithering idiot he seemed.

Then her gaze slid slowly down his chest to his belly . . . halted at his breeches . . . before jerking back up to his face. The new blush that suffused her pretty cheeks took him by surprise.

And suddenly he saw her spying on him in a whole new light.

Well, I'll be damned.

Could she have been watching him for another reason entirely? The very thought of the curious and virginal Virginia watching him in his half-dressed state made his blood run hot.

She tipped up her chin. "You only say these things about Pierce because you want me for yourself."

Damned right, he did. Even more, he now suspected that she felt the same. "I say it because it's true. You deserve better."

"I deserve *you*, I suppose."

"You deserve a man who sees you for what you are."

She eyed him warily. "And what is that?"

"A woman in bad need of someone to look after *her* for a change. To consider her dreams and wants and needs." He dragged his gaze slowly down her body, his blood leaping to see how it agitated her. "Someone who can give you what you crave most."

Her breath quickened. "You don't know what I crave most."

"Oh, I think I do." He stepped nearer, exulting when her cheeks grew rosy beneath his stare. "Admit it: you didn't just come in here to talk."

Alarm spread over her face. "Of course I did! I-I mean, why else would I possibly—"

"Don't play the outraged innocent with me, sweetheart." He cast her a knowing smile. "Innocent young ladies don't hide in the hay watching half-dressed men work."

Her mouth dropped open. When it snapped shut and temper flared in her eyes, he realized he'd overplayed his hand.

Still, it took him by surprise when she shoved him hard enough to make him fall into the hay. "And innocent gentlemen don't work half-dressed on a property where innocent young ladies might wander."

She turned to stalk away, but he half-rose to yank

her down into the hay beside him. As she gasped and opened her mouth in outrage, he leaned over and kissed her.

For a moment, he feared he'd misread her entirely. But as he molded her lips with his, she softened beneath him and threw her arms about his neck.

After that he was lost. His head told him he should keep this tender, give her a kiss that didn't send her running in alarm. But he'd spent days watching her from afar, hiding the ache to touch her again, to show her that what lay between them was more powerful than any stupid wager. And now that he had his chance, he couldn't be easy, soft, or quiet.

As he parted her lips with his, he shifted until he lay half on top of her, half off. Then he plunged his tongue inside her mouth the way he wanted to plunge his aching cock into her.

And she kissed him back, thank God. She tangled her tongue with his and met him with enough enthusiasm to set them both aflame. Desire exploded inside him. He burned to take her right here, to lift her skirts and put an end to days of mindless want. But he had enough presence of mind to know that wasn't wise.

Instead, he laid his hand on her breast. And she *let him*. She even arched into his hand as he kneaded her through her gown. It was enough to send a man out of his mind. Feverish to touch her bare skin, he tore loose the scrap of lace she wore about her neck, then fumbled with the bows that held her gown together in front.

It took him a few seconds to realize that they disguised

the hooks and eyes that were the real fastening, but he soon had them undone, then spread her gown open to slip his hand inside and drag down her corset cup.

"Sweet Lord," she whispered against his mouth as he fondled her breast through her shift, rolling the nipple between his thumb and forefinger.

"Sweet Virginia." Not content with just touching, he untied her shift and bared her breast to his gaze.

Her flesh flamed but she made no move to stop him, so he looked his fill. Her breast was every bit as exquisite as he'd imagined, pert and delicate and perfectly shaped, with a rosy nipple that begged to be sucked. And he was more than eager to answer the call.

When his mouth closed over her breast, she buried her hands in his hair. "Gabriel . . . you shouldn't . . . we shouldn't . . ."

He filled his hand with her other breast as he lifted his head to stare at her flushed face. "It's what you came here for, vixen. Admit it."

"No! I . . . I just came to talk to you."

Swirling his tongue over the tip of her breast, he exulted as her breath hitched in her throat. "And you were hiding here in the straw because . . ."

"I . . . was looking for something, that's all. Something I lost when I came up here . . . to wait for you to be . . . finished working."

He stifled a laugh. She was so damned transparent. He rubbed her breast shamelessly, delighting in the little gasp of pleasure she uttered. "And what exactly were you looking for?"

"Um . . . a . . . a piece of jewelry." When he sucked hard on her breast, she moaned. "Yes. A . . . a locket. It must have fallen in the straw."

Her hands slid to his neck and kneaded his shoulders convulsively as he sucked and teased her pretty little breasts. "Did you find what you were looking for?" he rasped against her nipple.

Her eyes were sliding shut. "I . . . I . . . no . . ."

"What a shame. I'll have to help you look."

Her eyes shot open. "No! I-I mean—"

"Who knows where it went?" He undid more hooks and eyes until he had her gown entirely open. "Perhaps it fell down inside your clothing."

She blinked. "I doubt that."

"Here, perhaps," he murmured, skimming his hand down her corset to the juncture between her legs. "Or here." He rubbed her there through her shift and petticoats.

How would she react to such a blatant invasion— would she be appalled? Given her lame excuse for why she'd been watching him, he was hoping for curious.

Virginia was torn between shock and fascination. She'd been dying to have him touch her since the moment she'd seen him half-naked, but *that* wasn't the part she'd wanted him to touch.

Then he rubbed her again, and she realized that was *exactly* the part she wanted him to touch. "Oh my. Good gracious. That is . . . oh! Ohhh."

"Found what you're looking for?" A smug smile crossed his face.

He was so blessed sure of himself, and she couldn't even bring herself to protest. Because what he was doing down there was making her insane. *Nothing* should feel that good.

No wonder everyone urged respectable females to stay away from rogues. Because every woman would throw her respectability out the window if she knew how it felt to have a man put his hands on her like this.

And now he was drawing up her petticoats, and sliding his hand beneath her shift . . .

"Or how about this?" he said, in a husky voice that made her pulse do a funny little dance. "Is this more of what you were looking for?"

Oh. Sweet. Lord. As his hand slid inside the slit in her drawers to cover her thatch of hair, a moan escaped her.

"I'll take that as a yes," he drawled.

A *definite* yes. She dug her fingers into his broad, naked shoulders, marveling at the silk-over-steel feel of skin over sinew. Then his finger slipped into the cleft between her legs, and she nearly came out of her skin. He delved inside her with one finger, making her want to squirm beneath his hand. Making her want to have him do it more . . . and more . . .

Her hands slid over his bared chest, which was every bit as firm as she'd thought. She couldn't stop touching him. He was so gloriously well muscled, and just feeling the warm flesh grow taut beneath her fingers made her ache for him down *there* even more.

His breathing grew strained. "I'll have to take a look," he growled.

She could scarcely think. "At what?"

"At you. Beneath your clothes." His eyes held a raw hunger that made her shiver deliciously. "How else can I find what you were looking for?"

He was already sliding down her body.

She really ought to put an end to the farce of the missing locket. "I don't think you need—"

He covered her down there with his mouth. His *mouth*.

"Gabriel!"

His tongue slid inside her.

"*Gabriel* . . ." she sighed. "What . . . how . . . Oh . . . my . . . word. You are wicked. So *wicked*."

A muffled chuckle escaped him as he started doing things with his tongue that gave new meaning to the word *wicked*. Good gracious. Who could have guessed . . . How could she have known . . .

Her body was on fire. She strained up against his mouth, wanting to feel every delicious stroke of his tongue. He was using lips and teeth and tongue to arouse her in an amazing fashion. It was the most glorious thing she'd ever felt! It was like thundering up a hill on a massive charger, hurtling toward the top, racing, straining . . .

And leaping off a cliff at the end.

She screamed. And screamed again as she went hurtling down into an ocean, where waves of pleasure crashed over her. They went on for what seemed like forever, until at last they lessened and he drew his mouth from her.

As she lay there gasping, he pressed a kiss into her thigh. "I think we found it," he said in a guttural voice.

A long breath escaped her. "I think so, too."

She wasn't sure exactly *what* she'd found, but she wanted to find it again, whenever she could. And clearly he wanted to help her find it, watching her with a stark need that turned her insides into jelly. He slid up her body to lie on his side next to her, his head propped up on his hand.

"This had nothing to do with any locket," he said, running his thumb over her lower lip.

She kissed it. "No."

He arched an eyebrow. "You just wanted to see me half-naked."

"You really are annoyingly full of yourself," she said petulantly.

"But I'm very happy that you did." His voice fell to a ragged murmur. "I daresay we wouldn't be up here otherwise. Besides, the thought of your watching me half-clothed arouses me something fierce."

"Does it?"

"See for yourself." He caught her hand and drew it down to his breeches. "When coupled with what we were just doing—"

He sucked in a breath as her hand swept the prominent bulge in his breeches. And when she rubbed him, he muttered a low curse that pleased her enormously. For once, he didn't seem quite so cocky.

"You were saying?" she asked. It was her turn to be smug.

His eyes slid shut. "You're a teasing little vixen who . . . Oh God . . ." With a moan he pressed himself into her hand. "Yes, sweetheart. Touch me just like that. Right there . . . God save me . . ."

"Sharpe!" called a voice from outside the stable.

It might as well have been the voice of God Himself, only he wasn't coming to save anyone.

She jerked her hand from Gabriel's breeches in a panic. "That's Poppy! He can't find us like this."

Gabriel stared at her uncomprehendingly for a second.

She shook him. "If he finds you here with me, there will be no wedding, no duel, no nothing except your handsome body speared on that pitchfork over there."

A lazy grin crossed his face. "You think I'm handsome?"

"Gabriel!"

"Oh, all right." He stood and brushed the straw from his skin and breeches.

"Sharpe!" came Poppy's voice, closer now. "Where the devil are you?"

Frantically, she sought to fasten her gown.

"We really must stop meeting where people can find us, sweetheart," Gabriel drawled as he tossed her fichu-pelerine to her. "It spoils the mood every time."

She glared at him.

When the door rattled downstairs, he muttered, "Stay down," then walked over to the pitchfork that was always kept in the loft.

It wasn't a moment too soon, for Poppy walked into

the stable just then. She sank into the straw, praying he couldn't see her. It helped that Gabriel managed to throw a dusting of hay over her as he faced the edge of the loft.

"Yes, General," he called out. "Did you want something?"

A short silence fell, during which she died a hundred deaths, sure that Poppy had guessed she was up here.

"What the devil are you doing?"

Gabriel forked some hay over the side. "What you asked me to."

"Didn't you hear me calling?"

"Sorry, no. Hard to hear up here."

"Well, I need your help with this damned mare that Lord Danville just brought in. He said he wasn't coming till tomorrow, and now he shows up with the bloody horse, expecting me to drop everything and see her well settled. The grooms are with Ghost Rider, and there's no one else. So come down. And put your damned clothes on, too. I don't want my granddaughter seeing you naked."

"Too late for that," Gabriel muttered under his breath as he sauntered past her to lay the pitchfork against the wall, then climb down the ladder.

She held her breath, waiting for them to leave.

"What do you know about Arabians?" Poppy asked.

She could hear Gabriel moving around, probably donning his clothes.

"I've heard they can be temperamental."

"Only if handled badly. By nature, they are even

tempered. Roger used to say that an Arabian was only as temperamental as his owner, but you could probably say that of most horses."

The conversation continued as the men left the stable, but she lay there a long moment, frozen by Poppy's mention of her brother.

She'd forgotten all about him. Caught up in her foolish desires and Gabriel's sweet words, she'd let her brother slip her mind completely.

"Roger, I'm sorry," she whispered as she sat up, but it did nothing to assuage her guilty conscience.

As she stood and finished restoring her clothing, she vacillated between defending Gabriel in her mind and hating herself for betraying her brother's memory. After a few moments of that, she realized one thing.

It was time she found out exactly what had happened during the night before their fateful race, and the morning when it had happened. She would never rest easy with Gabriel until she did.

And there was only one way to do that. She had to ask Gabriel. No matter how uncomfortable it made him— and her—she had to know the truth. Until she did, she could never move forward.

Chapter Thirteen

$\mathcal{L}$ate in the afternoon the next day, Virginia headed for the stable with an earthenware jug of ale, hoping to see Gabriel before he left for Halstead Hall. She'd had no chance to be alone with him since their encounter in the hay; Poppy or one of the grooms was always around.

When she entered the stable now, Poppy and the others sat on a bench cleaning their boots while Gabriel was putting away tack. He looked up as she entered, and the warm smile he flashed her made her tingle to her toes.

Having spent last night reliving every moment of their interlude in the stable, it was all she could do not to blush when his gaze trailed down her. *As if he can see right through your clothes.*

Now she knew what Poppy had meant. And now she could easily imagine being married to Gabriel, being able to do the things they'd done yesterday whenever they wished.

That was precisely why she had to talk to him. Her guard eroded more and more with every day she spent near him.

She went over to hand him a mug of ale, and his hand brushed her fingers as he took it from her. The knowing look in his eyes said he'd done it on purpose. This time she couldn't restrain the heat that rose to her cheeks. When he responded by winking at her, she caught her breath. Her pulse was racing, and her stomach was doing funny little flips that made it hard for her to think straight. If she wasn't careful, Poppy would notice.

"This ale is delicious." Gabriel sipped it with a slow sensuality that made her body hum. "Did you brew it here at Waverly Farm?"

"I'm afraid not." She glanced at Poppy, but fortunately he wasn't paying attention to how Gabriel was looking at her. "I've tried my hand at home brewing but haven't been terribly successful."

"Tastes like swill, it does," said Hob, one of the grooms.

She scowled at him, though he was right.

"Perhaps my sister-in-law could help you with it," Gabriel said. "She's a brewer, you know."

"If she has easy instructions I could follow," Virginia said, "I'd be most grateful."

"So would we," Hob said.

Gabriel shot the groom a foul look. "Yes, because it's not enough that Miss Waverly makes sure you're well fed and your ailments treated. She should brew a good small beer, too, right?"

As Hob gave a sullen shrug, Virginia smiled warmly at Gabriel. His unexpected defense of her touched her deeply.

But it also gained Poppy's attention. He glanced over at her and Gabriel, his eyes narrowing. "So, Sharpe, do you think you could come by earlier than usual tomorrow?"

Gabriel stiffened. "Why?"

"Tomorrow is the fair at Langsford. I'm taking some yearlings to market, so the grooms and I will have our hands full. We're not setting off until nine, but I could use some help earlier getting everything ready."

"I'm sorry, I can't."

Poppy sat back on the bench, looking smug. "I should have known. All you chaps enjoy your Friday nights in town, gambling and drinking. Makes it hard to rise early on a Saturday."

Shooting her grandfather a glare, Virginia walked over to pour ale for the two grooms.

"That's not the reason." Gabriel's voice held a trace of irritation. "Actually, I wasn't planning to come at all tomorrow."

"So you've finally tired of working this hard, have you? Want to end your little adventure?"

"Not in the least." Gabriel downed his ale with a scowl. "I have a prior engagement."

"Then come here for a while beforehand."

"Poppy," Virginia chided, "his lordship isn't one of your servants to be ordered about."

"I'd come if I could," Gabriel said, "but my engagement is quite early."

Her grandfather eyed him with suspicion. "Early in the morning there's only one kind of engagement a man can have, and that's with a woman."

Anger flared in Gabriel's face. "As it happens, I'm meeting with a gentleman. We're settling a wager."

As it dawned on her what kind of wager that must be, Virginia whirled to face Gabriel. "You're racing," she accused him.

His face carefully expressionless, Gabriel held out his empty mug. "And what if I am?"

Their gazes locked as she took it from him. He showed no sign that her feelings on the matter were of any consequence to him. He might be full of sweet words about her work on the farm, but that didn't change his character. He was still the Angel of Death, still as reckless as ever.

Well, she'd had enough of that. Time to settle once and for all what kind of man he truly was. She couldn't go on without knowing exactly what had happened between him and Roger.

She turned to her grandfather. "You said that if Lord Gabriel worked here a week, which he has, you would allow us a drive together. I want to take it now."

Poppy puffed up like a horse with colic. "I also said I'd have to go along. And I can't leave the farm right now with Lord Danville coming over to check on his mare."

"I'll take Hob. He should be a sufficient chaperone."

"Now, lambkin—"

"You owe us this, Poppy." She stared him down. "I've been very patient, but I deserve to spend time with my suitor. The least you can do after all the work he has done this week is to allow it."

Her grandfather glowered at her, then at Gabriel. But he had to know that he'd worked Gabriel like a dog, and that Gabriel had taken it with astonishing equanimity.

"Oh, very well, go on with you, then," he finally grumbled. "But don't be gone too long. It's no more than an hour before sunset, and you shouldn't be out after dark with him." He glanced at Hob. "And don't you let either of them out of your sight for one minute, do you hear?"

"Yes, sir," Hob answered.

A short while later, Gabriel was handing her up into the curricle as Hob climbed into the groom's seat on the back. Virginia took the reins as a matter of habit since it was her curricle, and Gabriel said nothing.

Although there was a hood between them and the groom, she needed far more privacy than the curricle could provide. "We're going to a place where we can talk."

When his eyes darkened and slid down her body with aching slowness, she regretted how she'd put that. She didn't want him to get the wrong idea. Much as she wanted to lose herself in his arms, she couldn't. Not until they settled a few things.

She drove half a mile, then pulled the curricle down a dirt track off the road, which soon ended in a little clearing. Before she was even fully to a halt, he jumped down. When he handed her out his hands lingered on her waist, prompting a little curl of excitement in her belly that she squelched ruthlessly. Casting him a reproving glance, she headed to the back of the curricle.

"Hob, if you will please take the horses for a bit of exercise down the road, I'd be most appreciative."

Hob jumped down, his jaw set as he glanced from her to Gabriel. "The master said I wasn't to let you out of my sight. The master said—"

"Perhaps I should tell our housekeeper that you and Molly have been meeting secretly in the stable at night." There was a reason she'd asked for Hob, and it wasn't just because he was the more shatter-brained of the two grooms.

All Hob's bravado fled. "Please, miss, the housekeeper would turn Molly out, she would, and—"

"So you'll exercise the horses for, say, the next half hour?"

Hob hesitated a long moment. Then with a sigh, he gave a curt nod and jumped into the driver's seat.

After he drove off, Gabriel drawled, "That was a neat little piece of blackmail. How did you know about him and Molly?"

She snorted. "The girl comes in to lay my fire at night with hay in her hair. And since our other groom has a sweetheart in town, that leaves Hob. I'm not the idiot my staff takes me for, you know."

"I know only too well," he said in a husky voice. He reached for her, but she moved away.

"Oh, no. I didn't go to all this trouble just so you could fog my head with kisses. I want to know about this race you're running tomorrow."

A low curse escaped him, and for a moment she feared he wouldn't tell her. Then he shoved his hands into his coat pockets with that devil-may-care manner that she both admired and hated, and said, "If you must know, a fellow named Wheaton challenged me. The wager is a hundred pounds, so I accepted."

"Of course you did," she said bitterly. "The money is always the most important thing to you."

Anger flared in his face. "It should be important to you, as well. If Celia is stubborn and refuses to marry, the money I win from races is what will support us. If I win tomorrow, the hundred pounds will be enough to cover the cost of hiring a jockey and paying the entry fee so that Flying Jane can run in the St. Leger Stakes. And if I win *that* prize—"

"If, if, *if*! That sounds like a great many ifs."

"So what do you suggest? That I take a position as a groom in your grandfather's stable?"

"No, of course not. Your grandmother won't help you with Flying Jane?"

With a cold laugh, he began to pace the clearing. "She doesn't approve of Thoroughbred racing. She fears I'll follow in the steps of my idiot grandfather, the old marquess, who lost thousands upon thousands of pounds trying to compete. I know that I can succeed in it, but she doesn't believe me."

She could see how much that hurt him. It hadn't occurred to her that he might have a plan for his life beyond gaining his inheritance. He'd mentioned that he wanted to build a racing stable, but she hadn't taken that seriously. Now that she knew he really meant it— now that she knew him better—it made sense. "Your grandmother is being foolish."

He halted to stare at her.

She colored. "I've seen how you are. You have a gift for recognizing a horse's particular strengths. Even Poppy has commented on it, though he'd never say anything to you."

His gaze steadied on her, dark and wary. "Gran would argue that succeeding in Thoroughbred racing requires more than an ability to pick a horse."

"And she'd be right. Training is important, too. But you're good at that, as well. If you start racing Thoroughbreds seriously, I daresay you'll give most of the important owners a run for their money." She smiled faintly. "No pun intended."

"Thank you." A determined expression settled on his face. "So you understand why I have to run this race tomorrow. The wagers I win on private races will pay for the Thoroughbred racing, and the Thoroughbred racing is where the real money is."

When she said nothing to that, he added, "I know I'm starting small with Flying Jane, but if things go as planned, I could one day have a whole stable full of Thoroughbreds to race. I might even have a stud farm of my own." He glanced away. "That's my hope, anyway."

She could see how much his plan meant to him. But it had distinct disadvantages, too, which he must surely realize. "So you need lots of private races, and lots of wagers. *High* wagers. Which means dangerous races."

His gaze shot back to her, instantly wary. "The more dangerous the race, the higher the wager. You know that."

Her heart sank. "So what dangerous course are you and Mr. Wheaton racing tomorrow?"

"*Lord* Wheaton. And it's not that dangerous, I swear. It's not even a carriage race. Just a plain old regular race, horse against horse."

"You know perfectly well that those can be just as dangerous, if not more so. What course are you racing?"

"You probably haven't even heard of it."

"What *course*?" she persisted.

A muscle ticked in his jaw. "The one that runs beside the stream on Lyons's estate in Eastcote."

Alarm seized her. "The one with all the jumps?"

He blinked, clearly surprised that she knew of it. "It's just two jumps, and they're not that bad."

"Not that bad! I remember Poppy talking about it. Didn't Lyons break his leg on one of them?"

Gabriel stiffened. "Only because he can't ride worth a farthing."

"Oh my word," she muttered, fear for him making her dizzy. "You're utterly daft."

That made him bristle. "No more daft than you, who raced Letty Lade and then challenged *me* to a race. Since when do you disapprove of racing?"

"Since I've seen how you race," she shot back. "Since I've seen firsthand how you take risks that no one with good sense should."

"You're going to lecture me about good sense?" He bore down on her. "You're the one who wanted to race at Turnham Green, despite the risk to your future."

"Yes, because I got tired of watching you build a

reputation for recklessness on the back of my dead brother!"

Shock filled his face, rapidly replaced by pain. Still, she couldn't take back the words. Now that it was out in the open, she couldn't let it go.

Her breath came in harsh gasps as she fought back tears. "You paint your phaeton black, and you prance about town in your black clothing and—"

"I don't *prance* anywhere, sweetheart," he said hollowly.

"Don't you dare make a joke of this! You talk about earning money from these dangerous races, when we both know that no one would be wagering against you if not for my brother!" Her voice fell to a whisper. "If not for Roger, there would be no Angel of Death."

"I didn't choose to be the Angel of Death, blast it!" He practically spat the words. When she blinked, taken aback by his vehemence, he added, "That was some fool's idea of a joke."

She kept staring at him, speechless. A joke? Her brother's death was a *joke* to someone?

Seeing her reaction, he went on in a low, tortured voice, "After Roger's accident, I wore black to mourn him. Since Roger wasn't my family, Chetwin commented on it, saying that I dressed in black because Death was my constant companion. He pointed out that everyone I touched died—my parents, my best friend . . . everyone."

He began to pace the clearing, pain etched in his features. "Chetwin was right, of course. Death *was* my constant companion. So it was no great surprise when other people started calling me the Angel of Death." His voice grew choked. "I fit the part, after all."

And in that moment she realized that she'd seen everything all wrong. The Angel of Death wasn't his way of bragging. It was his curse, laid upon him by people who didn't care about his torment.

"Oh, Gabriel," she whispered.

But he didn't seem to hear her, lost in the past. "I had two choices. I could let those arses cow me with their taunts, or I could show them I wasn't afraid of them *or* of Death." He whirled to face her, his gaze so deeply haunted it broke her heart. "So yes, I painted my phaeton black and wore all black and dared them to call me whatever they pleased, as long as they left me alone."

A mad laugh escaped him. "But of course they didn't. Every stupid fool who'd ever tooled a rig wanted to challenge me to a race. At first I refused. For nearly a year I said no to every challenge, until the wagers got so high that I couldn't ignore them any longer."

Stabbing his fingers through his hair, he returned to pacing. "It finally dawned on me that the money could be my salvation. If I could make enough to do what I really wanted, what Gran was never going to let me do on my own, I could free myself of society completely down the road."

So that was what he'd wanted? To earn enough so he could hide away?

"I never wanted to be the Angel of Death," he said

fiercely. "But once I was, I was damned well going to make it pay."

His gaze shot to her, vulnerable in its agony, and his voice fell to a ragged whisper. "I told myself I was honoring Roger's memory. That every time I won, I did it for him, to make up for the fact that he could never race again as he so loved to do. But I suppose you could see that as just my excuse for getting to do what *I* loved to do."

"Roger did love to race," she said softly. "It wasn't a bad way to honor his memory."

Guilt mingled with anger in his gaze. "You don't really believe that."

"I believe his death has tortured you more than I realized." Clearly she and Poppy hadn't been the only ones suffering. "It's been seven years, Gabriel. It's time that you put it behind you. But before you can do that—before either of us can—you have to tell me the truth."

He tensed.

Virginia gathered her courage. "I've heard Poppy's secondhand version, and I've heard the rumors, but I've never heard the truth from your lips. So why don't you tell me what really happened the night of the wager and the day of Roger's death?"

His eyes turned bleak and hopeless.

She wanted to draw him back from whatever place he was retreating to, but she couldn't.

This Gabriel, the one who stood cold and unmoving, was the Angel of Death. And she refused to let him intimidate her. "Tell me the truth. Who initially laid down the challenge: you or Roger?"

"You don't want the truth," he said in a remote voice. "You're merely looking for a reason to refuse my suit."

"I don't need a reason for that. What I need is a reason to accept it."

"There's no answer to your question that will make you happy," he snapped. "If I say that I made the challenge, you'll be angry at me. If I say that he laid it down you'll be angry at him, and then you'll resent me for destroying your perfect image of your brother."

"That's not true," she said steadily.

"You know in your heart that it is. I can't win." He stepped nearer and lowered his voice. "If we're to make this courtship work, our only choice is to put the past behind us. We have to stop discussing what happened that night—who was at fault, what could have been done differently."

She shook her head. "That's not our only choice."

"It's the only one I'll accept."

"Gabriel—"

"I won't talk about that night!" he ground out. "Not now, not ever. And if you can't accept that, then you leave me no choice but to withdraw my suit."

A week ago, she would have told him to take his suit and trot back to Ealing with it. But a week ago, she hadn't come to know him.

Yes, he could be reckless and wild, but he could also be responsible. He worked hard, he fit seamlessly into life at the farm when Poppy would let him, and he made her want to have a future. A real future, not one dependent upon Pierce's largesse or Poppy's prospects for a long life.

Most of all, he understood her as no one else did. He spoke to the restlessness inside her. And though her mind told her that should be the least of her reasons for accepting his suit, her heart and her body told her something different.

If only he'd proved to be as obnoxious and cold-hearted as she'd assumed. But at the farm he'd worked tirelessly without calling attention to his accomplishments. He joked with the grooms and laughed in the face of Poppy's displeasure, but she saw now that it was only a mask, only a way to hide the deep unhappiness in his soul.

Unfortunately, that deep unhappiness could easily poison them both if it continued.

"I don't know if I *can* accept your refusal to talk about that race," she said. "I don't even know if I should."

"Fine." He squared his shoulders as if against a blow. "I hereby declare that you've met the terms of our wager. You need not go on with it."

When he turned as if to leave the clearing, she called out, "At least give me time to think about it."

He halted. "I'm not going to change my mind."

Perhaps not now. But if he could come to trust her, to let her into his heart . . .

His heart?

Was that what she wanted? Gabriel's heart?

If it was, she was mad. He had his heart locked in the past. Bringing it to the future might take a herculean effort. It might break her own heart.

But the chance at having him for her own might be worth the risk. If she could endure looking into his secrets. And without knowing what they were, she didn't know if she could.

She walked up behind him to lay her hand on his arm. "Come back on Monday. That will give me a chance to consider what I want to do. All right?"

He gazed down at her hand, then up into her face. Hope warred with wariness in his eyes. "You're a very stubborn woman," he ventured.

"Strange words, coming from a man who has honed his own stubbornness to a fine point," she teased.

His expression softened. "True."

She glanced up at the sky. "And speaking of the perennially stubborn, we had best return or Poppy will ban you from the farm forever."

When she started to walk off, Gabriel snagged her about the waist and pulled her close for a heady kiss that rivaled the sunset for brilliance. For a moment she just let him have his way. It was so sweet to be in his arms once more, so easy to forget that his desire for intimacy didn't stretch beyond the physical.

Only when he had her reeling did he let her go. "There," he said, his gaze hot on her. "That should give you something to consider while you're thinking about whether to accept my suit."

Then he sauntered off toward the road as if he hadn't just kissed her into obliviousness.

Lord help her, she was in a world of trouble. The man already had her so captivated that she didn't know which way was up. The only way she could come out of this with her heart intact was to shore up her defenses. And she feared it might already be too late for that.

Chapter Fourteen

It was still fairly early in the morning when Gabe rode away from Marsbury House the next day. Lyons had invited him and Wheaton to stay for breakfast, but though Gabe knew it made him appear boorish, he'd refused. He couldn't stand one more of the duke's jokes.

Because the unfathomable had happened. He'd lost. He couldn't remember the last time he'd lost a race.

And he'd injured himself in the process, though not badly. He'd followed Wheaton under a tree, and a branch that Wheaton had pushed past had swung back into him with such force it had sliced into his head. The wound was superficial, but it looked a fright—dried blood and matted hair. Gran and the girls would fuss if they saw it.

Still, his wound didn't concern him nearly as much as the fact that he'd lost a hundred pounds. Damn it to blazes. If he'd won, that money would easily have paid for entering Flying Jane in the St. Leger Stakes.

Virginia's voice sounded in his head: *If, if, if! That sounds like a great many ifs.*

Blasted woman. She was the reason he'd lost. Normally before he raced, a cold calm came over him that allowed him to concentrate on winning, on blotting out the dangers. But today that calm had deserted him, thanks to the thoughts that had churned in his mind ever since yesterday's encounter with the wench.

He'd slept badly, spending half of last night wishing he'd never embarked upon this idea to court her, and the other half thinking about how she'd accused him of building his reputation upon Roger's back.

He'd never dreamed she might look at it like that. Enhancing his reputation had never been his intention. But once she'd said those words, he'd felt compelled to refute her accusation, and soon she'd been digging things up out of the grave where he'd kept them buried for years.

A curse escaped him. Why couldn't she let Roger's death stay in the past? And how the blazes was he going to make her stop asking her damned questions?

He couldn't tell her what she wanted to know. If he even hinted at the truth, she would refuse to have anything to do with him again. He had some chance of winning her if she didn't know, but no chance at all if she did.

And why should he expose himself like that to her or her grandfather or anyone? Let the past remain in the past. That was best for them all.

But what if he couldn't make Virginia see that? What if she refused to marry him?

Then he'd find someone else.

He groaned as he settled his horse into a trot. He

didn't *want* anybody else. He didn't want a demure society chit who tittered behind her fan and said one thing while meaning another. He wanted the sunny-natured vixen who saw to everyone's needs with a brightness that sweetened even the sourest souls on her staff. He wanted the woman whose cheery words calmed the servants, heartened her grandfather, and made Gabe ache—to taste and touch her again, to have her in his arms sighing her pleasure.

He might as well admit it—he couldn't think straight for wanting her. Now he knew exactly how the damned studs felt when they scented the mares in heat. All she'd had to do in the past week was slide one of her smiles at him, and his blood rose. The thought of her giving up on him now . . .

No, he wouldn't allow it. He had to make her see that the past didn't matter. That they could start afresh. But he wasn't going to do it by racing every idiot who challenged him.

He scowled as Oliver's words drifted into his mind: *She lost her brother in a race. She won't want to risk marrying a man she could lose in one, wager or no wager.*

Blast it all. She worried about him, incredibly enough. But he couldn't stop the racing until Celia married. What if he and his siblings lost their inheritance? He'd need money and he knew no other way than by racing.

Unless he joined forces with her grandfather. He could be what Roger had been groomed to be before his death—the general's right-hand man. If he was going to marry the general's granddaughter anyway . . .

He sighed. At the moment, that was a big if. Besides, he refused to spend his time and energy building up a stud farm that Devonmont would inherit. He needed his own income. And that meant racing.

Virginia would just have to learn to accept it, that's all.

He reached the turn that led toward Ealing and reined in. He ought to go home. But then he'd have to tell his blasted family about losing the race. He'd have to endure his idiot brothers' jokes about it. Then there was the gash on his head. He could try to sneak in and keep his hat on until he could clean his wound, but his family always turned up in the most unlikely places, and they would find his refusal to take off his hat suspicious. The last thing he needed was a bunch of females chiding him for a paltry gash on the head.

Besides, the general had wanted his help with taking the yearlings to market. It might not be too late to catch them. He'd rather help the general than deal with his family's questions about the race. The man probably wouldn't even bring it up—he'd be too preoccupied with other concerns.

Virginia wouldn't have a chance to ask him about it, either, since he'd be with the general dealing with the livestock. Outside, he'd have no reason to remove his hat, so she wouldn't know he'd hurt himself.

And he'd get to see her. Not that seeing her had anything to do with his desire to ride over to Waverly Farm. That was just incidental.

He snorted as he turned his horse toward Waverly

Farm. Incidental, right. He'd better watch himself. He was becoming besotted, and that wouldn't do. If she guessed it, she would try to wrap him about her finger, and next thing he knew, she'd be commanding him to stop racing.

Still, he couldn't keep his heart from pounding as he approached the farm half an hour later. The place looked deserted. No one was in the stable, not even the grooms, and the general was nowhere to be seen. Blast it all, he'd missed them.

But perhaps he could catch up to them on the road. One of the house servants might know which one they'd taken.

Dismounting, he tied his horse off and strode up to the door. He knocked. No answer. He knocked again, and was about to turn away when he heard a muffled response from inside.

When the door swung open, however, it wasn't one of the maids or the footman standing there. It was Virginia.

He sucked in a breath. Her hair was loose about her shoulders, and she wore nothing but a night rail with a thin cotton wrapper over it. Clearly he'd awakened her.

She rubbed sleep from her eyes. "I thought you had a race."

"I did. It's over."

"So soon?"

"Soon? It's past nine, sweetheart, and we raced at dawn."

"Oh. I just got to bed a few hours ago. Molly's sick.

That's why I didn't go to the fair—someone had to stay and take care of her." She blinked. "Wait, it's past nine? I've got to give her more barley water. With her fever, she needs plenty of it." She headed down the hall to the kitchen.

He entered and closed the door behind him, then followed her into the kitchen. "Is there no one here to help you with her?"

"Poppy had to take everyone to the fair. She and I were both supposed to go, but with us staying here, he needed whoever could attend him." She thrust a glass into his hand. "Hold this."

He watched as she filled a bowl with vinegar, but when she went to take the glass from him, he murmured, "I'll carry it for you."

With a nod, she hurried up the servants' stairs. He followed.

Molly's room was on the top floor. It was small but neat, with a cozy rug on the floor and a decent dresser. The windows were open, which made the summer heat bearable. Molly slept in the bed, snoring loudly.

Virginia set the glass on the tiny table beside the bed, then laid the back of her hand against Molly's forehead. "Thank heaven, her fever seems to have broken. I won't wake her. I'll just leave the barley water here."

Taking the bowl from him, she began to sprinkle vinegar around the room.

"What are you doing?" he asked.

"Dr. Buchanan's says it will refresh the patient."

"You brought in a doctor for Molly?"

"No, that seemed premature. I suspect she just has an ague. But I refer to Dr. Buchanan's *Domestic Medicine* whenever one of us is ill. He gives very sensible advice."

Gabe tried to imagine one of the simpering ladies that he met in society poring over a medical book, but he couldn't. About the only thing that lot ever consulted was *The Lady's Magazine*.

Setting the half-empty bowl on the dresser, she ushered him out the door. As he followed her down the stairs, she said, "You shouldn't be here."

"But I am," he said. "Might as well stay awhile."

It was dawning on him that he finally had her alone. Molly was clearly not going to be good for much in the next few hours, and if everyone else was gone, this might be his chance to win her.

Giles had won Minerva by compromising her. Why shouldn't that work for him? "I could help you with Molly," he said as Virginia hurried down the stairs to the front hall.

"I don't need help with Molly." She headed for the front door so fast, he had to catch her by the arm to halt her.

"Then I could help you with whatever else you need," he persisted.

"The only thing I need right now is to fall into bed." The minute the words left her lips, she blushed. "I mean, I . . . I need sleep."

He caught her by the chin. "I could help you sleep," he drawled.

Her eyes darkened to the troubled blue of a storm-tossed lake as she lifted her hands to push against his chest. "Gabriel——"

He kissed her. How could he resist? Fresh from her bed, she looked as wild and wanton as a French opera dancer, yet somehow innocent, too, in all that white linen and lace. He wanted to ravish her and cherish her all at the same time.

For a moment, she remained rigid in his arms. Then her arms crept about his waist, and she melted into him like the sweet vixen that she was. Her mouth opened beneath his, and he drove his tongue inside, craving her soft warmth, aching to make her his.

He couldn't keep his hands still, not with so much glorious femininity in his grasp, but when he slid them up to cup her breasts, she thrust him away.

Her eyes were wide, but not frightened. "You should go."

"You don't want me to go."

Her quickening breath showed he was right. "It's not wise that you stay."

"Since when do you always do what's wise?"

She shook her head at him. "I haven't made up my mind about you."

"Then let me help you with that," he whispered and hauled her into his arms again.

This time their kisses went longer, grew hotter, until they were both gasping, and her body was plastered to his. He managed to stay clear of the parts he yearned to touch, but then she flung her arms about his neck, dislodging his hat, and buried her hands in his hair——

And drew back with a cry of alarm. "What's this?" Her fingers probed the gash on his head. "You're hurt!"

Damn it, he'd completely forgotten about that. "It's fine, just a little cut."

"You're bleeding!" Grabbing him by the arm, she tugged him down the hall and into the kitchen.

"Honestly, Virginia, it's nothing."

"Sit down," she ordered. "That is not nothing." When he hesitated, she added, more firmly, "Sit down before I *make* you sit down."

He let out a laugh and she glowered at him. He dropped into a chair. "I had no idea you were so bossy."

"What choice do I have when faced with fools like you and Poppy?" She poured some water from a pitcher over a rag. "*Nothing*, indeed. You men always say that while you're trailing blood and sporting broken bones." Still grumbling, she came over to sponge his wound. "Looks like you've got a piece of wood in there. We have to get that out."

She left his side to fetch what she needed. "What did you do, run into a tree?"

"You could say that." He was rather enjoying having her fuss over him.

Until she came back and probed his head with the point of a paring knife.

"Good God almighty," he muttered under his breath. "Can't you do that less vigorously?"

"I'm only trying to help," she said primly.

"You seem to be enjoying it just a little too much."

"No more than you enjoy risking your life for a few pounds," she snapped.

A clink sounded as she dropped something into a tin bowl. He peered into it to see a sizable splinter of wood.

"And you claimed this wouldn't be a dangerous race," she muttered as she dabbed at his wound. "Every race you run is dangerous—it's the only kind you know. I daresay you gave your mother fits when you were a child, running into things and playing with sharp sticks." She drew back to assess the gash. "Sweet Lord, do you realize how close this is to your eye?"

"Not *that* close," he protested.

"You could have gouged your eye out! The wound won't stop bleeding, so I'll have to treat it with something. Take off everything down to your waist."

"I beg your pardon?"

She was already bustling off to a chest in the corner. "I don't want to ruin your clothes." It was clear from her no-nonsense demeanor that she meant that and only that.

With a sigh he untied his cravat, then rose to peel off his coat, waistcoat, and shirt.

Meanwhile, she rummaged through the chest. "It's a wonder you didn't rip off an ear, although that might have been a good thing. Might have made you think twice the next time you set out to kill yourself for a foolish wager." She stopped to glare at him. "Was that hundred pounds worth nearly killing yourself?"

He scowled as he tossed his clothes onto the table. "Actually, I didn't win."

Her eyes widened. "But you never lose."

"Don't remind me," he grumbled, dropping back into the chair.

"What happened?"

"What do you mean, what happened? He outrode me." He'd be damned if he told her it was because he'd been thinking of *her*.

But if he'd thought his loss would gain him her sympathy, he was vastly mistaken. "That makes it even worse." Plucking a stoppered bottle out of the chest, she brought it and a rag over to him. "You lost a hundred pounds risking your life, and now you have a gash on your head that might still kill you."

"Don't be ridiculous. I won't die from a little scratch."

"Little scratch, my eye." She poured some liquid over the wound.

"Ow!" he protested as it dripped onto his shoulder and she sponged it away with the rag. "What the hell is that?"

"Spirits of wine, to stop the bleeding. Now hold that on there." Pressing the rag to his head, she put his hand on it. "I'm going to fetch some sticking plaster."

He grabbed her by the arm. "Absolutely not. I'd be the laughingstock of London. Bandage it if you must, but—"

"I suppose you think a bandage would look more dashing." Fire blazed in her eyes. "So now I have to hunt up some black linen to wrap around your idiot head so it'll match your black—"

She broke off. "Wait a minute." Her eyes scanned him, then darted to the pile of clothes on the table. When she lifted her gaze to meet his, her anger had been replaced by shock. "You're not wearing black."

Chapter Fifteen

Virginia couldn't believe she hadn't noticed before. But she was certainly noticing now. He wore fawn-colored buckskin breeches, and on the table lay a chocolate-brown coat, a buff waistcoat, a white linen shirt, and a snowy cravat.

"What happened to your black shirt?" she asked.

He looked suddenly uncomfortable. "I got tired of it."

A lump caught in her throat. "And the rest of your black clothes? You got tired of those, too?"

He shrugged. "I figured it was time to give it a rest, is all."

There was more to it than that, and they both knew it. He'd stopped wearing black because of what she'd said yesterday.

She couldn't believe it. He'd made such an enormous change for *her*. If he could do that after so many years, then might he eventually do more? Might he even let her into that wary heart of his one day?

Trying to regain control of her feelings, she murmured, "You look good in brown."

His darkening gaze sent a shaft of need straight to her belly and below. Even with his hand on his head reminding her of his wound, she couldn't keep from reacting to his nearness. It had been two days since he'd caught her in the stable, two days since he'd woven his spell about her. It felt like forever.

It felt like a second.

"You look good in white," he rasped.

Sweet Lord, she'd completely forgotten how inappropriately she was dressed. He reached up with his free hand to untie her wrapper, then open it and slide it off her shoulders. It swished down to crumple at her feet, leaving her in only her night rail. Her flimsy, semi-transparent night rail.

She couldn't let him do this. She'd sworn not to give in to him until he was willing to share his secrets—yet here she was, already half-naked with him, her blood heating and her pulse stammering and her body yearning to have him . . .

No! She had to get away from him, to gain some air. "I'll go get a bandage for your head. I-I think I have some cloth I can use." Scooping up her wrapper, she hastened to the door. If she just had a moment to think, to put proper clothes on, so she didn't feel so exposed . . .

"Virginia, wait!" he cried, but she ignored him as she hurried out and raced up the stairs.

In her bedchamber she stood staring blankly into space, fighting for equilibrium, her wrapper still clutched in her hand. If she weren't careful, she just might—

"Are you running away from me, sweetheart?" Gabriel asked from behind her.

She whirled to find him standing in the open doorway. She hadn't expected him to follow her. "What are you doing here?"

When he stepped inside and closed the door, a thrill shot through her, equal parts alarm and excitement. Naked from the waist up, he looked sinful and dangerous. Deliciously dangerous.

"You shouldn't be in my bedroom," she said, attempting to sound firm.

He scanned her room. "This isn't what I expected."

She followed his gaze to the bed coverings of red damask that she'd made out of fabric belonging to her late mother, and the golden patterned wallpaper that she'd put up herself. She was rather proud of her bedroom. "Why not?" she asked defensively.

"After a week of watching you here at the farm, I thought your room would be more plain and practical." He gave a rueful laugh. "I should have known better. You have a romantic streak running through you as wide as that fancy rug you're standing on."

She sniffed. "If you don't like my room——"

"Ah, but I do. It suits you. The inner sanctum of Miss Virginia Waverly. On the outside is the efficient lady of the manor running the farmhouse. On the inside is the bold enchantress who challenges men to races and spies on them in stables." His voice deepened. "And tempts them to riot." With stark hunger in his eyes, he pushed away from the door. "Who knew that beneath the crisp linen and starched apron lay so much velvet and lace?"

She swallowed. Why must he be the only man who ever saw that? Who truly understood her? "And you claim you're not a poet."

"I guess you bring it out in me." His eyes took a slow, intimate survey of her thinly clad body, making her blood clamor with need. "The same way I bring out the recklessness in you."

"This is too reckless, even for me," she said in a vain attempt at protest.

"I doubt that. Anyway, I just came to tell you that I don't need a bandage." Dropping into the nearest chair, he tapped his head. "See for yourself."

Warily, she approached him, keeping well to the side as she peered at his head. She moved a lock of his hair to get a better look. He was right. The wound had stopped bleeding and was crusting over.

He caught her hand and brought it to his lips. With his gaze on hers, he kissed the back of her hand, so gently that it stopped her breath in her throat. Then he turned her hand over to kiss her palm. And next, her wrist.

Her pulse jumped into a frenzy beneath his lips.

"Don't," she whispered, tugging her hand free and turning to walk away.

Snagging her about the waist, he pulled her down onto his lap.

"What do you think you're doing?" she said hoarsely as she struggled against his grip. "You shouldn't—"

"Do you want to know the real reason I lost the race today?" he growled against her ear.

She stilled, her heart in her throat. With her back to him she couldn't see his face, but she could feel his arousal beneath her bottom. And it was stoking her own desire.

He reached up to unbutton her nightdress, and she let him, even when he parted the edges to expose her breasts. "I lost because my concentration was shattered. My mind was elsewhere." He covered one bare breast with his hand. "On you. On how badly I wanted you. How badly I wanted to be here with you."

A deep need seized her that wouldn't be denied. She wanted him here with her, perish his soul.

He fondled her breast, and a sigh of pleasure left her lips. "So," she gasped, "you're blaming . . . me for your . . . loss."

"Something like that. Though if you'd been standing at the end of the course dressed like this, I promise I would have won."

A purely feminine delight swirled through her. She tried to tell herself they were the practiced words of a practiced seducer, but she no longer believed it. Not after seeing his agony yesterday. Gabriel was many things, but a vain flatterer wasn't one of them.

He filled both hands with her breasts, teasing the nipples until she grew all fuzzy and agitated inside. Nothing this wonderful had ever happened to her, and while she shouldn't indulge him or herself, she wanted to badly. So very badly.

He slowly dragged her nightdress up her thighs so he could slip his hand beneath it. His breath came hot against her ear. "You're not wearing any drawers."

She blushed. "I never do when I sleep."

"I'll have to catch you in your nightdress more often." His hand found the place between her legs where she felt damp and warm and eager, and he rubbed it deliciously. When he slid his finger inside her, she let out a gasp. It was every bit as luscious as when he'd used his tongue on her in the stable.

"Are you trying to seduce me, sir?" she whispered.

"Absolutely. Is it working?"

Of course it was working. He was devilish good at this sort of thing. "Certainly not."

His husky chuckle made her heart flip over in her chest. "Then I'll have to try harder."

Oh, dear, that might be her undoing. But it was so enticing to have him touch her everywhere, one hand caressing her breast as the other fondled her below. The man had a talent for seduction that was downright diabolical. "You should not . . . We cannot . . ."

"We can, and we will." He pressed a hot, open-mouthed kiss to her neck. "You're going to marry me, after all. Who cares if we consummate the marriage early?"

She stiffened. "I have *not* agreed to marry you."

"Yes, you're being stubborn about that." He stroked her deeply, making her squirm, making her want more. "That's why I must resort to such tactics."

"You just want to gain your fortune," she accused, though she didn't really believe that anymore.

He paused. "If that fear is all that keeps you from marrying me, I can solve that problem right now. I'll give up my fortune. As long as I marry, Gran will be satisfied and not cut off the others. I'll just tell her to split my portion among my siblings."

Shocked, she turned on his lap so she could gaze into his face. He would really give up his inheritance for *her*? "You're joking."

His expression of solemn sincerity shook her to her toes. "The money means nothing to me."

"Even if it would enable you to reach your dream?"

"I can reach my dream without it."

Her heart constricted. "By racing for wagers, you mean."

Something glinted in his eyes. "Without the inheritance, I'll need the racing to support us."

"Then I'd rather you kept the inheritance."

"Careful, sweetheart," he murmured. "Or I'll think you're marrying me for the money."

Annoyed, she pushed at his chest. "And what else would I be marrying you for, you troublesome lout?"

A dark smile curved his lips. "For this."

Then he was kissing her, hot and deep and slow. And all the while he fondled her, rousing her to a fever pitch below. She squirmed, then tore her mouth from his so she could catch her breath. Except that she couldn't. Bending her back over his arm, he moved his mouth to suck at her breast while his hand deftly caressed her, seeming to know what she needed before *she* knew it.

"I want you, sweetheart," he growled against her breast. "I want to make love to you. Will you let me?"

A sensible woman would say no. Once she gave herself to him, there was no going back. They'd have to marry. And he still kept much of himself locked behind a door with no knob.

But he'd stopped wearing black for her. He was willing to give up his fortune. It was more than she'd hoped for. And the only other choice—to send him away now and draw out this courtship until she was more sure of him—didn't appeal to her, either. She couldn't endure more days of Poppy's hovering, with Gabriel so near, yet so inaccessible.

She was tired of giving everyone else what they wanted and never taking something for herself. She was tired of endlessly yearning for her own home and family, for a husband of her own. What Gabriel proposed wasn't perfect, but what was?

And part of her was sure that one day he would let her in. He'd already let her in further than she'd hoped.

She gazed into his fathomless eyes. "All right."

With a fierce growl of satisfaction, he set her on the floor so he could tug off his boots and toss them aside. Then he rose to drag her nightdress off her shoulders. It slithered down her body, leaving her naked as a birch in winter.

His eyes drank her in, dark, searing, and worshipful. "You're the most beautiful woman I've ever seen."

"I know there are a great many beautiful women in your circle," she whispered, torn between the urge to believe him and her fear that she lacked the physical attributes to hold a rogue like him.

He laughed. "Contrary to popular opinion, my 'circle' is mostly horses and the men who race them. I stay out of respectable society as much as possible, and the few women I have met there are either boring, stupid, or both. You are neither."

"And the women who aren't in society? You must be used to bedding women who have—" She gazed down at her breasts and swallowed. "Bigger . . . er . . . curves."

With a scowl, he tugged her close. "Don't you dare malign your curves. They're perfect. *You're* perfect." He bent his head to kiss each of her breasts. "I lie awake at night thinking of these beauties. And I daresay that once we marry and you're presented in society, I won't be the only one doing so. Half the men of the *ton* are going to envy me my wife, and the other half are going to try to seduce her."

"Don't be silly." He was being outrageous, and she loved it.

"I'm serious." He lifted his hands to smooth her hair over her shoulders. "Thank God, you never had a season, or some other fellow would have snapped you up before I could."

She couldn't resist teasing him. "Perhaps one of them still will."

The possessive light that flared in his face made her throat go raw. "Oh no, you lost your chance at that, vixen. You're going to belong to me now. Only me."

Pierce's accusation that day at the maze came into her mind: *Once you get your hands on your grandmother's money, you'll be spending every night in the stews.* Gabriel hadn't exactly denied it.

"And you?" she asked softly. "Will you belong to me, and only me?"

Pain flashed in his features. "My father's infidelity destroyed my mother and quite possibly caused their deaths. I promise you that the one thing I will *never* be is unfaithful. I wouldn't put you through that."

The words had the feel of a vow. They were as close to words of love as she'd heard from him. Not that she was even sure of her own feelings.

Still, it was nice that he cared so much.

She let out a breath. "So when do I get to see *you* naked?"

He blinked, then released her to swiftly dispense with the rest of his clothes. Then he stood back with that cocky grin of his. "Happy now?"

As his flesh sprang up, thick and long and hairy at the base, she caught her breath. Happy? Fascinated, more like. Who would have guessed that his *thing* would be so long? She'd spent some time thinking about the subject, having seen many a horse's appendage, but horses and men weren't as alike as she'd thought.

It seemed to bob beneath her gaze, as if liking the attention.

"Does it hurt when it sticks out like that?" she asked.

"No." His voice sounded strained. "Not when I'm naked, anyway. It's a bit uncomfortable in clothes."

"Can I touch it?" she asked.

"God, yes," he ground out. Seizing her hand, he closed it about his flesh.

That was interesting. It twitched when she held it, as

if her hand agitated it. Smooth and hard, it was rather like the leather-bound handle of a crop. Only bigger. Much bigger.

And growing even bigger, the more she stroked it.

"Doesn't it give you trouble when you ride?"

"Not usually," he bit out.

"How large does it get?"

"Large enough," he growled.

"That's no kind of ans—"

Next thing she knew she was flat on her back on the bed, and he was on top of her, staring hungrily down into her face. "A man can only bear a certain amount of teasing, Virginia."

"I was just curious about—"

"I know," he said, then forced a smile. "But much more of your curiosity, and this would have been over before it started."

"What do you mean?"

He slid his knee between her legs, parting them so he could kneel between them. "Just trust me when I say I need to be inside you. *Now.*"

Apparently men did have *one* thing in common with horses. Impatience.

She was feeling a bit impatient herself. As he began fondling her again between the legs, the restlessness returned that she'd felt in the stable. Then he was kissing her, roughly, savagely, and it was so delicious that she almost forgot he was naked and she was naked, and he was about to take her innocence.

Until something larger than his finger pressed into her.

She really was going to do this. She really was letting him make her his.

She ought to feel panicked. She ought to be afraid. Instead, a glorious excitement swelled through her. Even the thick pressure of him forging up inside her couldn't quell it.

This was what she'd been yearning for, this reckless act, this heady joining with a man who made her feel alive for once. Who made her feel like a woman, not just the female who looked after everyone's needs.

He dragged his mouth from hers to whisper, "I don't suppose I have to tell you about the pain."

"No." She buried her fingers in his hair, careful not to touch his wound. "But it doesn't feel that bad."

"Good," he rasped. "Because it feels amazing to me. Even better than I imagined."

She gazed shyly into his face. "Did you really lie in bed thinking of my . . . um . . . bosom?"

He inched farther in, sweat beading his brow. "Sweetheart, if you knew just how often, you'd slap the tar out of me."

The admission pleased her. She figured she owed him an admission of her own. "I . . . thought of you, too."

Raw heat suffused his face. "Like this?"

"No, silly." She shifted a little under him, seeking a more comfortable position, and he slid into her more deeply. She caught her breath. "But after I saw you half-naked that day in the stable . . ."

He gave a strained laugh. "I was right. In your soul, you're a seductress."

She should be insulted, but she wasn't. "I do believe . . . I might be."

"Then hold on. Because you're about to be a seductress in truth." And with that, he drove into her.

A gasp escaped her, but it was more in surprise than pain. She'd felt a pinch, nothing more.

"Are you all right?"

"I think so," she said, too embarrassed to admit that she felt fine. There was a pressure, and a certain awkwardness about having him thrust up inside her, but nothing like what she'd expected.

"Ready for more, my wife-to-be?" he asked in a husky voice. One hand fondled her breast as he held himself off her with his other.

Lord, but he was strong. "Oh, yes."

"Thank God," he growled.

He began to slide out of her and back in, in slow easy strokes. At first it felt quite peculiar. But when he bent to kiss her, thrusting his tongue inside her mouth, she giggled.

He tore his lips from hers. "And what do you find so amusing?"

"I just realized why you kiss that way. It mimics what we're doing."

His eyes gleamed at her. "Not entirely."

"No," she said. "Not entirely." While the kissing was always marvelous, it hardly compared to the strange heat building between her legs as he drove in and pulled out, over and over and over.

Some instinct made her draw her knees up just as he

thrust deep, and an intense pleasure pierced her. "Oh!" she cried. "Ohhhh, *Gabriel.*"

He gave a hoarse chuckle. "Like that, do you?" Deliberately he plunged deeply into her, provoking the same sensation as before.

She cried out, then blushed. "Lord help me . . . I suppose I'm . . . some sort of wanton."

"No." He nuzzled her cheek. "Just a woman in the throes of desire. Thank God. Because I ache for you every night, and every day."

"So do I," she admitted. Feeling more free to explore now that they'd fallen into a steady rhythm, she ran her hands over the taut muscles of his shoulders. "You feel so firm . . ."

He choked back a laugh. "I should hope so. And you feel like silk. Sweet, hot silk . . . "

She swept her hands over his chest, enjoying the play of muscles beneath her fingers. He was such a fine figure of a man. Was it wrong of her to love that about him?

He tweaked her nipple and sent a tremor through her to join with the others quaking up from below. The tremors were all twisting together now, making her ache and yearn and shake beneath his glorious thrusting.

Sweet Lord, this was beyond desire. This was him and her, locked together, headed for the future. She stared up into his hot gaze and felt her heart breaking open to let him in.

As if he saw her feelings in her eyes, he rasped, "Remember you belong to me . . . Only me . . ."

"And you to me—only me," she echoed. "Forever."

His eyes widened but the words seemed to push him over the edge, for he plunged deep one last time, and they erupted together. His body filled hers with his essence as hers shattered so powerfully that she could only hold onto him while the earthquake wracked her body.

And he rode it out with her, his scent and taste and touch filling her as he collapsed atop her with a groan.

That's when she realized she'd fallen in love with him. Her wild, tempestuous lord was the only man who'd ever seen into her soul.

He was also the only man she had ever let close enough to hurt her.

Now she could only pray to God that he never did.

Chapter Sixteen

Gabe lay beside Virginia in the aftermath of their lovemaking, panic gripping his heart.

Forever.

How was it that he hadn't thought of it that way until she'd said it? He'd been so focused on making sure he got what he wanted—making sure he got *her*—that he hadn't stopped to think what he was getting.

A wife, forever. Someone depending on him, forever. Someone who needed him more than anyone ever had.

Turning onto his side so he could gaze down at her, he saw the blood smearing her thighs. That only increased his panic. He'd taken his future bride, and now he was responsible for her.

Forever.

He'd never considered having a forever, because Death could end forever in one beat of the heart. He'd skated close to Death so many times that *future* and *forever* had meant nothing to him.

Now they *had* to mean something. *Then why marry if you're just going to make some woman a widow?* He'd ignored the words when she'd said them, but he couldn't ignore them now. Having a wife changed everything. He couldn't win races if he had to worry about dying and leaving a widow behind. Just look at what had happened this morning.

A cold chill shook him. How could he support a wife if he didn't get his inheritance and he couldn't win races?

Virginia stared up at him with a tremulous smile, and something clutched at his chest. God save him, what if he couldn't take care of her?

It was too late to consider that now. He'd ruined her. They had to marry.

"Are you all right?" he asked.

"Marvelous."

The trust in her eyes made his throat go dry. His anxiety must have shown, for her joy abruptly faded. "But you don't look so good."

He forced a smile. "I was just worried that I hurt you too much."

She relaxed. "You didn't."

He buried his fear beneath a joke. "Because we could always do it over, and I could try to improve on it."

A laugh burst out of her. "If you improved on that any more, I'd perish from the pleasure."

"Death by pleasure?" he said. "I could arrange that. I *am* the Angel of Death, you know."

The minute her eyes turned sad, he wanted to kick himself. What an idiotic thing to say.

"What does that make *me*?" she asked, perfectly serious. "Mrs. Angel of Death?"

"Of course not." He shifted onto his back, staring up

at the lush red damask of her tester bed. "It's just a stupid nickname, one I hope to be rid of soon."

"How, if you intend to keep racing?"

Clearly he wasn't the only one considering such matters. "I'll think of something."

And he would, too. He wasn't going to let her worries about him, or any foolish fears he felt right now over the possibility of leaving her a widow, alter his plans for the future.

He changed the subject. "How soon can we be married? Shall I ask the general for your hand when he returns from the fair?"

"Lord, no!" It was her turn to look alarmed. She sat up and dragged the sheet over herself. "If he found you here and had any inkling that we'd been alone in the house together, he'd skewer you on his cavalry sword."

"You're not worried about Molly telling him?"

"She'd have to wake up and find you here, and that's unlikely. Her fever may have broken, but she was sleeping hard. She won't rouse for a few hours yet. Even if she does, she won't leave her bed if she doesn't have to. She'll take the opportunity to get some rest. Lord knows we don't get much of it around here these days."

"Yes, I've seen how hard you work. All the more reason we should marry quickly. Then I could move in and start helping—"

"You're helping already." She cast him a plaintive look. "And why be in such a hurry to marry? You've got a few months yet before your grandmother's deadline."

"If you think I'll wait months, sneaking around to see

you, never being able to do more than touch your hand in public, you're out of your mind." He sat up to loop his arm about her shoulders. "I want to claim you as my wife. I don't want to wait."

She let out a frustrated breath. "Neither do I. But you have to give me the chance to break it to Poppy gently. He'll claim that you're only marrying me to gain your fortune."

"And you'll tell him that I'm giving it up. For you."

"Don't be ridiculous. It was lovely of you to offer, but I don't want you doing such a fool thing. The money will enable us to live more freely." She cast him a quick glance. "And it will help keep you from racing."

He said nothing. She was right, but only if Celia married, too, and that was by no means certain.

"So I have to convince Poppy that you're worthy of me, even with the matter of the fortune. Besides, he still has the daft notion that Pierce and I are going to marry."

The shaft of jealousy that arrowed to his heart took him by surprise. "I suppose Devonmont has the same daft notion."

She laughed. "My cousin has no illusions on that score, believe me." Turning her face up to his, she kissed his cheek. "But it's sweet of you to be jealous."

"Sweet?" he grumbled. "If he ever kisses you again as he did when he left, the throttling I give him will be anything but sweet."

"Pierce could use a throttling. He gets away with far too much." Her eyes gleamed at him. "As do you."

He shifted to face her. "Which is why you should marry me right away. Before I get into any more trouble."

"Tempting as that sounds," she said dryly, "I need some time to prepare Poppy."

Gabe scowled at her. "How much?"

"A few days, at least."

"One day."

"Gabriel!"

"I mean it. When I come here Monday, I'll be coming with a marriage proposal. And if you don't say yes, I'll throw you over my shoulder and carry you off on my trusty steed."

A laugh sputtered out of her. "I should like to see *that*. Then Poppy really would come after you with his cavalry sword."

"He'd have to catch me first. And I'm very quick on horseback."

Her gaze turned sultry. "Except when you're thinking of *me*. Like today."

He smiled ruefully. "You don't forget anything I say, do you?"

"Not when it's something as sweet as that."

She leaned up to kiss him and he cupped her head in his hands to lengthen the kiss. Within seconds it grew heated, and to his surprise he found himself hardening again. God, she already had him slavering after her like a blood-crazed stallion. He'd better watch his step, or he'd be as besotted with her as his brothers were with *their* wives.

And that would be a mistake. Unlike his brothers,

if he didn't gain his inheritance, he had no way to live except by racing. So he couldn't let himself become so drawn in that her worries altered his plans.

But it was difficult to stay aloof when the only woman who'd ever fired his blood *and* his mind was rousing him to madness.

"About that offer to do it over . . ." she whispered with her enchantress's smile.

"You're not too sore?" he asked as he filled his hand with her breast.

"Why don't we find out?"

That was all it took to have him pressing her back down. All right, so he had no self-control when it came to her in his bed. That didn't mean he was besotted. It merely meant he was the same randy fellow as always. He just happened to prefer satisfying his urges with *her*.

And this time he would drive from her mind the memory of her uncomfortable deflowering. He might not be able to keep her happy anywhere else, but he could certainly do it here, in the bedchamber.

So he devoted all his extensive experience with women to making her crazed by desire. By the time he plunged into her again, he had made sure she was begging him for it, meeting him thrust for thrust, shimmying her perfect little body beneath him exactly as a wife with a taste for passion should. And he forced himself to wait until she was climaxing before he allowed himself the same release.

It was every bit as wonderful as the first time. And even better, since he didn't have to worry about hurting her.

Afterward, they both fell into a doze, since neither of them had slept much the night before. It seemed like only moments passed before someone was shaking him.

"Gabriel, you have to get out of here!"

The panic in Virginia's voice roused him fully awake. "What?"

"We slept too long. It's nearly nightfall. Poppy will be driving up any minute, and if he sees your mount in front—"

"Right." He forced his sluggish limbs to move, forced himself out of the bed.

She thrust his drawers at him. "You have to get dressed!"

"And here I was planning to ride home naked," he quipped as he tugged on his drawers.

"This is no time to joke!" she said, urgency in her voice. "Gabriel, please . . ."

"All right, all right!" He hurried into his clothes. "But once we're married, sweetheart, I'm never going to be rushed out of your arms—or your bed—again."

That at least made her smile. "I should hope not."

He drew her to him for a hard, quick kiss, made all the quicker when she shoved him away.

She scowled at him. "If you get murdered by Poppy because you were doing fool things like kissing me, I'll never forgive you!"

She looked so adorably worried that he kissed her again.

"Gabriel!" she protested.

He winked, not the least perturbed. "Don't worry

about *me,* vixen. I cheat Death. It's what I do, what I've done more times than I can count."

Her troubled expression deepened. "That only means your luck might run out any day."

The words sent a chill down his spine that he tried to shrug off. Gran had been saying that for years, and so far it hadn't happened.

Still, as he dressed and hurried down the stairs, he couldn't ignore a deep feeling of foreboding. But that didn't stop him from pausing in the entrance hall to draw Virginia close for a searing kiss.

"I meant what I said earlier," he murmured as he took one last glance at her reddened mouth and thinly clad form. "I'll be here Monday, come hell or high water. So you'd best make sure that the general knows it."

"I will, I promise." She touched his head where his wound was. "Take care of this, will you? And try not to get yourself hurt in any more races."

Heartened by the fact that she hadn't asked him not to race at all, he nodded. Within moments, he was on the road and headed back for Halstead Hall.

He did have one scare about three miles from the farm. A coach was coming up the road ahead of him. Fortunately, he saw it in time to pull off into some trees. Thank God he had, for as it rumbled past, he saw that it was the general's carriage.

That was a little too close for comfort. If the general had seen him on this road, he would have guessed that Gabe had been to the farmhouse. Much as Gabe wanted to marry Virginia right away, he understood her desire to have her grandfather's blessing.

Besides, there was no point in antagonizing the old man. They quite possibly would be living in each other's pockets for a while, at least until Gabe's inheritance was freed up. *If* it was freed up.

That thought gave way to thoughts of their future and how it should be managed, which preoccupied him all the way back to Halstead Hall. He was so engrossed that he didn't notice the hue and cry that went up when he neared the stables.

But when Jarret came striding out, face wrought with worry, it brought Gabe up short.

"Where the devil have you been?" Jarret growled as Gabe dismounted.

That put Gabe instantly on alert. "Why?"

"The last thing we heard from one of the grooms, you'd gone out to race Wheaton at Lyons's property." Jarret's voice held an edge. "So when Pinter came with his news—"

"What news?" Gabe asked sharply.

Jarret ignored him. "—I rode over to Lyons's to fetch you, but he said you'd left hours before, and with a head wound, too. We've been scouring the countryside for you, assuming that you'd fallen into a ditch somewhere from loss of blood."

"Oh, for God's sake," Gabe snapped. "It was a scratch, nothing more."

Oliver came up just then. "That's not what Lyons said. I've had men riding the route, looking for you."

"We even checked all the taverns in Ealing," Jarret added.

"Well, I'm here now," Gabe snapped. He wasn't about to tell them where he'd been. "So would someone please tell me what the bloody hell Pinter's news is?"

"Benny May has been found."

Gabe gaped at Jarret. "Good. Is Pinter going to talk to him?"

"I'm afraid that's impossible," Oliver said. "Benny was found dead."

Dragging in a harsh breath, Gabe turned to stare blindly at the stables, a million thoughts jumbling together. Once again, someone connected to him had died. And though he knew it had nothing to do with him, it still felt as if it did. "How?" he asked hoarsely.

Jarret and Oliver exchanged glances. Then Jarret softened his tone. "We're not sure. But there's some indication it might have been foul play."

"The constable in Woburn remembered Pinter having asked about Benny a couple of weeks ago," Oliver explained. "So when the body of a man the right size and with the right hair color turned up in the woods near there, he sent word to Pinter. He's holding the body until Pinter can be there for the inquest."

Gabe swung his gaze back to them. "I want to be there, too."

"We thought you might," Jarret said. "Oliver can't leave the estate right now, but you and I can accompany Pinter. He's at his office giving instructions to his clerk about his other cases. We're to meet him there as soon as you're ready to go."

"I can be ready in minutes." Gabe strode toward the house.

It was only after he'd reached his bedchamber that it dawned on him. There was no way in hell he could get to Woburn, witness an inquest, since they wouldn't do it on a Sunday, and get back home by Monday to be at Waverly Farm. It would be Tuesday at the earliest.

Damn it to blazes.

Well, it couldn't be helped. He wasn't about to miss being at Benny May's inquest. If it was murder, that might mean that his parents' deaths really had been more than they seemed. And that he'd lost his chance to learn who the mysterious man in the stables had been.

But he had to get a message to Virginia.

Annabel happened to come down the hall at that moment, and an idea occurred to him.

"Annabel, would you do me a favor?"

"Of course."

"Here's what I need . . ."

Chapter Seventeen

"How was church?" Poppy asked Virginia when she came into the dining room. He'd clearly been reading the paper as he awaited her return, but now that she was home, he motioned to the footman to serve dinner.

She sat down and removed her gloves. "Church was fine."

Poppy never went to services. He hadn't gone since Roger's death, having apparently blamed God for that. She understood his feelings, but she wasn't brave enough to stay home herself. People talked about them and their troubles with the farm enough already; no point in having the whole town consider them godless heathens, too.

Especially when she'd *felt* like a godless heathen, sitting in church and fearing she might be struck by lightning any minute. After what she'd done with Gabriel yesterday, she must have been mad to show up in a house of God.

Still, she couldn't regret her fallen state. Since she and Gabriel were to be married anyway, what they'd done wasn't too awful, was it?

And she needed to tell Poppy that she meant to marry Gabriel. How the dickens was she going to do that?

The footman brought out their weekly roast beef and turnips, and she and Poppy made small talk as they ate. There had to be some way to bring up Gabriel without sending Poppy into a fit of temper.

"By the way," Poppy said as he finished off a large portion of gooseberry cream, "one of the yearlings fetched a fine price at the fair yesterday. So if you'd like a few new gowns, we should be able to manage it. Can't have you looking dowdy when you marry Pierce."

Her heart sank. "I'm not marrying Pierce."

He rose and crossed the room to pour himself a tot of brandy. "Of course you are. It's the perfect arrangement. You marry Pierce, he inherits the farm, the two of you can live here and run it together—"

"Pierce? Run the farm?" She snorted. "He can't tell the difference between a grass shoe and a frost shoe, and the only haunch he cares about is the pork he eats for Sunday dinner."

An uneasy look crossed Poppy's face. "Still, you'd have a home with him, even if you lived on the estate in Hertfordshire."

"You mean, the one he can't stand to live on himself?" She often wondered why that was. It had something to do with her aunt, Pierce's mother, but she wasn't sure what. He clearly avoided his childhood home. He did his duty by it, but no more.

"Then you'll live here and someone else will run the place," Poppy said, clearly exasperated. "It doesn't matter where you live, as long as you're together." He shot her a long look. "As long as you're taken care of."

"I can't marry him," she said softly. "He's like a brother to me. It would never work."

"It will if you give it a chance." There was a note of desperation in his voice now. "Come, lambkin, he's eager to marry you."

A curse upon Pierce and his nonsense. She should never have let him carry it so far. "Pierce is no more eager to marry me than I am him, Poppy."

He faced her with a scowl. "Then why did he propose?"

"To annoy Lord Gabriel, that's all. You know Pierce—he likes to tease."

"You're wrong, I tell you. Pierce would never—"

"Sir?" said the footman from the doorway. "There's a visitor for Miss Waverly."

She gazed at the footman in surprise.

Poppy scowled. "Who is it?"

"Lady Jarret Sharpe."

"Damned Sharpes. They're all invading us now." He drained his brandy glass. "I suppose she brought the rest of them with her, too?"

"No, sir. Only a footman."

"Send her in," Virginia said at the same time that Poppy snapped, "Tell her Miss Waverly is indisposed."

"Poppy!" Virginia jumped to her feet. "Don't you dare tell her that! Honestly, what is wrong with you? Do you want to cut me off from *every* female companion?"

He looked guilty. "Of course not. But it's Sunday, and

early besides. Why, we've barely finished eating. It's not proper."

She snorted. "As if you've ever been concerned about propriety before. She's probably here to give me instructions for home brewing. Lord Gabriel promised to have his sister-in-law help me with it, and obviously he made good on his promise."

"And got another ally to help plead his case," he grumbled. "That's the real reason she's here, to make him sound good. There's no point in that if you're marrying Pierce."

Actually, Virginia suspected that the woman was here for something else entirely. It would be just like Gabriel to send a message through one of his relations. It would have to be covert, however, since unmarried ladies weren't allowed to receive letters from gentlemen unless their families approved.

"Whatever her reason, I have a right to entertain whom I please whenever I please." She stared him down. "Unless you've decided to start keeping me prisoner here."

"Don't be a ninny," he grumbled. "I just don't think anything good can come of your associating with those Sharpes."

The footman still stood there, waiting to see the outcome of the argument. Virginia turned to him and said, "Please show Lady Jarret into the drawing room. And tell Cook to bring us some tea and lemon tarts."

As soon as the footman was gone, she headed for the door. "You needn't join us. Our talk is sure to bore you."

His eyes narrowed on her. "If you think I'm leaving you alone with any Sharpe, you're out of your mind."

She forced a shrug. "Suit yourself. But don't say I didn't warn you when we start talking about ale recipes."

Poppy poured himself another brandy, and she hid a smile. Perhaps she wouldn't have to worry about him interfering after all. With two brandies in his belly, he'd be unable to keep his eyes open. They could talk while he napped in his favorite chair.

Moments later, she breezed into the drawing room with a smile. "How lovely it is to see you again, my lady," she said, holding out her hands.

But before Lady Jarret could take them, Poppy said, "Lady Jarret," and sketched a bow. "What brings you all the way to Waverly Farm so early on a Sunday?"

If Lady Jarret noticed her grandfather's pointed remark about her chosen time for visiting, she gave no indication. "First, I came to pass on a message to you both. My husband and Gabriel were called away on a matter of family business late last night, so my brother-in-law won't be able to be here tomorrow to help you with the farm."

As Virginia sought to hide her disappointment, Poppy muttered, "I'm not surprised. The man was bound to tire of this sort of work eventually."

Fire glinted briefly in Lady Jarret's eyes before she banished it with a smile. "Actually, he wanted me to say that he expects to be here Tuesday morning, first thing. By then, they should have completed their business."

"Well then," Poppy said, "you've given the message. I'm sure you're eager to return home, so—"

"Oh no, I had another purpose for coming as well. Gabriel said your granddaughter wanted advice concerning home brewing. So I've come to talk to her about that."

"You see, Poppy?" Virginia gestured to a nearby settee. "Do take a seat, my lady."

"Please, I was just a miss until I married Jarret, and it still feels odd to be called 'my lady.' I'd prefer you call me Annabel."

"And please call me Virginia." With a furtive glance at Poppy, she added, "We may soon be family, after all."

"Over my dead body," Poppy growled.

Annabel blinked. "I beg your pardon?"

Poppy sat on the settee, making it impossible for Virginia and Annabel to sit next to each other as Virginia had planned. If Annabel *did* have a private message for her from Gabriel, Virginia was going to have a devil of a time retrieving it without Poppy noticing.

"Please excuse my grandfather's rudeness." Virginia gave Poppy a hard stare. "He doesn't approve of Lord Gabriel as a husband for me, so he's doing his best to annoy you. And me."

With a laugh, Annabel perched on a chair near the settee. "He'll have to do better than that. I live with Mrs. Plumtree, who has perfected the fine art of annoying suitors and their families. She put Mr. Masters through his paces very well when he was courting Lady Minerva."

Poppy seemed to sit a little straighter. "That's because

she has the good sense to know that a man must have more than a handsome face and a sly tongue to woo a lady."

"Yes, he must have property in Hertfordshire," Virginia retorted as she sat down across from Annabel. When the woman looked blank, Virginia added, "Poppy wants me to marry my cousin."

"Not because of the money," Poppy protested.

"No?" Virginia said archly. "You haven't given me any other good reasons."

"Lord Gabriel is a scoundrel!"

"So is Pierce. And he, too, has a handsome face and a sly tongue."

"But he cares for you," Poppy snapped.

"So does my brother-in-law," Annabel put in. "You should hear how he speaks of Virginia at home. He calls her the lively marshal of your farm. He says that your inadequate staff may march to her beat like any crack regiment, but they do it with a smile on their lips and a spring in their step."

That made Virginia go all soft and wobbly inside. "He truly said that?"

Poppy jumped up from the settee. "I'm not going to let him use you to spout his idle flattery, Lady Jarret!"

Annabel blinked. "It's not idle flattery, I assure you, sir."

It was to *him*, Virginia thought with a pang. "Please, Poppy, you're embarrassing me." She used the soft voice that usually calmed his quick temper. "I don't want my friend thinking that we're rude to guests."

He stood there sullenly. "She's no friend to you if she's here on his behalf."

Annabel smiled sweetly at Poppy. "Truly, sir, I do wish to help your granddaughter with her brewing. If you'll allow it, of course. I always think it's important for a home to have decent ale available for meals."

"Poppy likes a nice bitter ale," Virginia chimed in, "and it's difficult to find one like that in this area. All they have is mild. We used to go to London for it, but we're so busy these days, I thought it might be nice if I could make some myself. Don't you agree, Poppy?"

He glanced from Virginia to Annabel, then let out a sigh. "I suppose." Dropping back onto the settee, he crossed his arms over his chest. "Well, get on with it, then."

"If it's bitter you want," Annabel told Virginia, "then you have to get the hops right."

The tea and lemon tarts were brought in just then, so the two women talked over their refreshments. For the next half hour they discussed brewing, a subject that interested Virginia anyway. But since she was more concerned today with trying to get Poppy to fall asleep so she and Annabel could have a few moments alone, she asked some ridiculously mundane questions.

Apparently Annabel realized what she was doing, for the woman described the ale-making process in long, elaborate terms that would put any man to sleep, especially an aging one who'd just drunk two brandies.

Sure enough, after a while Poppy's head began to droop onto his chest. As soon as Virginia noticed that, she gave Annabel a speaking look. Annabel glanced over at Poppy, then nodded to show she'd understood.

They talked of hops and roasting and the advantages of using malt over barley for a few more moments. Once Poppy started to snore, Annabel said, "I've written down some instructions that I hope you'll find helpful. They contain recipes and such." She cast Virginia a meaningful glance. "But you must read *all* the instructions. They make everything clear."

Virginia nodded. Gabriel *had* sent her a private message.

Keeping an eye on Poppy, Annabel drew out a folded piece of paper. She leaned forward to hand it to Virginia, who rose a little from her chair to reach it. That was just enough to startle Poppy from his doze.

As he caught sight of the folded paper, he snatched it from Annabel. "And what is this?" he growled.

"It's brewing instructions, sir," Virginia retorted as she rose, her heart in her throat.

He opened the paper and scanned it. Then a sheepish look crossed his face. "Oh. It *is* brewing instructions."

Virginia shot Annabel a quizzical glance, but the lady's gaze was fixed on him, her eyes full of worry. Poppy started to hand the sheet to Virginia, then thought to turn the paper over.

A scowl darkened his brow. He turned to Annabel. "It's time for you to leave, Lady Jarret."

As Annabel rose, Virginia reached for the piece of paper he was glaring at. "Poppy, I believe that's for me."

"It is indeed. And we'll discuss it as soon as Lady Jarret is gone." With that, he pocketed it, then went to the door and called for the footman.

Annabel came up to press Virginia's hand. "I'm sure we'll meet again soon."

"So am I," Virginia said, with an extra dose of emphasis for her grandfather. She was dying to know what was on that piece of paper. If he thought he could keep it from her, he was mad.

As soon as the footman entered, Poppy instructed him to see that Lady Jarret was escorted safely off the premises. But he stopped the woman as she was heading out the door with the footman.

"I have a message for your brother-in-law," Poppy said. "Tell him that if he shows up on my property on Tuesday morning, I will shoot him. Is that clear?"

Annabel's eyes went wide. "Very clear, sir."

The minute she was gone, Virginia rounded on her grandfather. "Have you gone mad? Why would you threaten such a thing? He's done nothing to warrant it!"

Drawing out the letter, Poppy read aloud, " 'My dearest Virginia—' " He glanced at her. "The damned fellow thinks he can use your Christian name now? When did *that* start?"

She refused to answer him when he was in such a temper. She just folded her arms over her waist and glared at him.

With a scowl, he continued reading. " 'Forgive me for not keeping to my promise.' And when was he making promises to you, young lady?"

She fought the urge to blush. "We went riding on Friday, remember?"

Poppy cast her a baleful glance, then went back to the letter. "'But since you said you needed more time to convince your grandfather to accept my suit, you have it now.'"

So much for breaking it to Poppy gently.

Poppy glowered at her. "Did you agree to *marry* the damned scoundrel?"

She squared her shoulders. "I did."

"You are not marrying that arse!"

Forcing herself to remain calm, she tried logic. "You've seen how hard he's worked all week. Admit it—he's proved perfectly well that he's not the soft, indolent noble you took him for."

"All he's proved is that he can play a role when there's something he wants. He'll do anything to gain his fortune."

Her temper flared. "He offered to give up that fortune if I'd marry him."

Poppy snorted. "As I said, he'll do anything to get what he wants—lie, cheat—"

"Is it so hard to believe that a man might just want me for myself?" She choked back tears as years of feeling unappreciated welled up inside her. "Is it really that impossible to comprehend?"

Her grandfather looked as if he'd been kicked in the gut. "No!" He came close. "That's not what I—"

"That's what it sounds like." Tears ran down her cheeks. "You can't fathom that a lord of his station and family wealth might truly want me. That's why you were so eager to promote Pierce's proposal. Because what man would want me otherwise, without lots of money to tempt him?"

"Oh, lambkin, no." Grabbing her in his arms, he held her close. "It's not like that at all. It's because you're so precious that I worry. I want you to find a man who deserves you. A man of good character."

"He *is* a man of good character," she whispered. "You won't even give him a chance."

"How can you say that when he killed Roger?"

She lifted her tearstained face to him. "That was an accident, Poppy, and you know it. He's deeply sorry about what happened to Roger."

Poppy turned mulish. "What kind of man bullies his supposed friend into risking death?"

"You don't know that he bullied him."

"I certainly do."

The icy certainty in his voice froze her blood. "How could you?" She slipped free of his arms. "You weren't there."

He glanced away. "But I know what happened, all the same."

"How? What do you know about that night?"

He stiffened. "Enough. You'll have to trust me on this."

"I see." Her anger sparked. "You won't talk about it, *he* won't talk about it, and you both expect me just to meekly accept your nonsense and choose between you—is that it?"

He stood there stoically, saying nothing.

"Right. Well, it seems to me that if you won't say what you know, it's because you're protecting Roger's memory. You certainly wouldn't hide the truth if it meant that Lord Gabriel was at fault." She thrust out her chin. "And from what I know of his character, he's probably hiding the truth for the same reason: to protect Roger's memory. That speaks well of him—not ill."

"Damn it, girl, that's not what—"

When he broke off, she lifted an eyebrow. "Feel free to correct my mistaken impression at any time."

He muttered an oath. "Why won't you believe me when I say the truth is more complicated than you think? He isn't the man he seems."

"Yet you give me no proof of that." She held out her hand. "I'd like my letter now, please."

He hesitated, then handed her the paper. She scanned it swiftly. The part Poppy hadn't read aloud said, "I'm counting the hours until I see you again, sweetheart." It was signed only, "Your Gabriel."

With her heart full, she tucked it into her apron pocket to read again when she was alone. Gabriel had spoken no words of love, but she hadn't expected that. And it didn't matter. He was offering her what Poppy wanted to deny her—a future with a man she loved.

Even if that love wasn't returned, it was better than the sort of life she would have with Pierce. *If* Pierce was even sincere, which she doubted. And she truly believed that in time Gabriel would grow to love her, would feel secure enough in her love to tell her his secrets. She had to believe it. Because she'd given herself to him now, and the thought of a future without him was too bleak to contemplate.

When she turned for the door, Poppy said, "I mean it, lambkin. If he comes here Tuesday morning, I'll shoot him."

She didn't answer, because it didn't matter. Gabriel would never let a threat like that deter him. Somehow he would find a way for them to be together.

If she didn't find it first.

GABE, JARRET, AND Pinter were allowed to attend the entirety of the inquest, held in a small, upstairs room at the coroner's office in George Street. Gabe wondered if they would have been better off being spared it. The scent of death fogged the air, made even worse by the summer heat and the sight of Benny's body . . .

Gabe shuddered. He'd been present at Roger's inquest, too, but only briefly as a witness, and he hadn't looked at Roger. Here he *had* to look at Benny, who lay swollen and practically unrecognizable on a table. There was no other way he could grasp what the coroner was pointing out about Benny's injuries.

Gabe had never been forced to see a body so decayed, and he hoped he never had to again. It gave new meaning to the idea of staring Death in the face.

He began to understand why Virginia had been so angry at him for his Angel of Death role. In thumbing his nose at Death, he'd somehow glorified it as well. And there was nothing glorious about a man's body slowly disintegrating in the cloying warmth of a coroner's office while his family worried over where he was.

Just as there was nothing admirable in risking life and limb in some sort of futile battle with Death. If Death came for you, there was nothing you could do to stop it. Benny had proved that.

The inquest was blessedly short. The coroner easily determined that Benny had died of a gunshot wound to the chest; the ball was lodged between two of Benny's ribs.

The local authorities had delayed the inquest in hopes that Pinter might be able to identify the body for certain as Benny's. Fortunately, despite the amount of decay, Pinter was able to oblige. When he'd interviewed Benny months before, he'd noticed the unusual ring the man wore to commemorate one of the few races he'd won as a former jockey. The body bore that same ring.

The fact that it was still on Benny's finger made Gabe wonder why the murderer hadn't stolen it. This hadn't been highway robbery.

Beyond the information that Benny had definitely been shot to death, the inquest told them little else. No one could determine for certain whether the shooting was accidental, perhaps done unwittingly by a hunter. A couple of witnesses came forth to testify that they'd seen Benny in town two and a half weeks before his body was found, but none of them had seen him with anyone. And no one knew why he had been in town. He'd stayed in an inn for a single night, saying only that he was headed home.

After the inquest, Pinter convinced the constable to take them out to where the body had been found by a boy looking for firewood. Pinter said he wanted to make sure that no crucial evidence had been overlooked in the constable's haste to get the body into town for an inquest.

After a few moments of tramping through heavy overgrowth, the constable stopped in a small clearing he'd marked earlier with a stake. If they hadn't known that a body had once been there, they wouldn't have guessed it now.

Pinter gazed about them. "Surely Benny didn't come this far into the woods himself," he told the constable. "Sunlight barely penetrates the trees here. What purpose could he have for being so deep in the forest?"

"Hunting perhaps?" the constable remarked.

"Benny was never much of a hunter," Gabe said. "He was strictly a horse man. He left the shooting to others. And why would he stop to hunt while on a trip to visit a friend?"

Jarret made a wide circuit of the area in which they stood. He knelt to pick something up, then rose to show them a piece of fabric. "This was caught on some scrub. It's stained with blood, and it matches the clothing Benny was wearing at the inquest. It looks as if he might have been dragged here after he was killed."

"If so, it seems unlikely that the shooting was accidental," Pinter said. "At the very least, someone sought to hide the body. At the worst, he was murdered."

Gabe's unease deepened into a chilling fear. "Pinter, do you think this could have anything to do with Mother's and Father's deaths? What if Benny saw something back then, and their killer knew it?"

"Then the killer would have murdered him before now," Pinter said. "It's been nineteen years."

"Unless the killer got nervous about our asking questions."

Pinter let out a long breath. "Honestly, I don't know what to think. It's odd that Benny chose to leave his home after I spoke with him, and odd that he would die in a shooting. But it might merely be a series of coincidences. We need more information."

"Someone has to know more about why he traveled to Manchester," Jarret said. "If not any of the townsfolk here or there, then Benny's family. One of us should stay in town a while longer to ask questions. I can't do it—I have to be back at the brewery tomorrow for a meeting, but what about you, Pinter?"

"I have a week or so before I need to return to London," Pinter said.

"We have to send a letter to the Mays, anyway," Jarret said, "so they can come claim his body. While you await their arrival, you can ask questions here, then question them when they arrive."

"If I have any time left afterward, I'll travel up to Manchester," Pinter said. "Now that a death is involved, some of the people I questioned before might be more forthcoming with information. It's worth a try, at any rate."

"Excellent idea." Jarret glanced at Gabe. "What about you? Are you staying?"

"I can't. I made a promise to Virginia."

"What sort of promise?"

"That I'd ask her grandfather for her hand formally

tomorrow morning. If we leave now, I can still arrive home in enough time to be there at first light."

"Then by all means, we should go," Jarret said with a broad smile. "You can handle it on your own, can't you, Pinter?"

"Certainly."

"Let us know what you learn." Gabe hated to leave, but he meant to keep his promise to Virginia, no matter what.

Still, he dreaded the journey home with Jarret. His brother had spent half the inquest watching Gabe with concern, and Gabe was in no mood to endure that same scrutiny for the next several hours.

As soon as they got started, Jarret said, "Have you ever been to an inquest before?"

"Only Roger's," Gabe said tersely.

"This one must have been nearly as difficult, given your childhood friendship with Benny."

That was an understatement. "If you don't mind, I'd rather not talk about it. I need to sleep. I didn't get much last night in that noisy inn, and I have to rise early tomorrow."

Jarret nodded. "Probably a good idea for both of us."

Thank God. Gabe leaned against the squabs and closed his eyes, but sleep was impossible. He couldn't get the image of Benny's bloated body out of his mind. The stench of it seemed to cling to him, and he wondered if it would cling for days—if people would smell it on him and see the horror lurking in his soul.

For the first time in his life, he really felt like the Angel of Death. And he did not like that feeling.

Chapter Eighteen

Virginia and her grandfather hadn't spoken since yesterday, keeping out of each other's way as if by mutual agreement. She'd even taken her meals in her room, which he hadn't questioned.

Thankfully, he hadn't questioned her writing to Pierce, either. After her conversation with Poppy yesterday, she'd sent an express to her cousin saying only, *I need you.* He had to set Poppy straight once and for all about their not marrying. The rascal had raised Poppy's hopes, and now he must help her dash them.

But since Pierce wouldn't receive the express until today, he might not arrive by tomorrow morning. And with night falling now, she grew anxious. She needed a plan for when Gabriel showed up.

Would Poppy really meet him with a rifle? Even if he did, would he actually use it? She couldn't imagine that, but neither could she imagine him backing down.

Nor could she imagine Gabriel doing so, even when staring down the barrel of a gun. The man was as stubborn as Poppy, and more reckless. No telling what either of them would do if forced to confront each other.

How could Poppy be so blind? Hadn't he seen how much interest Gabriel had taken in the farm? Granted, Gabriel wouldn't inherit it, which meant that eventually she and he would have to leave, but that might be a long time off, and in the meantime Gabriel could be a great help to him.

As long as he's not off getting himself killed in a race.

She pushed that thought from her mind. Dwelling on it would only increase her doubts, and she was determined to put those to rest. Marrying Gabriel was what she wanted, racing or no.

So she needed to warn him off before Poppy did something daft. Annabel would tell him of Poppy's threat, but that wouldn't stop Gabriel from coming here. Perhaps she could slip out at 7:30 tomorrow morning and waylay him on the road—

A knock came at the door and she tensed. "Who is it?"

"It's Molly, Miss. The general is wanting a word with you in his study."

She sighed. She should have known she couldn't avoid him forever. "Tell him I'll be right there."

When Virginia got to Poppy's study, she was surprised to find him sitting at his desk with his head in his hands. He looked quite weary—and when he lifted his head to stare at her, his eyes held an uncharacteristic bleakness.

"Close the door and have a seat, lambkin."

The softness in his voice made her instantly wary. She did as he bade, but he didn't speak right away. He just stared past her as if contemplating a ghost.

"Poppy?"

His gaze finally went to her, and he stiffened his spine. "I've thought and thought about it, but I can see no way around it. You were right yesterday. Much as I hate it, I can't keep secrets from you when you're letting that scoundrel Sharpe wriggle into your heart."

She swallowed hard. "What sort of secrets?"

"You asked how I know what happened that night. Well, I'll tell you." With a haunted look on his face, he took a long breath. "Your brother came home and told me about it before he went out to face Sharpe."

The words stunned her. "You knew that Roger was going to race, and you didn't even try to stop him?"

"No!" He picked up a letter opener, turning it round and round in his hands. "He didn't tell me specifics. He came in and said, 'If a man agrees to a wager while he's in his cups, is there any gentlemanly way he can get out of it? Or does he have to see it through?'

"I thought he was talking about card wagers, and that he'd gambled more than he could afford. And I didn't want the lad thinking he could agree to a bet, then cry off just because he'd been drinking. It was dishonest and dishonorable."

Pain carved heavy lines into his weathered features. "So I told him only a blackguard reneged on a wager. If he couldn't hold his liquor, he shouldn't be gambling. The right thing to do was to stand up and pay his debts."

Oh, Poppy. Her mind reeled. She could easily imagine what Roger would have thought about those words from the great cavalry general. Her brother had always wanted to impress their larger-than-life grandfather, and was angry that his swaggering about town with a marquess's son and a duke's son didn't accomplish that. He would have taken Poppy's advice to heart, while balking at sharing the whole story. Why risk another quarrel?

And there had been many quarrels between Roger and Poppy, about Roger's gambling and drinking and his late hours.

How could she have forgotten that? She'd been dwelling on the brother she missed desperately, whom she'd made into a saint. But he'd never been a saint. He'd been an orphan struggling to find his place in the world, with a grandfather whom he'd thought he'd disappointed.

Poppy's gaze shifted to her. "I swear, I had no idea he was speaking of some idiotic race where he could kill himself, or I would never have—"

"It's all right, Poppy," she said softly. "You couldn't have known."

All these years, he'd held this guilt inside him. Gabriel had said, *He needs someone to blame, so he blames me. But that doesn't mean he has a reason for it.*

He was right.

"But I should have pressed him on it," Poppy said. "I should have made him tell me what happened." He curled his hand around the letter opener. "Instead, I asked him how much he owed and to whom." His voice hardened. "That's all I cared about—the money. When he said it was nothing much and not to worry about it, I let it go. I was relieved, to tell the truth. I thought it was a sign he was finally taking responsibility for his recklessness."

He let out a heavy breath. "Why didn't I press him? If he had said it was a race at Turnham Green between him and Sharpe—"

"You mustn't torture yourself over it." She leaned across the desk to take the letter opener from him, then caught his tense hand in hers. "You were trying to teach him to do the right thing."

"Was I?" His eyes were full of ancient remorse. "Or was I just embarrassed at the idea of my grandson looking less than he was in front of his lofty friends?"

He got to his feet and began to pace. "My last words to him were about how he had to be a man. What kind of monster sends his own grandson to his death because he doesn't want to be shamed in front of a lot of idiots?"

She rose to go to his side. "You didn't send him to his death. You gave the only advice you could give without having all the facts. That wasn't your fault—it was his."

Poppy rounded on her, seizing her shoulders in his hands. "But now do you understand? I *know* Sharpe took advantage of your brother's drunken state to get him to agree to that fool wager."

"It could just as easily have been Roger who made it."

"Then why did your brother say, 'If a man agrees to a wager'? That implies accepting a challenge. Sharpe laid down the challenge, and Roger agreed to it. Otherwise why regret it later? Men regret things they've been bullied into, not things they did themselves."

"That's not true, Poppy. Men regret all sorts of things they do when they're drunk. You know that as well as I."

But *If a man agrees to a wager* definitely sounded as if Roger had accepted the challenge.

"The point is," Poppy said, "a man of good character doesn't bully his drunken friend into doing something that might kill him."

"You don't know that he bullied him."

"Yes, I do. I know it in my heart."

She gazed sadly at him. His heart. His guilt-stricken, grief-laden heart that couldn't let go of that night. Gabriel was right—it was time to put the past to rest. It had caused enough pain already.

The trouble was, neither man could let go of it. They kept gnawing on that same old bone, worrying it to death. And as long as the truth of what had happened lay shrouded in secrecy, as long as they kept blaming themselves, they would never stop.

Someone had to make it stop. Someone had to clear the air. And it looked like that someone would have to be her.

What if you learn terrible things about Gabriel? What if the truth only makes everything worse?

No, she couldn't believe that. The Gabriel she'd come to know wouldn't bully a man into anything. It wasn't in his nature. He was a good man; she knew that as surely as she knew that she loved him.

So she had only one choice. She couldn't wait until morning, when something tragic might happen once Gabriel arrived. If she slipped out tonight, she could ride over to Halstead Hall and catch Gabriel. With a full moon, she shouldn't have any trouble on the road.

She had to impress upon him the importance of being honest with Poppy. It was the only way to mend the rift between the two men, the only way to gain Poppy's permission to marry. For though she was of age and didn't need that permission, she really wanted it.

Once she talked to Gabriel, he might be able to persuade Mrs. Plumtree to come here *with* him in the morning. Poppy wouldn't dare shoot him in front of Mrs. Plumtree. He seemed to like the woman.

Yes, that plan just might work.

GABE STARED BLANKLY out the window as Jarret's carriage headed up the drive to Halstead Hall. His brother had managed to sleep, but Gabe hadn't.

Unfortunately, they still had a long night ahead of them. Despite the late hour, the family would expect a report about Benny. And before Jarret went off to bed with his wife, Gabe must find out from Annabel whether her visit to Virginia had been successful.

Too bad he couldn't just ride over to Waverly Farm and sneak in to see her. But it would be nearly impossible to get inside the house without being detected, and the last thing he needed was a midnight confrontation with the general.

The very fact that he was willing to risk it showed how far he'd fallen. When had that happened? He'd bedded plenty of women through the years, but none of them had invaded his thoughts every waking moment. None of them had ever made him yearn and ache for them, body and soul.

In bedding her, he'd set off a craving that intensified the longer he was away from her. Especially after his day in Death's den. She made him want Life, in all its color and beauty.

The carriage stopped in front of Halstead Hall, rousing Jarret. When they climbed out, one of the grooms came up to tell Gabe, "My lord, you had better look in on Flying Jane."

His heart dropped into his stomach. "Why?"

With a furtive glance at Jarret, the groom murmured, "You really must see for yourself."

Jarret asked, "Do you want me to go with you?"

"No, Annabel will probably be waiting up for you, and Gran, too." They'd sent a rider on ahead to alert the family to their arrival. "I'll be in shortly."

As he followed the groom back, he asked, "Is the horse ill?"

"No, my lord. You have a visitor, and she doesn't want anyone to know she's here except you."

That was all the preparation Gabe got before they entered the old stable and he saw Virginia.

Shock and delight froze him in his tracks. How was she here? *Why* was she here? How the hell had she known he was aching to see her?

Then she turned toward him, and he no longer cared why.

He barely noticed the groom slipping out and closing

the door. All he could see was her, and her smile welcoming him home.

He strode up to catch her face in his hands, holding her for a hard, urgent kiss that she returned with great fervor.

Had he thought he needed her, craved her?

He was *starved* for her—the way a man in a dungeon was starved for light. Because she was his light. She was warmth and beauty and sweet succor, everything he needed to banish what he'd seen in Woburn.

She tore free. "Gabriel, we have to talk."

"Not now." He dragged his mouth down her neck, fragrant with lavender, and tongued her throat. "If you had any idea what I'd gone through today . . ."

The image of Benny rose in his mind, and he buried it beneath the desire that had him by the ballocks.

As he fumbled with the ties of her gown, her breath came heavy and hot against his cheek. "I thought you were traveling on a matter of family business."

"Yes, an awful matter of family business. I'll tell you about it later—right now I need you too badly. I missed you. You have no idea how much."

"I missed you, too. But the groom—"

"Is gone. He won't come back." He pulled her gown off her shoulders. "No one else knows you're here."

"Good," she said with a shy smile. She tugged at his coat and he pulled it off, then she went to work on the buttons of his waistcoat.

He got her gown open enough to bare one lovely breast. "You got my message?" he murmured just before he closed his mouth over her sweet, tender nipple.

She gasped, and the pleasure echoed through his every vein, sinew, and bone. She still belonged to him. She'd be his forever. And suddenly forever didn't seem nearly as frightening as before.

"I did . . . " She clutched his head to her breast. "That's why I came here . . . Poppy said he'd shoot you if you showed up tomorrow."

"Then we'll elope." He backed her toward the nearest wall. "Tonight. But first . . ."

He opened his breeches and drawers. As he hoisted her up to straddle his waist, her eyes went wide. He knew he shouldn't take her like some whore in an alley. But the need to drive out the chill in his soul, to be enveloped in her warmth, was so powerful, he couldn't help himself.

"Sorry, sweetheart, but I can't move slow and easy tonight." He worked a hand between them and into the slit in her drawers. She was slick and hot, as eager as he was, and his cock stiffened even more. "I have to have you now, right here. Will you let me?"

Desire flared in her face, and he saw the vixen's smile he so adored. "I'm already letting you."

"Thank God," he choked out, and entered her with one deep thrust.

"*Gabriel* . . ." she gasped against his mouth. "Oh . . . sweet . . . *Lord*. It's amazing."

Amazing was definitely the word. With her silky thighs bracketing his hips and her delicate arms clasping him about the neck, she cocooned him in a lush tropic of female heat. Life at its most basic; a counter to the ice of Death.

He drove into her in strokes that he feared were too rough, but when she undulated against him, he knew it would be all right. She was a wonder, his wife-to-be.

"My sweet Virginia," he whispered. "You have me utterly enthralled."

"Really?"

"Can't you see how you've addled my brain? Why else would I be taking you here like a wild animal?"

"I like it when you're wild," she whispered. "At least when we're . . . you know." She rubbed her breasts against his waistcoat, and he wished he'd peeled it off. And his shirt. And her gown.

Later. If they eloped tonight, they could make love in the carriage all the way to Gretna Green.

For now, his instinct was telling him to swive her senseless. Or perhaps he just wanted to be senseless himself, to be taken out of himself by her. By *this*.

He tried to hold back his release, but it was impossible. She felt too good, and he needed it too much. He couldn't even finger her in this position, but her moans told him she was feeling *something*. And when he shifted his angle to drub her little button of flesh over and over with each thrust, she dug her fingernails into his shoulders.

"Oh, yes." She tightened her legs about his hips. "Oh, Gabriel . . . Please . . . oh, please . . . I want . . . I want . . ."

"Whatever you want . . . is yours." He thrust into her in quickening strokes that brought him right over the edge.

She followed him over with a cry that he muffled with his mouth. And as she shuddered and shook, and he pumped his seed into her, he kept hearing, *I want . . . I want . . .*

So did he. Oh, how he wanted. He wanted far more than he'd realized. He wanted her to know every dark secret in his heart, every bit of the past he'd buried. He wanted her to know the real him.

The unexpected thought terrified him. If he gave in to *that* desire, he could lose her. And suddenly the thing he wanted most of all was not to lose her.

Chapter Nineteen

Virginia felt bereft when Gabriel withdrew from her and her legs came down. The words "I love you" were on the tip of her tongue, but something held her back. She couldn't bear to not have him return her feelings. Perhaps it would be easier once he was her husband.

As Gabriel left her arms, he looked embarrassed. "I didn't mean to be so rough," he said as he fastened up his drawers, then his trousers. "You must think me more of a scoundrel than ever."

"If that's what you're like when you're a scoundrel," she said lightly, "then thank God for scoundrels."

He looked startled. Then he flashed her the grin that always made her quiver. "Enjoyed that, did you?"

She smoothed back an errant lock of his hair. "Very much. Though it did take me by surprise."

"I know. I just . . ." He turned her around so he could fasten up her gown. "I just needed to forget for a while what I saw today."

"And what was that?"

"Death."

She pivoted to stare at him, the harsh word shivering across her skin. "What do you mean?"

"Jarret and I traveled up north to view an inquest. Not since Roger's have I—"

"You were at Roger's inquest?"

He stiffened. "Of course. He died racing me. There are official rules for such things. All of us who'd been present had to answer questions and give testimony. Your grandfather appeared, as did other witnesses."

Did that mean Gabriel had been questioned publicly about how the race had come about? And wouldn't Poppy have heard that testimony? Because then he would know who'd laid down the challenge, yet he'd acted as if he didn't. But no one else had ever claimed to have heard the truth, either.

Gabriel went on, clearly eager to leave the subject behind. "This inquest was a different matter entirely. Benny was found after being outdoors in the weather for a while."

She shuddered. She could imagine how awful that must have been. "Was he a friend?"

"You might say that. He was head groom here at Halstead Hall until shortly after my parents died."

In a few terse words, he explained that over the past few months he and his siblings had been investigating their parents' deaths. They hadn't told anyone because they wanted to be sure of the truth first. That was why he hadn't allowed Annabel to reveal to her grandfather the reason for his sudden trip.

He told Virginia of their attempts to question the

family's head groom and how that had led to their being informed of the man's possible murder.

"I've never witnessed Death quite like that. After being left in the woods for a couple of weeks, Benny's body was . . . was . . ."

"Unspeakable?" she finished softly.

He nodded. "I hadn't seen him in nineteen years. After our parents died, Gran took us into town to live and Oliver kept the estate closed up, so most of the staff was let go. But I wouldn't have known him even if I'd seen him every day. His face . . ." A ragged breath escaped him. "It wasn't easy to look at. We were only able to identify him by a ring he'd worn when Pinter had questioned him."

"I'm sorry you had to go through that."

"I'm not. It finally impressed upon me that I don't want to die." He leveled a bleak gaze on her. "I don't want to end up broken and bleeding in some field somewhere. I don't want to be left in the ground to rot before my time.

"But I don't know how to stop it from happening. If Celia doesn't marry, then racing is all I have. And if I let fear of death make me cautious, I can't win."

The fact that he shared his fears touched her. "Surely you can make money some other way than by racing. You could bring Flying Jane to Waverly Farm. If Poppy or one of your brothers could be persuaded to lend you the entrance fee for that first race—"

He snorted. "Your grandfather isn't going to give me money, and you know it. And my brothers don't have lots to spare for a risky investment. I wouldn't feel right asking them."

"But it would be just this once. And if you won a race with her, they'd get their money back with interest."

With a rueful smile, he reached up to tuck a lock of hair behind her ear. "As you said last week, that's a lot of ifs."

"But it's something. In the meantime, you could help Poppy race his horses and run the stud farm."

"So that Pierce can inherit it all when your grandfather dies? Where will that leave us?"

She swallowed. "At least it won't leave you dead. Besides, why are you so sure that Celia won't marry?"

"You did *meet* my sister, didn't you?" he said dryly.

"She's very pretty."

"It's not her looks I'm worried about. It's her strong disinclination to marry."

"She seemed very eager to champion you." She cupped his cheek. "I'm sure she'll do the right thing when the time comes. Don't borrow trouble, Gabriel. It will all work out."

"Ever the sunny optimist, aren't you?" He pressed her hand to his lips. "You're assuming that your grandfather will even let me within a mile of your place. He already said he wants to shoot me. Are you willing to elope?" he asked, a hopeful note in his voice. "We could leave tonight."

"I'd prefer that you settle your differences with him beforehand."

He pulled away from her, then went to pick his coat up off the floor. "How the blazes am I to do that?"

"He needs to know the truth about the night when you and Roger made the wager. And he needs to hear it from you."

His jaw went taut. "You mean *you* need to hear it from me," he snapped. "You won't let it alone."

"That's not true," she said steadily. "I know in my heart that you're a good man. But Poppy needs to be sure you're a man of good character. He has to feel you're worthy of me, and that means knowing the truth. Otherwise he'll never—"

The door to the stable swung open. "Good God, Gabe. Are you ever going to come—" Lord Jarret stopped short, glancing from Virginia to Gabriel. "Sorry, old chap. I assumed you were still coddling your Thoroughbred." His gaze shot to the coat in Gabriel's hand. "I . . . um . . . didn't mean to interrupt. Annabel said she needed to talk to you, and I guess that's probably moot now. I'll just leave you two to . . . whatever you were doing."

"No need." Gabriel donned his coat. "Virginia and I were merely discussing our elopement. It seems her grandfather is opposed to the marriage and is out for my blood, so we're going to eliminate that problem by hastening to Gretna Green."

"Gabriel." He was running from everything, from the truth, from the past. He had to stop. "You know perfectly well that I didn't agree—"

"If you're planning on an elopement," Lord Jarret said, "you'd best come inside. Gran needs to hear this."

Looping an arm about Virginia's waist, Gabriel led her toward the door.

"Listen to me—" she began.

"How long do you think it will take us?" Gabriel asked his brother, pointedly ignoring her. They proceeded to discuss the logistics of the elopement as the three of them crossed the courtyard.

Perish the man. Why wouldn't he listen?

They'd entered the house and were headed for the drawing room, when they were accosted in the hall by his grandmother.

"What the devil is taking you so— Oh." Mrs. Plumtree spotted Virginia and smiled. "Good evening, Miss Waverly. Annabel said that your grandfather threatened to shoot my grandson if he went to Waverly Farm to propose marriage tomorrow. Are you here to warn Gabe?"

"Actually—"

"We're eloping, Gran," Gabriel broke in. "I know what you said about no elopements, but—"

"No, no, my boy, you go on and elope," Mrs. Plumtree said cheerily. "Just make sure it's legal. Make them give you something written—none of that havey-cavey Scottish nonsense about your word being good enough."

"Of course," Gabriel said.

"But I don't want—" Virginia began.

"What can I do to help?" Mrs. Plumtree went on. "If the general is anything like me, he'll be up in a few hours, and you'll want to be well under way before he discovers that Miss Waverly has gone. He'll probably come here first, and we'll stall him, which will gain you some time."

Virginia was growing annoyed. "I really don't think—"

Lord Jarret said, "The phaeton won't be as comfortable for traveling, but it'll be quicker. You can take my coach, but the coachman hasn't had a chance to rest from our journey. Then again, neither have you."

"Stop it, all of you!" Virginia cried. "I don't *want* to elope!"

Muttering a low oath, Gabriel tightened his arm about her waist like a manacle.

"You don't want to marry my grandson?" Mrs. Plumtree asked, casting a pointed glance at Gabriel's intimate grip on her.

Virginia colored. "Of course I want to marry him. But I want to do it right. I want Poppy's permission."

Mrs. Plumtree clucked her tongue. "Given what your grandfather told me the night of our dinner, he's unlikely to give it. His exact words were, 'One way or the other, I'll make sure that she *never* marries your scoundrel of a grandson.' And if he's talking about shooting Gabe, it doesn't sound as if he's changed his mind."

"You're damned right I haven't changed my mind!" cried yet another voice from the doorway.

Sweet Lord. Poppy, with a footman trailing him.

"I'm sorry, madam," the footman said, "but General Waverly refused to wait in the—"

"It's all right, John," Mrs. Plumtree said.

Virginia eyed her grandfather with concern. He looked harried and tired, his hair sticking up everywhere. "What are you doing here, Poppy?"

He strode up to her with a scowl. "After our discussion, I couldn't sleep. I went to your room, thinking I'd talk to you again about it, but you were gone." He shot Gabriel a murderous glance. "How did you convince my granddaughter to do something so blasted idiotic as to ride over here in the middle of the night? Anything could have happened to her. She could have been accosted on the road or lost her way in the dark—"

"He had nothing to do with it," Virginia cut in. "I came here because you were talking about shooting him in the morning."

"She came to warn him," Mrs. Plumtree pointed out, a gleam in her eyes. "You can't blame her for that. It speaks well of the girl."

Poppy turned his glower on Mrs. Plumtree. "The only thing it speaks well of, woman, is your machinations. And I don't blame Virginia. I blame you and your blasted family, and their interference in matters that aren't their concern." He turned to scowl at Lord Jarret. "Next time you send your wife to my house passing messages behind my back, sir, you'd better be prepared for trouble."

"I did not send my wife to your house," Lord Jarret protested.

"That was my doing." Gabriel tugged Virginia closer. "I wanted Virginia to know I'd be back to marry her as soon as possible."

"She's Miss Waverly to you, boy. And you'll marry her over my dead body." Poppy held out his arm. "Come, Virginia, we're going home."

Virginia gazed up at Gabriel and said softly, "Tell him. Tell him now."

He stiffened, then scowled at her. "This is not the time."

"There's no better time. You said on that night we waltzed that you wanted to make amends to my family. Well, this is your chance. He needs to hear it."

She could see him withdrawing, see him pulling into himself like a turtle into its protective shell, but she persisted anyway. "Make him understand."

"I won't discuss this *here*, damn it!"

"Discuss what?" Mrs. Plumtree asked.

"Then I'm going home with him." Tearing herself from his grip, she moved a few feet away. She had to force Gabriel's hand. "You have to choose. Tell him the truth or watch me leave."

She didn't know if she could hold to that, but she had to try. His refusal to face the past would only poison their love, and an elopement wouldn't solve anything.

Something flickered deep in his eyes. Anger. And regret. "Don't ask me to do this."

Why must he be so stubborn? Without a word, she turned and walked toward her grandfather.

"Damn it, Virginia, ask me to do anything but that!"

The pain in his words made her heart twist in her chest, but she kept walking.

"I *can't* tell you the truth," he ground out.

"You mean you won't."

"I *can't.* Because I don't know what it is."

That halted her. Not sure she'd heard him right, she faced him. "What do you mean?"

Though the others didn't know what she was talking about, they seemed to hold their breaths, as did she, waiting for his answer.

He spiked his hand through his hair, then let out a foul curse. "I don't actually know what happened that night. I was so drunk that I have no memory of it." His breathing sounded harsh in the sudden stillness. "People have always assumed I didn't speak of it either to hide my culpability or to protect Roger's memory. But the truth is, I don't *know* which of us laid down the challenge. I never have."

Her mind whirled. "How can that be?"

He let out a harsh laugh. "Have you no idea how Roger and I were back then? We spent our evenings with our heads in tankards of ale."

"Many a young man does, Gabe," Lord Jarret offered.

Gabriel scowled at his brother. "So much that he utterly forgets if he caused his best friend's death?" He shot her a hard glance. "You said your grandfather needed to know if I was a man of good character. I can't tell him."

His voice grew choked. "All I remember is Roger quarreling with Lyons. The duke left, and Roger and I drank ourselves into oblivion. I don't remember leaving the tavern, I don't remember the ride home, and I bloody well don't remember making that bloody wager!"

He paced in agitation. "There's nothing in my memory between the time we began drinking heavily and the time I awoke midmorning to find Roger standing at the foot of my bed saying, 'Well, old chap, are we doing this or not?'"

"You didn't even ask him what he was talking about?" she whispered.

"Of course, I asked him!" He whirled on her, his voice so full of anger that she backed away out of reflex.

He noticed and went pale. When he continued, it was in a carefully controlled voice that was more chilling than his anger. "He said, 'You know, the race.' Then he got that smug look on his face that he always got when he'd bested me and said, 'You don't remember our wager.'

"And would I admit it? Oh, no, I would never admit to Roger that I couldn't hold my liquor. That I didn't know what the bloody hell he was talking about. That would make me appear a fool."

Her heart broke to see his pain.

He glanced away from her. "It was enough for me to know that we'd agreed to a bet. Because every gentleman knows that if you make a wager, in your cups or not, you stick to it."

Reminded of what Poppy had said, she gave him a furtive glance, but he was held rapt by Gabriel's story. "So you just went with him like some young fool?" her grandfather asked.

"Exactly like some young fool. He said, 'Well, let's get on with it. I'm going to win this time, Sharpe,' and I dragged myself out of bed and went out to saddle my horse. I didn't care where the race was or what it involved. I just cared about beating him." His voice was bitter.

"Because he always had to beat you," Lord Jarret said softly.

It was true, she remembered. Their rivalry had not been one-sided. Roger would come home claiming that Gabriel had somehow bewitched his horses, or Gabriel had won a card game because he had the devil's own luck.

And she'd said those very words to Gabriel at the race they'd run. She winced.

Gabriel's gaze was distant, as if he saw it all again. "When it became apparent where we were headed, I had a moment of sanity. I knew that the course in Turnham Green was too dangerous; I'd seen other men get hurt running it."

He swallowed convulsively. "But we'd already dragged Lyons from his bed to judge the outcome of the race, and I wasn't about to back out of it in front of them both. Better to kill myself than do that, right?" His voice turned icy, remote. "Better to kill my best friend."

"You didn't kill him, Gabriel," she said softly, unable to take any more.

"Are you sure?" His eyes glittered at her. "Because I'm not. Your grandfather says I got him drunk and bullied him into running the race—and that's very possible. I might have goaded him into it. I might have called him a coward. I might even have threatened him. We'll *never know.*"

He came up to her, his face as dead and cold as his tone. "But we know one thing for sure. I was too proud to admit that I didn't remember. I was too arrogant to back out, or even just let my best friend win. Because when I raced, then by God, I had to win, even if it meant . . ."

His breath caught in his throat. "So there's my character for you. The general is right, Virginia. I don't deserve you."

"I don't believe that," she whispered.

He stared her down. "Don't you? Then why did you press so hard to make me bare my soul? And don't say it was for your grandfather. We both know it was for you, so *you* could know if I was a man of 'good character.' Because you never were quite sure."

Was that true? Had it been *her* need all along that had brought them to this terrible place?

His breathing was rough. "No matter who made the wager, your brother died because I was too full of myself to stop the race, too eager for glory to let him win. Do you really think you'll ever be able to forget that? Or forgive me for it?"

For a moment, an image flashed into her mind—of Roger laid out in his bedchamber, unnaturally still. Gabriel could have stopped the race, but he hadn't.

Then again, Roger could have stopped it, too.

But if he hadn't realized that Gabriel didn't remember . . .

"That's what I thought," he said coldly when she didn't answer. "At least now that you have the facts, you can hate me with good reason."

He pushed past her, headed for the door.

"Wait!" Her mind whirled with everything he'd revealed. "Where are you going?"

Though he paused in the doorway, he refused to look at her. "Where I always go to forget what I *do* remember." He glanced at her grandfather. "Tell Devonmont to take good care of her."

Then he strode out the door.

"Gabriel!" She headed after him, but Poppy caught her by the arm. "Let me go!" she protested, struggling.

Lord Jarret said, "I'll fetch him back," and hurried out.

"Leave it be, lambkin," Poppy said. "I told you what Roger said that night: 'If a man agrees to a wager while he's in his cups, is there any gentlemanly way he can get out of it?' Clearly your brother didn't want to make that wager, and Lord Gabriel pushed him into it."

"He isn't like that," Mrs. Plumtree protested.

Virginia agreed. The Gabriel she knew would never bully anyone into anything. She might not be sure what had happened that night, but one thing she *was* sure of—Gabriel was no more culpable than Roger.

Mrs. Plumtree glowered at Poppy. "You've made up your mind that Gabe's some monster, based solely on some words said by your grandson. For all you know, he was lying. You're so blinded by your anger that you can't see beyond your bias."

"And what about *your* bias?" Poppy growled.

"It was an *accident*," Mrs. Plumtree said. "A tragic, stupid accident. Gabriel didn't set out to murder your grandson. He behaved as foolish young men often do, yes. But it was Roger who rousted him out of bed, Roger who got them to the race course. Think about that when you start accusing my grandson."

Mrs. Plumtree's words seemed to stun Poppy. She had

a point. If Gabriel were to be believed—and Virginia knew in her heart that he wouldn't lie—then Roger had been the one to push the matter.

More importantly, it had happened seven years ago. And no matter what Gabriel thought, it didn't change the fact that she loved him.

I don't deserve you.

She'd been a fool to let him believe even for one moment that he wasn't worthy of her. Believe he wasn't worthy of love. "I have to talk to Gabriel."

Just then, Lord Jarret came back in. "He's gone, I'm afraid. He was saddling a horse when I entered the stable, and he told me to leave him be. I tried to talk to him, but he just leaped into the saddle and rode out."

"To go where?" she asked.

"I don't know," Lord Jarret said, his eyes full of sympathy.

"He'll return eventually," Mrs. Plumtree said. "He always does."

"He's done this before?" Virginia asked.

"A few times, when he gets morose over Roger's death. He goes off God knows where, and the next thing we know, he's agreeing to another fool race."

She'd lost him. She'd let him leave here hating himself, and now she'd lost him. She hadn't even told him she loved him! "Why is he so obsessed with racing? He says it's for the money, but I'd swear it's more than that."

Sadness filled Mrs. Plumtree's features. "It's his way of shielding himself from his fear that he might end up like Roger and his parents, dead before his time."

I don't want to be left in the ground to rot before my time. But I don't know how to stop it from happening.

Yet there was something else there, too. Something she was missing. Something more.

"Let's go home," Poppy said softly. "No point in remaining here. If you must speak to the man, I'll bring you back tomorrow. But you need sleep."

"I'm not leaving," she said firmly. "Not until Gabriel returns."

"Your grandfather is right, you need sleep," Mrs. Plumtree surprised her by saying. "But you can do that here. We have plenty of room."

Poppy stared at Mrs. Plumtree. "If she stays, I stay."

"That can be arranged." Mrs. Plumtree's steady gaze made Poppy flush. "Your granddaughter isn't the only one who needs sleep, I daresay."

It shocked her when he said, "All right. We'll stay the night. But if he hasn't returned by morning . . ."

"We'll handle that when it happens," Mrs. Plumtree said firmly. She glanced at Lord Jarret.

He nodded. "I'll find him, Miss Waverly, don't you worry."

"Thank you," she murmured through the lump in her throat. They were being so kind. Lord Jarret had just returned from a long trip; the last thing he probably wished to do was go hunting for his brother.

As Lord Jarret left, Mrs. Plumtree guided them down the hall. "Halstead Hall has an entire private apartment you can use," she said. "It was built to accommodate a foreign prince and his wife in the seventeenth century."

Virginia scarcely listened, remembering Gabriel's parting words.

Tell Devonmont to take good care of her.

He meant to turn his back on her, after everything they'd said and meant to each other. How could he?

In a daze of pain, she entered the massive suite with two bedrooms and a sitting room as large as the dining room at Waverly Farm. Mrs. Plumtree ordered servants about, getting fires going and dust cloths removed in such a short time that soon Virginia and Poppy were left alone.

When she made no move toward her bedchamber, Poppy came up to her with a worried look. "Go to bed, lambkin. I'm sure the scoundrel will return soon."

She shook her head. "I can't sleep. Not until I know he's safe."

"He'll be fine," Poppy said, an edge in his voice. "Besides, this might be just as well. Now you can reconsider the possibility of you and Pierce—'"

"I am not going to marry Pierce!" she cried, unable to take it anymore. "I'm in love with Gabriel!"

Poppy blinked. "In love? You barely know the man. Surely you're not foolish enough to believe that a marriage can be built on kisses and flattery and soft words."

"Is it foolish to want to be treated like a desirable woman for once, and not like a cog in the wheel of the farm?" she choked out. When Poppy looked stricken, she released a ragged breath. "Can't you understand? Gabriel sees all of me—not just the efficient parts. He sees the woman who wants to be thought pretty and receive flowers, who wants to dance, who wants to feel something more than just relief that the foal who got loose didn't trample the turnips."

Her voice fell. "At least he did until I pushed him into talking about the past. Now all he can see is his guilt. And he thinks that's all I can see, too."

Was he out there even now, searching for some new challenge to blot the heartache from his mind, some new race in his ongoing battle with death?

I cheat Death. It's what I do.

And suddenly she understood.

He'd said it as a joke, but it wasn't a joke. It explained everything—the racing, the recklessness, the times when he'd withdrawn and become that cold, frightening person she thought of as the real Angel of Death.

She prayed that she got the chance to make *him* understand. Because until he did, they could never marry. And she couldn't bear the thought of that.

Chapter Twenty

*M*ust. Beat. Roger.

The chant from Gabe's dream haunted him. So did the image of Roger lying with his neck broken as Lyons ran toward them and Gabe fought to rein in the horses.

With a scowl, Gabe gulped some ale. He had to put that image from his mind. Had to find that perfect state of blessed numbness, of cold calm, that he felt when he was racing. He didn't usually seek it in drink, but tonight if it took half the liquor in London, he was going to drive the memories from his mind. He gave a bitter laugh as he stared into his tankard. The irony didn't escape him.

"You're devilishly hard to find," Jarret said from behind him. "I've been scouring the stews for hours."

Damn it. "Well, you found me. Now go away."

He gulped more ale. He had to be drunker than this to deal with his brother.

Jarret moved the tankard away from him. "You'd think you'd have learned by now that this won't help."

True, but tonight he was desperate. He dragged the

tankard back. "Get your own damned ale. Or better yet, leave."

"You should have stayed to see everything out. She wanted you to stay."

"Yes, I could tell by the way she asked me not to leave." Why was he even talking to Jarret? It wouldn't change anything.

"You didn't give her a chance."

He cursed under his breath. He'd seen the confusion in her face, the shock as he'd told her the truth. Perhaps she would have forgiven him, perhaps not. He couldn't stay around to find out. Leaving meant he didn't have to watch the light die in her eyes as she realized what he truly was. "It wouldn't have mattered."

"Of course it would have mattered. She's in love with you."

The words seared a path through the encroaching numbness, sparking a tiny hope in the glacier of Gabe's heart. "She told you that?"

Jarret paused. "She didn't have to. I saw it in her face."

The hope winked out. "You saw what you wanted to see. I saw a woman who'd finally got the truth she'd been clamoring for and didn't like it."

He lifted the tankard to drink, but it was empty. He held the tankard out to a nearby tavern maid. "Another!" She bustled off to refill it.

"You barely gave Miss Waverly the chance to take it all in," Jarret snapped. "What did you expect?"

"I expected . . ." What? That once he bared his soul for her, the pain would stop? That was naïve.

It would never stop—not even if she could forgive him for what had happened. Her brother would still be dead. And he would still be the reckless wretch who had put him in the grave.

"I got exactly what I expected," he lied.

"So you're going to punish her for her momentary lapse by abandoning her?" Jarret asked.

"Punish her?" Gabe scowled at him. "I'm doing her a favor. I was an idiot to think we could marry. There's too much of the past between us."

"She seems willing to work through it."

"Then she's a fool. She deserves a man who's worthy of her. And I'm not that man." The tankard was set down in front of him, and he grabbed it up. He needed not to feel. It used to be so easy—he just found some race to run and became the Angel of Death. Why couldn't he do that anymore? All he wanted was to sink into the numbness, let it surround him like the grave . . .

"But Miss Waverly isn't likely to get a more worthy man in her present situation, is she?" Jarret said coolly.

"She's got her cousin," he ground out, though the very thought made his fingers itch to throttle the man. "He'll marry her."

"She doesn't want Devonmont. God only knows why, but she wants *you*."

Judging from how his pulse leapt at those words, he hadn't yet consumed enough liquor. "She doesn't know what she wants. And anyway, she'll be better off with him than me."

Jarret snorted. "You are such a damned coward."

When that sparked his temper, he cursed. Where was the numbness? "Watch it, big brother. The last man who called me that got his teeth knocked down his throat."

"Yes, you're brave when it counts the least. You're perfectly happy to race any idiot who challenges you, but God forbid you should admit that you need Virginia. That you might even love her. It's easier to turn tail and run."

Gabe stiffened. "Not easier. Better for her. I can't give her what she wants."

"What? Some sort of penance for racing her brother? She doesn't want that. She wants you to open your heart to her, to trust her with it. And that scares the hell out of you."

Gabe drank deeply, fighting to ignore the truth in Jarret's words.

"Believe me, I understand," Jarret continued. "I've been in your place. So have Oliver and Minerva. We've all spent the last nineteen years protecting our hearts, because we know how awful it feels to be abandoned by those we love most. It has made us slow to trust. But until you can trust someone with your heart, you'll only be half living. Loving someone and being loved is worth any risk."

The words pounded in his brain, warring with the effects of the ale. "Are you finished?" he growled. "Because none of this concerns you. The general and Devonmont have concocted a tidy little plan for her future, and I won't stand in the way of it."

"Fine," Jarret said coolly as he stood. "But I should mention one thing. Does your willingness to give her up to Devonmont mean that I misunderstood what was going on when I burst in on the two of you in the stable? I had assumed that you'd just bedded her."

Gabe froze.

"But that can't be possible. Because taking her innocence and then walking away, leaving her to handle the consequences alone, would be ten times worse than anything you ever did to Roger Waverly."

And with that parting shot, Jarret left.

Gabe shoved the tankard aside with a string of curses. He couldn't believe he'd forgotten that. He'd ruined Virginia, and Jarret was right—he couldn't just leave her to handle it. Devonmont might be as indulgent as Virginia had claimed, but he wouldn't be indulgent about *that*. No man would.

He'd seduced her twice. That meant he had to marry her.

If she wanted to marry him. He stared blindly at the tankard. Despite Jarret's optimistic observations, he wasn't sure of that. Once she had time to think about his revelations, she might not want anything to do with him.

And who could blame her? He couldn't even tell her the one thing she wanted to know—what had happened between him and Roger that night. She deserved to know, and he couldn't tell her.

Or . . . could he?

His mind began to race, clipping through possibilities. For the past seven years he'd avoided trying to learn the truth, afraid of what he might learn. But perhaps he could find out now. Someone must have heard him and Roger talk about that wager. Perhaps someone present that night had witnessed everything, but their tale blended in with the rest of the gossip, so no one recognized it as the truth.

If he could learn what really happened, then Virginia and her grandfather would have the whole truth at last.

Gabe tossed some money down on the table and lurched out of the tavern, then stumbled down the street. He needed to clear his head, needed to think.

Who'd been in the tavern when he, Roger, and Lyons had arrived? There had to have been somebody who'd heard them. God knows he and his chums had never been quiet drinkers. Perhaps if he returned to the place, it might jog his memory.

Gabe spent the next couple of hours wandering the stews. He entered the tavern where they'd been that night. Just being there didn't resurrect anything from the burial ground of his memory, so he started asking questions. He had no pride left. He wanted only the truth, even if half the world started gossiping about his strange new obsession with the events leading up to Roger's death.

Unfortunately, the tavern had changed hands a couple of times, so the owner could only guide him to the previous owners. He questioned the regulars and the barmaids, but none of them had any idea what he was talking about.

He headed out to ask questions in one tavern after another. Before long, he was chasing shadows, looking for people who might know someone who knew someone who'd been there that night.

The less foxed he grew, the more he began to realize how futile his search was. No one remembered a pair of drunken fools making a wager in a tavern seven years ago. The one time he came across someone who was there, the man had little to tell him. Clearly people who spent long evening hours in taverns weren't the best sources of information. The drink had pickled their brains.

After finally hunting down the original owner of the tavern, only to hear the fellow say he had no idea about any wager, Gabe sat down in the man's new establishment to contemplate his choices.

None of them were good, and they all involved marrying Virginia with the questions of the past hanging between them. They'd have to elope, since her grandfather would never approve a marriage.

He was just about to order some food, having not eaten for hours, when a man dropped into the seat across from him.

Chetwin, damn his eyes. The last person he wanted to see tonight.

"I hear you've been asking questions around town about the night you and Roger made your wager," Chetwin said.

Though he hated to have his search laid bare to an arse like Chetwin, he didn't let on.

"And I find it very interesting, especially in light of your courtship of Miss Waverly."

Gabe scowled but didn't rise to the bait.

"Everyone is talking about that, you know. You won the right to court her, so we're all waiting to see if she'll marry you." Chetwin called for a tankard. "I'm guessing that your questions about what happened that night have something to do with Miss Waverly."

"I don't have time for this," Gabe snapped as he rose to his feet.

"You don't remember it, do you?"

That held Gabe in place. "Don't be absurd. Why wouldn't I remember it?"

"Because you were fairly cupshot, from what I hear. And if you did remember," Chetwin continued, "why would you be looking for someone who might have witnessed it? The only reason you'd need a witness is if you wanted to shore up your memory."

Stiffening, Gabe stared down at Chetwin. "What's your point?"

"My point is that you obviously have a sudden need to set the story straight for Miss Waverly. I always assumed that she knew what happened from her grandfather or even Waverly himself, but perhaps she didn't. So she'd want to know the truth before she married you." Chetwin cast Gabe a smug smile. "And I happen to know someone who knows."

Though Gabe's pulse went into triple-time, he managed a shrug. "Do you? Who might that be?"

"I'll tell you, but only under one condition. That you race me at Turnham Green again."

Gabe laughed even as disappointment sliced through him. "I'm not going to fall for your attempt to set a rematch. You don't know a damned thing, and I'm not going to race you."

As he turned to walk off, Chetwin said, "I know that Lyons argued with Waverly and left the tavern before the wager was made."

Gabe froze. That was something only someone who'd been there—or who'd spoken to someone who'd been there—would know.

Slowly he faced Chetwin. "If you've known the truth all these years, why haven't you said anything to anyone?"

"I didn't say I know the truth. I said I know someone who does." Chetwin's face darkened. "One night when I was speculating to some friends about what had provoked the wager, a fellow told me I ought to keep my mouth shut when I didn't have all the facts. He let slip the bit about Lyons and the quarrel. When I realized that he must know the truth himself, I tried to get him to say more, but he refused. Said that the families deserved not to be gossiped about by the likes of me."

Gabe racked his brain for who might have defended him, but for the life of him, he couldn't think who it might be. He remembered the argument with Lyons but didn't remember any friend of his being there when it was going on. It had to have been a stranger—but what man who knew Chetwin wouldn't know Gabe as well?

Gabe thrust his face down into Chetwin's. "Tell me who it is, or I'll throttle you until you do."

Chetwin just sneered up at him. "Then you'll never know, will you?"

Gabe straightened, fighting to keep his temper in check. "I could ask every one of your friends—"

"The man is no friend of mine. I thought I made that clear. Just a chap I once talked to in a tavern." Chetwin leaned back in the chair, smug and insolent as always. "So here's what I propose. We race at Turnham Green tomorrow at noon for a wager of three hundred pounds. Whoever wins the race wins the money, but no matter who wins, I give you the name. Surely that pot is sweet enough to tempt you."

Three hundred pounds was a lot of money. If he won, he could go into marriage with Virginia in a far more financially secure position than he was now. But if he lost, he'd be in dire straits. Either way, though, he could give her and her grandfather the truth at last.

Of course, Chetwin might be lying. But it made no difference; he had no other choice.

Besides, he had beaten Chetwin once—he could beat him again.

But this would be the last time Gabe ever ran the course at Turnham Green. Virginia would have his head on a platter if she knew he was planning to run it. She might even balk at marrying him, and that wouldn't solve anything.

"I have a condition of my own," Gabe said. "The race has to be kept between the two of us for now. Bring one of your friends to witness it, and I'll bring Lyons. No one else. Once I'm married to Miss Waverly you can tell whomever you please about the outcome, but not until then. Do you agree?"

Chetwin didn't look happy about it, but he nodded.

"All right," Gabe told Chetwin. "Then you'll have your race."

Chapter Twenty-one

$\mathcal{M}$idmorning on Tuesday, Celia slipped across the courtyard, headed for the far field in the northwest corner of the estate. In the distance she could hear the huntsmen—grouse-hunting season had begun Saturday. Now she could practice target shooting without anyone being the wiser. And with the Waverlys here, everyone had forgotten about her, thank goodness. With a house party coming up that was sure to include shooting matches, she wanted to be ready.

She sighed. Poor Miss Waverly. Much as Celia hadn't wanted Gabe to marry and force her own hand, she also hadn't wanted to see Miss Waverly suffer. She seemed a decent sort, and that whole business with her brother dying was very sad.

Celia rounded the stable and nearly collided with Gabe, who was leading his phaeton and horses out through the doors along with young Willy, one of the grooms.

"Gabe! What are you doing?" she cried as she thrust her rifle behind her back. "Everyone's beside themselves with worry. Gran gave Jarret quite the tongue-lashing when he returned from London alone." Should she tell him that the Waverlys were here? Perhaps not. That might spook him. He already looked like hell. "You need to go in and talk to Gran—"

"Later. If you don't mind, I'd rather you kept it quiet that you'd seen me. Just for a few hours, that's all."

She glanced at his phaeton, then at him, and awareness dawned. "You're going off to race someone, aren't you?"

He muttered an oath under his breath. Then his gaze shifted slightly to the left of her, and his eyes narrowed. "And you're going off to shoot, aren't you?"

"Why do you say that?" she squeaked.

"I can see the rifle you're unsuccessfully hiding behind your back," he drawled. "I thought Gran forbade you to practice shooting anymore."

"What she doesn't know won't hurt her." She cast him a worried look. "You won't tell, will you?"

"You keep my secret, I'll keep yours." He paused, as if considering something, then said, "In fact . . ." And turning to Willy, he gestured to the lad's coat pocket.

The groom took out an envelope and handed it to Gabe, who stared down at it. Then he lifted his gaze to Celia. "If something should happen to me, I want you to give this to Miss Waverly. Will you do that?"

A chill chased down her spine. "Where are you racing, Gabe?" she asked.

He lifted an eyebrow. "Where are you shooting?"

She chewed on her lip. Keeping each other's secrets suddenly seemed very unwise.

He held out the envelope, but when she reached for it, he didn't release it. "Promise me you won't look at it. Or pass it on unless something happens to me."

She hesitated. But if she wanted to find out what was going on, she'd better do as he asked. She crossed her fingers behind her back, just in case. "I promise."

He let go of the envelope and she tucked it into her apron pocket. Then she watched as he climbed up into his phaeton and sent the horses into a trot.

As soon as he disappeared, she turned to Willy. "Do you know where he's going?"

"No, miss, he didn't say."

She drew out the envelope and stared at it. It wasn't like Gabe to leave notes for anyone before he raced. He always assumed he would win handily, without any injury. That's what got him into trouble.

But lately he'd been different, more moody, more snappish. He wasn't even wearing black anymore. On top of what she'd heard about last night's revelations, it all seemed to add up to her brother being in serious trouble. Jarret seemed to think that Gabe was at some sort of crossroads, having to do with Miss Waverly. He'd even speculated that Gabe was in love, an opinion Jarret's wife seemed to share.

Contrary to what the rest of the family thought about Celia, she believed in love. That was precisely why she didn't want to marry at Gran's whim.

Out of nowhere rose Mr. Pinter's words from over a

week ago: *I'm merely pointing out that your grandmother has your best interests at heart, something you seem incapable of recognizing.*

What did he know about it? That dratted Bow Street runner didn't have an ounce of passion in him. It was always business with him. He couldn't understand what it was like to want things routinely denied to females—the security of knowing that no one could ever hurt you unless you allowed it, the delicious thrill of putting a bullet squarely in a target, the intense pleasure of beating a bunch of idiotic, pompous men who thought themselves better than you. She might be able to tolerate Mr. Pinter if the man had any capacity to *feel*—

A curse escaped her. It didn't matter if he could or not. He worked for Gran, that's all. Nothing to do with her.

She returned her attention to the envelope. She'd been hurt when Gabe had given in to Gran's demands by courting Miss Waverly. But that didn't matter if he truly were in *love* with the woman, which the letter seemed to imply.

The envelope and all its implications seared her hand, making her uneasy. *If something should happen to me . . .*

She sighed. So much for spending the afternoon shooting.

She turned and headed back into the house.

Isaac paced the sitting room, wondering if he should wake Virginia. He'd finally persuaded her to go to bed around four a.m. and she was still asleep, thank God. But he wanted to be back at Waverly Farm. This mansion reminded him too much of his childhood at the estate in Hertfordshire that Pierce now owned as heir to the title.

A soft knock came at the door into the sitting room. Assuming it was a servant, he went to open it, only to find Hetty standing there with a vase of fresh-cut flowers. She looked harried and wan, yet still managed to look pretty, too.

"May I come in?"

"Of course."

"How is she?" Hetty asked as he stood aside to let her pass.

"Sleeping. I was trying to decide when to wake her. I need to be at home. Have you heard anything from Lord Gabriel?"

"I'm afraid not." Hetty walked over to place the vase on a table. "I brought her some lavender from our garden. Gabe said it was her favorite, and I thought it might cheer her. I had a time of it finding some, since someone has been cutting it like mad."

He sees the woman who wants to be thought pretty and receive flowers . . .

A groan escaped him. "I am such an old fool."

She blinked. "Why?"

"I thought she was filling our vases with *our* lavender." He shook his head. "I had some idiot notion that if I kept your grandson busy working in the stable, he wouldn't have the chance to court her. Meanwhile, he was doing so right under my nose the whole time. I just saw what I wanted to see."

Hetty busied herself with arranging the flowers. "We often do that."

He shot her a rueful glance. "You don't. You told me she had a passionate nature, but I didn't see it. She's always so responsible that I forgot she had other needs, a woman's needs." His voice wavered. "Something your grandson noticed better than I."

Too late, he remembered Sharpe standing up for her with Hob, paying attention to what she wore, thanking her for the sandwiches . . . behaving like a gentleman.

If he examined the man's actions honestly in the last week, he had to admit that Sharpe had always behaved like a gentleman. Indeed, he'd behaved better. He'd never once complained about mucking out the stalls, and he hadn't done a slipshod job of it, either. He'd shown genuine interest in how Isaac trained his horses. And he'd offered a few tips of his own concerning feed for the Thoroughbreds.

The man was either a consummate actor or a gentleman. Isaac had been convinced of the former for so long it was hard to think of him being the latter. But last night had shaken his perceptions.

"I know you don't want to hear this, Isaac," she said softly, "but I think they suit each other. Virginia has just enough fire to keep him interested, and he has just enough sense to listen to her when she's setting him straight. They would make a good marriage, if you could see your way to allowing it. A better marriage than she could make with Lord Devonmont, I dare say."

I can't marry Pierce when I'm in love with Gabriel!

Hell and damnation. "She made it quite clear last night that she'll never marry Pierce. That was something else I've been blind about."

Had he really believed that those two could marry? He'd hoped they could, but somewhere deep inside, he'd known they behaved more like siblings than lovers. He'd just been so eager for the marriage that he'd ignored what his instincts told him.

He seemed to do that a great deal with his lambkin. "I'm used to giving orders, even with my granddaughter, and she bears it well. But you were right—love isn't something even a general can dictate."

"She loves Gabriel?" Hetty asked, her voice quavering.

"She says she does. But she thinks his guilt will keep him from loving her in return."

"It might." Hetty sighed. "I'm sorry for what I said to you last night about Roger lying. I didn't mean to imply—"

"No, you were right to say it." He dragged in a heavy breath. "I've had plenty of time to think since then. Virginia has always put Roger on a pedestal, and I had sanctified his memory fairly well myself. Roger liked to gamble and drink, and he lied to me about both on occasion. He was troubled, and I knew that. But I couldn't do anything about it, so after his death, it was just easier . . ."

He swallowed hard. This was difficult to say, especially to her.

"To blame Gabe," she murmured.

He nodded. Briefly, he related what he'd told Virginia about his conversation with Roger that night. "Roger said naught about being bullied or forced. That was my own contribution. But you were right, damn it. The fact that Roger rousted your grandson from bed for the race says much about who was at fault. I tried to tell myself Sharpe lied about that, but if he were lying, why not just claim that Roger laid down the challenge? Why admit to being so drunk?"

"Why tell Virginia he didn't deserve her?" Hetty pointed out.

"He doesn't," Isaac bit out. When he saw her bristle, he added, "But no one does, in my estimation."

A smile touched Hetty's lips. "Perhaps you're right. But I still say Gabe will make her a good husband."

Sharpe married to his granddaughter. It griped him to think of it, but if she wanted him so very badly . . . He sighed. "Every general recognizes when he's outgunned and outmaneuvered. Between you and Virginia . . ." He cast her a serious glance. "I only want her happiness, you know."

"I know. I want that, too. For both of them." She walked up close to him. "Thank you, Isaac, for keeping an open mind about it."

She stretched up on tiptoe to kiss his cheek, but before she could draw back, he caught her chin in his hand and kissed her squarely on the lips. When he lifted his head, she was staring up at him, eyes wide, with a blush turning her papery cheeks a youthful, rosy hue.

There was surprise in her gaze, and womanly awareness, as well.

He slipped his arm about her waist to steady her against him, then gave her a more thorough kiss. She melted, as he'd known she would, for Hetty was old enough to know how the battle was waged—and it wasn't with words.

Surrender had never tasted so sweet.

A knock at the door made him release her regretfully. Especially when she slid a soft half-smile up at him before going to open the door.

Lady Celia hurried in. "Gran, I've been searching for you everywhere! I just saw Gabe—"

"He's returned?" said Virginia as she came out of her bedroom, looking dazed. She was still wearing her clothes from yesterday, though they were rumpled as if she'd slept in them. "He's here?"

"Not anymore. I couldn't make him stay. He was headed out to race somewhere, but he gave me this to give to you." She held up a sealed letter, but when Virginia hurried over to get it, she added, "I should warn you that he made me promise *not* to give it to you—unless something happened to him."

As Hetty cursed, the blood drained from Virginia's face.

"He's never left a letter for anyone before," Celia said, "so knowing what that might mean, I figured you'd better take a look at it. Perhaps it will say where he's racing."

As Virginia tore open the envelope and read, Isaac cursed under his breath. Sharpe was making it awfully hard to forgive him anything right now.

Virginia lifted her gaze to them, looking as if she might faint. Hetty took the letter from her, and read it aloud for his and Lady Celia's benefit.

> *Dearest Virginia,*
> *If you're reading this, then the unthinkable has happened. I've lost the race and my life. I couldn't bear to leave you wondering how it came about, the way you were left wondering about my race against Roger, so this is to explain.*
> *Chetwin claims to know someone who can tell me what happened that night seven years ago. He won't reveal the name unless I race him at Turnham Green, so I agreed.*
> *Do not blame yourself for it. I did it so you would know exactly what sort of man you were marrying. Just make sure that Chetwin meets the terms of our wager, which is that he give me (or my representative should I die) the person's name, regardless of who wins. If you finally learn the truth, my life won't be in vain.*
> *I only wish I could be there to give the truth to you myself. I would do anything to make that right for you.*

"Anything except not race at Turnham Green," Virginia said bitterly. She cast Poppy an urgent glance. "We have to stop him. If something happens to him . . ." Her voice broke.

"Of course." He turned to Lady Celia. "How long ago did he leave?"

"Fifteen minutes or so."

He glanced at Hetty. "We should take my gig. I already sent down to have it readied. But only three of us will squeeze into it."

"I'll stay here," Lady Celia said.

Isaac nodded. "If we leave now, we ought to reach Turnham Green before the race begins. They won't jump to it immediately upon his arrival, I imagine." Turning to Virginia, he added, "And if we don't make it, my dear, the lad has run that race three times now—surely he can escape it unscathed again."

Her gaze narrowed. "Oh no, he can't. Because he'll have to face me afterward. And he will *not* escape *me* unscathed, I assure you."

With his blood pumping and sweat beading his brow, Gabe stood watching for Chetwin.

Lyons frowned as he studied his pocket watch. "It's ten after."

"He's playing with me," Gabe bit out. "Trying to rattle me, that's all." Worse yet, it was working.

Never had a race meant so much to him. And that worried him. It meant he couldn't get to that place of cold control that he needed in order to win.

He stared down the course to where the boulders

loomed large. The last two times he was here, there had been so many people that the memory of his race with Roger had receded before the roar of the spectacle. And the time of day had been different, the season different. Nor had Lyons been present. He'd been abroad for the other two races with Chetwin.

But today was just like that day seven years ago. Summer. Noon. Nobody around but him and Lyons. Gabe was even suffering the effects of a night spent drinking. *Everything* was eerily the same.

A shudder wracked him. That shouldn't bother him, but it did.

"Are you sure you want to do this?" Lyons asked.

That was different—Lyons hadn't asked him a damned thing before his race against Roger. Back then they'd all been far more foolish.

"I have no choice. It's the only way to know what happened."

"I always assumed that you did, that you were keeping silent because you didn't want to tarnish his memory."

"I know." He didn't know whether to laugh or cry. All these people attributing such noble motives to him, when all the while—

"I'm sorry I never questioned you both myself," Lyons said. "I was half-asleep when we came out here. It was just another race; I didn't care who'd laid down the challenge." His voice held an edge. "For years I thought that if I had questioned it, if I'd just said something . . . But of course I didn't, and you didn't, and there you have it."

A chill swept over Gabe. It had never occurred to him that Lyons might feel guilt over it, too. Given that, it was surprising that he'd come today.

"So this time I shall satisfy my conscience by asking again," Lyons went on. "Are you *sure* you want to do this?"

Before Gabe could answer, the sound of hoofbeats came to them. He turned to see Chetwin driving his rig toward them with a soldier sitting next to him. Briefly, Gabe wondered if that might be the man Chetwin had mentioned. But his mysterious informant hadn't been a friend—or so Chetwin claimed.

Chetwin reined in next to his rig.

"You're late," Gabe said as Chetwin's friend got down and went to stand beside Lyons.

The smug smile Chetwin shot him confirmed his suspicions. "Worried I wouldn't show up?"

"And lose a chance at making an arse of yourself?" Gabe gathered up his reins. "Not damned likely."

That banished Chetwin's smile. "We'll see who's the arse when this is over, and I've won."

"Just remember what we agreed to," Gabe drawled. "This is the last time you plague me to race you here, regardless of whether your horse picks up a stone or your axle breaks or any number of freak occurrences keep you from winning."

That really got Chetwin's goat. "Watch it, Sharpe, or I'll change my mind about racing you, and you'll *never* know the name."

Gabe gritted his teeth. Baiting Chetwin was no fun when the man had something he wanted.

"Shall I recite the rules so we can get on with this?" Lyons asked.

"We know the rules," Gabe said.

With a nod, Lyons took up the flag and went to stand between them.

Then Gabe heard more hoofbeats coming from behind him. With a scowl, he glared over at Chetwin. "Damn it, you said you wouldn't tell anyone!"

"They're not friends of mine, I swear," Chetwin retorted.

Gabe shifted in his seat to look back, then cursed. Gran. Celia must have broken her promise, damn her.

Then his heart skipped a beat. Not just Gran. Virginia.

At the sight of her, his heart began to pound. She'd come to stop him. She'd cared enough to try to stop him—even after what he'd told her.

That made it imperative that he run this race. Because no matter how much she worried about him, she deserved the truth. And now he was certain he could do it.

For her. Only for her.

"Drop the damned flag, Lyons!"

Chapter Twenty-two

As the gig halted, Virginia heard Gabriel's command. Jumping down and breaking into a run, she shouted at the duke, "If you drop that flag, Your Grace, I will shove it down your throat!"

Lyons blinked, no doubt unused to being threatened with violence by a woman. Then he broke into a smug grin and raised the flag higher.

She reached Gabriel in moments. "Don't you *dare* run this race, Gabriel Sharpe, or I swear I will not marry you!"

"Lyons, you bloody arse," Chetwin snapped, "if you don't drop that flag, I'll run it without him and declare that he forfeited!"

"Poppy!" she called.

She held Gabriel's gaze as Poppy hurried to stand at the head of Chetwin's team, grabbing the harness of the lead horse.

"Damn it, get out of the way!" Chetwin cried.

"Not till my granddaughter is done," Poppy said, easily keeping control of Chetwin's team.

Gabriel scowled at Chetwin. "Give me a few minutes,

will you? We'll have our race. Just let me talk to her." He leaped down from his perch, caught her by the arm, and led her away from the rest of them.

"Virginia, sweetheart—" he began.

"Don't you 'sweetheart' me!" she cried. "You can't run this race. I'll throw myself in front of the rig before I let you."

That seemed to startle him. "You don't understand—"

"I do understand. I read the letter you left for me."

Beyond them, his grandmother climbed down from the carriage, but thankfully kept her distance.

"If you did," he said in the patient tone one uses with children or fools, "then you know this is the only way to learn the truth."

"I don't *care* about the truth! I don't care what happened that night, or the next day or the years between then and now. I know that you're a good man, Gabriel—a fine man." Her voice broke. "I fell in love with that man."

The leap of joy in his face made her think that all he'd needed was to hear those words. Until a sad smile touched his lips. "Then you should understand even more why I must race Chetwin."

She swallowed her disappointment. "*Why?*"

"Because I can't marry you without knowing if I have any right to that love. I know you don't think the past matters now, but down the road it will poison whatever you feel for me at the moment. I'm doing this for us."

"No," she said, grabbing his arms. "You're doing it for *you*."

He stared at her, and she could see him withdrawing into himself, into that cold, wary creature—

Not *this* time, drat it. "Listen to me," she said urgently. "You told me that you kept on playing the Angel of Death because you figured you might as well make it pay. And your grandmother said you kept on with it because it was your way of fighting your fears. But we both know it's something more."

He tensed, sinking further into the icy detachment that frightened her more than any race he could ever run. But at least he didn't pull away. "I don't know what you're talking about."

"You said it yourself: 'I cheat Death. It's what I do.'" She dug her fingers into his arms, determined to make him see. "You think somehow you cheated Death that day with Roger. You think Death should have taken *you* instead of him."

When a muscle flicked in his jaw, she knew she'd struck home. She pressed her advantage ruthlessly.

"Since then, you've been challenging Death over and over, sure that one day it will come for you. You figure that it might as well be at a time of *your* choosing, right? But what you can't accept is that sometimes people just die. They strike out in a moment of passion, like your parents, or they're in the wrong place at the wrong time, like your friend Benny. Or they run foolish races, like Roger."

Anger shone in his gaze now, which was better than the detachment. "You don't understand. If I had just—"

"It had naught to do with you!" she cried. "It doesn't

matter that you didn't call off the race. He wouldn't have done it, either. Or Lyons. And neither you nor Lyons made him run it. Neither of you made him take a risk and not rein in when he should have."

She swallowed, realizing she would have to expose her own vulnerabilities if she was to win this. "I should never have blamed you for it; I had no right. I was angry and hurt, and I missed my brother. But I realize now that he ran the race the way *he* chose to. He always made his own choices."

She cupped his face between her hands. "You want to believe you have some sort of power over Death, that every time you race and don't die, you've cheated it out of its rightful prize. But the truth is, Death has had you in its grip for seven years."

Gabe wanted to ignore the truth in her words, but they resonated too deeply for him to do so. He felt rooted to the spot, unable to tear his gaze from her desperate one. If only he could take refuge in the blessed numbness that had kept him sane for the past seven years . . .

But that had grown less and less possible from the moment he'd met her. Every time he was with her she showered him with warmth and feeling, no matter how much he fought it.

And she was still doing it, his fierce enchantress, still fighting. "The clothes and the phaeton and the endless races are all your dance with Death. If you keep them up, you *will* die. But you won't win anything, except what you foolishly think you deserved to have won seven years ago—*your* place in the grave, instead of Roger."

The words pounded in his ears. Oh, God, it was true. How many times had he wished he hadn't survived that day?

The pain he always avoided surged through him, staggering him, until he finally admitted the truth that had scored his soul all these years. "It should have been me." Unshed tears clogged his throat. "Then you wouldn't have been left with no one to take care of you. It's not right that he died. He didn't deserve—"

"Neither of you deserved it." Her hands gripped him tightly, so tightly. "I wish to God that you had both come home hale and hearty, but since you didn't, there's nothing wrong with being happy that you're still here, with me, *alive*. Lord knows, I'm happy that you are."

"How can you say that?" he said hoarsely. "Roger lies in the grave while I get to have a *life*."

"He wouldn't begrudge you that. And I don't, either."

The healing words dove straight into his heart, planting a seed of hope.

She smoothed back a lock of his hair. "Nothing you do can change what happened, Gabriel. Getting the truth from Chetwin or racing this course over and over certainly won't, nor even marrying me as a sort of penance. There's no dishonor in bowing out of a battle with Death. It's not a battle you can win. And it's time you accept that."

The seed of hope took root and blossomed. He'd been slamming his head against the past ever since Roger's death, and for what? Nothing but a sore head. Perhaps it was time he took the love she offered—without questioning, without remorse.

"All right."

She froze. "All right, what?"

"All right, I won't race Chetwin." As she sagged against him in relief, he brought her hands to his lips and kissed them. "After all, I can't have the woman I love refusing to marry me over some foolish race."

Her eyes began to shimmer with tears. "You . . . you love me?"

His heart seemed permanently lodged in his throat. "More than life. God only knows why you love *me*, because I sure as hell don't, but I know why I love *you*. You're my beacon in the darkness, and my compass on a night sea. When I'm with you, I don't want to dance with Death. I want to dance with Life. I want to dance with *you*. And whatever it takes, I mean to spend the rest of my life trying to deserve you."

She began to cry, sobbing and clinging to him. He didn't know what to do, so he went on instinct and lifted her tear-drenched face for a long, tender kiss that he hoped showed her just how much he loved her.

When he drew back he flashed her a smile, hoping to stop her tears. "So if you don't want me to race Chetwin, I won't race Chetwin." He chucked her under the chin as she tried mightily to regain control over her emotions. "After all, the last thing I need is you throwing yourself in front of my horses."

"I'd do it, too," she choked out.

"I have no doubt of that. I can just see you, standing in the gap between the boulders and daring us to run you down."

"I hadn't thought of that," she said gamely, "but it's a good idea."

With a laugh, he kissed her again. Then taking her hand in his, he led her back toward where Lyons paced and Chetwin stood scowling.

As they neared the rigs, Chetwin snapped, "Well? Are you ready?"

"Sorry, old chap. The race is off."

Lyons said, "Thank God," and ambled toward Gabe's family.

"You can't do this," Chetwin said.

"Sure I can," Gabe drawled. "I changed my mind."

Chetwin scowled. "Then I swear you'll never hear the truth."

Gabe looked down at Virginia, who was gazing up at him with eyes full of love. "It doesn't matter. I have everything I want already."

"And the three hundred pounds?" Chetwin sneered at him. "That doesn't matter, either?"

Gabe lifted an eyebrow at Virginia. "Sweetheart? Shall I race Chetwin for three hundred pounds?"

"Absolutely not," she said stoutly. "We'll do just fine without it."

Gabe told Chetwin, "No race today, or ever again. The Angel of Death is retiring."

That earned him a kiss on the cheek from Virginia.

"Balderdash," Chetwin spat. "You'll be back once

your pockets are to let and you need some blunt for that new Thoroughbred of yours."

"I don't see why," Gran said, stepping into the fray. "I have every intention of investing in my grandson's Thoroughbreds. I can't wait to see him double my money."

Gabe gaped at her, and she colored a little. "The general and I had a conversation on the way here. He says you have a knack for training horses, and with his help, he thinks you might make a go of it. I'm willing to invest a bit to see if that's true." She tipped up her chin. "A tiny bit, mind you, but it should be enough to fund entering a horse in the race."

"Thank you, Gran," Gabe said, biting back a smile. Occasionally she could be quite the soft touch. Especially when it came to her grandchildren.

The sound of more horses approaching caught his attention. They all looked over to see Devonmont and Lady Celia barreling toward them in Devonmont's curricle with his tiger on the back.

"Pierce!" Virginia cried as she ran up to greet him. "What are you doing here?"

After climbing down from the carriage and handing Celia down, he gave Virginia a quick peck on the cheek. "I arrived at Waverly Farm late last night. I figured you were all sleeping, so I didn't worry until this morning when I awoke to find nobody there but the servants. They told me that you were both at Halstead Hall, so I went there. Then Lady Celia showed me a letter that Sharpe had written, and I came here straightaway."

"Why?" Gabe came up to snake a possessive arm about Virginia's waist. "Were you hoping I'd break my neck, and you could take my place with her?"

"I was hoping to stop you." He turned a hard gaze on Chetwin. "I believe the lieutenant knows why, too."

Chetwin looked belligerent. "I don't know what you mean."

"No?" Devonmont snapped. "So you don't recall a conversation we had years ago, when you were blathering a lot of nonsense about Sharpe and Roger and what had happened the night before their race?"

Gabe forgot to breathe. "*You're* Chetwin's mysterious source?"

Virginia froze. "You were there for the wager, Pierce?"

"No," he said, "I was at Waverly Farm. But after Roger stumbled in drunk that night, he came to talk to me before he talked to Uncle Isaac. He told me everything."

"And you never said a word of it?" she cried. "How could you?"

"Until I read Sharpe's letter a short while ago and Lady Celia explained its import, I assumed that Sharpe knew exactly what had happened that night."

"But *I* didn't know what happened that night!" she said, betrayal in her voice. "*Poppy* didn't know. Why didn't you tell us? You *knew* it was important to us!"

"Which is why, if you'll recall, I told you to ask Sharpe about it," Devonmont retorted. "How was I to know that he didn't remember? I assumed he was keeping it to himself for the same reason *I* never said anything—

because I wanted to protect you and Uncle Isaac from knowing the worst about Roger."

As it dawned on Gabe what that meant, a relief coursed through him so profound that he began to shake. "So I didn't . . . I wasn't the one who . . ."

"No," Devonmont said. "Roger told me *he* laid down the wager. Apparently he was smarting over something Lyons had said in their argument, and when you agreed with Lyons, he challenged you to that fool race."

With a sigh, Lyons moved up behind Gabe. "I remember that. He complained because the general wouldn't let him play jockey in some horse race. Roger said his grandfather had gone soft in his old age. I told him that a man who had stared down Boney had more courage than all three of us put together. He took exception to that, especially when Sharpe agreed with me. When he started railing at me for it, I decided I'd had enough, and I went home."

"He then felt compelled to demonstrate his bravery by challenging Sharpe to run the most dangerous course in London," Devonmont said.

"Damned fool," the general muttered.

Devonmont looked at Gabe. "He said you balked at first. He was very proud of that, seemed to think it made him somehow superior. I told him he was an arse, that he could easily kill himself on that course and that at least you had the good sense to recognize it. I told him he ought to get out of it however he could, honor be damned."

"Then he came to me," the general said hoarsely. "And I countered your advice, Pierce."

Virginia cast her grandfather a concerned glance. "You didn't know what you were advising him about, Poppy. It wasn't your fault." She swept them all with a fierce look. "It was no one's fault. Not Gabe's or Pierce's or the duke's. Roger always made his own decisions. And that one proved to be his worst."

"While this is all very interesting," Chetwin put in, "it doesn't change the fact that Sharpe agreed to race me and is now trying to back out." He strode up to Gabe. "This is your last chance, Sharpe. If you don't race me as agreed, I'll make sure every man in London knows you're a coward. I'll blacken your name from one end of London to the other for backing down from a challenge."

"You laid down a challenge?" General Waverly put in. "Sounded more like blackmail to me: if Sharpe didn't agree to race you, you refused to tell him what any decent fellow would have told him when asked." His tone hardened. "There's no dishonor in a gentleman's refusing to give in to blackmail."

He strode over to Chetwin. "I happen to know your superior officer, and I'd be happy to give him a truthful account of your actions here today. He's a gentleman. He won't look kindly upon your preying on another gentleman's grief. Are you willing to risk your future in the army for one last go at threading the needle?"

Chetwin went utterly pale, but the general wasn't done.

"So I'd better not hear one word about this incident ever again. My granddaughter is about to marry this man, and I will *not* have the reputation of my future grandson-in-law besmirched by an arse like you. Is that understood, soldier?"

Gabe had to dig his fingers into his palm to keep from laughing. Chetwin looked as if he were about to piss in his pants.

"Yes, General," Chetwin finally choked out. Then he grabbed his friend and headed back to his rig.

"Apparently Chetwin has some sense after all," Gabe drawled as the man swiftly drove away.

"Obviously more than you," Gran snapped. "I can't believe you were going to thread the needle again with that blasted—"

"Hetty," the general said, halting her tirade. "It's done. He came to his senses in the end, so leave the man be."

That shocked Gabe more than anything the general had said to Chetwin. Especially when, instead of giving the general a blistering retort, his grandmother gazed softly up at him and said, "I suppose he *has* suffered enough."

Gabe glanced down to find Virginia gaping at her grandfather, and he bent close to whisper, "Looks like I'm not the only one who fell in love with a Waverly."

Tucking her hand in his arm, he strode up to the general. "Thank you for stepping in, sir. I don't much care what Chetwin calls me, but I appreciate your nipping it in the bud."

The general's gaze hardened. "Just don't make me regret it." His gaze flicked to Virginia. "Make her happy.

Or I'll make good on my promise to shoot you." He offered his arm to Gran. "Now, shall we adjourn somewhere a little more comfortable?"

"Sounds like an excellent idea to me," Devonmont drawled as he handed Celia up into his curricle.

"We'll be along in a moment." Gabe drew Virginia aside. "There is one thing I need to make clear, my love."

She stared up at him with a soft look that made his blood hum. "Yes?"

"You said earlier that I was marrying you as some sort of penance. I'm not. Don't think that for even one moment."

The sudden vulnerability in her face clutched at his heart. "You did say you wanted to marry me to make amends, to keep me from a bleak future."

"I said a lot of stupid things," he admitted, "and perhaps it started out that way." He took her hands in his. "But that reason for courting you vanished the first time I kissed you. The first time I realized that you were the light to my darkness, and the only woman I could ever imagine marrying."

As her eyes began to glisten, he added, "You are my *reward*. God only knows what for, but I'm not going to question it. I'm just going to take the prize and thank God for letting me win it."

He drew her close and pressed a soft kiss to her lips. "Because of all the prizes I have ever won, you are definitely the best."

Epilogue

"*A*ll hail the conquering hero!"

The cry greeted Virginia and her husband of one week as they descended from their carriage at Halstead Hall, and the Sharpes swiftly surrounded them to congratulate Gabriel on Flying Jane's win in Doncaster.

Virginia smiled as Gabriel hoisted the gold cup for the benefit of his brothers, who cheered and slapped each other's backs as if they'd ridden the horse to glory themselves.

Celia was the only one of his siblings who'd attended the race. His brothers hadn't wanted to leave their wives, who'd both entered the periods of their confinements, and Mrs. Masters had chosen to remain in London with her husband, who couldn't leave his law practice at the moment. But now they were all together again, and clearly excited by the news.

"The *Times* said it was a brilliant race," Stoneville told Gabriel. "I quote, 'Flying Jane flew to the finish line.'"

"I told you that jockey would do you proud," Jarret said.

"And you were right," Gabriel said. "Thanks to him, I have two gentlemen clamoring to buy Flying Jane."

"You're not selling, are you?" Annabel asked.

"Not on your life."

Virginia smiled. "Poppy wants to breed her with Ghost Rider."

A carriage drove up behind theirs just at that moment.

"And speaking of Ghost Rider," Gabriel said, "here's the other conquering hero."

Another cheer went up as Poppy descended from his carriage and handed Mrs. Plumtree down. Pierce followed, helping Lady Celia disembark.

Gabriel and Poppy had decided to run the better of the two horses in the St. Leger Stakes, which in trials had proved to be Ghost Rider. Then both horses had run the second race for the gold cup since, as winner of the St. Leger Stakes, Ghost Rider had to carry additional weight. Gabriel had thought the weight might tip the balance toward Flying Jane, and it had indeed. Flying Jane had won the gold cup, so it was a triumph all around. Poppy and Gabriel had been celebrating all the way from Doncaster.

"So what do you think of Thoroughbred racing now, Gran?" Jarret called as she took the general's arm.

"They were lucky, is all," she said primly.

"Don't listen to her." Poppy patted her hand. "She won a hundred pounds in bets on the two races."

"Gran gambled on a horse race?" Minerva exclaimed. "Will wonders never cease!"

"Oh, hush," Mrs. Plumtree retorted. "Isaac told me if I didn't bet I would regret it, but I damned near had heart failure watching those races. That second one was a very near thing."

"So they said in the papers." Oliver grinned. "I guess you were glad you listened to 'Isaac.'"

The two spots of pink that appeared in her pale cheeks showed that she hadn't meant to slip up and use Poppy's Christian name.

Virginia stifled a laugh. He and Mrs. Plumtree had grown quite chummy of late, and she and Gabriel had begun to speculate on whether there was a marriage in the offing. Mrs. Plumtree kept saying she was too old for such nonsense, but her protests had weakened quite a bit lately.

"And what did you think of the races, Devonmont?" Jarret asked as they all headed for the arched entranceway.

Pierce shrugged. "One horse race is like any other, to me." With a sly glance at Gabriel, he tucked Celia's hand in the crook of his elbow. "Thank heaven, Lady Celia was there to keep me entertained."

At Gabriel's frown, Virginia whispered, "You know he's just trying to provoke you. He can't make you jealous of me, now, so he's trying to worry you about your sister. It's his idea of entertainment. But Lady Celia is far too clever to fall for Pierce. You should know that."

"I hope you're right," Gabriel grumbled.

They were crossing the courtyard when they heard the sound of another horse approaching, and Mr. Pinter came through the archway.

He halted at the sight of the entire family. "Am I interrupting something?" His gaze took in Pierce and Lady Celia, and hardened.

Oliver came forward. "Not at all. The racing enthusiasts have returned home and we were just heading in to celebrate. You're welcome to join us."

"Thank you, but first I should tell you my news."

Virginia felt the instant tension vibrating through her husband. He'd told her about the investigation into their parents' deaths, but nothing much had happened in the past month. Mr. Pinter had been busy trying to hunt down various old servants, as well as retrace Benny May's steps in Manchester.

"Is this about Benny's death?" Gabriel asked.

"No, I'm still working on that," Mr. Pinter said. "I'm headed back to Manchester now."

"Then what's your news?" Jarret asked.

"When we began all this, I asked the constable for a chance to examine the gun used to kill your parents. He said it had been moved into storage in town somewhere, and it would take him a while to hunt it down. He found it yesterday, and I got a look at it." Mr. Pinter paused, as if to be sure he had their full attention. "I know for sure that your mother didn't kill your father."

"How?" Gabriel asked eagerly.

"Because that gun did not kill them. It had never been fired. Clearly, it had been taken down from the wall where it hung and placed near their bodies, so it would look as if it were the weapon. The killer must not have realized it was only ornamental."

At last, the Sharpes had confirmation that their parents had been murdered. All these years, they had lived with what they thought was a domestic tragedy. They'd borne that shame together, shaped their lives around it, lived daily with the painful knowledge that their mother had killed their father. To learn otherwise was monumental.

"You're certain?" Oliver asked with a quaver in his voice.

"Yes."

"But why didn't the constable notice it hadn't been fired?" Gabriel asked.

Pinter eyed him askance. "Constables aren't trained in such matters—they're regular citizens who serve a turn as peace officers for one year. No doubt that particular year's constable wasn't experienced with weapons. Or perhaps he didn't even examine the weapon closely, since your grandmother paid him to keep quiet about the night's events. When she told him what had happened, he might have just taken her at her word."

Mrs. Plumtree colored. "I should never have interfered. But at the time it seemed obvious who'd killed whom, and I only wanted to protect my family."

"It seemed obvious to me, too," Oliver said. "This is the first concrete evidence we've had that it was not Mother who shot him!"

They all began to talk at once, questioning Pinter, revising former theories, telling each other that they'd been sure of it all along. Oliver herded them inside so they could be more comfortable for the discussion. But after discussing it for some time without coming to any conclusion except that Mr. Pinter should investigate further, the conversation eventually returned to the races and the wins.

"So what are you going to do with that gold cup?" Oliver asked Gabriel. "Melt it down so you can buy another Thoroughbred?"

"Bite your tongue," Gabriel said. "It's going on display at Waverly Farm, until Virginia and I can buy our own stud farm."

Their own farm. The words had such a nice ring, she thought. And who'd have ever guessed she'd be sitting here amid the people she'd once hated, next to the man whom she'd once considered her enemy? Now she couldn't imagine life without him. And she liked to think that Roger would approve.

"My offer still stands," Pierce said. "If you want to rent and run the place once it passes to me, I'll happily give you a long lease."

"Thank you," Gabriel said, with a squeeze of Virginia's hand, "but we'd rather have a place of our own. If we can ever afford it."

"Why wouldn't you, once you get your inheritance from Mrs. Plumtree?" Mr. Masters asked. The barrister had come over from London for the day at his wife's request.

Gabriel snorted. "Unless someone I don't know about is planning on offering for Celia, I doubt any of us is going to inherit."

All eyes turned to Celia. She blinked. "Now see here, are you saying that I *can't* get a husband?"

"No one's saying that, I'm sure," Virginia said.

"Oh yes, they are. Gabe is, anyway." Celia glared at him. "You think I can't get a husband. You think no one will marry me!"

Gabriel shrugged. "There's four months left in the year and I don't see anyone but Devonmont at our door, and Virginia says you're too clever to fall for him."

Pierce lifted an eyebrow at her.

Gabriel continued, "By all means, tell me if you have someone else waiting in the wings. But I won't wait around hoping for a slew of suitors to appear. I'm making my own plans for the future, since Gran seems determined to hold to her ultimatum."

Celia rose to plant her hands on her hips and survey the rest of the family. "Is that what *all* of you think? That I'm incapable of finding a husband? That no one would ever offer for me?"

The women murmured reassurances, and the men blinked like startled deer—except for Gabriel, who kept staring at Celia with his taunting smile, and Mr. Pinter, who was watching Pierce with a shuttered expression.

Celia colored deeply. "To hell with all of you. "I'll have a husband by Christmas—you'll see!" She hurried from the room.

Virginia jumped up and ran after her, but she'd barely reached the stairs before Gabriel caught up to her. "Leave her be, sweetheart."

"You don't understand. Now she thinks that we all believe her to be unmarriageable."

"Good."

"Gabriel! That's cruel!"

"No, Celia has a contrary side. When Gran said we had to marry to inherit, that made her dig in her heels and say she would *never* marry. Someone had to push her in the opposite direction. Now that she has a challenge to rise to, she'll kill herself trying to meet it. If she says she'll be married by Christmas, I promise you, she'll be married by Christmas."

Virginia stared at him. His grandmother was famous for such manipulation, but she'd never seen it in him. "Is the money so very important to you?"

"No, but my sister is." He drew her into his arms, lowering his voice to a husky murmur. "Gran has been right about one thing all along—none of us would have pursued love if she hadn't pushed us. And now that I know what love is, I want nothing less than that for Celia."

Those words made her heart soar, but there was one more thing she wanted to know. "Do you ever miss the racing, my love?"

He stared solemnly down at her. "The truth? I don't. Racing is for the young and foolish, for those who have nothing to lose." He brushed a kiss to her lips. "These days I have far too much to ever risk it for something as stupid as a horse race. Watching my Thoroughbred run a race course with you at my side is plenty enough excitement for me now."

Death had finally lost its hold over him. "For a man who once said he wasn't adept at giving pretty compliments, you certainly know how to turn a woman up sweet."

He flashed her that cocky grin she so adored. "Really? On the very night we met, Lyons informed me that I wasn't good with respectable women."

"You're not," she teased. "But with women who challenge men to races and have a secret yearning to be swept off their feet by scoundrels?" She looped her arms about his neck and stretched up so she could whisper in his ear. "With those women, my love, you are very, very good."

Then he kissed her, hot and sweet and slow, and she met it with all the recklessness and yearning in her soul. Because as any clever woman knows, sometimes the only way to true happiness is to wed a wild lord.

Turn the page
for a special look
at the final delightful romance in

Hellions of Halstead Hall series

A LADY NEVER SURRENDERS

featuring the fiercely independent Lady Celia Sharpe

by *New York Times* bestselling author

SABRINA JEFFRIES

Coming soon from Pocket Books

*B*ow Street runner Jackson Pinter gaped at Lady Celia, wondering how this conversation had turned so terribly wrong. The woman was clearly daft. Bedlam-witted.

And trying to drive him in the same direction. "You can't be serious. Since when do you know anything about investigating people?"

She planted her hands on her hips. "You refuse to investigate my suitors, so I will have to do it."

God save him, she was the most infuriating, maddening— "How do you propose to manage that?"

She shrugged. "Ask them questions, I suppose. The house party for Oliver's birthday is next week. Lord Devonmont is already coming, and it will be easy to convince Gran to invite my other two prospects. Once they're there, I could try sneaking into their rooms and listening in on their conversations, or perhaps bribing their servants—"

"You've lost your bloody mind," he hissed.

Only after she lifted an eyebrow at his choice of words did he realize he'd cursed so foully in front of her. But by thunder, the woman would turn a sane man into a blithering idiot! The thought of her wandering in and out of men's rooms, risking her virtue and her reputation, made his blood run cold.

"You don't seem to understand," she said in a clipped tone, as if speaking to a child. "I have to catch a husband *somehow*. I need help, and I've nowhere else to turn. Minerva is rarely here, and Gran's matchmaking efforts are about as subtle as a sledgehammer. And even if my brothers and their wives could do that sort of work, they're preoccupied with their own affairs. That leaves *you*, who seems to think that suitors drop from the skies at my whim. If I can't even entice you to help me for money, then I'll have to manage on my own."

Turning on her heel, she headed for the door.

Hell and blazes, she was just liable to attempt such an idiotic thing, too. She had some fool notion she was invincible. That's why she spent her time target shooting with her brother's friends, blithely unconcerned that her rifle might misfire or the other gentlemen might shoot her by mistake.

The wench did as she pleased, and the men in her family just let her. Someone had to curb her insanity, and it looked as if it would have to be him.

"All right!" he called out. "I'll do it."

She halted, but didn't turn around. "You'll find out what I need in order to snag one of my choices as a husband?"

"Yes."

"Even if it means being a trifle underhanded?"

He gritted his teeth. This would be pure torture. The underhandedness didn't bother him. He'd be as under-handed as necessary to get rid of those damned suitors who didn't deserve her. But to manage that he'd have to be around her a great deal, if only to make sure the idiots didn't compromise her.

Still, he had no choice. So he must find something in their backgrounds to send her running the other way. She said she wanted facts? By thunder, he'd give her enough damning facts to blacken every one of those men in her mind.

And then what?

If you know of some eligible gentlemen you can strong-arm into courting me, then by all means, tell me. I'm open to suggestions.

All right, so he had no gentlemen to suggest. But he couldn't let her marry any of her ridiculous choices, could he? They would all make her miserable. To keep her from making the same foolish mistake as his mother, he must impress upon her that she was court-ing disaster.

Then he'd find someone more eligible for her. Some-how.

She faced him. "Well?"

"Yes," he said, suppressing a curse. "I'll do whatever you want."

A skeptical laugh escaped her. "*That* I'd like to see." When he scowled, she added hastily, "But thank you. Truly, I mean that. And I'm happy to pay you extra for your efforts, as I said."

He stiffened. "No need."

"Nonsense," she said firmly. "It will be worth it to have your discretion."

His scowl deepened. "My clients always have my discretion."

"Ah, but the only client actually paying you at the moment is Oliver. I want to be your client on my own terms—especially since you must keep my plans secret from him and Gran."

That roused his suspicions. "And why is that?"

Her expression grew guarded. "In case this doesn't turn out how I want."

Under his pointed stare, she flushed. Damn if it didn't make her look even prettier.

She dropped her gaze to the jewel-encrusted bracelet she kept twisting about her slender wrist. "They think me incapable of gaining a husband, and I mean to prove them wrong. But I don't want them knowing that I've been forced to stoop to such devious tactics. It's embarrassing." She cut a glance up at him. "Do you understand?"

He nodded. Pride was a powerful motivator. Sometimes the urge to prove people wrong was the only thing that kept a man—or a woman—moving forward.

"This conversation will stay between us," he said tightly. "You may depend upon that."

Relief shone in her lovely face. "All the same, I wish to pay you for your discretion. And for whatever work isn't covered by your arrangement with Oliver."

He was *not* taking money from her for this. "I tell you

what. Assuming that all goes well and you gain one of these gentlemen as a husband, you may cover my fee with the money you'll inherit from your grandmother."

"But what if it *doesn't* go well? You still deserve to be compensated for your efforts. Gran gives me an allowance. Just tell me what you want."

What he wanted was her, naked in his bed, gazing up at him with a smile as she drew him down to kiss that thoroughly enchanting mouth.

But that was impossible, for more reasons than he could count. Desiring her didn't change that.

"My clients only pay me if they get results," he lied. "So until you achieve your goal, there's no fee."

She eyed him skeptically. "Come now, surely you require at least a pledge of some kind, so you'll receive *something* for your trouble." She unclasped her bracelet and held it out to him. "Take this. I'll warrant it's worth a few pounds."

More like a few *hundred* pounds. Leave it to a fine lady to act as if it were some bauble.

When he merely stood there, she added softly, "I insist. I don't want to be obligated to you in case this . . . doesn't work out. You could always sell it or give it to your sweetheart. Or perhaps your mother."

He tensed. "I don't have a sweetheart, and my mother is dead."

Her face fell. "I'm sorry, I forgot that your mother . . . that is . . ." She drew back the bracelet. "How awful of me to remind you of it."

The soft regret in her voice clutched at his gut. He'd

never seen this side of her. "It's fine. She died a long time ago."

Her eyes searched his face. "Some wounds even time can't heal, no matter what people say."

They shared a glance of their mutual loss, both of their mothers vilified in death as they'd been wronged in life. A lump caught in his throat.

"You live with your aunt," she said hesitantly. "Is that right?"

He cleared his throat. "Actually, she lives with me. My uncle willed their house in Cheapside to me when he died last year, with the condition that she be allowed to live there until her death. I was going to remain in my regular lodgings, but she's been so lonely. . . ." Realizing he was revealing more of his life than he wanted, he said, "Anyway, I moved in last week."

She held out the bracelet again. "Then keep this as a surety and give it to *her* if our agreement doesn't prove fruitful."

"She could never wear that," he countered. It was too expensive for the widow of a magistrate to sport at church or in the shops.

A flush filled her cheeks. "Oh, of course. I see."

He hadn't expected her to take his meaning, but her mortification showed that she had. He'd never thought Lady Celia was so perceptive. Or sensitive.

"My aunt's wrists aren't as delicate as yours," he added hastily. "It wouldn't fit her." When relief showed in her eyes, he was glad he'd lied. "Still, I'll accept it as a gesture of good faith on your part." He took the bracelet from her. "Though I fully expect to be returning it in a few weeks."

"Of course." Her bright smile warmed him. "So, what do you think of the idea of inviting the gentlemen to the house party? Halstead Hall is large enough to accommodate a few more guests."

What an understatement. The marquess's seat was called a "calendar house," because it had three hundred and sixty-five rooms, seven courtyards, fifty-two staircases, and twelve towers. It had been given to the first marquess by Henry VIII.

"And if you attend, too," she went on, "you'll be able to investigate the gentlemen more easily. Plus, it will give me more chances to get to know them."

Damn. Attending a house party would mean vails to pay the servants and fine clothes for him, a definite strain on his funds. Especially now that he was trying to do improvements on the house he'd inherited.

But if her idiot suitors were going to stay at Halstead Hall, then by thunder, he'd be here, too. They wouldn't take advantage of her on *his* watch. "We're agreed that you won't do any of that foolish nonsense you mentioned, like spying on them, right?"

"Of course not. That's what I have you for."

Her private lackey, meant to jump at her command. He was already beginning to regret this.

"We shouldn't have any trouble tempting the gentlemen to accept our invitation," she went on blithely. "It's hunting season, and the estate has some excellent coveys."

"I wouldn't know."

She cast him an easy smile. "Yes, you generally hunt men, not grouse. And apparently you do it very well."

A compliment? From *her*? "No need to flatter me, my lady," he said dryly. "I've already agreed to your scheme."

Her smile vanished. "Really, Mr. Pinter, sometimes you can be so . . ."

"Honest?" he prodded.

"Irritating." She tipped up her chin. "It will be easier to work together if you're not always so prickly."

He was more than prickly, and for the most foolish reasons imaginable. Because he didn't like her trawling for suitors. Or using him to do it. And because he hated her "lady of the manor" role. It reminded him too forcibly of the difference in their stations.

"I am who I am, madam," he bit out. "You knew what you were purchasing when you set out to do this."

She colored. "Must you make it sound so sordid?"

He stepped as close as he dared. "You want me to gather information you can use in playing a false role to catch a husband. *I* am not the one making it sordid."

"Tell me, sir, will I have to endure your moralizing at every turn?" she said in a voice dripping with sugar. "Because I'd happily pay extra to have you keep your opinions to yourself."

"There isn't enough money in all the world for that," he said in a low voice.

Her eyes blazed up at him. Good. He much preferred her in a temper. At least then she was herself and not putting on some show.

I prefer not *to marry a fortune hunter.*

With a scowl, he tucked her bracelet into his coat pocket as he walked out the door. No, she only preferred fools and lechers and sons of madmen. As long as they were rich and titled, she was perfectly content. Because then she knew they weren't after her money.

Yet he couldn't despise her for that. He might travel between two worlds with apparent ease, but it made him all the more aware of how hard it would be to actually take up residence in the world he hadn't been born to.

And yet . . .

I know what you think of me.

If he wasn't careful, one day he would show her exactly what he thought of her. But if that day came, he'd better be prepared for the consequences. Because he suspected they would not be easy ones.

She seemed to catch herself, pasting an utterly false smile on her lips. "Well then, do you think you can manage to be civil for the house party? It does me no good to bring suitors here if you're going to be skulking about, making them uncomfortable."

He tamped down the urge to provoke her further. If he pressed her too far she'd strike off on her own, and that would be disastrous. "I shall try to keep my 'skulking' to a minimum."

"Thank you." She thrust out her hand. "Shall we shake on it?"

The minute his fingers closed about hers, he wished he'd refused. Because having her soft hand in his roused everything he'd been trying to suppress during this interview.

He couldn't seem to let go. For such a small-boned female, she had a surprisingly firm grip. Her hand was just like her—fragility and strength all wrapped in beauty. He had a mad impulse to lift it to his lips and press a kiss to her creamy skin.

But he was no Lancelot to her Guinevere. Only in legend did lowly knights dare to court queens.

Releasing her hand before he could do something stupid, he sketched a bow. "Good day, my lady. I'll begin my investigation at once and report to you as soon as I learn something."

He left her standing there, a goddess surrounded by the aging glories of an aristocrat's mansion. God save him, this had to be the worst mission he'd ever taken on, one he was sure to regret down the road.